PRAISE FOR
JEFFREY ARCHER AND HIS NOVELS

FIRST AMONG EQUALS

MORE . . .

"Archer invests his novels with drama, irony and suspense—
First Among Equals is no exception . . . fascinating."

—The Boston Herald

"Not since Gore Vidal's *1876* has there been such a
cliffhanger aspect to an election and to the selection of a
head of government . . . at the conclusion, Archer brings
the reader to a moment of truth . . . a surprising finish."

—The San Diego Union

"A razzle-dazzle fictional turn . . . engaging . . . pertinent and
compelling."

—The Washington Times

THE PRODIGAL DAUGHTER

"Chalk up another smash hit for Jeffrey Archer . . . an excep-
tional storyteller."

—John Barkham Reviews

"Fast-moving and compelling."   *—Library Journal*

KANE & ABEL

"A smashing good read!"   *—The Des Moines Register*

"I defy anyone not to enjoy this book, which is one of the
best novels I have ever read."

—Otto Preminger

"A sprawling blockbuster!"   *—Publishers Weekly*

"Grips the reader from the first page to the last. A smash hit."
—John Barkham Reviews

"Archer is a master entertainer."   *—Time*

AS THE CROW FLIES

"A certified page-turner." —*New York Daily News*

"Archer . . . has an extraordinary talent for turning notoriety into gold, and telling fast-moving stories."
—*The Philadelphia Inquirer*

"An endearing story." —*The Wall Street Journal*

"Archer plots with skill, and keeps you turning the pages."
—*The Boston Globe*

"Top flight . . . Mr. Archer tells a story to keep you turning those pages."
—*The Washington Post*

"Great fun!" —*Kirkus Reviews*

JEFFREY ARCHER

FIRST AMONG EQUALS

St. Martin's Paperbacks

FIRST AMONG EQUALS

Copyright © 1984 by Jeffrey Archer.

Political cartoons by Charles Griffin.

ISBN: 978-1-250-10199-0

Hodder & Stoughton (UK) edition published 1984
HarperPaperbacks edition / October 1993
St. Martin's Paperbacks edition / May 2004

St. Martin's Paperbacks are published by St. Martin's Press, 175 Fifth Avenue, New York, NY 10010.

P1

To Alan and Eddie

PROLOGUE

WEDNESDAY 10 APRIL 1931

IF CHARLES GURNEY Seymour had been born nine minutes earlier he would have become an earl, inherited a castle in Scotland, 22,000 acres in Somerset, and a thriving merchant bank in the City of London.

It was to be several years before young Charles worked out the full significance of coming second in life's first race.

His twin brother, Rupert, only just came through the ordeal, and in the years that followed contracted not only the usual childhood illnesses but managed to add scarlet fever, diphtheria and meningitis, causing his mother, Lady Seymour, to fear for his survival.

Charles, on the other hand, *was* a survivor, and had inherited enough Seymour ambition for both his brother and himself. Only a few years passed before those who came into contact with the brothers for the first time mistakenly assumed Charles was the heir to the earldom.

As the years passed Charles's father tried desperately to discover something at which Rupert might triumph over his brother—and failed. When they were eight the two boys were sent away to Summer Fields where generations of Seymours had been prepared for the rigors of Eton. During his first month at the Oxford prep school Charles was voted form captain and no one hindered his advance *en route* to becoming head boy at the age of twelve, by which time Rupert was looked upon as Seymour Minor. Both boys proceeded to Eton, where in their first half Charles beat Rupert at every subject in the classroom, outrowed him on the river, and nearly killed him in the boxing ring.

When in 1947 their grandfather, the thirteenth Earl of Bridgwater, finally expired, the sixteen-year-old Rupert became Viscount Seymour while Charles inherited a meaningless prefix.

The Hon. Charles Seymour felt angry every time he heard his brother deferentially addressed by strangers as "My Lord."

At Eton, Charles continued to excel and ended his schooldays as President of Pop before being offered a place at Christ Church, Oxford, to read History. Rupert covered the same years without over-burdening the examiners, internal or external. At the age of eighteen the young viscount returned to the family estate in Somerset to pass the rest of his days as a landowner. No one destined to inherit 22,000 acres could be described as a farmer.

At Oxford, Charles, free of Rupert's shadow, progressed with the air of a man who found the university something of an anticlimax. He would spend his weekdays reading the history of his relations and the weekends at house parties or riding to hounds. As no one had suggested for one moment that Rupert should enter the world of high finance, it was assumed once Charles had left Oxford that he would succeed his father at Seymour's Bank: first as a director and then in time as its chairman: although it would be Rupert who would eventually inherit the family shareholding.

This "best laid plan" changed, however, when one evening the Hon. Charles Seymour was dragged off to the Oxford Union by a nubile undergraduate from Somerville, who demanded he should listen to the Eights Week motion, "I would rather be a commoner than a lord." The President of the Union had achieved the unique coup of having the motion proposed by the Prime Minister, Sir Winston Churchill.

Charles sat at the back of a hall packed with eager students mesmerized by the elder statesman's performance. Never once did he take his eyes off the great war leader during his witty and powerful speech, although what kept flashing across his mind was the realization that, but for an accident of birth, Churchill would have been the ninth Duke of Marlborough. Here was a man who had dominated the world stage for three decades and then turned down every hereditary honor a grateful nation could offer, including the title of Duke of London.

From that moment Charles never allowed himself to be referred to as "the Hon." again: his ultimate ambition was now above mere titles.

Another undergraduate who listened to Churchill that night was also considering his future. But he did not view proceedings crammed between his fellow students at the back of the crowded hall. The tall young man dressed in white tie and tails sat alone in a large chair on a raised platform, for such was his right as President of the Oxford Union.

Although Simon Kerslake *was* the first-born, he had otherwise few of Charles Seymour's advantages. The only son of a family solicitor, he had come to appreciate how much his father had denied himself to ensure that his son should remain at the local public school. Simon's father had died during his son's last year at Lancing College, leaving his widow a small annuity and a magnificent MacKinley grandfather clock. Simon's mother sold the clock a week after the funeral in order that her son could complete his final year with all the "extras" the other boys took for granted. She also hoped that it would give Simon a better chance of going on to university.

From the first day he could walk Simon had always wanted to outdistance his rivals. The Americans would have described him as "an achiever," while many of his contemporaries thought of him as pushy, or even arrogant, according to their aptitude for jealousy. During his last term at Lancing Simon was passed over for head of school and he still found himself unable to forgive the headmaster his lack of foresight. Later that year, some weeks after he had completed his S-levels and been interviewed by Magdalen, a circular letter informed him that he would not be offered a place at Oxford; it was a decision Simon was unwilling to accept.

In the same mail Durham University offered him a scholarship, which he rejected by return of post. "Future Prime Ministers aren't educated at Durham," he informed his mother.

"How about Cambridge?" she inquired, continuing to wipe the dishes.

"No political tradition," replied Simon.

"But if there is no chance of being offered a place at Oxford, surely —?"

"That's not what I said, Mother," replied the young man. "I shall be an undergraduate at Oxford by the first day of term."

After eighteen years of forty-yard goals Mrs. Kerslake had learned to stop asking her son, "How will you manage that?"

Some fourteen days before the start of the Michaelmas Term at Oxford Simon booked himself into a small guest house just off the Iffley Road. On a trestle table in the corner of lodgings he intended to make permanent he wrote out a list of all the colleges, then divided them into five columns, planning to visit three each morning and three each afternoon until his question had been answered positively by a resident Tutor for Admissions: "Have you accepted any freshmen for this year who are now unable to take up their places?"

It was on the fourth afternoon, just as doubt was beginning to set in and Simon was wondering if after all he would have to travel to Cambridge the following week, that he received the first affirmative reply.

The Tutor for Admissions at Worcester College removed the glasses from the end of his nose and stared at the tall young man with a mop of dark hair falling over his forehead.

Alan Brown was the twenty-second don Kerslake had visited in four days.

"Yes," he replied. "It so happens that a young man from Nottingham High School, who had been offered a place here, was tragically killed in a motorcycle accident last month."

"What course—what subject was he going to read?" Simon's words were unusually faltering. He prayed it wasn't Chemistry, Anthropology, or Classics. Alan Brown flicked through a rotary index on his desk, obviously enjoying the little cross-examination. He peered at the card in front of him. "History," he announced.

Simon's heartbeat reached 120. "I just missed a place at Magdalen to read Politics, Philosophy, and Economics," he said. "Would you consider me for the vacancy?"

The older man was unable to hide a smile. He had never in twenty-four years come across such a request.

"Full name?" he said, replacing his glasses as if the serious business of the meeting had now begun.

"Simon John Kerslake."

Dr. Brown picked up the telephone by his side and dialed a number. "Nigel?" he said. "It's Alan Brown here. Did you ever consider offering a man called Kerslake a place at Magdalen?"

Mrs. Kerslake was not surprised when her son went on to be President of the Oxford Union. After all, she teased, wasn't it just another stepping stone on the path to Prime Minister— Gladstone, Asquith . . . Kerslake?

Ray Gould was born in a tiny, windowless room above his father's butcher's shop in Leeds. For the first nine years of his life he shared that room with his ailing grandmother until she died at the age of sixty-one.

Ray's close proximity to the old woman who had lost her husband in the Great War at first appeared romantic to him. He would listen enraptured as she told him stories of her hero husband in his smart khaki uniform—a uniform now folded neatly in her bottom drawer, but still displayed in the fading sepia photograph at the side of her bed. Soon, however, his grandmother's stories filled Ray with sadness, as he became aware that she had been a widow for nearly thirty years. Finally she seemed a tragic figure as he realized how little she had experienced of the world beyond that cramped room in which she was surrounded by all her possessions and a yellowed envelope containing 500 irredeemable war bonds.

There had been no purpose in Ray's grandmother making a will, for all he inherited was the room. Overnight it became his study—full of ever-changing library and school books, the former often returned late, using up Ray's meager pocket money in fines. But as each school report was brought home it became increasingly apparent to Ray's father that he would not be extending the sign above the butcher's shop to proclaim "Gould and Son."

Shortly after his eleventh birthday Ray won the top scholarship to Roundhay School. Wearing his first pair of long trousers—turned up several inches by his mother—and horn-rimmed spectacles that didn't quite fit, he set off for the opening day at his new school. Ray's mother hoped there were other boys as thin and spotty as her son, and that his wavy red hair would not cause him to be continually teased.

By the end of his first term Ray was surprised to find he was far ahead of his classmates, so far in fact that the headmaster considered it prudent to put him up a form—"to stretch the lad a little," as he explained to Ray's parents.

By the end of that year, one spent mainly in the classroom, Ray managed to come third in the form, and top in Latin and English. Only when it came to selecting teams for any sport did Ray find he came bottom in anything. However brilliant his mind might have been, it never seemed to coordinate with his body. His single greatest academic achievement during the year, though, was to be the youngest winner of the prize essay competition in the school's history.

Each year the winner of the essay was required to read his entry to the assembled pupils and parents on Speech Day. Even before he handed in his entry Ray rehearsed his efforts out loud several times in the privacy of his study-bedroom, fearing he would not be properly prepared if he waited until the winner was announced.

Ray's form master had told all his pupils that the subject of the essay could be of their own choosing, but that they should try to recall some experience that had been unique to them. Thirty-seven entries arrived on his desk by nine o'clock on the closing date six weeks later. After reading Ray's account of his grandmother's life in the little room above the butcher's shop the form master had no inclination to pick up another script. When he had dutifully struggled through the remainder he did not hesitate in recommending Gould's essay for the prize. The only reservation, he admitted to its author, was the choice of title. Ray thanked him for the advice but the title remained intact.

On the morning of Speech Day the school hall was packed with 700 pupils and their parents. After the headmaster had delivered his speech and the applause had died down, he announced, "I shall now call upon the winner of the prize essay competition to deliver his entry: Ray Gould."

Ray left his place in the hall and marched confidently up on to the stage. He stared down at the 2,000 expectant faces but showed no sign of apprehension, partly because he found it difficult to see beyond the third row. When he announced the title of his essay some of the younger children began to snigger, causing Ray to stumble through his first few lines. But by the time he had reached the last page the packed hall was still, and after he had completed the final paragraph he received the first standing ovation of his career.

Twelve-year-old Ray Gould left the stage to rejoin his parents in the body of the hall. His mother's head was bowed but he could still see tears trickling down her cheeks. His father was trying not to look too proud. Even when Ray was seated the applause continued, so he too lowered his head to stare at the title of his prize-winning essay: "The First Changes I Will Make When I Become Prime Minister."

*   *   *

Andrew Fraser attended his first political meeting in a pram. True, he was left in the corridor while his parents sat on the stage inside another drafty hall, but he quickly learned that applause signaled his mother would soon be returning. What Andrew did not know was that his father, who had made his name as Scotland's finest scrum-half since the Great War, had delivered yet another speech to the citizens of Edinburgh Carlton in his efforts to capture a marginal seat on the City Council. At that time few believed Duncan Fraser was more than a rugby hero, and consequently he failed to win the seat for the Conservatives, if only by a few hundred votes. Three years later Andrew, a sturdy four-year-old, was allowed to sit at the back of several sparsely filled halls as once again he and his mother trailed round the city to support their candidate. This time Duncan Fraser's speeches were almost as impressive as his long pass, and he won his place on the City Council by 207 votes.

Hard work and consistent results on behalf of his constituents ensured that the marginal seat remained in the hands of Councillor Fraser for the next nine years. By the age of thirteen, Andrew, a stocky wee lad with straight black hair and a grin that no one seemed to be able to remove from his face, had learned enough about local politics to help his father organize a fifth campaign, by which time neither party considered Edinburgh Carlton a marginal seat.

At the Edinburgh Academy it came as no surprise to his fellow pupils that Andrew was chosen to captain the school debating society; however, they were impressed when under his leadership the team went on to win the Scottish Schools debating trophy. Although Andrew was destined to be no taller than five-foot-nine it was also widely accepted that he was the most complete scrum-half the Academy had produced since his father had captained the school side in 1919.

On matriculating from the Academy Andrew took up a place at Edinburgh University to read Politics, and by his third year he had been elected President of the Union and captain of rugby.

When Duncan Fraser became Lord Provost of Edinburgh he

made one of his rare visits to London, to receive a knighthood from the Queen. Andrew had just completed his final exams and, along with his mother, attended the investiture at Buckingham Palace. After the ceremony Sir Duncan traveled on to the House of Commons to fulfill an engagement with his local member, Ainslie Munro. Over lunch Munro informed Sir Duncan that he had contested the Edinburgh Carlton seat for the last time, so they had better start looking for a new candidate. Sir Duncan's eyes lit up as he savored the thought of his son succeeding Munro as his Member of Parliament.

After Andrew had been awarded an honors degree at Edinburgh, he remained at the university to complete a thesis entitled "The history of the Conservative party in Scotland." He planned to wait for his father to complete the statutory three years as Lord Provost before he informed him of the most significant outcome the research for his doctorate had produced. But when Ainslie Munro announced officially that he would not be contesting the next election Andrew knew he could no longer hide his true feelings if he wanted to be considered for the seat.

"Like father, like son," read the headline in the center-page of the *Edinburgh Evening News*, who considered that Andrew Fraser was the obvious candidate if the Conservatives hoped to hold on to the marginal seat. Sir Duncan, fearing the local burghers would consider Andrew too young, reminded them at the first selection meeting that eight Scots had been Prime Ministers and every one had been in the House before the age of thirty. He was pleased to find members nodding their agreement. When Sir Duncan returned home that night he phoned his son and suggested that they should have lunch at the New Club the following day to discuss a plan of campaign.

"Think of it," said Sir Duncan, after he had ordered a second whisky. "Father and son representing the same constituency. It will be a great day for the Edinburgh Conservative party."

"Not to mention the Labour party," said Andrew, looking his father in the eye.

"I am not sure I take your meaning," said the Lord Provost.

"Precisely that, Father. I do not intend to contest the seat as a Conservative. I hope to be selected as the Labour candidate—if they'll adopt me."

Sir Duncan looked disbelieving. "But you've been a Conservative all your life," he declared, his voice rising with every word.

"No, Father," replied Andrew quietly. "It's you who have been a Conservative all my life."

BOOK ONE

1964–1966
THE BACK BENCHES

CHAPTER ONE

THURSDAY 10 DECEMBER 1964

MR. SPEAKER ROSE and surveyed the Commons. He tugged at his long black silk gown, then nervously tweaked the full-bottomed wig that covered his balding head. The House had almost got out of control during a particularly rowdy session of Prime Minister's questions, and he was delighted to see the clock reach three-thirty. Time to pass on to the next business of the day.

He stood shifting from foot to foot waiting for the 500-odd members present to settle down before he intoned solemnly, "Members desiring to take the oath." The packed assembly switched its gaze from the Speaker to the far end of the Chamber, like a crowd watching a tennis match. There, standing at the bar of the Commons, was the victor of the first by-election since the Labour party had taken office some two months before.

The new member, flanked by his proposer and seconder, took four paces forward. Like well-drilled guardsmen, they stopped and bowed. The stranger stood at six-foot-four. He looked like a man born with the Tory party in mind, his patrician head set on an aristocratic frame, a mane of fair hair combed meticulously into place. Dressed in a dark gray, double-breasted suit and wearing a Guards' tie of maroon and blue, he advanced once again toward the long table that stood in front of the Speaker's chair between the two front benches which faced each other a mere sword's length apart.

Leaving his sponsors in his wake, he passed down the Government side, stepping over the legs of the Prime Minister and Foreign Secretary before being handed the oath by the Clerk of the House.

He held the little card in his right hand and pronounced the words as firmly as if they had been his marriage vows.

"I, Charles Seymour, do swear that I will be faithful, and bear true allegiance to Her Majesty Queen Elizabeth, her heirs and successors according to law, so help me God."

"Hear, hear," rose from his colleagues on the benches opposite as the new MP leaned over to subscribe the Test Roll, a parchment folded into book-shape. Charles was introduced to the Speaker by the Clerk. The new member then proceeded toward the chair where he stopped and bowed.

"Welcome to the House, Mr. Seymour," said the Speaker, shaking his hand. "I hope you will serve this place for many years to come."

"Thank you, Mr. Speaker," said Charles, and bowed for a final time before continuing on behind the Speaker's chair. He had carried out the little ceremony exactly as the Tory Chief Whip had rehearsed it with him in the long corridor outside his office.

Waiting for him behind the Speaker's chair and out of sight of the other members was the leader of the Opposition, Sir Alec Douglas-Home, who also shook him warmly by the hand.

"Congratulations on your splendid victory, Charles. I know you have a great deal to offer to our party and indeed your country."

"Thank you," replied the new MP, who after waiting for Sir Alec to return to take his place on the Opposition front bench made his way up the steps of the side gangway to find a place in the back row of the long green benches.

For the next two hours Charles Seymour followed the proceedings of the House with a mixture of awe and excitement. For the first time in his life he had found something that wasn't his by right or by effortless conquest. Glancing up at the Strangers' Gallery he saw his wife Fiona, his father the fourteenth Earl of Bridgwater and his brother, the Viscount Seymour, peering down at him with pride. Charles settled back on the first rung of the ladder. He smiled to himself: only six weeks ago he had feared it would be many more years before he could hope to take a seat in the House of Commons.

At the general election a mere two months before, Charles had contested a South Wales mining seat with an impregnable Labour majority. "Good for the experience, not to mention the soul," the vice-chairman in charge of candidates at Conservative Central Office had assured him. He had proved to be right on both counts, for Charles had relished the contest and brought the Labour majority down from 22,300 to 20,100. His wife had aptly described it as a "dent," but it had turned out to be enough of a dent for the party to put Charles's name forward for the Sussex Downs seat when Sir Eric Koops had died of a heart attack only a few days after Parliament had assembled. Six weeks later Charles Seymour sat in the Commons with a 20,000 majority of his own.

Charles listened to one more speech before leaving the Chamber. He stood alone in the Members' Lobby not quite certain where to begin. Another young member strode purposefully toward him. "Allow me to introduce myself," the stranger said, sounding to Charles every bit like a fellow Conservative. "My name is Andrew Fraser. I'm the Labour member for Edinburgh Carlton and I was hoping you hadn't yet found yourself a pair." Charles admitted that so far he hadn't found much more than the Chamber. The Tory Chief Whip had already explained to him that most members paired with someone from the opposite party for voting purposes, and that it would be wise for him to select someone of his own age. When there was a debate on less crucial issues a two-line whip came into operation: pairing made it possible for members to miss the vote and return home to their wife and family before midnight. However, no member was allowed to miss the vote when there was a three-line whip.

"I'd be delighted to pair with you," continued Charles. "Am I expected to do anything official?"

"No," said Andrew, looking up at him. "I'll just drop you a line confirming the arrangement. If you'd be kind enough to reply letting me have all the phone numbers where you can be contacted we'll just take it from there. Any time you need to miss a vote just let me know."

"Sounds a sensible arrangement to me," said Charles as a rotund figure wearing a light gray three-piece suit, blue shirt, and a pink-spotted bow tie trundled over toward them.

"Welcome to the club, Charles," said Alec Pimkin. "Care to join me for a drink in the smoking room and I'll brief you on how this bloody place works."

"Thank you," said Charles, relieved to see someone he knew. Andrew smiled when he heard Pimkin add, "It's just like being back at school, old chum," as the two Tories retreated in the direction of the smoking room. Andrew suspected that it wouldn't be long before Charles Seymour was showing his "old school chum" just how the bloody place really worked.

Andrew also left the Members' Lobby but not in search of a drink. He had to attend a meeting of the Parliamentary Labour party at which the following week's business was due to be discussed. He hurried away.

Andrew had been duly selected as the Labour candidate for Edinburgh Carlton and had gone on to capture the seat from the Conservatives by a majority of 3,419 votes. Sir Duncan, having completed his term as Lord Provost, continued to represent the same seat on the City Council. In six weeks Andrew—the baby of the House—had quickly made a name for himself and many of the older members found it hard to believe that it was his first Parliament.

When Andrew arrived at the party meeting on the second floor of the Commons he found an empty seat near the back of the large committee room and settled down to listen to the

Government Chief Whip go over the business for the following week. Once again it seemed to consist of nothing but three-line whips. He glanced down at the piece of paper in front of him. The debates scheduled for Tuesday, Wednesday, and Thursday all had three thick lines drawn under them: only Monday and Friday had two-liners which at least after his agreement with Charles Seymour he could arrange to miss. The Labour party might have returned to power after thirteen years but, with a majority of only four and a full legislative program, it was proving almost impossible for members to get to bed much before midnight during the week.

As the Chief Whip sat down the first person to jump to his feet was Tom Carson, the new member for Liverpool Dockside. He launched into a tirade of abuse against the Government, complaining that they were looking more like Tories every day. The under-the-breath remarks and coughing that continued during his speech showed how little support there was for his views. Tom Carson had also made a name for himself in a very short time, for he had openly attacked his own party from the first day he had arrived.

"*Enfant terrible,*" muttered the man sitting on the right of Andrew.

"Those aren't the words I'd use to describe him," muttered Andrew. "Altogether too many letters." The man with wavy red hair smiled as they listened to Carson ranting on.

If Raymond Gould had acquired any reputation during those first six weeks it was as one of the party's intellectuals, and for that reason older members were immediately suspicious of him, although few doubted he would be among the first from the new intake to be promoted to the front bench. Not many of them had really gotten to know Raymond as the north-countryman appeared remarkably reserved for someone who had chosen a career in public life. But with a majority of over 10,000 in his Leeds constituency he looked destined for a long career.

Leeds North had chosen Raymond to be their candidate from a field of thirty-seven, when he showed himself to be so much better informed than a local trade-union official whom the press had tipped as favorite for the seat. Yorkshire folk like people who stay at home and Raymond had been quick to point out to the selection committee—in an exaggerated Yorkshire accent—that he had been educated at Roundhay School on the fringes of the constituency. But what really tipped the vote in his favor had been Raymond's refusal of an open scholarship to Cambridge. He had preferred to continue his education at Leeds University, he explained.

Raymond took a first-class honors degree in Law at Leeds before moving to London to complete his studies for the bar at Lincoln's Inn. At the end of his two-year course Raymond joined a fashionable London chambers to become a much sought-after junior counsel. From that moment he rarely mentioned his family background to his carefully cultivated circle of Home Counties friends, and those comrades who addressed him as Ray received a sharp "Raymond" for their familiarity.

When the last question had been asked, the party meeting broke up, and Raymond and Andrew made their way out of the committee room—Andrew for his tiny office on the second floor to finish off the day's mail, Raymond to return to the Chamber as he hoped to deliver his maiden speech that day. He had waited patiently for the right moment to express his views to the House on the subject of widows' pensions and the redemption of war bonds, and the debate in progress on the economy was an obvious opportunity. The Speaker had dropped Raymond a note earlier in the day saying he expected to call him some time that evening.

Raymond had spent many hours in the Chamber, carefully studying the techniques demanded by the House and noting how they differed from those of the law courts. F. E. Smith had been right in his assessment of his colleagues when he had described the Commons as nothing more than a noisy court-room with over 600 jurors and absolutely no sign of a judge. Raymond was dreading the ordeal of his maiden speech; the dispassionate logic of his arguments had always proved more appealing to judges than to juries.

As he approached the Chamber an attendant handed him a

note from his wife Joyce. She had just arrived at the Commons and had been found a seat in the Strangers' Gallery so that she could be present for his speech. After only a cursory glance Raymond scrunched up the note, dropped it into the nearest wastepaper basket, and hurried on toward the Chamber.

The door was held open for him by a Conservative member who was on his way out.

"Thank you," said Raymond. Simon Kerslake smiled back, trying in vain to recall the man's name. Once Simon was in the Members' Lobby he checked the message board to see if the light under his name was lit up. It wasn't, so he continued on through the swing doors to the right of the lobby on his way down past the cloisters to the Members' Car Park. Once he had found his car he headed off in the direction of St. Mary's, Paddington, to pick up his wife. They had seen little of each other during Simon's first six weeks in Parliament which made the thought of tonight even more enjoyable. Simon couldn't see any easing of the pressure until there was another general election and one party had gained a sensible working majority. But what he feared most—having won his seat by the slimmest of margins—was that such a working majority would not include him and he might end up with one of the shortest political careers on record. After such a prolonged stretch of Tory rule the new Labour Government was looking fresh, idealistic, and certain to increase their numbers whenever the Prime Minister chose to go to the country.

Once Simon had reached Hyde Park Corner he headed on up toward Marble Arch thinking back over how he had become a member. On leaving Oxford he had completed two years' national service with the Sussex Yeomanry, finishing his military days as a second lieutenant. After a short holiday he had joined the BBC as a general trainee. He spent five years moving from drama, to sport, to current affairs before being appointed a producer on "Panorama." During those early days in London he had rented a small flat in Earl's Court and continued his interest in politics by becoming a member of the Tory Bow Group. When he became the Group's secretary he helped to organize meetings, and had then progressed to writing pamphlets and speaking at weekend conferences before being invited to work at Central Office as personal assistant to the chairman during the 1959 election campaign.

Two years later Simon met Elizabeth Drummond when "Panorama" carried out an investigation into the National Health Service and she had been invited to be a participant. Over drinks before the program Elizabeth made it perfectly clear to Simon that she distrusted media men and detested politicians. They were married a year later. Elizabeth had since given birth to two sons, and with only a small break on each occasion she had continued her career as a doctor.

Simon had left the BBC somewhat abruptly when, in the summer of 1964, he had been offered the chance to defend the marginal constituency of Coventry Central. He held on to the seat at the general election by a majority of 918.

Simon drove up to the gates of St. Mary's and checked his watch. He was a few minutes early. He pushed back the mop of brown hair from his forehead and thought about the evening ahead. He was taking Elizabeth out to celebrate their fourth wedding anniversary, and had prepared one or two surprises for her. Dinner at Mario & Franco, followed by dancing at the Establishment Club, and then home together for the first time in weeks.

"Um," he said, savoring the thought.

"Hi, stranger," said the lady who jumped in beside him and gave him a kiss. Simon stared at the woman with a perfect smile and long fair hair that turned up at the shoulder. He had stared at her when she had first arrived at the "Panorama" studio that night nearly five years before and he had hardly stopped staring since.

He switched on the ignition. "Want to hear some good news?" he asked, and answered his own question before she could reply. "I'm paired for tonight. That means dinner at Mario & Franco, dancing at the Establishment, home and . . . "

"Do you want to hear the bad news?" asked Elizabeth, also not waiting for a reply. "There's a shortage of staff because of the flu epidemic. I have to be back on duty by ten o'clock."

Simon switched off the ignition. "Well, which would you prefer?" he asked. "Dinner, dancing, or straight home?"

Elizabeth laughed. "We've got three hours," she said. "So we might even find time for dinner."

Chapter
Two

RAYMOND GOULD STARED down at the invitation. He had never seen the inside of No. 10 Downing Street. During the last thirteen years few Socialists had. He passed the embossed card across the breakfast table to his wife.

"Should I accept or refuse, Ray?" she asked in her broad Yorkshire accent.

She was the only person who still called him Ray, and even her attempts at humor now annoyed him. The Greek tragedians had based their drama on "the fatal flaw," and he had no doubt what his had been.

He had met Joyce at a dance given by the nurses of Leeds General Infirmary. He hadn't wanted to go but a second-year undergraduate friend from Roundhay convinced him it would make an amusing break. At school he had shown little interest in girls as his mother kept reminding him that there would be occasion enough for that sort of thing once he had taken his degree. By the time he graduated he felt certain that he was the only virgin left at the university.

He had ended up sitting on his own in the corner of a room decorated with wilting balloons and Day-Glo orange crêpe paper. He sucked disconsolately at a shandy through a bent straw. Whenever his school friend turned round from the dance floor—each time with a different partner—Raymond would smile broadly back. With his National Health spectacles tucked away in an inside pocket, he couldn't always be certain he was smiling at the right person. He began contemplating at what hour he could possibly leave without having to admit the evening had been a total disaster. He wouldn't even have answered her question if it hadn't been for that familiar accent.

"You at the university as well?"

"As well as what?" he asked, without looking directly at her.

"As well as your friend," she said.

"Yes," he replied, looking up at a girl he guessed was about his age.

"I'm from Bradford."

"I'm from Leeds," he admitted, aware he was going redder by the second.

"My name is Joyce," she volunteered.

"Mine's Ray—Raymond," he said.

"Like to dance?"

He wanted to tell her that he had rarely been on a dance floor before in his life but he didn't have the courage. Like a puppet he found himself standing up and being guided by her toward the jivers. So much for his assumption that he was one of nature's leaders.

Once they were on the dance floor he looked at her properly for the first time. She wasn't half bad, any normal Yorkshire boy might have admitted. She was about five-foot-seven, and her auburn hair was tied up in a ponytail, matching the dark brown eyes that had a little too much makeup round them. She wore pink lipstick, the same color as her short skirt from which emerged two very attractive legs. They looked even more attractive when she twirled to the music of the four-piece student band. Raymond discovered that if he twirled Joyce very fast he could see the tops of her stockings, and he remained on the dance floor for longer than he would ever have thought possible. After the quartet had put their instruments away Joyce kissed him goodnight. He walked slowly back to his small room above the butcher's shop.

The following Sunday, in an attempt to gain the upper hand, he took Joyce rowing on the Aire, but his performance was no better than his dancing, and everything on the river overtook him, including a hardy swimmer. He watched out of the side of his eyes for a mocking laugh but Joyce only smiled and chatted about missing Bradford and wanting to return home to nurse. After only a few weeks at university Raymond knew he wanted to get away from Leeds, but he didn't admit it to anyone. When he eventually returned the boat Joyce invited him back to her digs for tea. He went scarlet as they passed her landlady. Joyce hustled him up the worn stone staircase to her room.

Raymond sat on the end of the narrow bed while Joyce made two milkless mugs of tea. After they had both pretended to drink she sat beside him, her hands in her lap. He found himself listening intently to an ambulance siren as it faded away in the distance. She leaned over and kissed him, taking one of his hands and placing it on her knee.

She parted his lips and their tongues touched: he found it a peculiar sensation, an arousing one; his eyes remained closed as she gently led him through each new experience, until he was unable to stop himself committing what he felt sure his mother had once described as a mortal sin.

"It will be easier next time," she said shyly, maneuvering herself from the narrow bed to sort out the crumpled clothes spread across the floor. She was right: he wanted her again in less than an hour, and this time his eyes remained wide open.

It was another six months before Joyce talked about their future and by then Raymond was bored with her and had his sights set on a bright little mathematician in her final year. The mathematician hailed from Surrey.

Just at the time Raymond was summoning up enough courage to let her know the affair was over Joyce told him she was pregnant. His father would have taken a meat ax to him had he suggested an illegal abortion. His mother was only relieved that she was a Yorkshire girl; like the county cricket selection committee, Mrs. Gould did not approve of outsiders.

Raymond and Joyce were married at St. Mary's in Bradford during the long vacation. When the wedding photos were developed Raymond looked so distressed and Joyce so happy they resembled father and daughter rather than husband and wife. After a reception given at the church hall the newly married couple traveled down to Dover to catch the night ferry. Their first night as Mr. and Mrs. Gould was a disaster. Raymond turned out to be a particularly bad sailor. Joyce only hoped that Paris would prove to be memorable—and it was. She had a miscarriage on the second night of their honeymoon.

"Probably caused by all the excitement," his mother said on their return. "Still, you can always have another, can't you? And this time folk won't be able to call it a little . . ."

She checked herself.

Raymond showed no interest in having another. Ten years had passed since that memorable honeymoon; he had escaped to London and become a barrister, but had long since accepted that he was tethered to her for life. Although Joyce was only thirty-two she already needed to cover those once-slim legs that had first so attracted him. How could he be so punished for such a pathetic mistake? Raymond wanted to ask the gods. How mature he had thought he was: how immature he had turned out to be. Divorce made sense, but it would have meant the end of his political ambitions: Yorkshire folk would not have considered selecting a divorced man. To be fair, it hadn't all been a disaster: he had to admit that the locals adored her, and his parents seemed every bit as proud of Joyce as they did of their son. She mixed with the trade unionists and their frightful wives far better than he ever managed. He also had to acknowledge that Joyce had been a major factor in his winning the seat by over 10,000 votes. He wondered how she could sound so sincere the whole time: it never occurred to him that it was natural.

"Why don't you buy yourself a new dress for Downing Street?" Raymond said as they rose from the breakfast table.

She smiled: he had not volunteered such a suggestion for as long as she could remember. Joyce had been left with no illusions about her husband and his feelings for her, but hoped that eventually he would realize she could help him achieve his unspoken ambition.

On the night of the reception at Downing Street Joyce made every effort to look her best. She had spent the morning at Harvey Nichols searching for an outfit appropriate for the occasion, finally returning to a suit she had liked the moment she had walked in to the store. It was not the perfect fit but the sales assistant assured Joyce that "Modom looked quite sensational in it." She only hoped that Raymond's remarks would be half as flattering. By the time she reached home she realized she had nothing to match the unusual color.

Raymond was late returning from the Commons and was pleased to find Joyce ready when he leaped out of the bath. He bit back a remark about the incongruity of her shoes and new suit. As they drove toward Westminster he rehearsed the names of every member of the Cabinet with her, making Joyce repeat them as if she were a child.

The air was cool and crisp that night so Raymond parked his Sunbeam in New Palace Yard and they strolled across Whitehall together to No. 10. A solitary policeman stood guard at the door. Seeing Raymond approach, the officer banged the brass knocker once and the door was opened for the young member and his wife.

Raymond and Joyce stood awkwardly in the hall as if they were waiting outside a headmaster's study. Eventually they were directed to the first floor. They walked slowly up the staircase, which turned out to be less grand than Raymond had anticipated, passing photographs of former Prime Ministers. "Too many Tories," muttered Raymond as he passed Chamberlain, Churchill, Eden, Macmillan, and Home, with Attlee the only framed compensation.

At the top of the stairs stood Harold Wilson, pipe in mouth, waiting to welcome his guests. Raymond was about to introduce his wife when the Prime Minister said, "How are you, Joyce? I'm so glad you could make it."

"Make it? I've been looking forward to the occasion all week." Her frankness made Raymond wince; he failed to notice that it made Wilson chuckle.

Raymond chatted to the Prime Minister's wife about the difficulty of getting poetry published until she turned away to greet the next guest. He then moved off into the drawing room and was soon talking to Cabinet ministers, trade union leaders, and their wives, always keeping a wary eye on Joyce, who seemed engrossed in conversation with the General Secretary of the Trades Union Congress.

Raymond moved on to the American Ambassador, who was telling Andrew Fraser how much he had enjoyed the Edinburgh Festival that summer. Raymond envied Fraser his relaxed clubbable manner and had already worked out that the Scotsman would be a formidable rival among his contemporaries.

"Good evening, Raymond," said Andrew. "Do you know David Bruce?" he asked, as if they were old friends.

"No," Raymond replied, rubbing his palm on his trousers before shaking hands. "Good evening, Your Excellency," he said, glad to see Andrew slipping away. "I was interested to read Johnson's latest communiqué on Vietnam and I must confess the escalation . . ."

Andrew had spotted the Minister of State for Scotland arriving and went over to chat to him.

"How are you, Andrew?" Hugh McKenzie asked.

"Never better."

"And your father?"

"In great form."

"I'm sorry to hear that," said the minister, grinning. "He's giving me a lot of trouble over the Highlands and Islands Development Board."

"He's a sound chap basically," said Andrew, "even if his views are a little misguided." They both laughed as a slight, attractive woman with long brown hair came up to the minister's side. She wore a white silk blouse and a McKenzie tartan skirt.

"Do you know my daughter Alison?"

"No," Andrew said, holding out his hand. "I've not had that pleasure."

"I know who you are," she said, in a slight lowland accent, her eyes flashing. "Andrew Fraser, the man who makes Campbells look trustworthy. The Tories' secret mole."

"It can't be much of a secret if the Scottish Office know about it," said Andrew.

A waiter, wearing the smartest dinner-jacket in the room, approached them carrying a silver tray of thinly-cut sandwiches.

"Would you care for a smoked salmon sandwich?" Alison asked mockingly.

"No, thank you. I gave them up with my Tory background. But beware—if you eat too many you won't appreciate your dinner tonight."

"I wasn't thinking of having dinner."

"Oh, I thought you might enjoy a bite at Sigie's," teased Andrew.

Alison hesitated, then said, "It'll be the first time anyone's picked me up at No. 10."

"I hate to break with tradition," said Andrew. "But why don't I book a table for eight?"

"Is Sigie's one of your aristocratic haunts?"

"Good heavens no, it's far too good for that lot. Why don't we leave in about fifteen minutes? I must have a word with one or two people first."

"I'll bet." She grinned as she watched Fraser comb the room. His years as a Tory party fellow-traveler had taught Andrew all he needed to know about how to make the best use of a cocktail party. His trade union colleagues would never understand that it was not in pursuit of endless smoked salmon sandwiches drowned by whisky. When he arrived back at Alison McKenzie's side she was chatting to Raymond Gould about Johnson's landslide victory at the polls.

"Are you trying to pick up my date?" asked Andrew.

Raymond laughed nervously and pushed his spectacles back up his nose. A moment later Andrew was guiding Alison toward the door to say their farewells, and Raymond, watching them, wondered if he would ever learn to be that relaxed. He looked around for Joyce: it might be wise not to be the last to leave.

Andrew was ushered discreetly to a corner table at Sigie's Club and it became quickly evident to Alison that he had been there several times before. The waiters ran around him as if he were a Tory Cabinet minister, and she had to admit to herself that she enjoyed the experience. After an excellent dinner of roast beef that wasn't burnt and a *crème brûlée* that was they strolled over to Annabel's where they danced until the early morning. Andrew drove Alison back to her Chelsea flat a little after two a.m.

"Care for a nightcap?" she asked casually.

"Daren't," he replied. "I'm making my maiden speech tomorrow."

"So this maiden is to be rejected," she said to his retreating back.

The House of Commons was well attended at five o'clock the following afternoon when Andrew rose to address his fellow members. The Speaker had allowed him to follow the front-bench contributions, an honor Andrew would not be granted again for some considerable time. His father and mother looked down over the railings from the Strangers' Gallery as he informed the commoners that the Lord Provost of Edinburgh had spent a lifetime teaching him all he knew about the constituency he was now proud to represent. The Labour party chuckled at the Opposition's obvious discomfort, but they abided by tradition and made no interruption during a maiden speech.

Andrew had chosen as his subject the question of whether Scotland should remain part of the United Kingdom despite the recent oil discoveries. He delivered a well-argued case, assuring members that he saw no future for his country as a tiny independent state. His rhetoric, and his relaxed turn of phrase, had members laughing on both sides of the House. When he came to the end of his argument, never having once referred to a note, he sat down to loud cheers from his own benches and generous acknowledgment from the Tory side. In his moment of glory he glanced up toward the Strangers' Gallery. His father was leaning forward, following every word. To his surprise sitting in front of his mother on the benches reserved for distinguished visitors was Alison McKenzie, her arms folded on the balcony. He smiled.

Andrew's success was considerably enhanced when later that afternoon another member from the Labour benches rose to address the House for the first time. Tom Carson cared nothing for convention and even less for keeping to tradition and made no attempt to avoid controversy in his maiden speech. He began with an attack on what he described as "the Establishment conspiracy," pointing an accusing finger as much at the ministers on his own front bench as at those opposite him, describing them all as "puppets of the capitalist system."

Members present in the Chamber restrained themselves from interrupting the scowling Liverpudlian, but the Speaker stirred several times as the accusing finger appeared to cross his path as well. He was painfully aware that the member from Liverpool Dockside was going to cause all sorts of problems if this was the way he intended to conduct himself in the House.

When Andrew left the Chamber three speeches later he went to look for Alison, but she had already left; so he took the members' lift up to the Public Gallery and invited his parents to join him for tea in the Harcourt Rooms.

"The last time I had tea here was with Ainslie Munro . . ." Sir Duncan began.

"Then it may be a very long time before you're invited again," Andrew interrupted.

"That may depend on whom we select as Tory candidate to oppose you at the next election," retorted his father.

Several members from both sides of the House came up one by one to congratulate Andrew on his speech. He thanked them all individually but kept glancing hopefully over his father's shoulder, but Alison McKenzie did not appear.

After his parents had finally left to catch the last flight back to Edinburgh Andrew returned to the Chamber to hear Alison's father summing up the debate on behalf of the Government. The Minister of State described Andrew's contribution as one of the finest maiden speeches the House had heard in years. "Maiden it may have been but virginal it was not," concluded Hugh McKenzie.

Once the debate was over and the usual ten o'clock division had been declared by the tellers Andrew left the Chamber. One final vote on a prayer detained members for a further forty-five minutes and Andrew found the tea room—the traditional haunt of the Labour party—as crowded as it had been earlier in the afternoon.

Members jostled for the remains of unappetizing-looking lettuce leaves that any self-respecting rabbit would have rejected, accompanied by blobs of plastic-covered sweating cheese, described optimistically on the billboard as salad. Andrew contented himself with a cup of Nescafé.

Raymond Gould sat alone, slumped in an armchair in the far corner of the tea room, apparently engrossed in a week-old copy of the *New Statesman*. He stared impassively as several of his colleagues went over to Andrew to congratulate him. His own maiden speech the previous week had not been as well received and he knew it. He believed just as passionately about war widows' pensions as Andrew did about the future of Scotland but reading from a prepared manuscript he had been unable to make members hang on his every word. He consoled himself with the thought that Andrew would have to choose the subject for his next speech very carefully as the Opposition would no longer treat him with kid gloves.

Andrew was not concerning himself with such thoughts as he slipped into one of the many internal telephone booths and after checking in his diary dialed a London number. Alison was at home, washing her hair.

"Will it be dry by the time I arrive?"

"It's very long," she reminded him.

"Then I'll have to drive slowly."

When Andrew appeared on the Chelsea doorstep he was greeted by Alison in a housecoat, her newly dry hair falling down well below shoulder level.

"The victor come to claim his spoils?"

"No, only last night's coffee," he said.

"But won't that keep you awake?"

"I certainly hope so."

By the time Andrew left Alison's home at eight the next morning he had already decided he wanted to see a lot more of Hugh McKenzie's daughter. He returned to his own flat in Cheyne Walk, showered, and changed before making breakfast for himself and going over his mail. There were several more messages of congratulations including one from the Secretary of State for Scotland, while *The Times* and the *Guardian* carried brief but favorable comments.

Before leaving for the Commons Andrew checked over an amendment he wanted to move in committee that morning. When he had reworded his efforts several times he picked up his papers and headed off toward Westminster.

Arriving a little early for the ten-thirty committee meeting, Andrew found time to collect his mail from the Members' Post Office just off the Central Lobby. He set off, head down, along the corridor toward the library, flicking through the envelopes to see if he recognized any familiar hand or official-looking missive that demanded to be opened immediately.

As he turned the corner he was surprised to find the House ticker-tape machine surrounded by Conservative members, including the man who had agreed to be his "pair" for voting purposes.

Andrew stared up at the tall figure of Charles Seymour, who, although standing on the fringe of the crowd, still found it possible to read the tapped-out message on the telex machine.

"What's causing so much interest?" he asked, prodding Seymour's elbow.

"Sir Alec has just announced the timetable that'll be followed when we select the new Tory leader."

"We all await with baited breath," said Andrew.

"As well you might," said Charles, ignoring the sarcasm, "since the next announcement will undoubtedly be his resignation. Then the real politics will begin."

"Be sure you back the winner," said Andrew, grinning.

Charles Seymour smiled knowingly but made no comment.

CHAPTER THREE

CHARLES SEYMOUR DROVE his Daimler from the Commons to his father's bank in the City. He still thought of Seymour's of Cheapside as his father's bank although for two generations the family had been only minority shareholders, with Charles himself in possession of a mere two percent of the stock. Nevertheless as his brother Rupert showed no desire in representing the family interests the two percent guaranteed Charles a place on the board and an income sufficient to ensure that his paltry parliamentary salary of £1,750 a year was adequately supplemented.

From the day Charles had first taken his place on the board of Seymour's he had no doubt that the new chairman, Derek Spencer, considered him a dangerous rival. Spencer had lobbied to have Rupert replace his father on retirement and only because of Charles's insistence had Spencer failed to move the old earl to his way of thinking.

When Charles went on to take his seat in Parliament Spencer at once raised the problem of his burdensome responsibilities at the House preventing him from carrying out his day-to-day duties for the board. However, Charles was able to convince a majority of his fellow directors of the advantages of having someone on the board at Westminster, although he knew that would cease if he was ever invited to be a minister.

As Charles left the Daimler in Seymour's courtyard it amused him to consider that his parking space was worth twenty times the value of the car. The area at the front of Seymour's was a relic of his great-grandfather's day. The twelfth Earl of Bridgwater had insisted on an entrance large enough to allow a complete sweep for his coach and four. That conveyance had long disappeared, to be replaced by twelve car spaces for Seymour directors. The bank's new management-conscious chairman, despite all his grammar school virtues, had never suggested the land be used for any other purpose.

The young girl seated at the reception desk abruptly stopped polishing her nails in time to say "Good morning, Mr. Charles," as he came through the revolving doors and disappeared into a waiting lift. A few moments later Charles was seated behind a desk in his small oak-paneled office, a clean white memo pad in front of him. He pressed a button on the intercom and told his secretary that he did not want to be disturbed during the next hour.

Sixty minutes later the white pad had twelve names penciled on it, but ten already had lines drawn through them. Only the names of Reginald Maudling and Edward Heath remained.

Charles tore off the piece of paper and the indented sheet underneath and put them both through the shredder by the side of his desk. He tried to summon up some interest in the agenda for the bank's weekly board meeting; only one item, item seven, seemed to be of any importance. Just before eleven, he gathered up his papers and headed toward the boardroom. Most of his colleagues were already seated when Derek Spencer called item number one as the boardroom clock chimed the hour.

During the ensuing predictable discussion on bank rates, the movement in metal prices, Eurobonds, and client investment policy Charles's mind kept wandering back to the forthcoming leadership election and the importance of backing the winner if he were to be quickly promoted from the back benches.

By the time they reached item seven on the agenda Charles had made up his mind. Derek Spencer opened a discussion on the proposed loans to Mexico and Poland, and most of the board members agreed with him that the bank should participate in one but not risk both.

Charles's thoughts, however, were not in Mexico City or Warsaw. They were far nearer home and when the chairman called for a vote, Charles didn't register.

"Mexico or Poland, Charles. Which of the two do you favor?"

"Heath," he replied.

"I beg your pardon," said Derek Spencer.

Charles snapped back from Westminster to Cheapside to find everyone around the boardroom table staring at him. With the air of a man who had been giving the matter considerable thought Charles said firmly, "Mexico," and added, "The great difference between the two countries can best be gauged by their attitudes to repayment. Mexico might not want to repay, but Poland won't be able to, so why not limit our risks and back Mexico? If it comes to litigation I'd prefer to be against someone who won't pay rather than someone who can't." The older members round the table nodded in agreement; the right son of Bridgwater was sitting on the board.

When the meeting was over Charles joined his colleagues for lunch in the directors' dining room. On the walls hung two Hogarths, a Brueghel, a Goya, and a Rembrandt that could distract even the most indulgent gourmet: just another reminder of his great-grandfather's ability to select winners. Charles did not wait to make a decision between the Cheddar and the Stilton as he wanted to be back in the Commons for question time.

On arrival at the House he immediately made his way to the smoking room, long regarded by the Tories as their preserve. There in the deep leather armchairs and cigar-laden atmosphere the talk was entirely of who would be Sir Alec's successor.

Charles could not avoid overhearing Pimkin's high-pitched voice. "As Edward Heath is Shadow Chancellor while we debate the Finance Bill on the floor of the House, it is he who is bound to be the center of attention."

Later that afternoon Charles returned to the Commons Chamber. He wanted to observe Heath and his Shadow team deal with the Government's amendments one by one.

He was about to leave the Chamber when Raymond Gould rose to move an amendment. Charles listened with grudging admiration as Raymond's intellectual grasp and force of argument easily compensated for his lack of oratorial skill. Although Gould was a cut above the rest of his intake on the Labour benches he didn't frighten Charles. Twelve generations of shrewd business acumen had kept large parts of Leeds in the hands of the Bridgwater family without the likes of Raymond Gould even being aware of it.

Charles took supper in the Members' Dining Room that night and sat at the large table in the center of the room frequented by Tory back-benchers. There was only one topic of conversation and as the same two names kept emerging it was obvious that it was going to be a very close run thing.

When Charles arrived back at his Eaton Square home after the ten o'clock division Fiona was already tucked up in bed reading Philip Larkin's *The Whitsun Weddings*.

"They let you out early tonight."

"Not too bad," said Charles, and began regaling her with how he had spent his day, before disappearing into the bathroom.

If Charles imagined he was cunning, his wife, Lady Fiona, only daughter of the Duke of Falkirk, was in a different league. She and Charles had been selected for each other at an early age and neither had questioned or doubted the wisdom of the choice. Although Charles had squired numerous girlfriends before their marriage in between he had always assumed he would return to Fiona. Charles's grandfather always maintained that the aristocracy was becoming far too lax and sentimental about marriage. "Women," he declared, "are for bearing children and ensuring a continuation of the male line."

The old earl became even more staid in his convictions when he was made aware that Rupert showed little interest in the opposite sex, and was rarely to be found in the company of women. Fiona would never have dreamed of disagreeing with the old man to his face as she was determined that it would be a son of hers that would inherit the earldom. But despite enthusiastic and then contrived efforts Charles seemed unable to sire an heir. Fiona was later assured by a Harley Street physician that there was no reason *she* could not bear children. The specialist had suggested that perhaps her husband pay the clinic a visit. She shook her head, knowing Charles would dismiss such an idea out of hand, and never mentioned the subject to anyone again.

Fiona spent a considerable amount of her spare time in their Sussex Downs constituency furthering Charles's political career. She had learned to live with the fact that theirs was not destined to be a romantic marriage and resigned herself to its other advantages. Although many men confessed covertly and overtly that they found the tall elegant lady desirable she either ignored their overtures or pretended not to notice them.

By the time Charles returned from the bathroom in his blue silk pajamas Fiona had formed a plan, but first she needed some questions answered.

"Whom do you favor?"

"I'd like Sir Alec to carry on: after all, the Homes have been friends of our two families for over 400 years."

"But that's a non-starter," said Fiona. "Everyone knows Alec is on the way out."

"I agree, and that's exactly why I spent the entire afternoon observing the worthwhile candidates."

"Did you come to any serious conclusions?" Fiona asked.

"Heath and Maudling are out on their own, though to be honest I've never had a conversation with either of them that lasted for more than five minutes."

"In that case we must turn a disadvantage into an advantage."

"What do you mean, old girl?" Charles asked as he climbed into bed beside his wife.

"Think back. When you were President of Pop at Eton, could you have put a name to any of the first-year boys?"

"Certainly not," said Charles.

"Exactly. And I'd be willing to bet that neither Heath nor Maudling could put a name to twenty of the new intake on the Tory benches."

"Where are you leading me, Lady Macbeth?"

"No bloody hands will be needed for this killing. Simply, having chosen your Duncan you volunteer to organize the new intake for him. If he becomes leader, he's bound to feel it would be appropriate to select one or two new faces for his team."

"You could be right."

"Well, let's sleep on it," said Fiona, turning out the light on her side of the bed.

Charles didn't sleep on it but lay restless most of the night turning over in his mind what she had said. When Fiona awoke the next morning she carried on the conversation as if there had been no break in between. "Do you have to be rushed into a decision?"

"No, but if I let it drift I could be accused of jumping on the bandwagon and then I would have lost my chance to be seen as a leader among the new intake."

"Better still," she continued, "before the man you choose announces he is a candidate, demand that he stand on behalf of the new members."

"Clever," said Charles.

"Whom have you decided on?"

"Heath," Charles replied without hesitation.

"I'll back your political judgment," said Fiona. "Just trust me when it comes to tactics. First, we compose a letter."

In dressing gowns, on the floor at the end of the bed, the two elegant figures drafted and redrafted a note to Edward Heath. At nine-thirty it was finally composed and sent round by hand to his rooms in Albany.

The next morning Charles was invited to the small, bachelor flat for coffee. They talked for over an hour and later, as the two men stood below a Piper landscape in the drawing room, the deal was struck.

Charles thought Sir Alec would announce his resignation in the late summer which would give him eight to ten weeks to carry out a campaign. Fiona typed out a list of all the new members and during the next eight weeks every one of them was invited to their Eaton Square flat for drinks. Fiona was subtle enough to see that members of the Lower House were outnumbered by other guests, often from the House of Lords. Heath managed to escape from his front-bench duties on the Finance Bill to spend at least an hour with the Seymours once a week. As the day of Sir Alec Douglas-Home's resignation drew nearer Charles realized the leadership result could be almost as important to him as it would be to Heath, but he also remained confident that he had carried out his plan in a subtle and discreet way. He would have been willing to place a wager that no one other than Edward Heath had worked out how deeply he was involved.

One man who attended the second of Fiona's soirées saw exactly what was going on. While many of the guests spent their time admiring the Seymour art collection Simon Kerslake kept a wary eye on his host and hostess. Kerslake was not convinced that Edward Heath would win the forthcoming election and felt confident that Reginald Maudling would turn out to be the party's natural choice. Maudling was, after all, Shadow Foreign Secretary, a former Chancellor, and far senior to Heath. More important, he was a married man. Simon doubted the Tories would ever pick a bachelor to lead them.

As soon as Kerslake had left the Seymours he jumped into a taxi and returned immediately to the Commons. He found Reginald Maudling in the Members' Dining Room seated at the table frequented only by the Shadow Cabinet. He waited until Maudling had finished his meal before asking if they could have a few moments alone. The tall shambling figure—not altogether certain of the name of the new member—

leaned over and invited Simon to join him for a drink in his room.

Maudling listened intently to all the enthusiastic young man had to say and accepted the judgment of the well-informed member without question. It was agreed that Simon should try to counter the Seymour campaign and report back his results twice a week.

While Seymour could call on all the powers and influence of his Etonian background, Kerslake could rely on the knowledge and arm-twisting skills gained from his time as President of the Oxford Union. Simon weighed up the advantages and disadvantages he possessed. He did not own a palatial home in Eaton Square in which Turners, Constables, and Holbeins were not to be found in books but on the walls. He also lacked a glamorous society wife. Simon lived in a small house in Beaufort Street in Chelsea and Elizabeth was a gynecologist at St. Mary's Hospital, Paddington. Although Elizabeth gave Simon's political aspirations her full backing she still considered her own career every bit as important, an opinion with which Simon concurred. The local Coventry press had on several occasions recalled in their columns how Elizabeth had left her three-day-old child to help perform a Caesarian section on a mother in the adjoining ward and, two years later, had to be dragged off night duty just as she went into labor with their second child.

This independence of character was one of the reasons Simon had admired Elizabeth when they first met, but he realized she was no match for Lady Fiona Seymour as a hostess and he never wanted her to be. He despised pushy political wives.

Simon spent the following days trying to work out the certain Maudling and certain Heath supporters, although many members claimed they would favor both candidates, according to who asked them. These he listed as doubtfuls. When Enoch Powell threw his cap into the ring Simon could not find a single new member other than Alec Pimkin who openly supported him. That left forty members from the new intake who still had to be followed up. He estimated twelve certain

Heath, eleven certain Maudling, and one Powell, leaving sixteen undecided. As the day of the election drew nearer it became obvious that few of the remaining sixteen actually knew either candidate well, and were still not sure for whom they should vote.

Simon realized that he could not invite them all round to Beaufort Street between Elizabeth's ward duties, so he would have to go to them. During the last eight weeks he accompanied his chosen leader as he addressed the party faithfuls in twenty-three new members' constituencies. Simon traveled from Bodmin to Glasgow, from Penrith to Great Yarmouth, briefing Maudling studiously before every meeting.

Gradually it became obvious to everyone that Charles Seymour and Simon Kerslake were the chosen lieutenants among the new intake. Some members resented the whispered confidences at the Eaton Square cocktail parties, or the discovery that Simon Kerslake had visited their constituencies under false pretenses, while others were simply envious of the reward that would inevitably be heaped on the victor.

"But why do you support Maudling?" Elizabeth had asked him one evening over dinner.

"Reggie has a great deal more experience of Government than Heath—and in any case he's more caring about those around him."

"But Heath appears to be so much more professional," Elizabeth insisted, pouring her husband a glass of wine.

"That may well be the case, but the British have always preferred good amateurs to preside over their affairs."

"If you believe all that stuff about amateurs why become so involved yourself?"

Simon considered her question for some time before answering. "Because I don't come from the type of background that automatically commands the center of the Tory stage," he admitted.

"Neither does Heath," commented Elizabeth dryly.

* * *

Although everyone inside and outside of Parliament knew it could not be long before Sir Alec formally announced his resignation it did not become official until 22 July 1965, when he addressed the 1922 Committee of Tory back-benchers.

The date chosen for the leadership election was just five days later. During that time Simon Kerslake and Charles Seymour worked almost round the clock but, despite many national papers' commissioned polls, columns of newsprint offering statistics and opinions, no one seemed certain of the outcome, other than to predict that Powell would come third.

Charles and Simon began avoiding each other and Fiona started referring to Kerslake, first in private then in public, as "that pushy self-made man." She stopped using the expression when Alec Pimkin asked in all innocence whether she was referring to Edward Heath.

On the morning of the secret ballot Simon and Charles voted early and spent the rest of the day pacing the corridors of the Commons trying to assess the result. By lunchtime they were both outwardly exuberant, while inwardly despondent.

At two-fifteen they were seated in the large committee room to hear the chairman of the 1922 Committee make the historic announcement:

"The result of the first election for leader of the Conservative parliamentary party," said Sir William Anstruther-Gray, "is as follows:

Edward Heath	150 votes
Reginald Maudling	133 votes
Enoch Powell	15 votes."

An hour later Reginald Maudling, who had been lunching in the City, telephoned Heath to say he would be happy to serve under him as the new leader. Charles and Fiona opened a bottle of Krug while Simon took Elizabeth to the Old Vic to see *The Royal Hunt of the Sun*. He slept the entire way through Robert Stephens's brilliant performance, before Elizabeth drove him home.

"How come you didn't fall asleep? After all, you've been just as busy as I have the last few weeks," Simon asked.

Elizabeth smiled. "It was my turn to want to be involved with what was happening on the center of the stage."

Two weeks later, on 4 August, Edward Heath announced his Shadow team. Reggie Maudling was to be deputy leader. Sir Alec accepted the Foreign Office brief while Powell went to Defense. Charles Seymour received an invitation to join the Housing and Local Government team as its junior spokesman, thus becoming the first of the new intake to be given front-bench responsibilities.

Simon Kerslake received a handwritten letter from Reggie Maudling thanking him for his valiant efforts.

BOOK TWO

1966–1974
JUNIOR OFFICE

CHAPTER
FOUR

WHEN ALISON MCKENZIE moved into Andrew Fraser's Cheyne Walk flat everyone, including her father, the Minister of State for Scotland, assumed they would soon announce their engagement.

For the previous three months Andrew had had his head down in committee helping out with the public bills relating exclusively to Scotland which were referred to the committee from the House itself. He found much of the committee work boring, as so many members repeated the views of their colleagues, less and less articulately, and for some time only his doodling improved. Even so, Andrew's energy and charm made him a popular companion through the long summer months and he quickly gained enough confidence to suggest first minor and later major changes to amendments considered by the committee. The disparity between penalties under English and Scottish law had long worried him, and he pressed hard for changes that would bring the two systems closer together. He soon discovered that the Scottish Labour members were more traditional and clannish than even the most hidebound of Tories.

When the session came to an end Andrew invited Alison to spend a long weekend with his parents at their country home in Stirling at the end of the recess.

"Do you expect me to sleep under the same roof as a former Conservative Lord Provost of Edinburgh?" she demanded.

"Why not? You've been sleeping with his son for the past six months."

"Well, the same roof perhaps, but there's one weekend we won't be able to sleep in the same bed."

"Why not? The Tories may be snobs but they're not hypocrites."

Alison didn't want to admit that she was actually quite nervous about spending the weekend with Andrew's father, as she had heard him continually maligned at her parents' breakfast table for over twenty years.

When she did meet "Old Dungheap," as her father referred to the former Lord Provost, Alison liked him immediately. He reminded her so much of her own father, while Lady Fraser was not at all the snobbish little battle-ax her mother had prepared her for.

It was immediately agreed that during the weekend nobody would talk politics. Andrew and Alison spent most of the Friday afternoon walking through the heather-covered hills and discussing in detail how they saw their future. On the Saturday morning the minister telephoned Sir Duncan and invited them over to Bute House—the official residence of the Secretary of State for Scotland—for dinner.

After so many years of opposing each other both families were nervous of the social get-together, but it seemed the children were to bridge the political gap they had failed to build for themselves. The McKenzies had invited two other Edinburgh families to dinner in the hope that it would ease the tension of the occasion, a branch of the Forsyths who owned the departmental store in Princes Street, and the Menzies, who ran the largest chain of newsagents in the country.

Andrew had decided to use the gathering to make an announcement at the end of dinner, and having spent longer shopping than he originally intended was the last to arrive at Bute House.

After they had all found their place cards around the long dining room table the fourteen guests remained silent as a lone piper played a lament before the chef entered carrying a silver salver which bore on it a large haggis for the minister's inspection. Sir Duncan's opinion was sought: "Warm—reekin rich!" he declared. It was the first occasion the two men had wholeheartedly agreed on anything.

Andrew did not eat as much as the others because he couldn't take his eyes off the guest who had been placed opposite him. She didn't pay much attention to Andrew, but seemed always to be smiling or laughing, making those around her enjoy her company. When Andrew had last seen Louise Forsyth it had been scoring goals on a hockey pitch. She had been a dumpy little girl with long pigtails and a tendency to go for one's ankles rather than for the ball. Now the jet black hair was short and curly, while the body had become slim and graceful. After dinner Andrew mixed among the guests and it was well after one o'clock when the party broke up: he never managed a moment alone with her. Andrew was relieved to discover that Alison wanted to spend the night with her parents at Bute House while the Frasers traveled back to their home in Stirling.

"You're very silent for a Socialist," his father said in the car on the way home.

"He's in love," said his mother fondly.

Andrew made no reply.

The next morning he rose early and traveled into Edinburgh to see his agent. The minister had caught the first flight back to London but had left a message asking if Andrew would be kind enough to see him at ten o'clock in Dover House, the London headquarters of the Scottish Office, the following day, "on an official matter."

Andrew was delighted but it didn't change his attitude.

Having answered his local post and dealt with some constituents' problems he left his office and made his way over to the New Club to make a private phone call. He was relieved to find her still at home. She reluctantly agreed to join him for lunch. Andrew sat alone for forty minutes, checking the grandfather clock every few moments while pretending to read the *Scotsman*. When she was eventually ushered in by the steward, Andrew knew this was the woman with whom he wanted to spend the rest of his life. He would have laughed, if he had been told—before the previous evening—that he could change his well-ordered plans on what was nothing more than a casual meeting. But then he had never met anyone like Louise before and was already convinced he never would again.

"Miss Forsyth," said the man wearing the green livery uniform of the club. He inclined his head slightly and left them alone.

Louise smiled and Andrew guided her to a table in the corner.

"It was kind of you to come at such short notice," he said nervously.

"No," she said. "It was very stupid of me."

Over a lunch which he ordered but didn't eat Andrew learned that Louise Forsyth was engaged to an old friend of his from university days and that they planned to be married the following spring. By the end of lunch he had convinced her they should at least meet again.

Andrew caught the five-ten flight back to London and sat alone in his flat and waited. Alison returned a little after nine o'clock and asked why he hadn't traveled down from Scotland with her or at least phoned. Andrew immediately told her the truth. She burst into tears while he stood helplessly by. Within the hour she had moved all her possessions out of Andrew's flat and left.

At ten-thirty he phoned Louise again.

The next morning Andrew dropped into the Commons to collect his mail from the Members' Post Office, and to check with the Whips' office as to what time they were anticipating the votes that day.

"One at six and two at ten," shouted a junior Whip from

behind his desk. "And we could lose the second so be certain you're not far away if we need you."

Andrew nodded and turned to leave.

"By the way, congratulations."

"On what?" queried Andrew.

"Oh hell, another indiscretion to start the week on. It's penciled in on the morning sheet," said the Whip, tapping a piece of paper in front of him.

"What is?" asked Andrew impatiently.

"Your appointment as Parliamentary Private Secretary to Hugh McKenzie. For pity's sake don't let him know I told you."

"I won't," promised Andrew, breathing a sigh of relief. He checked his watch: perfect timing to stroll over to Dover House and keep his appointment with the minister.

He whistled as he walked down Whitehall and the doorman saluted as he entered the ministry. They had obviously been briefed as well. He tried not to show too much anticipation. He was met at the top of the stone steps by the minister's secretary.

"Good morning," Andrew said, trying to sound as if he had no idea what was in store for him.

"Good morning, Mr. Fraser," replied the secretary. "The minister has asked me to apologize for not being available to see you, but he has been called away to a Cabinet committee to discuss the new IMF standby credit."

"I see," said Andrew. "Has the minister rearranged my appointment?"

"Well, no, he hasn't," replied the secretary, sounding a little surprised. "He simply said that it was no longer important, and he was sorry to have wasted your time."

Charles Seymour was enjoying the challenge of his new appointment as a junior Opposition spokesman. Even if he was not actually making decisions on future policy he was listening to them, and at least he felt he was near the center of affairs. Whenever a debate on housing took place in the

Commons he was allowed to sit on the front bench along with the rest of the team. He had already caused the defeat of two amendments on the Town and Country Planning Bill in standing committee, and had added one of his own, relating to the protection of trees, during the report stage of the bill on the floor of the House. "It isn't preventing a world war," he admitted to Fiona, "but in its own way it's quite important because if we win the election I'm confident of being offered junior office and then I'll have a real chance to shape policy."

Fiona continued to play her part, hosting monthly dinner parties at their Eaton Square house. By the end of the year every member of the Shadow Cabinet had dined with the Seymours at least once and Fiona never wore the same dress twice or allowed a menu to be repeated.

When the parliamentary year began again in October Charles was one of the names continually dropped by the political pundits. Here was someone to watch. "He makes things happen," was the sentiment that was expressed again and again. He could barely cross the Members' Lobby without a correspondent trying to solicit his views on everything from butter mountains to rape. Fiona cut out of the papers every mention of her husband and couldn't help noticing that, if any new member was receiving more press coverage than Charles, it was a young Socialist from Leeds called Raymond Gould.

Raymond's name began to disappear from political columns soon after his success on the budget debate; his colleagues assumed it was because he was busy building a career at the bar. Had they passed his room at the Temple they would have heard the continual tap of a typewriter and been unable to contact him on his off-the-hook phone.

Each night Raymond could be found in chambers writing page after page, checking then rechecking his proofs, and often referring to the piles of books that cluttered his desk. When his *Full Employment at Any Cost? Reflections of a Worker Educated After the Thirties* was published it caused an immediate sensation. The suggestion that the unions would become impotent and the Labour party would need to be more radical to capture the young vote was never likely to endear him to the party activists. Raymond had anticipated that it would provoke a storm of abuse from union leaders, and even among some of his more left-wing colleagues. But A. J. P. Taylor suggested in *The Times* that it was the most profound and realistic look at the Labour party since Anthony Crosland's *The Future of Socialism*, and had given the country a politician of rare honesty and courage. Raymond soon became aware that his strategy and hard work was paying dividends. He found himself a regular topic of conversation at political dinner parties in London.

Joyce thought the book a magnificent piece of scholarship and she spent a considerable time trying to convince trade unionists who had only read out-of-context quotations from it in the *Sun* or *Daily Mirror* that it in fact showed a passionate concern for the trade union movement, while at the same time realistically considering the Labour party's future in the next decade.

The Labour Chief Whip took Raymond on one side and told him, "You've caused a right stir, lad. Now keep your head down for a few months and you'll probably find every Cabinet member quoting you as if it was party policy."

Raymond took the Chief Whip's advice, but he did not have to wait months. Just three weeks after the book's publication the Prime Minister quoted a whole passage at the Durham Miners' Rally. A few weeks later Raymond received a missive from No. 10 requesting him to check over the Prime Minister's speech to the TUC conference and add any suggestions he might have.

Simon Kerslake had sulked for about twenty-four hours after Maudling's defeat for the leadership. He then decided to turn his anger and energy toward the Government benches. It hadn't taken him long to work out that there was a fifteen-minute period twice a week when someone with his skills of oratory could command notice. At the beginning of a new session each week he would carefully study the order paper and in particular the first five questions listed for the Prime Minister on the Tuesday and Thursday. Every Monday morning he would prepare a supplementary for at least three of them. These he worded, then reworded, so that they were biting and witty and always likely to embarrass the Government. Although preparation of such supplementary questions could take several hours Simon would make them sound as though they had been jotted down on the back of the order paper during question time—and in fact would even do so. Elizabeth teased him about how long he took on something she considered trivial. He reminded her of Churchill's comment after being praised for a brilliant rejoinder, "All my best off-the-cuff remarks had been worked on days before."

Even so Simon was surprised at how quickly the House took it for granted that he would be there on the attack, probing, demanding, harrying the Prime Minister's every move. Whenever he rose from his seat the party perked up in anticipation, and many of his interruptions reached the political column of the daily newspapers the following day.

Unemployment was the subject of that day's question. Simon was on his feet leaning forward jabbing a finger in the direction of the Government front bench.

"With the appointment of four extra Secretaries of State this week the Prime Minister can at least claim he has full employment—in the Cabinet."

The Prime Minister sank lower into his seat, looking forward to the recess.

CHAPTER
FIVE

When the Queen opened Parliament the talk was not of the contents of her speech, which traditionally lists the aims of the Government of the day, but of how much of the legislation could possibly be carried out while the Labour party retained a majority of only four. Any contentious legislation was likely to be defeated at the committee stage and everyone knew it. The Conservatives were convinced they could win the forthcoming election whatever date the Prime Minister chose until the by-election held in Hull increased the Labour majority from 1,100 to 5,350. The Prime Minister couldn't believe the result and asked the Queen to dissolve Parliament immediately and to call a general election. The date announced from Buckingham Palace was 31 March.

Simon Kerslake began spending most of his spare time in his Coventry constituency. The local people seemed pleased with the apprenticeship of their new member, but the disinterested statisticians pointed out that a swing of less than one percent would remove him from the House for another five years. By then his rivals would be on the second rung of the ladder.

The Tory Chief Whip advised Simon to stay put in Coventry and not to participate in any further parliamentary business. "There'll be no more three-line whips between now and the election," he assured him. "The most worthwhile thing you can do is pick up votes in Coventry, not give them in Westminster."

Elizabeth could only manage two weeks' leave of absence from St. Mary's, and yet between the two of them they covered the entire constituency before election day. Simon's opponent was the former member, Alf Abbott, who became progressively confident of victory as the national swing to Labour accelerated during the campaign. The slogan "You know Labour Government works" was sounding convincing after only eighteen months in power. The Liberals fielded a third candidate, Nigel Bainbridge, but he admitted openly that he only hoped to save his deposit.

Alf Abbott felt assured enough to challenge Simon to a public debate. Although it was usual for the sitting member to refuse to be drawn on such occasions Simon jumped at his opponent's challenge and prepared for the encounter with his usual diligence. Seven days before the election Simon and Elizabeth stood in the wings behind the stage of Coventry town hall with Alf Abbott, Nigel Bainbridge, and their wives. The three men made stilted conversation while the women eyed each other's outfits critically. The political correspondent of the *Coventry Evening Telegraph*, acting as chairman, introduced each of the protagonists as they walked on to the stage, to whipped-up applause from different sections of the hall. Simon spoke first and held the attention of the large audience for over twenty minutes. Those who tried to heckle him ended up regretting having brought attention to themselves. Without once referring to his notes, he quoted figures and clauses from Government bills with an ease that impressed even Elizabeth. Abbott followed him and made a bitter attack on the Tories, accusing them of still wanting to tread down the workers at any cost, and was greeted by large cheers from his section of the audience. Bainbridge claimed that neither understood the real issues and went into an involved dissertation on the problem of the local sewers. During the questions that followed Simon once again proved to be far better informed than Abbott or Bainbridge, but he was aware that the packed hall only held 700 that cold March evening while elsewhere in Coventry were 50,000 more voters, most of them glued to "Coronation Street."

Although the local press proclaimed Simon the victor of a one-sided debate he remained downcast by the national dailies which were now predicting a landslide for Labour.

On election morning Simon and Elizabeth were up by six and among the first to cast their votes at the local primary school. They spent the rest of the day traveling from polling station to committee room to party checking posts, trying to keep up the morale of their supporters. Everywhere they went the committed believed in his victory but Simon knew that the national swing would be impossible to ignore. A senior Conservative back-bencher had once told him that an outstanding member could be worth a thousand personal votes and a weak opponent might sacrifice another thousand. It wasn't going to be enough.

By nine o'clock the last polling station had been locked and Simon and Elizabeth collapsed into a local pub and ordered two halves of bitter. They sat and watched the television above the bar. The commentator was saying that during the day a straw poll had been taken outside six constituencies in London and from those figures they were predicting a Labour majority of sixty to seventy seats. Up on the screen flashed the seventy seats most vulnerable to siege by Labour. Ninth on the list was Coventry Central: Simon ordered the other half.

"We should be off to watch the count soon," said Elizabeth.

"There's no hurry."

"Don't be such a wimp, Simon. And remember you're still the member," she said, surprisingly sharply. "You owe it to your supporters to remain confident after all the work they've put in."

In the town hall black boxes were being delivered by police

vehicles from every ward in the constituency. Their contents were tipped on to trestle tables which made up three sides of a square on the vast cleared floor. The town clerk and his personal staff stood alone in the well made by the tables, while council workers sat around the outside carefully stacking up the votes into little piles of a hundred. These in turn were checked by party scrutineers who hovered over them, hawklike, often demanding that a particular hundred be rechecked.

The little piles grew into large stacks which were then placed next to each other, and as the hours passed it became obvious even to a casual observer that the outcome was going to be extremely close.

The tension on the floor mounted as each hundred, then each thousand, was handed over to the clerk. Rumors that began at one end of the room had been puffed up like soufflés long before they had reached the waiting crowd standing in a chill wind outside the hall. By midnight, several constituencies' results around the country had been declared. The national swing seemed to be much as predicted, around three percent to Labour, which would give them the promised majority of seventy or over.

At twelve-twenty-one the Coventry town clerk invited all three candidates to join him in the center of the room. He told them the result of the count.

A recount was immediately demanded. The town clerk agreed, and each pile of voting slips was returned to the tables and checked over again.

An hour later the town clerk called the three candidates together again and briefed them on the result of the recount; it had changed by only three votes.

Another recount was requested and the town clerk reluctantly acquiesced. By two o'clock in the morning Elizabeth felt she had no nails left. Another hour passed, during which Heath conceded defeat while Wilson gave an extended interview to ITN spelling out his program for the new Parliament.

At two-twenty-seven the town clerk called the three candidates together for the last time and they all accepted the result. The town clerk walked up on to the stage accompanied by the rivals. He tapped the microphone to check the speaker was working, cleared his throat, and said:

"I, the undersigned, being the acting returning officer for the constituency of Coventry Central, hereby announce the total number of votes cast for each candidate to be as follows:

Alf Abbott	19,716
Nigel Bainbridge	7,002
Simon Kerslake	19,731

I therefore declare Simon Kerslake to be the duly elected Member of Parliament for the constituency of Coventry Central."

Even though the Labour party ended up with an overall majority in the House of ninety-seven, Simon had still won by fifteen votes.

Raymond Gould increased his majority to 12,413 in line with the national swing, and Joyce was ready for a week's rest.

Andrew Fraser improved his vote by 2,468 and announced his engagement to Louise Forsyth on the night after the election.

Charles Seymour could never recall accurately the size of his majority because, as Fiona explained to the old earl the following morning, "They don't count the Conservative vote in Sussex Downs, darling, they weigh it."

CHAPTER
SIX

IN MOST DEMOCRATIC countries a newly elected leader enjoys a transitional period during which he is able to announce the policies he intends to pursue and whom he has selected to implement them. In Britain MPs sit by their phones and wait for forty-eight hours immediately after the election result has been declared. If a call comes in the first twelve hours they will be asked to join the Cabinet, the second twelve given a position as a Minister of State, the third twelve made an Under-Secretary of State, and the last twelve a Parliamentary Private Secretary to a Cabinet minister. If the phone hasn't rung by then, they remain on the back benches.

Andrew Fraser had not bothered to be anywhere near a phone when the BBC midday news announced that Hugh McKenzie had been promoted from Minister of State to Secretary of State for Scotland, with a seat in the Cabinet. Andrew and Louise Forsyth decided to spend a quiet weekend at Aviemore, he to relax and climb other mountains before returning to the House, she to make plans for their forthcoming wedding.

It had taken Andrew countless trips to Edinburgh to convince Louise what had happened to him at Bute House that night had not been mere infatuation that would soon pass, but held long-term conviction. When the one weekend he couldn't travel to the Scottish capital and she came down to London he knew she no longer doubted his resolve. Andrew had found in the past that once the conquest was achieved interest soon waned. For him, though, his love for "the wee slip of a thing," as his mother had come to describe Louise, grew and grew.

Although Louise was only five foot three she was so slim she appeared far taller, and her short black hair, blue eyes, and laughing smile had many tall men bending down to take a closer look.

"You eat like a pig and look like a rake. I don't know how you manage it," grumbled Andrew over dinner one night. He played regular games of squash and swam three times a week to keep his own heavy frame in trim. He stared in admiration and not a little envy as Louise's eyes twinkled mischievously before she devoured another portion of Black Forest *gâteau*.

Although she had been brought up in a strict Calvinist household in which politics were never discussed Louise quickly learned about the machinery of Government and soon found herself debating long into the night with Sir Duncan. At first he scored points off her with ease, but it was not long before he had to answer her demands with more and more reasoned arguments, and sometimes even that was not enough.

By the time the election had taken place Louise had become a total convert to Andrew's views. The squalor in some of the parts of the Edinburgh Carlton constituency, which she had never set foot in before, made her sick at heart. Like all converts, she became zealous and began by trying to reform the entire Forsyth clan. She even paid twelve shillings to join the Scottish Labour party.

"Why did you do that?" asked Andrew, trying not to show his pleasure.

"I'm against mixed marriages," she replied.

Andrew was delighted and surprised by the interest she

took, and the local constituency's suspicions of "the wealthy lady" soon turned to affection.

"Your future husband will be Secretary of State for Scotland one day," many of them shouted, as she walked down the narrow cobbled streets.

"It's Downing Street, not Bute House, that I want to live in," he had once confided to her. "And in any case I've still got to become a junior minister."

"That could change in the very near future."

"Not while Hugh McKenzie is Secretary of State," he said, not under his breath.

"To hell with McKenzie," she said. "Surely one of his Cabinet colleagues has the guts to offer you the chance to be his PPS?" But despite Louise's sentiments the phone did not ring that weekend.

Raymond Gould returned from Leeds the moment the count was over, leaving Joyce to carry out the traditional "thank you" drive around the constituency.

When he wasn't sitting by the phone the following day he was walking around it, nervously pushing his glasses back up his nose. The first call came from his mother who had rung to congratulate him.

"On what?" he asked. "Have you heard something?"

"No, love," she said, "I just rang to say how pleased I was about your increased majority."

"Oh."

"And to add how sorry we were not to see you before you left the constituency, especially as you have to pass the shop on the way to the A1."

Not again, Mother, he wanted to say.

The second call was from a colleague inquiring if Raymond had been offered a job.

"Nothing so far," he said before learning of his contemporary's promotion.

The third call was from one of Joyce's friends.

"When will she be back?" another Yorkshire accent inquired.

"I've no idea," said Raymond, desperate to get the caller off the line.

"I'll call again this afternoon, then."

"Fine," said Raymond, putting the phone down quickly.

He went into the kitchen to make himself a cheese sandwich, but there wasn't any cheese, so he ate stale bread smeared with three-week-old butter. He was halfway through a second slice when the phone rang.

"Raymond?"

He held his breath.

"Noel Brewster."

He exhaled in exasperation as he recognized the vicar's voice.

"Can you read the second lesson when you're next up in Leeds? We had rather hoped you would read it this morning—your dear wife . . ."

"Yes," he promised. "The first weekend I am back in Leeds." The phone rang again as soon as he placed it back on the receiver.

"Raymond Gould?" said an anonymous voice.

"Speaking," he said.

"The Prime Minister will be with you in one moment."

Raymond waited. The front door opened and another voice shouted, "It's only me. I don't suppose you found anything to eat, poor love." Joyce joined Raymond in the drawing room.

Without looking at his wife he waved his hand at her to keep quiet.

"Ray," said a voice on the other end of the line.

"Good afternoon, Prime Minister," he replied, rather formally in response to the more pronounced Yorkshire accent.

"I was hoping you would feel able to join the new team as Under-Secretary for Employment?"

Raymond breathed a sigh of relief. It was exactly what he'd hoped for. "I'd be delighted, Prime Minister."

"Good, that will give the trade union leaders something new to think about." The phone went dead.

Raymond Gould, Under-Secretary of State at the Department of Employment, sat motionless on the third rung of the ladder.

As Raymond left the house the next morning he was greeted by a driver standing next to a gleaming black Austin Westminster. Unlike his secondhand Sunbeam, it glowed in the morning light. The rear door was opened and Raymond climbed in to be driven off to the department. Thank God he knows where my office is, thought Raymond as he sat alone in the back. By his side on the back seat was a red leather box the size of a very thick briefcase with gold lettering running along the edge: "Under-Secretary of State for Employment." Raymond turned the small key, knowing what Alice must have felt like on her way down the rabbit hole. The inside was crammed with buff files. He opened the first to see, "A five-point plan for discussion by Cabinet on how to keep unemployment under one million." He immediately started to read the closely typed documents.

When Charles Seymour returned to the Commons on the Tuesday there was a note from the Whips' office waiting for him on the Members' Letter-board. One of the Housing and Local Government team had lost his seat in the general election and Charles had been promoted to number two on the Opposition bench. "No more preservation of trees. You'll be on to higher things now," chuckled the Chief Whip. "Pollution, water shortage, and exhaust fumes . . ."

Charles smiled with pleasure as he walked through the Commons, acknowledging old colleagues and noticing a considerable number of new faces. He didn't stop and talk to any of the newcomers as he could not be certain if they were Labour or Conservative and, given the election result, most of them had to be Socialist. A doorkeeper in white tie and black tail-jacket handed him a message to say that a constituent was waiting to see him in the Central Lobby. He hurried off to find out what the problem was, passing some of his older colleagues who wore forlorn looks on their faces. For some it would be a considerable time before they were offered the chance of office again, while others knew they had served as ministers for the last time. As Macmillan had proclaimed, even the most glittering political career always ends in tears.

But at thirty-five Charles dismissed such thoughts as he marched toward the waiting constituent. He turned out to be a red-faced Master of Hounds who had traveled up to London to grumble about the proposed private member's bill banning hare coursing. Charles listened to a fifteen-minute monologue before assuring his constituent that any such bill was doomed through lack of parliamentary time. The Master of Hounds went away happy and Charles returned to his room to check over the constituency mail. Fiona had reminded him of the 800 letters of thanks to the party workers that had been franked but still needed topping and tailing after every election. He groaned.

"Mrs. Blenkinsop, the chairman of Sussex Ladies' Luncheon Club, wants you to be their guest speaker this year," his secretary told him once he had settled.

"Reply yes—what's the date?" asked Charles, reaching for his diary.

"16 June."

"Stupid woman, that's Ladies Day at Ascot. Tell her that I'm delivering a speech at a Housing Conference, but I'll be certain to make myself free for the function next year."

The secretary looked up anxiously.

"Don't fuss, she'll never know any better."

She moved on to the next letter. "Mr. Heath wonders if you can join him for a drink on Thursday, six o'clock?"

Simon Kerslake also knew it was going to be a long slog. He was aware the Tories would not change their leader until Heath had been given a second chance at the polls, and that could take every day of five years with a Government which had a ninety-seven majority.

He began writing articles for the *Spectator* and for the *Sunday Express* center pages, in the hope of building a reputation outside the House while at the same time supplementing his parliamentary salary of £3,400. Even with Elizabeth's income as a consultant he was finding it difficult to make ends meet, and soon their two young sons would have reached prep school age. He envied the Charles Seymours of this world who did not have to give a second thought about their next paycheck. Simon wondered if the damn man had any problems at all. He ran a finger down his own bank account: as usual there was a figure around £500 in the right-hand margin, and as usual it was in red. Many of his Oxford contemporaries had already established themselves in the City or at the bar and on a Friday evening could be seen being driven to large houses in the country. Simon laughed whenever he read that people went into politics to make money.

He pressed on with demanding questions to the Prime Minister, and tried not to show how frustrated he was by the expectations of his colleagues whenever he rose each Tuesday and Thursday. Even after it became routine he prepared himself thoroughly, and on one occasion he even elicited praise from his normally taciturn leader. But as the weeks passed he found that his thoughts continually returned to money—or to his lack of it.

That was before he met Ronnie Nethercote.

Andrew Fraser had often read that the anger or jealousy of one man could block the advance of a political career but he still found it hard to accept that it could apply to him. What annoyed him even more was that Hugh McKenzie's tentacles seemed to have spread through every other department.

Andrew's marriage to Louise Forsyth had been expansively covered in the national papers and the absence of the Secretary of State at the wedding did not escape the notice of the *Daily Express*'s William Hickey. They even published an out-of-date photograph of Alison McKenzie looking sorrowful.

Sir Duncan reminded his son that politics was for long-distance runners, not sprinters, and that he still had a few more laps to complete yet. "An unfortunate analogy," considered

Andrew as he had been a member of the Edinburgh University
4 × 110 relay team. Nevertheless he prepared himself for the
marathon.

"Don't forget, Harold Macmillan spent fourteen years on
the back benches before holding office," Sir Duncan added.

Louise accompanied Andrew all over the country for his
speeches "of major importance," usually to an audience of less
than twenty; she only stopped traveling to Scotland every
week when she discovered she was pregnant.

To Louise's surprise, Andrew turned out to be a keen an-
ticipatory father, determined his son would not think of him
only as a politician. Single-handed, he converted one of the
upstairs bedrooms in Cheyne Walk into a nursery and sought
her approval for a variety of blue decorative schemes.

Louise was anxious that Andrew should extend the same
feelings to their unborn child, if they had a daughter.

Raymond Gould quickly gained a reputation at the Department of Employment. He was thought of as extremely bright,
demanding, hard working and, not that it was ever reported to
him, arrogant. His ability to cut a junior civil servant off in
mid-sentence or to correct his principal Private Secretary on
matters of detail did not endear him even to his closest staff,
who always want to be loyal to their master.

Raymond's work load was prodigious and even the Permanent Secretary experienced Gould's unrelenting "Don't make
excuses" when he tried to trim one of the minister's private
schemes. Soon senior civil servants were talking of when, not
whether, he would be promoted. His Secretary of State, like
all men who were expected to be in six places at once, often
asked Raymond to stand in for him, but even Raymond was
surprised when he was invited to represent the department as
guest of honor at the annual CBI dinner.

Joyce checked to see that her husband's dinner jacket was
well brushed, his shirt spotless, and his shoes shining like a
guards officer's. His carefully worded speech—a combination
of civil-servant draftsmanship and a few more forceful phrases

of his own to prove to the assembled capitalists that not every member of the Labour party was a "raving commie"—was safely lodged in his inside pocket. His driver ferried him from his Lansdowne Road home toward the West End.

Raymond enjoyed the occasion; although he was nervous when he rose to represent the Government in reply to the toast of the guests. By the time he had resumed his seat he felt it had been one of his better efforts. The ovation that followed was certainly more than polite from what had to be classified as a naturally hostile audience.

"That speech was dryer than the Chablis," one guest whispered in the chairman's ear but he had to agree that, with men like Gould in high office, it was going to be a lot easier to live with the Socialists.

The man on Simon Kerslake's left was far more blunt in voicing his opinion of Gould. "Bloody man thinks like a Tory, talks like a Tory, so why isn't he a Tory?" he demanded.

Simon grinned at the prematurely balding man who had been expressing his equally vivid views throughout dinner. Corpulent and ruddy-faced, Ronnie Nethercote looked as if he was trying to escape from every part of his bulging dinner jacket.

"I expect," said Simon in reply, "that Gould would have found it hard to join the Young Conservatives, born in the thirties and living in Leeds."

"Balls," said Ronnie. "I managed it and I was born in the East End of London without any of his advantages. Now tell me, Mr. Kerslake, what do you do when you're not wasting your time in the House of Commons?"

Raymond stayed on after dinner and chatted for some time to the captains of industry. A little after eleven he left to return to Lansdowne Road.

As his chauffeur drove slowly away from Grosvenor House down Park Lane, the Under-Secretary waved expansively back to his host. Someone else waved in reply. At first Raymond only glanced across, assuming it was another dinner guest, until he saw her legs. Standing on the corner outside the petrol station on Park Lane stood a young girl smiling at him invitingly, her white leather miniskirt so short it might have been better described as a handkerchief. Her long legs reminded him of Joyce ten years before except that they were black. Her finely curled hair and the set of her hips remained firmly implanted in Raymond's mind all the way home.

When they reached Lansdowne Road Raymond climbed out of the official car and said "Good night" to his driver before walking slowly toward his front door, but he did not take out his latch key. He waited until he was sure the driver had turned the corner before looking up and checking the bedroom window. All the lights were out. Joyce must be asleep.

He crept down the path and back on to the pavement, then looked up and down the road, finally spotting the space where Joyce had parked the Sunbeam. He checked the spare key was on his key-ring and fumbled about, feeling like a car thief. It took three attempts before the car spluttered into life, and Raymond wondered if he would wake up the whole road as he moved off and headed back to Park Lane, not certain what to expect. When he reached Marble Arch he traveled slowly down in the center stream of traffic. A few dinner guests in evening dress were still spilling out of Grosvenor House. He passed the petrol station: she hadn't moved. She smiled again and he accelerated, nearly running into the car in front of him. Raymond traveled back up to Marble Arch but, instead of turning toward home, he drove down Park Lane again, this time not as quickly and on the inside lane. He took his foot off the accelerator as he approached the petrol station and she waved again. He returned to Marble Arch before repeating his detour down Park Lane, this time even more slowly. As he passed Grosvenor House for a third time he checked to be sure that there were no stragglers still chatting on the pavement. It was clear. He touched the brakes and his car came to a stop just beyond the petrol station. He waited.

The girl looked up and down the street before strolling over to the car, opening the passenger door and taking a seat next to the Under-Secretary of State for Employment.

"Looking for business?"

"What do you mean?" asked Raymond hoarsely.

"Come on, darling. You can't imagine I was standing out there hoping to get a suntan."

Raymond turned to look at the girl more carefully and wanted to touch her despite the aura of cheap perfume. Her black blouse had three buttons undone; a fourth would have left nothing to the imagination.

"It's ten pounds at my place."

"Where's your place?" he heard himself say.

"I use a hotel in Paddington."

"How do we get there?" he asked, putting his hand nervously through his red hair.

"Just head up to Marble Arch and I'll direct you."

Raymond pulled out and went off toward Hyde Park Corner, and drove round before traveling on up toward Marble Arch once again.

"I'm Mandy," she said, "what's your name?"

Raymond hesitated. "Malcolm."

"And what do you do, Malcolm, in these hard times?"

"I . . . I sell secondhand cars."

"Haven't picked out a very good one for yourself, have you?" She laughed.

Raymond made no comment. It didn't stop Mandy.

"What's a secondhand car salesman doing dressed up like a toff, then?"

Raymond had quite forgotten he was still in evening dress.

"I've . . . just been to a convention . . . at the . . . Hilton Hotel."

"Lucky for some," she said, and lit a cigarette. "I've been standing outside Grosvenor House all night in the hope of getting some rich feller from that posh party." Raymond's cheeks nearly turned the color of his hair. "Slow down and take the second on the left."

He followed her instructions until they pulled up outside a small dingy hotel. "I'll get out first, then you," she said. "Just

walk straight through reception and follow me up the stairs."
As she got out of the car he nearly drove off and might have
done so if his eye hadn't caught the sway of her hips as she
walked back toward the hotel.

He obeyed her instructions and climbed several flights of
narrow stairs until he reached the top floor. As he approached
the landing, a large bosomy blonde passed him on the way
down.

"Hi, Mandy," she shouted back at her friend.

"Hi, Sylv. Is the room free?"

"Just," said the blonde sourly.

Mandy pushed open the door and Raymond followed her
in. The room was small and narrow. In one corner stood a tiny
bed and a threadbare carpet. The faded yellow wallpaper was
peeling in several places. There was a washbasin attached to
the wall; a dripping tap had left a brown stain on the enamel.

Mandy put her hand out, and waited.

"Ah, yes, of course," said Raymond, taking out his wallet to
find he only had nine pounds on him.

She scowled. "Not going to get overtime tonight, am I, darling?" she said, tucking the money carefully away in the corner
of her bag before matter-of-factly taking off all her clothes.

Although the act of undressing had been totally sexless he
was still amazed by the beauty of her body. Raymond felt
somehow detached from the real world. He watched, eager to
feel the texture of her skin, but made no move. She lay down
on the bed.

"Let's get on with it, darling. I've got a living to earn."

The minister undressed quickly, keeping his back to the
bed. He folded his clothes in a neat pile on the floor as there
was no chair. Then he lay down on top of her. It was all over
in a few minutes.

"Come quickly, don't you, darling?" said Mandy, grinning.

Raymond turned away from her and started washing himself as best he could in the little basin. He dressed hurriedly,
realizing he must get out of the place as rapidly as possible.

"Can you drop me back at the petrol station?" Mandy asked.

"It's exactly the opposite direction for me," he said, trying not to sound anxious as he made a bolt for the door. He passed Sylv on the stairs accompanied by a man. She stared at him more closely the second time. Raymond was back in his car a few moments later. He drove home quickly but not before unwinding the windows in an attempt to get rid of the smell of stale tobacco and cheap perfume.

Back in Lansdowne Road he had a long shower before creeping into bed next to Joyce; she stirred only slightly.

CHAPTER
SEVEN

CHARLES DROVE HIS wife down to Ascot early to be sure to avoid the bumper-to-bumper traffic that always developed later in the day. With his height and bearing, Charles Seymour was made for tails and a topper and Fiona wore a hat which on anyone less self-assured would have looked ridiculous. They had been invited to join the McFarlands for the afternoon and when they arrived they found Sir Robert awaiting them in his private box.

"You must have left home early," said Charles.

"About thirty minutes ago," he said, laughing. Fiona looked politely incredulous.

"I always come here by helicopter," he explained.

They lunched on lobster and strawberries accompanied by a fine vintage champagne which the waiter kept pouring and pouring. Charles might not have drunk quite as much had he not picked the winners of the first three races. He spent the fifth race slumped in a chair in the corner of the box and only the noise of the crowd kept him from nodding off.

If they hadn't waited for a farewell drink after the last race

Charles might have gotten away with it. He had forgotten that his host was returning by helicopter.

The long tail of cars across Windsor Great Park all the way back to the M4 made Charles very short-tempered. When he eventually reached the motorway he put his Daimler into fourth gear. He didn't notice the police car until the siren sounded and he was directed to pull over.

"Do be sensible, Charles," whispered Fiona.

"Don't worry, old girl, I know exactly how to deal with the law," he said, and wound down the window to address the policeman who stood by the car. "Do you realize who I am, officer?"

"No, sir, but I would like you to accompany me—"

"Certainly not, officer, I am a Member of . . ."

"Do be quiet," said Fiona, "and stop making such a fool of yourself."

" . . . Parliament and I will not be treated . . ."

"Have you any idea how pompous you sound, Charles?"

"Perhaps you will be kind enough to accompany me to the station, sir?"

"I want to speak to my solicitor."

"Of course, sir. As soon as we reach the station."

When Charles arrived at the constabulary he proved quite incapable of walking in a straight line and refused to provide a blood sample.

"I am the Conservative MP for Sussex Downs."

Which will not help you, Fiona thought, but he was past listening and only demanded that she phone the family solicitor at Speechly, Bircham and Soames.

After Ian Kimmins had spoken first gently, then firmly to Charles his client eventually cooperated with the police.

Once Charles had completed his written statement Fiona drove him home, praying that his stupidity would pass unnoticed by the press the following day.

Andrew even bought a football but hid it from Louise.

As the months passed Louise's slight frame expanded alarmingly. Andrew would rest his head on the bulge and listen for the heartbeat. "It's a scrum-half," he declared.

"Perhaps she's a center forward," Louise suggested, "and will want to emulate the distaff side of the family."

"If he has to be a center forward he will play for Hearts," Andrew assured her.

"Male chauvinist pig," she called to his back as he headed off to the Commons that morning. Andrew toyed with the names of Jamie, Robert, Hector, and Iain and had settled on Robert before he had reached Westminster. On arrival at New Palace Yard he hailed the policeman on the gate and was surprised to see the familiar figure immediately rush toward him.

Andrew wound down the window. "What's the problem, officer?"

"Your wife's been taken to St. Mary's, Paddington, sir. Emergency wing."

Andrew would have broken the speed limit all the way to Marble Arch if it hadn't been for the traffic. He kept praying he would be there in time, but he couldn't help remembering that Louise was only six months pregnant. When he arrived the doctor on duty would not allow him to see her.

"How is Louise?" were Andrew's first words.

The young doctor hesitated, then said, "Your wife's fine, but I'm afraid she's lost the baby."

Andrew felt his whole body go limp. "Thank God she's all right," he said.

"I'm afraid I can't let you see her until she has come out of sedation."

"Of course, Doctor," said Andrew, glancing at the lapel badge on her white coat.

"But I can see no reason why you shouldn't have more children in the future," she added gently, before he had the chance to ask the question.

Andrew smiled with relief and began pacing up and down the corridor, unaware of the passing of time, until the doctor returned and said it would now be all right for him to see his wife.

"I hope you're not too disappointed?" were Louise's first words when eventually he was allowed to see her.

"Don't be silly—we'll have a dozen before we're through," he said, taking her hand.

She tried to laugh. "Do you know my doctor's husband?"

"Not that I'm aware of," said Andrew.

"Simon Kerslake."

"Good heavens, yes. Very capable fellow. Look aye, lass," said Andrew, putting on a deep brogue, "you'll be a new woman after a couple of days' rest, I'll guarantee it."

"And if I'm not?"

"I'll stick with the old one. And I'll tell you what: as soon as they let you out of this place we'll go down to the south of France for the weekend."

"You don't like him because he comes from the East End," said Simon, after she had read the letter.

"That's not true," replied Elizabeth. "I don't like him because I don't trust him."

"But you've only met him twice."

"Once would have been quite enough."

"Well, I can tell you I'm impressed by the not inconsiderable empire he's built up over the last ten years, and frankly it's an offer I can't refuse," said Simon, pocketing the letter.

"I know we could do with a little more money," said Elizabeth, "but surely not at any cost."

"I won't be offered many chances like this," continued Simon, "and frankly we could use the money. The belief people have that every Tory MP has some lucrative sinecure and two or three non-executive directorships is plain baloney and you know it. Not one other serious proposition has been put to me since I've been in the House, and another £2,000 a year for a monthly board meeting would come in very handy."

"And what else?"

"What do you mean, what else?"

"What else does Mr. Nethercote expect for his £2,000?

Don't be naive, Simon, he's not offering you that kind of money on a plate unless he's hoping to receive some scraps back."

"Well, maybe I have a few contacts and a little influence with one or two people . . ."

"I'll bet."

"You've just taken against him, Elizabeth."

"I'm against anything that might in the long term harm your career, Simon. Struggle on but never sacrifice your integrity, as you're so fond of reminding the people of Coventry."

On Friday morning, two weeks later, Andrew and Louise set out for London airport with one suitcase between them. As Andrew locked the front door the phone rang.

"No one's in," he shouted at the doorknob, "but we'll be back on Monday."

He had booked a suite at the Colombe d'Or nestled in the hills of St. Paul in the south of France. He was determined to prize Louise away from London and see she had some sun and rest.

The famous old hotel was everything the brochure had promised. On the walls hung paintings by Picasso, Monet, Manet, Utrillo—all of which the patroness, Madame Reux, had accepted many years before in place of payment from artists who needed lodging and a square meal. On the way up the winding staircase Louise was nearly knocked out by a Calder mobile and a Courbet hung above the bed in their room. But it was the bed itself, a sixteenth-century four-poster, that they both coveted. They were soon to discover it possessed a mattress so comfortable that visitors always overslept.

The food was memorable and they walked through the green hills each day to be sure they could tackle another full dinner at night. Three days of no radio, no television, no papers, and no telephone ensured that by Monday morning they were ready to face London. They swore they would return again soon.

Once their plane had landed at Heathrow they were made aware that the holiday was over. Twenty minutes passed before someone pushed the waiting steps up to the Vanguard's door. Then a crowded bus to the terminal that seemed miles away was followed by a route-march to customs. Despite their first-class tickets their bags were among the last off. By the time the taxi had crawled through the morning rush hour to their front door in Cheyne Walk all Louise could say was, "I need another holiday." As Andrew put his latch key in the door the telephone started ringing.

"I hope they haven't been trying all weekend," Louise said.

Andrew put the phone to his ear as it went dead.

"Just missed whoever it was," said Andrew, picking up several brown envelopes from the floor. "France already seems about a week ago." He kissed his wife. "Must get changed and be off to the House," he said, checking his watch.

"How has the nation managed to survive without you?" mocked Louise.

When the phone rang again Andrew was just stepping out of the bath.

"Can you take it, Louise?" he shouted. A moment later he heard her rushing up the stairs.

"Andrew, it's the Prime Minister's office."

He ran dripping and naked to the bedroom phone and picked up the extension.

"Andrew Fraser," he said.

"This is No. 10," said an official-sounding voice, "the Prime Minister has been wanting to contact you since Friday morning."

"I'm sorry, I took my wife to Provence for the weekend."

"Really, sir?" said the voice, not sounding at all interested. "May I tell the Prime Minister you are now free to speak to him?"

"Of course," said Andrew, frowning at his nude reflection in the mirror. He must have put on half a stone; it would have to be four games of squash this week and no more wine at lunch.

"Andrew."

"Good morning, Prime Minister."

"Sad news about Hugh McKenzie."

"Yes, sir," said Andrew, automatically.

"They warned me about his heart before the last election but he insisted he wanted to carry on. I've asked Bruce to be the new Secretary of State and Angus to take his place as minister. They both want you to be the new Under-Secretary—how do you feel about it?"

"I'd be delighted, Prime Minister," Andrew stammered, trying to take in the news.

"Good. And by the way, Andrew, when you open your first red box you won't find any tickets for Colombe d'Or, so I do hope Louise is fully recovered." The phone clicked.

They had tracked him down, but the Prime Minister had left him in peace.

The first official function Andrew Fraser attended as Her Majesty's Under-Secretary of State at the Scottish Office was Hugh McKenzie's funeral.

"Think about it, Simon," said Ronnie, as they reached the boardroom door. "Two thousand pounds a year may be helpful but if you take shares in my property company it would give you a chance to make some capital."

"What did you have in mind?" asked Simon, doing up the middle button of his blazer and trying not to sound too excited.

"Well, you've proved damned useful to me. Some of those people who you bring to lunch wouldn't have allowed me past their front doors. I'd let you buy in cheap . . . you could get hold of 50,000 shares at one pound so when we go public you'll make a killing."

"Raising £50,000 won't be that easy, Ronnie."

"When your bank manager has checked over my books he'll be only too happy to lend you the money, you see."

After the Midland Bank had studied the authorized accounts of Nethercote and Company and the area manager had interviewed Simon, they agreed to his request, on the condition that Simon lodge the shares with the bank.

How wrong Elizabeth was proving to be, Simon thought, and when Nethercote and Company went on to double their profits for the year he brought home a copy of the annual report for his wife to study.

"Looks good," she had to admit. "But that still doesn't mean I have to trust Ronnie Nethercote."

When Charles Seymour's drink-driving charge came up in front of the Reading Bench he listed himself as C. G. Seymour—no mention of MP. Under profession he entered "Banker."

He came sixth in the list that morning, and on behalf of his absent client Ian Kimmins apologized to the Reading magistrates and assured them it would not happen again. Charles received a fifty-pound fine and was banned from driving for six months. The whole case was over in four minutes.

When Charles was told the news by telephone later that day he was appreciative of Kimmins's sensible advice and felt he had escaped lightly. He couldn't help remembering how many column inches George Brown, the Labour Foreign Secretary, had endured after a similar incident outside the Hilton Hotel.

Fiona kept her own counsel.

At the time Fleet Street was in the middle of "the silly season," that period in the summer when the press are desperate for news. There had only been one cub reporter in the court when Charles's case came up, and even he was surprised by the interest the nationals took in his little scoop. The pictures of Charles taken so discreetly outside the Seymours' country home were now glaring from the pages the following morning. Headlines ranged from "Six months' ban for drink-drive son of earl" to "MP's Ascot binge ends in heavy fine." Even *The Times* mentioned the case on its home news page.

By lunchtime the same day every Fleet Street newspaper had tried to contact Charles—and so had the Chief Whip.

When he did track Charles down his advice was short and to the point. A junior Shadow minister can survive that sort of publicity once, not twice.

"Whatever you do, don't drive a car during the next six months and don't ever drink and drive again."

Charles concurred, and after a quiet weekend hoped he had heard the last of the case. Then he caught the headline on the front page of the *Sussex Gazette*, "Member faces no confidence motion": Mrs. Blenkinsop, the chairman of the Ladies' Luncheon Club, was proposing the motion—not for the drunken driving but for deliberately misleading her about why he had been unable to fulfill a speaking engagement at their annual luncheon.

Raymond had become so used to receiving files marked "Strictly Private," "Top Secret," or even "For Your Eyes Only" in his position as a Government Under-Secretary that he didn't give a second thought to a letter marked "Confidential and Personal" even though it was written in a scrawled hand. He opened it while Joyce was boiling his eggs.

"Four minutes and forty-five seconds, just the way you like them," she said as she returned from the kitchen and placed two eggs in front of him. "Are you all right, dear? You're white as a sheet."

Raymond recovered quickly, pushing the letter into a pocket before checking his watch. "Haven't the time for the other egg," he said. "I'm already late for Cabinet committee, I must dash."

Strange, thought Joyce, as her husband hurried to the door. Cabinet committees didn't usually meet until ten and he hadn't even cracked open his first egg. She sat down and slowly ate her husband's breakfast, wondering why he had left all his post behind.

Once he was in the back of his official car Raymond read the letter again. It didn't take long.

Dear "Malcolm,"

I enjoid our little get together the other evening and five hundrud pounds would help me to forget it once and for all.

> Love, Mandy.
> PS. I'll be in touch again soon.

He read the letter once more and tried to compose his thoughts. There was no address on the top of the notebook paper. Neither letter nor envelope gave any clue as to where they had come from.

After he had arrived outside the Department of Employment Raymond remained in the back seat for several moments.

"Are you feeling all right, sir?" his driver asked.

"Fine, thank you," he replied, and jumped out of the car and ran all the way up to his office. As he passed his secretary's desk he barked at her, "No interruptions."

"You won't forget Cabinet committee at ten o'clock, will you, Minister?"

"No," replied Raymond sharply and slammed his office door. Once at his desk he tried to calm himself and recall what he would have done had he been approached by a client as a barrister at the bar: first instruct a good solicitor. Raymond considered the two most capable lawyers in England to be Arnold Goodman and Sir Roger Pelham. Goodman was getting too high a profile for Raymond's liking whereas Pelham was just as sound but virtually unknown to the general public. He called Pelham's office and made an appointment to see him that afternoon.

Raymond hardly spoke in Cabinet committee, but as most of his colleagues wanted to express their own views nobody noticed. As soon as the meeting was over Raymond hurried out and took a taxi to High Holborn.

Sir Roger Pelham rose from behind his large Victorian desk to greet the junior minister.

"I know you're a busy man, Gould," Pelham said as he fell back into his black leather chair, "so I shan't waste your time. Tell me what I can do for you."

"It was kind of you to see me at such short notice," Raymond began and without further word handed the letter over.

"Thank you," the solicitor said courteously and, pushing his half-moon spectacles higher up his nose he read the note three times before he made any comment.

"Blackmail is something we all detest," he began, "but it will be necessary for you to tell me the whole truth, and don't miss out any details. Please remember I am on your side. You'll recall only too well from your days at the bar what a disadvantage one labors under when one is in possession of only half the facts."

The tips of Pelham's fingers touched, forming a small roof in front of his nose as he listened intently to Raymond's account of what had happened that night.

"Could anyone else have seen you?" was Pelham's first question.

Raymond thought back and then nodded. "Yes," he said. "Yes, I'm afraid there was another girl who passed me on the stairs."

Pelham read the letter once more. "My immediate advice," he said, looking Raymond in the eye and speaking slowly and deliberately, "and you won't like it, is to do nothing."

"But what do I say if she contacts the press?"

"She will probably get in touch with someone from Fleet Street anyway, even if you pay the £500, or however many other £500s you can afford. Don't imagine you're the first minister to be blackmailed, Mr. Gould. Every homosexual in the House lives in daily fear of it. It's a game of hide and seek. Very few people other than saints have nothing to *hide*, and the problem with public life is that a lot of busybodies want to *seek*." Raymond remained silent, trying not to show his anxiety. "Phone me on my private line immediately after the next letter arrives," said Pelham, scribbling a number on a piece of paper.

"Thank you," said Raymond, at least relieved that his secret was now shared with someone else. Pelham rose from behind his desk and accompanied Raymond to the door. "You'll be glad to see Yorkshire back as county champions," said the solicitor as he walked down the long passage with the minister. Raymond did not reply. When they reached the outer door they shook hands formally. "I'll wait to hear from you," said Pelham. A pity that the man showed no interest in cricket.

Raymond left the solicitor's office feeling better, but he found it hard to concentrate on his work the rest of that day and slept only in fits and starts during the night. When he read the morning papers he was horrified to see how much space was being given to Charles Seymour's peccadillo. What a field day they would be able to have with him. When the post came, he searched anxiously for the scrawled handwriting. It was hidden under an American Express circular. He tore it open. The same hand was this time demanding that the £500 should be deposited at a newsagent in Pimlico. Sir Roger Pelham saw the minister one hour later.

Despite the renewed demand the solicitor's advice remained the same.

Andrew Fraser never stopped moving from one city to another because the Scottish Office had to show a presence in Edinburgh and Glasgow as well as in London. Louise did not complain; she had never seen her husband so happy. The only moment of light relief during his first three months as a minister came when Andrew found it necessary to send a letter to his father addressed, "Dear Sir Duncan," which went on to explain why he had to reject his offered advice on a Highlands and Islands Board project. Andrew was particularly pleased with the line, "I have for some considerable time listened to both sides of the argument."

Once he had settled in his favorite chair that night with a large whisky in his hand Louise told him she was pregnant again. "When did I find the time?" he asked, taking her in his arms.

"Maybe the half-hour between your meeting with the Norwegian Fishing Minister and the address to the Oil Conference in Aberdeen?"

*   *   *

When the AGM of the Sussex Downs Conservative Association came round in October Charles was pleased to learn that Mrs. Blenkinsop's "no confidence" motion had been withdrawn. The local press tried to build up the story but the nationals were full of the Aberfan coal-tip disaster, in which 116 schoolchildren had lost their lives. No editor could find space for Sussex Downs.

Charles delivered a thoughtful speech to his association which was well received. During question time he was relieved to find no embarrassing questions directed at him.

When the Seymours finally said good night, Charles took the chairman to one side and inquired: "How did you manage it?"

"I explained to Mrs. Blenkinsop," replied the chairman, "that if her motion of no confidence was discussed at the AGM it would be awfully hard for the member to back my recommendation that she should receive an OBE in the New Year's Honors for service to the party. That shouldn't be too hard for you to pull off, should it, Charles?"

Every time the phone rang Raymond assumed it would be the press asking him if he knew someone called Mandy. Often it was a journalist, but all that was needed was a quotable remark on the latest unemployment figures, or a statement of where the minister stood on devaluation of the pound.

It was Mike Molloy, a reporter from the *Daily Mirror*, who was the first to ask Raymond what he had to say about a statement phoned in to his office by a girl with a West Indian accent called Mandy Page.

"I have nothing to say on the subject. Please speak to my solicitor, Sir Roger Pelham," was the Under-Secretary's succinct reply. The moment he put the phone down he felt queasy.

A few minutes later when the phone rang again Raymond still hadn't moved. He picked up the receiver, his hand still shaking. Pelham confirmed that Molloy had been in touch with him.

"I presume you made no comment," said Raymond.

"On the contrary," replied Pelham. "I told him the truth."

"*What?*" exploded Raymond.

"Be thankful she hit on a fair journalist because I expect he'll let this one go. Fleet Street are not quite the bunch of shits everyone imagines them to be," Pelham said uncharacteristically, and added, "they also detest two things, bent policemen and blackmailers. I don't think you'll see anything in the press tomorrow."

Sir Roger Pelham was wrong.

Raymond was standing outside his local newsagent the next morning when it opened at five-thirty and he surprised the proprietor by asking for a copy of the *Daily Mirror*. Raymond Gould was plastered all over page five saying, "Devaluation is not a course I can support while the unemployment figures remain so high." The photograph by the side of the article was unusually flattering.

Simon Kerslake read a more detailed account of what the minister had said on devaluation in *The Times*, and noted Raymond Gould's firm stand against what was beginning to look like inevitable Government policy.

Simon looked up from his paper and started to consider a ploy that might trap Gould. If he could make the minister commit himself again and again on devaluation in front of the whole House he knew that when the inevitable happened Gould would be left with no choice but to resign. Simon penciled a question on the top of the paper before returning to the political columns.

The devaluation news had caused a Tory lead in the opinion polls of eight percent, and despite a majority of ninety-five in the Commons the Government had actually lost a vote on the floor of the House the previous day. Nevertheless, Simon still could not envisage a general election for at least another two years.

On the business front Simon had advised Ronnie Nethercote not to allow his company shares to be traded on the Stock Exchange until the Tories returned to power. "The climate," he assured Ronnie, "should be much easier then."

Charles Seymour was glad to be behind the wheel again after his driving ban had been completed, and he had the grace to smile when Fiona showed him the photograph of the happy Mrs. Blenkinsop displaying her OBE outside Buckingham Palace to a reporter from the *Sussex Gazette*.

It was six months to the day of his first meeting with Sir Roger Pelham that Raymond Gould received an account from the solicitor for services rendered—£500. He sent the check by return of post in a parcel that also contained a copy of the recently published edition of *Wisden*.

CHAPTER
EIGHT

ANDREW HAD BEEN warned by his ministerial colleagues that the first day answering questions at the dispatch box would be an experience he was unlikely to forget.

Questions for the Scottish Office appear on the order paper on a Wednesday once every four or five weeks, and each minister answers on behalf of his own department between two-thirty-five and three-twenty. There are usually four or five ministers of the Crown, not including the law officer available to represent each great department of state. During the forty-minute to one-hour period the ministers would expect to reply to about twenty-five questions, but it is rarely the questions that are the problem; it is the supplementaries.

Any member can place a question through the table office to any minister, and can word it in a seemingly innocuous way. "When does the minister hope next to visit Aberdeen?" to which the minister concerned may reply anything from "next week" to "I have no plans to do so in the foreseeable future"—but when the member who put down the question rises from his seat to ask his supplementary he can change the subject completely. "Does the minister realize that Aberdeen has the highest rate of unemployment in the United Kingdom, and what new ideas does his department have to deal with this problem?" The hapless minister must then come up with a convincing reply on the spot.

In an attempt to see that a minister is adequately briefed, his department will spend the morning scrutinizing each tabled question and looking for pitfalls he might encounter. A variety of possible supplementaries will be placed in his brief with appropriate answers. Ministers can, of course, always ask colleagues on their own side what they are hoping to find out from their tabled questions, but Opposition members use question time to test a minister in the hope of discovering some weakness in his armory, thus making the Government appear incompetent.

Andrew spent a considerable time in preparation for his first encounter at the dispatch box although the more senior and experienced ministers in the Scottish Office had agreed to handle any questions that looked hostile.

He ended up having to respond to only one question from the Opposition benches, while fielding four from his own. Added to which, the timing was such that question number twenty-three from the Opposition member seemed unlikely to be reached by three-twenty, when the Solicitor General for Scotland would have to start answering questions himself.

Andrew's first four answers to questions numbers five, nine, eleven, and fourteen, went smoothly enough. He opened his dark blue file and was pleased to confirm the well-prepared briefs to everything that was thrown at him. By three-fifteen, when question number nineteen was being answered, Andrew sat back on the front bench and began to relax for the first time that day.

The Solicitor General for Scotland entered a now packed Commons and, moving alongside the table in the center of the Chamber, he crouched slightly to be sure he did not obscure the Speaker's view of the Government benches on his right. The Prime Minister had been left a place between the Chancellor and the Foreign Secretary and waited for the clock to reach three-twenty.

The Speaker called question number twenty-one but the member was not present. He called number twenty-two and once again the member was absent. Each had obviously considered that their question had little chance of being reached before three-twenty. At three-eighteen the Speaker called question twenty-three—Andrew's heart sank—which read on the order paper, "Had the minister been invited to visit the Kinross Nursing Home?"

Andrew rose, opened his folder, and said, "No, sir."

"No one in the House will be surprised by the minister's reply," said George Younger, the member for Ayr, "because the nursing home has forty-nine occupants, forty-seven of whom have their own television sets and yet the minister demands forty-seven separate license fees. If they were to congregate in one room, he would expect only one fee. Is this another example of the Labour party's 'Care for the Aged' program that we hear so much about nowadays?"

Andrew rose to the dispatch box to cries of "Answer, answer," from the Opposition benches. He had checked his crib sheet while sitting on the edge of his seat. Andrew had a prepared answer for medical facilities, old-age pensions, supplementary benefits, food allowances, medical charges—but nothing on TV licenses. As he stood stranded at the dispatch box he was aware for the first time of the pitfalls that a minister encounters when he is not fully prepared. Such a system might appear wonderfully democratic to onlookers, he thought, until you are the Christian facing the 300 hungry lions.

A handwritten note was quickly passed along the front bench to him from one of the civil servants who sit in the official box to the left behind the Speaker's chair. With no time to consider its implications Andrew crossed his fingers and read the note out to the House.

"This was a decision taken by the last administration, of which the Honorable Gentleman was a member. We have seen no reason to reverse that decision," he read, thinking how much like a parrot he sounded. He sat down to polite Government murmurs and some considerable relief.

Mr. Younger rose again and was allowed a second supplementary.

"Mr. Speaker, this is the sort of inaccuracy we have grown to expect from this Government. The decision he refers to was made by his Right Honorable friend, the Secretary of State, only last year, and I think the minister will find, if he does his research more fastidiously, that his party was in power at the time." The Opposition howled their delight.

Andrew rose again and gripped the sides of the dispatch box to avoid anyone seeing that he was shaking in fear. Several members of the Government front bench had their heads bowed. The Opposition had drawn blood and were baying in triumph. Lord Attlee's words came back to Andrew. "When you are caught out by the House admit it, apologize, and sit down."

Andrew waited for the noise to subside before he replied. "The Secretary of State warned me that a new minister will never forget his first question time and I feel bound to agree with him." Andrew, who knew how the atmosphere in the House can change in a moment, felt such a moment now, and before it could turn back added, "On the question of television licenses in the Kinross Nursing Home, I apologize to the Honorable Gentleman for Ayr for my mistake and I will look into the case immediately and send him a written reply within twenty-four hours." "Hear, hears" could now be heard from his own benches and the Opposition benches were quietened. Mr. Younger was trying to interrupt again but as Andrew didn't give way he had to resume his seat, knowing the Speaker would not call on him again once the clock had passed three-nineteen. Andrew waited for silence before adding, "And I blame my grandmother for this who, as President of the Kinross Nursing Home and a staunch Conservative, has always believed in increasing old-age pensions rather than looking for false subsidies that can never be fair to everyone." By now the Labour members were laughing and all the heads on the front bench were looking toward the new minister, who remained at the dispatch box until the House was silent again. "My grandmother would be delighted to learn that this administration has raised that old-age pension by fifty percent in the three years since we have taken office." The Labour back-benchers were now cheering and waving their order papers as Andrew resumed his seat, while the Opposition were silent and glum.

The hands of the clock touched three-twenty and the Speaker said, "The Solicitor General's questions."

Andrew Fraser had made a political reputation, and as the laughter echoed round the House the intense figure sitting on the end of the front bench put a hand through his red hair and wondered if he could ever match Andrew's skill at the dispatch box. On the Opposition back benches Simon Kerslake made a mental note to be cautious if he ever thought of putting a sharp question to Andrew Fraser.

As soon as the Solicitor General's questions were over Simon left the House and drove himself to Whitechapel Road. He arrived a few minutes after the four o'clock board meeting of Nethercote and Company had begun, quietly took his seat, and listened to Ronnie Nethercote describing another coup.

Ronnie had signed a contract that morning to take over a major city block at a cost of fifteen million pounds with a guaranteed rental income of over 1.1 million per annum for the first seven years of a twenty-one-year lease with seven-year rent reviews.

Simon formally congratulated him and asked if this made any difference to the company's timing for going public.

"Why do you ask?" said Ronnie.

"Because I still feel it might be wise to wait until we know the result of the next general election. If the Conservatives return to power, as the opinion polls forecast, that could change the whole atmosphere for launching a new company."

"If they don't, I shan't hold up going public much longer."

"I wouldn't disagree with that decision either, Mr. Chairman," said Simon.

When the meeting was over he joined Nethercote in his office for a drink.

"I want to thank you," Ronnie said, "for that introduction to

Harold Samuel and Louis Freedman. It made the deal go through much more smoothly."

"Does that mean you'll allow me to purchase some more shares?"

Ronnie hesitated. "Why not? You've earned them. But only another 10,000. Don't get ahead of yourself, Simon, or the other directors may become jealous."

In the car on the way to pick up Elizabeth Simon decided to take a second mortgage out on the house in Beaufort Street to raise the extra cash needed for the new shares. He thought it might be wise not to trouble her with the details. He savored the prospect of the Conservatives winning the next election, perhaps being given office in the Government and selling his shares for a sum that would make it possible for him to stop the continual worries of how he would finance his children's education. Perhaps he could even give Elizabeth that holiday in Venice she had talked about so often.

When he drove up to the hospital Elizabeth was waiting outside the gates. "We won't be late, will we?" were her first words.

"No," said Simon, checking the clock on the dashboard as he turned the car round in the direction of Beaufort Street.

They arrived at the hall five minutes before the curtain was due to rise. The occasion was their sons' pantomime, and both Peter and Michael had assured their parents that they had major parts. It was Charles Kingsley's *The Water Babies*, and Michael turned out to be a crab, who although he never left the stage lay on his stomach throughout the entire performance and never uttered a word. Peter, who had spent the week learning his words off by heart, was an unconvincing water baby standing at the end of a row of twelve. His speaking part turned out to be one sentence: "If grown-ups go on eating all the fish in the sea there will be none left for me." King Neptune fixed his imperial eye on Peter and said, "Don't blame us, it's your father who's the MP," upon which Peter bowed his head and blushed, though not as deeply as Elizabeth when the audience in front of them turned round and smiled at Simon, who felt more embarrassed than if he had been in the center of a raging debate in the Commons.

At coffee afterward the headmaster admitted that the sentence had been added without the approval of the late Charles Kingsley. When Simon and Elizabeth took the children home that night they insisted on repeating Peter's one line again and again.

"If the Government did an about-turn and devalued the pound, would the Under-Secretary find it possible to remain in office?"

Raymond Gould stiffened when he heard Simon Kerslake's question. His grasp of the law and his background knowledge of the subject made all except the extremely articulate or highly experienced wary of taking him on. Nevertheless Raymond had one Achilles' heel arising from his firmly stated views in *Full Employment at Any Cost?*: any suggestion that the Government would devalue. Time and again eager backbenchers would seek to tackle him on the subject but once more it was Simon Kerslake who felled his opponent.

Andrew, sitting on the front bench, composed in his mind a sharp reply about his colleagues' collective responsibility, but Raymond Gould said rather ponderously: "The policy of Her Majesty's Government is one hundred percent against devaluation, and therefore the question does not arise."

"Wait and see," shouted Kerslake.

"Order," said the Speaker, rising from his seat and turning toward Simon as Raymond sat down. "The Honorable member knows all too well he must not address the House from a sedentary position. The Under-Secretary of State."

Raymond rose again. "This Government believes in a strong pound, which still remains our best hope for keeping unemployment figures down."

"But what would you do if Cabinet does go ahead and devalue?" Joyce asked him when she read her husband's reply to Kerslake's question reported in *The Times* the next morning.

Raymond was already facing the fact that devaluation

looked more likely every day. A strong dollar causing imports to reach record levels coupled with a run of strikes during the summer of sixty-seven was causing foreign bankers to ask when, not if.

"I'd have to resign," he said in reply to Joyce's question.

"Why? No other minister will."

"I'm afraid Kerslake is right. I'm on the record and he's made sure everybody knows it. Don't worry, Harold will never devalue. He's assured me of that many times."

"He only has to change his mind once."

Pressure on the pound increased during the following weeks and Raymond began to fear that Joyce might turn out to be right.

Andrew Fraser had read *Full Employment at Any Cost?* and considered it a succinctly argued case although he did not agree with all the small print. He personally was in favor of devaluation but felt it should have been pushed through in the Labour party's first week in office, so that the blame could be left at the door of the Tories. After three years and a second election victory any such suggestion would rightly be considered outrageous.

As Louise's time of delivery approached she was getting larger by the day. Andrew helped to take pressure off her as much as he could, but this time he did not prepare so obviously for the birth, as he felt his unbridled enthusiasm might have contributed to her previous anxiety. He tried as often as possible to bring the red boxes home each night, but it remained an exception if he returned to Cheyne Walk before eleven o'clock.

"Voting every night at ten o'clock and sometimes on through the night into the next day is one system the rest of the world has *not* considered worth emulating," Andrew had told Louise after one particularly grueling session. He couldn't even remember what he had been voting on—although he didn't admit that to her. "But as no Government of whatever party has ever seriously considered the idea of limiting the time for ending business 'the troops', as back-benchers are known, go on charging through the lobbies day in and day out. That's why the press refer to us as 'lobby fodder.' "

"More like a bunch of unruly children," she chided.

When Louise went into hospital one week early Elizabeth Kerslake assured her there was nothing to be worried about, and two days later Louise gave birth to a beautiful girl.

Andrew was in a departmental meeting discussing Glasgow's high-rise housing program when the hospital staff nurse rang to congratulate him. He went straight to his fridge and took out the bottle of champagne his father had sent him the day he joined the Scottish Office. He poured a plastic mug of Krug for each of his team of advisers.

"Just better than drinking it out of the bottle," he suggested as he left his civil servants to go to the hospital.

On arrival at St. Mary's Andrew was relieved to find Elizabeth Kerslake was on duty. She warned him that his wife was still under sedation after a particularly complicated Caesarian delivery. Elizabeth took him to see his daughter who remained under observation in an isolation unit.

"Nothing to fret about," Elizabeth assured him. "We always take this precaution after any Caesarian birth as there are a number of routine tests we still have to carry out."

She left Andrew to stare at his daughter's large blue eyes. Although he knew it might change in time the soft down on the crown of her head was already dark.

He slipped out an hour later when she had fallen asleep to return to Dover House, where he had a second celebration in the Secretary of State's office, but this time the champagne was served in crystal glasses.

When Andrew climbed into bed that night the champagne helped him fall into a deep sleep with the only problem on his mind being what they should call their daughter. Claire had always been the name Louise favored.

The phone had rung several times before he answered it and as soon as he had replaced the receiver he dressed and drove to the hospital as quickly as possible. He parked the car and ran to the now-familiar ward. Elizabeth Kerslake was standing waiting by the door. She looked tired and disheveled, and even with all her training and experience she found it hard to explain to Andrew what had happened.

"Your daughter died forty minutes ago when her heart stopped beating. Believe me, we tried everything."

Andrew collapsed on the bench in the corridor and didn't speak for several moments. "How's Louise?" was all he could eventually manage.

"She hasn't been told yet. She's still under sedation. Be thankful she never saw the baby."

Andrew thumped his leg until it was numb. He stopped suddenly. "I'll tell her myself," he said quietly and remained on the bench, tears coursing down his cheeks. Elizabeth sat down beside him but didn't speak. When she left it was only to check that Mrs. Fraser was ready to see her husband.

Louise knew the moment Andrew walked in. It was over an hour before she managed to speak.

"I bet Alison McKenzie would have given you a dozen sons," she said, trying to make him smile.

"No doubt about that," said Andrew, "but they would have all been ugly and stupid."

"I agree with you," said Louise. "But that wouldn't have been her fault."

They both tried to laugh.

Andrew returned to Cheyne Walk a little after four o'clock, but he didn't sleep again that night.

The great orator Iain Macleod once remarked that it was the first two minutes of a speech that decided one's fate. One either grasps the House and commands it or dithers, and loses it, and once the House is lost it can rarely be brought to heel. When Charles Seymour was invited to present the winding-up speech for the Opposition during the Economic debate, he felt he had prepared himself well, and although he knew he could not expect to convert Government back-benchers to his argument he hoped the press would acknowledge the following day that he had won the argument and embarrassed the

Government. The Administration was already rocking over daily rumors of devaluation and economic trouble, and Charles was confident that this was the chance to make his name.

Full parliamentary debates usually start at three-thirty, after question time, but can be delayed if there are ministerial statements to be made. The senior minister in the department concerned makes the opening speech for approximately thirty minutes and then the Opposition spokesman addresses the House for the same period of time. Between four-thirty and nine the debate is thrown open to the floor and the Speaker tries to be scrupulously fair in calling a cross-section of backbenchers who have demonstrated an interest in the subject, as well as preserving a party and regional balance. These backbencher speeches are frowned on if they last for more than fifteen minutes. Some of the most memorable speeches delivered in the House have lasted eight or nine minutes, some of the worst over thirty.

At nine o'clock the Opposition spokesman makes his final comments, and at nine-thirty a Government minister winds up.

When Charles rose and stood at the dispatch box he intended to press home the Tory case on the Government's economic record, the fatal consequences of devaluation, the record inflation, coupled with record borrowing and a lack of confidence in Britain unknown in any member's lifetime.

He stood his full height and stared down belligerently at the Government benches.

"Mr. Speaker," he began, "I can't think . . ."

"Then don't bother to speak," someone shouted from the Labour benches. Laughter broke out as Charles tried to compose himself, cursing his initial over-confidence. He began again.

"I can't imagine . . ."

"No imagination either," came another voice. "Typical Tory."

". . . why this motion was ever put before the House."

"Certainly not for you to give us a lesson in public speaking."

"Order," growled the Speaker, but it was too late.

The House was lost and Charles stumbled through thirty minutes of embarrassment until no one but the Speaker was listening to a word he said. Several members of his own front bench had their feet up on the table and their eyes closed. Back-benchers on either side sat chattering amongst themselves waiting for the ten o'clock division: the ultimate humiliation the House affords to its worst debaters. The Speaker had to call for order several times during Charles's speech, once rising to rebuke noisy members, "The House does its reputation no service by behaving in this way." But his plea fell on deaf ears as the conversations continued. At nine-thirty Charles sat down in a cold sweat. A few of his own backbenchers managed to raise an unconvincing "Hear, hear."

When the Government minister opened his speech by describing Charles's offering as among the most pathetic he had heard in a long political career he may well have been exaggerating, but from the expressions on the Tory front benches not many Opposition members were going to disagree with him.

CHAPTER
NINE

THE DECISION WAS finally made by the inner Cabinet of twelve on Thursday, 16 November 1967. By Friday every bank clerk in Tokyo was privy to the inner Cabinet's closest secret, and by the time the Prime Minister made the announcement official on Saturday afternoon the Bank of England had lost 600 million dollars of reserves on the foreign exchange market.

At the time of the Prime Minister's statement Raymond was in Leeds conducting one of his fortnightly constituency "surgeries." He was in the process of explaining the new housing bill to a young married couple when Fred Padgett, his agent, burst into the room.

"Raymond, sorry to interrupt you, but I thought you'd want to know immediately. No. 10 have just announced that the pound has been devalued from two dollars eighty to two dollars forty." The sitting member was momentarily stunned, the local housing problem driven from his mind. He stared blankly across the table at the two constituents who had come to seek his advice.

"Will you please excuse me for a moment, Mr. Higginbottom," Raymond asked courteously, "but I must make a phone call." The moment turned out to be fifteen minutes, in which time Raymond had made contact with a senior civil servant from the Treasury and had all the details confirmed. He called Joyce and told her not to answer the phone until he arrived back home. It was several minutes before he felt composed enough to put his head round the office door.

"How many people are still waiting to see me, Fred?" he asked.

"After the Higginbottoms there's only the mad major, still convinced that Martians are about to land on the roof of Leeds town hall."

"Why would they want to come to Leeds first?" asked Raymond, trying to hide his anxiety with false humor.

"Once they've captured Yorkshire, the rest would be easy."

"Hard to find fault with that argument. Nevertheless, tell the major I'm deeply concerned but I need to study his claim in more detail and to seek further advice from the Ministry of Defense. Make an appointment for him to see me at the next surgery and by then I should have a strategic plan ready for him."

Fred Padgett grinned. "That will give him something to tell his friends about for at least two weeks."

Raymond returned to Mr. and Mrs. Higginbottom and assured them he would have their housing problem sorted out within a few days. He made a note on his file to ring the Leeds Council Housing Officer.

"What an afternoon," exclaimed Raymond after the door had closed behind them. "One wife-beating, one electricity turned off by the YEB with four children under ten in the house, one pollution of the Aire river, and one appalling housing problem—never forgetting the mad major and his itinerant Martians. And on top of all of that the devaluation news."

"How can you remain so calm?" asked Fred Padgett.

"Because I can't afford to let anyone know how I really feel."

After his surgery Raymond would normally have gone round to the local pub for a pint and an obligatory natter with the locals. This always gave him the chance to catch up on what had been happening in Leeds during the past fortnight. But on this occasion he bypassed the pub and returned quickly to his parents' home.

Joyce told him that the phone had rung so often that she had finally taken it off the hook, without letting his mother know the real reason.

"Very sensible," said Raymond.

"What are you going to do?" she asked.

"I shall resign, of course."

"Why do that, Raymond? It will only harm your career."

"You may turn out to be right, but that won't stop me going."

"But you're only just beginning to get on top of your work."

"Joyce, without trying to sound pompous, I know I have many failings but I'm not a coward and I'm certainly not so self-seeking as totally to desert any principles I might have."

"You know, you just sounded like a man who is destined to become Prime Minister."

"A moment ago you said it would harm my chances. Make up your mind."

"I have," she said.

Raymond smiled wanly before retreating to his study to write a short handwritten letter.

Saturday, 18 November 1967

Dear Prime Minister,

After your announcement this afternoon on devaluation and the stand I have continually taken on the issue I am left with no choice but to resign my position as Under-Secretary of State at the Department of Employment.

I would like to thank you for having given me the opportunity to serve in your administration. Be assured that I shall continue to support the Government on all other issues from the back benches.

Yours,
Raymond Gould.

When the red box arrived at the house that Saturday night Raymond instructed the messenger to deliver the letter to No.

10 immediately. As he opened the box for the last time he reflected that his department was answering questions on employment in the House that Monday. He wondered who would take his place.

Because of the paraphernalia surrounding devaluation, the Prime Minister did not get round to reading Raymond's letter until late Sunday morning. The Goulds' phone was still off the hook when an anxious Fred Padgett was heard knocking on the front door later that day.

"Don't answer it," said Raymond. "It's bound to be another journalist."

"No, it's not, it's only Fred," said Joyce, peeping through an opening in the curtain.

She opened the door. "Where the hell's Raymond?" were Fred's first words.

"Right here," said Raymond, appearing from the kitchen holding the Sunday newspapers.

"The Prime Minister has been trying to contact you all morning." Raymond turned round and replaced the phone on the hook, picked it up a few seconds later, and checked the tone before dialing London WHI 4433. The Prime Minister was on the line in moments. He sounded calm enough, thought Raymond.

"Have you issued any statement to the press, Ray?"

"No, I wanted to be sure you had received my letter first."

"Good. Please don't mention your resignation to anyone until we've met. Could you be at Downing Street by eight o'clock?"

"Yes, Prime Minister."

"Remember, not a word to the press."

Raymond heard the phone click.

Within the hour he was on his way to London, and arrived at his house in Lansdowne Road a little after seven. The phone was ringing again. He wanted to ignore the insistent *burr-burr* but thought it might be Downing Street.

He picked the phone up. "Hello."

"Is that Raymond Gould?" said a voice.

"Who's speaking?" asked Raymond.

"Walter Terry, *Daily Mail.*"

"I am not going to say anything," said Raymond.

"Do you feel the Prime Minister was right to devalue?"

"I said nothing, Walter."

"Does that mean you are going to resign?"

"Walter, nothing."

"Is it true you have already handed in your resignation?"

Raymond hesitated.

"I thought so," said Terry.

"I said nothing," spluttered Raymond and slammed down the phone—before lifting it back off the hook.

He quickly washed and changed his shirt before leaving the house. He nearly missed the note that was lying on the door-mat, and he wouldn't have stopped to open it had the envelope not been embossed with large black letters across the left-hand corner—"Prime Minister." Raymond ripped it open. The handwritten note from a secretary asked him on his arrival to come by the rear entrance of Downing Street and not the front door. A small map was enclosed. Raymond was becoming weary of the whole exercise.

Two more journalists were waiting by the gate and followed him to his car.

"Have you resigned, Minister?" asked the first.

"No comment."

"Are you on your way to see the Prime Minister?"

Raymond did not reply and leaped into his car. He drove off so quickly that the pursuing journalists were left with no chance of catching him.

Twelve minutes later, at five to eight, he was seated in the anteroom of No. 10 Downing Street. As eight struck he was taken through to Harold Wilson's study. He was surprised to find the Secretary of State for Employment seated in the corner of the room.

"Ray," said the Prime Minister. "How are you?"

"I'm well, thank you, Prime Minister."

"I was sorry to receive your letter and thoroughly understand the position you are in, but I hope perhaps we can work something out."

"Work something out?" Raymond repeated, puzzled.

"Well, we all realize devaluation is a problem for you after *Full Employment at Any Cost?* but I felt perhaps a move to the Foreign Office as Minister of State might be a palatable way out of the dilemma. It's a promotion you've well earned."

Raymond hesitated. The Prime Minister continued. "It may interest you to know that the Chancellor of the Exchequer has also resigned, but will be moving to the Home Office."

"I am surprised," said Raymond.

"What with the problems we are about to tackle in Rhodesia and Europe your legal skills would come in very useful."

Raymond remained silent as he listened to the Prime Minister; he knew what decision he must now make.

Monday usually gets off to a quiet start in the Commons. The Whips never plan for any contentious business to be debated, remembering that members are still arriving back from their constituencies all over the country. The House is seldom full before the early evening. But the knowledge that the Chancellor of the Exchequer would be making a statement on devaluation at three-thirty ensured that the Commons would be packed long before that hour.

The green benches, accommodating just 427 members, had deliberately been restored as they were after the Germans had bombed the Palace of Westminster on 10 May 1941. The intimate theatrical atmosphere of the House had remained intact. Sir Giles Gilbert Scott could not resist highlighting some of the Gothic décor of Barry, but he concurred with Churchill's view that to enlarge the Chamber would only destroy the packed atmosphere of great occasions.

The Commons filled up quickly, and by two-forty-five there was not a seat to be found. Members huddled up on the steps by the Speaker's canopied chair and around the legs of the chairs of the clerks at the table. One or two even perched like unfed sparrows on the empty petition bag behind the Speaker's chair. The galleries to the side and above the Chamber, which normally resembled empty benches at the Oval on a rainy day, had taken on the look of a crucial last Test match against Australia.

The chief doorkeeper checked his supply of snuff that it had been his office to keep since those days when "unpleasant odors" wafted through London.

Raymond Gould rose to answer question number seven on the order paper, an innocent enough inquiry concerning supplementary benefits for women. As soon as he reached the dispatch box the first cries of "Resign" came from the Tory benches. Raymond couldn't hide his embarrassment. Even those seated on the back benches could see he had gone scarlet. It didn't help that he hadn't slept the previous night following the agreement he had come to with the Prime Minister. He answered the question, but the calls for his resignation did not subside. The Opposition fell silent as he sat down, only waiting for him to rise for a further question. The next question on the order paper for Raymond to answer was from Simon Kerslake; it came a few minutes after three. "What analysis has been made by his department of the special factors contributing to increasing unemployment in the Midlands?"

Raymond checked his brief before replying. "The closure of two large factories in the area, one in the Honorable member's constituency, has exacerbated local unemployment. Both of these factories specialized in car components which have suffered from the Leyland strike."

Simon Kerslake rose slowly from his place to put his supplementary. The Opposition benches waited in eager anticipation. "But surely the minister remembers informing the House, in reply to my adjournment debate last April, that devaluation would drastically increase unemployment in the Midlands, indeed in the whole country. If the Honorable Gentleman's words are to carry any conviction, why hasn't he resigned?" Simon sat down as the Tory benches demanded, "Why, why, why?"

"My speech to the House on that occasion is being quoted out of context, and the circumstances have since changed."

"They certainly have," shouted a number of Conservatives

and the benches opposite Raymond exploded with demands that he give up his office.

"Order, order," shouted the Speaker into the tide of noise.

Simon rose again, while everyone on the Conservative benches remained seated to ensure no one else was called. They were now hunting as a pack. Everyone's eyes switched back and forth between the two men, watching the dark, assured figure of Kerslake once again jabbing his forefinger at the bowed head of Raymond Gould who was now only praying for the clock to reach three-thirty.

"Mr. Speaker, during the debate, which he now seems happy to orphan, the Honorable Gentleman was only echoing the views he so lucidly expressed in his book *Full Employment at Any Cost?* Can those views have altered so radically in three years, or is his desire to remain a minister so great that he now realizes that *his* employment can be retained at any cost?"

"This question has nothing to do with what I said to the House on that occasion," retorted Raymond angrily. His last few words were lost in Opposition shouts of "Resign, resign!"

Simon was up in a flash and the Speaker called him for a third time.

"Is the Honorable Gentleman telling the House that he has one set of moral standards when he speaks, and yet another when he writes?"

The House was now in total uproar and few members heard Raymond say, "No, sir, I try to be consistent."

The Speaker rose and the noise subsided slightly. He looked about him with an aggrieved frown. "I realize the House feels strongly on these matters, but I must ask the Honorable member for Coventry Central to withdraw his remark suggesting that the minister has behaved dishonorably."

Simon rose and retracted his statement at once, but the damage had been done. Nor did it stop members from calling "Resign" until Raymond left the Chamber a few minutes later.

Simon sat back smugly as Gould left the Chamber. Conservative members turned to nod their acknowledgment of his professional demolition of the Government's Under-Secretary of State. The Chancellor of the Exchequer rose to deliver his prepared statement on devaluation. Simon felt sick as he listened with horror to the Chancellor's opening words. "The Honorable member for Leeds North handed in his resignation to the Prime Minister on Saturday evening but graciously agreed not to make this public until I had had an opportunity to address the House."

The Chancellor went on to praise Raymond for his work in the Department of Employment, and to wish him well on the back benches.

Andrew visited Raymond in his room immediately after the Chancellor had finished answering questions. He found him slumped at his desk, a vacant look on his face. Andrew had never considered Raymond a natural friend but he wanted to express his admiration for the way he had conducted himself.

"It's kind of you," said Raymond, who was still shaking from the experience. "Particularly as you would have demolished the lot of them."

"Well, they're all demolished now," said Andrew. "Simon Kerslake must feel the biggest shit in town."

"There's no way he could have known," said Raymond. "He'd certainly done his homework and the questions were spot on. I suspect we would have approached the situation in much the same way given the circumstances."

Several other members dropped in to commiserate with Raymond after which he returned to his old department to say farewell to his team before he went home to spend a quiet evening with Joyce. There was a long silence before the Permanent Secretary ventured an opinion: "I hope, sir, it will not be long before you return to Government. You have certainly made our lives hard but for those you ultimately serve you have undoubtedly made life easier." The sincerity of the statement touched Raymond, especially as the civil servant was already serving a new master.

It felt strange to sit down and watch television, read a book, even go for a walk and not be perpetually surrounded by red boxes and ringing phones. Within forty-eight hours he missed it all.

He was to receive over a hundred letters from colleagues in the House but he kept only one.

Monday, 20 November 1967

Dear Gould,

I owe you a profound apology. We all in our political life make monumental mistakes about people and I certainly made one today.

I believe that most members of the House have a genuine desire to serve the country, and there can be no more honorable way of proving it than by resigning when one feels one's party has taken a wrong course.

I envy the respect in which the whole House now holds you.

Yours sincerely,
Simon Kerslake.

When Raymond returned to the Commons that afternoon, he was cheered by the members of both sides from the moment he entered the Chamber. The minister who had been in the middle of addressing the House at the time had no choice but to wait until Raymond had taken his seat on the back benches.

CHAPTER
TEN

SIMON HAD ALREADY left when Edward Heath called his home. It was another hour before Elizabeth was able to pass on the message that the party leader wanted to see him at two-thirty.

Charles was at the bank when the Chief Whip called, asking if they could meet at two-thirty that afternoon before Commons business began. Charles felt like a schoolboy who had been told the headmaster expected him to be in his study after lunch. The last time the Chief Whip had phoned was to ask him to make the winding-up speech and they had hardly spoken since. Charles remained apprehensive; he always preferred to be told what a problem was immediately.

He decided to skip lunch at the bank and join his colleagues in the House, to be certain he wouldn't be late for the afternoon appointment.

Charles did not enjoy eating at the House as the food, with the exception of the hors d'oeuvres trolley, was only a little better than Paddington station and rather worse than London airport.

He joined some of his colleagues at the large table in the

center of the Members' Dining Room and took the only seat available, next to Simon Kerslake. The two men had not really been on good terms since the Heath-Maudling leadership contest. Charles did not care much for Kerslake: he had once told Fiona that he was one of the new breed of Tories who tried a little too hard and he had not been displeased to see him embarrassed over the Gould resignation. Not that he allowed anyone other than Fiona to know his true feelings.

Simon watched Charles sit down and wondered how much longer the party could go on electing Etonian guardsmen who spent more time making money in the City and spending it at Ascot than they did working in the House—not that it was an opinion he would have expressed to anyone but his closest friend. The discussion over lunch centered on the remarkable run of by-election results the Tories had had at Acton, Meriden, and Dudley. It was obvious that most of those around the table could not wait for a general election, although the Prime Minister did not have to call one for at least another three years.

Neither Charles nor Simon ordered coffee.

At two-twenty-five Charles watched the Chief Whip leave his private table in the corner of the room and turn to walk toward his office. Charles checked his watch and waited a moment before leaving his colleagues to begin a heated discussion about entry into the Common Market.

He strolled past the smoking room before turning left at the entrance to the library. Then he continued down the old Ways and Means corridor, passed through the swing doors, and entered the Members' Lobby which he crossed to reach the Government Whips' office. He put his head round the secretary's door. Miss Norse OBE, the Chief's invaluable secretary, stopped typing.

"I have an appointment with the Chief Whip," said Charles.

"Yes, Mr. Seymour, he is expecting you. Please go through." The typing recommenced immediately.

Charles walked on down the corridor and found the Chief Whip blocking his own doorway.

"Come on in, Charles. Can I offer you a drink?"

"No, thank you," replied Charles, not wanting to delay the news any longer.

The Chief Whip poured himself a gin and tonic before sitting down.

"I hope what I'm about to tell you will be looked upon as good news." The Chief Whip paused and took a gulp of his drink. "The leader thinks you might benefit from a spell in the Whips' office, and I must say I would be delighted if you felt able to join us . . ."

Charles wanted to protest but checked himself. "And give up my Housing and Local Government post?"

"Oh yes, and more of course, because Mr. Heath expects all Whips to forgo outside commitments. Working in this office is not a part-time occupation."

Charles needed a moment to compose his thoughts. "And if I turn it down, will I keep my post at Housing and Local Government?"

"That's not for me to decide," said the Chief Whip, "but it is no secret that Ted Heath is planning several changes in the run-up to the election."

"How long do I have to consider the offer?"

"Perhaps you could let me know your decision by question time tomorrow."

"Yes, of course. Thank you," said Charles. He left the Chief Whip's office and drove to Eaton Square.

Simon arrived at two-twenty-five, five minutes before his meeting with the party leader. He had tried not to speculate as to why Heath wanted to see him, in case the meeting only resulted in disappointment. Douglas Hurd, the head of the private office, ushered him straight through to the Conservative leader.

"Simon, how would you like to join the Housing and Local Government team in the run-up to the election?" It was typical of Heath not to waste any time on small talk and the suddenness of the offer stunned Simon. He recovered quickly.

"Thank you very much," he said. "I mean er . . . yes . . . thank you."

"Good, let's see you put your back into it, and be sure the results at the dispatch box are as effective as they have been from the back benches."

The door was opened once again by the private secretary; the interview was clearly over. Simon found himself back in the corridor at two-thirty-three. It was several moments before the offer sank in. Then he suddenly felt elated and made a dash for the nearest phone. He dialed the St. Mary's switchboard and asked if he could be put through to Dr. Kerslake. As he spoke, his voice was almost drowned by the sound of the division bells, signaling the start of the day's business at two-thirty-five following prayers. A woman's voice came on the line.

"Is that you, darling?" asked Simon above the din.

"No, sir. It's the switchboard operator. Dr. Kerslake's in the operating theater."

"Is there any hope of getting her out?"

"Not unless you're expecting a baby, sir."

"What brings you home so early?" asked Fiona as Charles came charging through the front door.

"I need to talk to someone." Fiona could never be sure if she ought to be flattered, but she didn't express any opinion as it was all too rare these days to have his company at all.

Charles repeated to his wife as nearly verbatim as possible his conversation with the Chief Whip. Fiona remained silent when Charles had come to the end of his monologue. "Well, what's your opinion?" he asked anxiously.

"All because of one bad speech from the dispatch box," Fiona commented wryly.

"I agree," said Charles, "but nothing can be gained by tramping over that ground again."

"We'll miss the salary you earn as a director of the bank,"

said Fiona. "The tax on my private income has made the amount I now receive derisory."

"I know, but if I turn it down, and we win the next election . . .?"

"You'll be left out in the cold."

"More to the point, stranded on the back benches."

"Charles, politics has always been your first love," said Fiona, touching him gently on the cheek. "So I don't see that you have a choice, and if that means some sacrifices you'll never hear me complain."

Charles rose from his chair saying, "Thank you. I'd better go and see Derek Spencer immediately."

As Charles turned to leave, Fiona added, "And don't forget, Ted Heath became leader of the party via the Whips' office."

Charles smiled for the first time that day.

"A quiet dinner at home tonight?" suggested Fiona.

"Can't," said Charles. "I've got a late vote."

Fiona sat alone wondering if she would spend the rest of her life cohabiting with three-line whips.

At last they put him through.

"Let's have a celebration dinner tonight."

"Why?" asked Elizabeth.

"Because I've been invited to join the front-bench team to cover Housing and Local Government."

"Congratulations, darling, but what does Housing and Local Government consist of?"

"Housing, urban land, transport, devolution, water, historic buildings, Stansted or Maplin airport, the Channel tunnel, royal parks . . ."

"Have they left anything for anyone else to do?"

"That's only half of it, if it's out of doors it's mine. I'll tell you the rest over dinner."

"Oh, hell, I don't think I can get away until eight tonight, and we'd still have to get a baby-sitter. Does that come under Housing and Local Government, Simon?"

"Sure does," he said, laughing. "I'll fix it and book a table at the Grange for eight-thirty."

"Have you got a ten o'clock vote?"

"Afraid so."

"I see, coffee with the baby-sitter," she said. She paused. "Simon."

"Yes, darling?"

"I'm very proud of you."

Derek Spencer sat behind his massive partner's desk in Cheapside and listened intently to what Charles had to say.

"You will be a great loss to the bank," were the chairman's first words. "But no one here would want to hold up your political career, least of all me."

Charles noticed that Spencer could not look him in the eye as he spoke.

"Can I assume that I would be invited back on the board if for any reason my situation changed at the Commons?"

"Of course," said Spencer. "There was no need for you to ask such a question."

"That's kind of you," said Charles, genuinely relieved. He stood up, leaned forward, and shook hands rather stiffly.

"Good luck, Charles," were Spencer's parting words.

"Does that mean you can no longer remain on the board?" asked Ronnie Nethercote when he heard Simon's news.

"No, not while I'm in Opposition and only a Shadow spokesman. Only the Chief Whip receives a salary and is therefore disqualified, but if we win the next election and I'm offered a job in Government I would have to resign immediately."

"So I've got your services for another three years?"

"Unless the Prime Minister goes earlier, or we lose the next election."

"No fear of the latter," said Ronnie. "I knew I'd picked a winner the day I met you, and I don't think you'll ever regret joining my board."

Over the months that followed Charles was surprised to find how much he enjoyed working in the Whips' office, although he had been unable to hide from Fiona his anger at Kerslake taking over his shadow post at Housing and Local Government. The order, discipline, and camaraderie of the job brought back memories of his days in the Grenadier Guards. His duties were manifold and ranged from checking that members were all present in their committees to sitting on the front bench in the Commons and picking out the salient points members made in their speeches to the House. He also had to keep an eye out for any signs of dissension or rebellion on his own benches while remaining abreast of what was happening on the other side of the House. In addition he had fifty of his own members from the Midlands area to shepherd, and had to be certain that they never missed a vote unless paired, and only then when the Whips' office had been informed.

As Whips are never called on to make speeches in the House at any time Charles seemed to have discovered a role for which he was best cut out. Fiona reminded him once again that Ted Heath had a spell in the Whips' office on his way to becoming Shadow Chancellor. She was delighted to see how involved her husband had become with Commons life but still hated going to bed alone each night and regularly falling asleep before he had even arrived home.

Simon also enjoyed his new appointment from the first moment. As the junior member of the Housing and Local Government team he was given transport as his special subject. During the first year he read books, studied pamphlets, held meetings with national transport chairmen from air, sea, and rail, and frequently worked long into the night trying to master his new brief. Simon was one of those rare members who, after only a few weeks, looked as if he had always been on the front bench.

Both parties were surprised by the fourteen percent swing to the Conservatives at the Louth by-election toward the end of 1969. It began to look as if the Labour party did not have enough time to recover before they had to call an election. But in March 1970 the Labour party had a surprisingly good result in the Ayrshire South by-election; it caused the press to speculate that the Prime Minister might go to the country early. The May local elections in England and Wales showed a further swing to Labour, which was contrary to every other political trend of the previous two years. Talk of a general election was suddenly in the air.

When the following month's opinion polls confirmed the swing to Labour Harold Wilson visited the Queen at Buckingham Palace and asked her to dissolve Parliament. The date of the general election was set for 18 June 1970.

The press were convinced that Wilson had got it right again, and would lead his party to victory for the third time in a row, a feat no man in political history had managed. Every Conservative knew that would spell the end of Edward Heath's leadership of his party.

Andrew and Louise returned to Edinburgh as soon as the Queen had made the announcement. Parliament went into a limbo period while members dispersed all over the country only in order to try and return to Westminster.

Andrew found his local committee had been taken by surprise by the PM's announcement, and realized he only had a matter of days to prepare himself.

The evening he arrived back in Edinburgh he called his General Purposes Committee together and over coffee and sandwiches mapped out a demanding three-week timetable which would allow him to reach every part of the constituency not once but several times. Street cards were pinned on to an old trestle table, soon to be filled in with crayon of various colors according to the canvassing returns: a red line through a definite Labour vote, a blue line through a Conservative one, a yellow through a Liberal, and a black line through the growing Scottish Nationalist party.

Andrew began each day of the campaign with a press conference at which he discussed local matters that affected his constituents, answered criticisms made by the other candidates, and dealt with any national issues that had arisen during the previous twenty-four hours. He then spent the rest of the morning touring the constituency with a loudspeaker van, entreating people to "Send Fraser back to Westminster." He and Louise would fit in a pub lunch together before the dreaded door-to-door canvassing began.

"You'll enjoy this," said Andrew as they walked up to the first door on a cold Monday morning. The street list of names was on a card in his pocket. Andrew pressed the door bell, and a little jingle could be heard. A woman still in her dressing gown answered it a few moments later.

"Good morning, Mrs. Foster," he began. "My name is Andrew Fraser. I'm your Labour candidate."

"Oh, how nice to meet you. I have so much I need to discuss with you—won't you come in and have a cup of tea?"

"It's kind of you, Mrs. Foster, but I have rather a lot of ground to cover during the next few days." When the door closed, Andrew put a blue line through her name on his card.

"How can you be sure she's Conservative?" demanded Louise, "she seemed so friendly."

"The Conservatives are trained to ask all the other candidates in for tea and waste their time. Your own side will always say, 'You have my vote, don't spend your time with me,' and let you get on to those who are genuinely uncommitted."

"I always vote for Fraser," said Mrs. Foster's next-door neighbor. "Labour for parliament, Tory for the local council."

"But don't you feel Sir Duncan should be removed from the council?" asked Andrew, grinning.

"Certainly not, and that's what I told him when he suggested I shouldn't vote for you."

Andrew put a red line through the name and knocked on the next door.

"My name is Andrew Fraser and I—"

"I know who you are, young man, and I'll have none of your politics, or your father's for that matter."

"May I ask who you will be voting for?" asked Andrew.

"Scottish Nationalist."

"Why?" asked Louise.

"Because the oil belongs to us, not those bloody Sassenachs."

"Surely it's better for the United Kingdom to remain as one body?" suggested Andrew. "At least that way —"

"Never. The Act of 1707 was a disgrace to our nation."

"But —" began Louise enthusiastically. Andrew put a hand on her arm. "Thank you, sir, for your time," and prodded his wife gently down the path.

"Sorry, Louise," said Andrew, when they were back on the pavement. "Once they mention the 1707 Act of Union we have no chance; some Scots have remarkably long memories."

He knocked on the next door. A fat man answered it, a dog lead in his hand.

"My name is Andrew Fraser, I—"

"Get lost, creep," came back the reply.

"Who are you calling creep?" Louise retaliated as the door was slammed in their faces. "Charming man."

"Don't be offended, darling. He was referring to me, not you."

"What will you put by his name?"

"A question mark. No way of telling who he votes for. Probably abstains."

He tried the next door.

"Hello, Andrew," said a lady before he could open his mouth. "Don't waste your time on me, I always vote for you."

"Thank you, Mrs. Irvine," said Andrew, checking his house list. "What about your next-door neighbor?" he asked, pointing back.

"Ah, he's an irritable old basket, but I'll see he gets to the polls on the day and puts his cross in the right box. He'd better, or I'll stop keeping an eye on his greyhound for him when he's out."

"Thank you very much, Mrs. Irvine," said Andrew, laughing.

"One more red," he told Louise as they returned to the pavement.

"And you might even pick up the greyhound vote."

They covered four streets during the next three hours, and Andrew put red lines through those names he was certain would support him on polling day.

"Why do you have to be so sure?" asked Louise.

"Because when we pick them up to vote on election day we don't want to remind the opposition, let alone arrange a lift for someone who then takes pleasure in voting Tory."

Louise laughed. "Politics is so dishonest."

"Be relieved you're not married to an American senator," said Andrew, putting a red line through the last name in the street. "At least we don't have to be millionaires to stand. Time for a quick bite before the evening meeting," he added, taking his wife's hand. On their way back to their headquarters they came across their Conservative opponent, but Andrew didn't respond when Hector McGregor tried to engage him in conversation, again holding him up.

Louise never joined her husband again on these sessions, deciding she could be of more use working back in the Committee Rooms.

In the public meetings held each evening, Andrew made the same speech thirty-two times in twenty-four days with only slight variations to account for national developments. Louise sat loyally through every one of them, always laughing at his punch lines and starting the clapping whenever he made a telling point. Somehow she managed to remain fresh and lively even at the end of the day when she drove her husband home.

By the eve of the election all the press were predicting a clear majority for Labour, but Andrew observed the gleam in his father's eye when he passed him in the street canvassing for McGregor.

At five-thirty on the morning of the election Louise woke Andrew with a cup of tea. He didn't see another cup that day. To his relief the sun was shining when he pulled back the curtains after he had had his bath: bad weather invariably helped the Tories with their never-ending pool of cars, ferrying voters to the polling booths. He returned to the bedroom to find his wife pinning to the lapel of his jacket a vast red rosette bearing the exhortation, "Send Fraser back to Westminster."

He was strolling through the streets of Edinburgh shaking hands, chatting to well-wishers, trying to convince last-minute "don't knows" when he spotted his father heading toward him. They ended up facing each other in the middle of the street.

"It's going to be a close-run thing," said Sir Duncan.

"Then I'll know who to blame if I lose by one vote," said Andrew.

Sir Duncan looked conspiratorially about him, then lowered his voice. "If you win by one vote you'll have me to thank, laddie." He marched away entreating the citizens of Edinburgh to remove the turncoat Fraser.

The next time father and son met was at the count that evening. As the little piles of votes began to grow it became obvious that Andrew would be returned to Parliament, and Hector McGregor was soon shaking his head in disappointment.

But when the first result was announced in Guildford and showed a four percent swing to the Tories all the previous predictions of a strong Labour victory began to look unrealistic. As each return was announced from town hall platforms all over the country it became progressively more obvious that the Tories were going to end up with a large enough majority to govern.

"I would have thought," Sir Duncan said to his son as the trend was confirmed across the nation, "that you'll be in for a wee spell of Opposition."

"Wee is the important word," was all that Andrew replied.

Andrew retained his seat, keeping the swing against him down to one percent and his majority a safe 4,009. Scotland wasn't as sure about Heath as the rest of the country, which showed an average swing against Labour of 4.7 percent.

Simon Kerslake managed a four-figure majority for the first time when he won Coventry Central by 2,118.

When Fiona was asked by the old earl how many votes Charles had won by, she said she couldn't be certain but she did recall Charles telling a journalist it was more than the other candidates put together.

Raymond Gould suffered an adverse swing of only two percent and was returned with a 10,416 majority. The people of Leeds admire independence in a member, especially when it comes to a matter of principle.

The Conservatives captured Parliament with an overall majority of thirty. Her Majesty the Queen called for Edward Heath and asked him to form a Government. He kissed the hands of his sovereign and accepted her commission.

CHAPTER ELEVEN

WHEN SIMON AWOKE on the morning after the election he felt both exhausted and exhilarated. He lay in bed trying to imagine how those Labour ministers, who only the previous day had assumed they would be returning to their departments, would be feeling now.

Elizabeth stirred, let out a small sleep-filled sigh. Simon stared down at his wife. In the seven years of their marriage she had lost none of her attraction for him, but he still took pleasure in just looking at her sleeping form. Her long fair hair rested on her shoulders and her slim, firm figure curved gently beneath the silk nightgown. He started stroking her back and watched her slowly come out of sleep. When she finally awoke she turned over and he took her in his arms.

"I admire your energy," she said. "If you're still fit after three weeks on the trail I can hardly claim to have a headache."

He smiled, delighted to catch a moment of privacy between the seeming lunacy of electioneering and the anticipation of office. No voter was going to interrupt this rare moment of pleasure.

"Mum," said a voice, and Simon quickly turned over to see Peter standing at the door in his pajamas. "I'm hungry."

On the way back to London in the car Elizabeth asked, "What do you think he'll offer you?"

"Daren't anticipate anything," said Simon. "But I would hope—Under-Secretary of State for Housing and Local Government."

"But you're still not certain to be offered a post?"

"Not at all. One can never know what permutations and pressures a new Prime Minister has to consider."

"Like what?" asked Elizabeth.

"Left and right wings of the party, north and south of the country—countless debts to be cleared with those people who can claim they played a role in getting him into No. 10." Simon yawned.

"Are you saying he could leave you out?"

"Oh yes. But I'll be livid if he does, and I'd certainly want to know who had been given my job—and why."

"And what could you do about it?"

"Nothing. There is absolutely nothing one can do and every back-bencher knows it. The Prime Minister's power of patronage is absolute."

"It won't matter, if you continue driving on the center line," she said. "Are you sure you wouldn't like me to take a turn at the wheel?"

Louise let Andrew lie in on the Friday morning. She knew he had been expecting to return to a higher ministerial office and had been shattered by the election result.

By the time Andrew woke it was nearly eleven. He sat in silence in his dressing gown, unshaven, and tapped a hard-boiled egg that refused to crack. An unopened *Times* lay by his side.

"Thank you for all your hard work," he said once the second cup of coffee had taken effect. She smiled.

An hour later, dressed in sports jacket and gray flannels, he toured the constituency in a loudspeaker van, thanking his supporters for returning him to Westminster. Louise was by his side, often able to jog his memory on names he couldn't recall.

After they had shaken the last hand they spent a quiet weekend with Sir Duncan in Stirling—who found it extremely hard to remove the smirk from his face.

Raymond was astonished by the election result. He couldn't believe that the opinion polls had been so wrong. He didn't confide in Joyce that he had hoped a Labour victory would bring him back into office after languishing on the back benches for what seemed an interminable time.

"There's nothing for it," he told her, "but to rebuild a career at the bar. We may be out of office for years."

"But surely that won't be enough to keep you fully occupied?"

"I have to be realistic about the future," he said slowly. "Although I don't intend to let Heath drag us into Europe without putting up one hell of a fight."

"Perhaps they'll ask you to Shadow someone?"

"No, there are always far fewer jobs available in Opposition, and in any case they always give the orators like Fraser the dispatch box when all you can do is to sit and make noises while we wait for another election."

Raymond wondered how he would broach what was really on his mind and tried to sound casual when he said, "Perhaps it's time we considered having our own home in the constituency."

"That seems an unnecessary expense," said Joyce, "especially as there's nothing wrong with your parents' home. And, in any case, wouldn't they be offended?"

"My first interest should be my duty to the constituents and this would be a chance to prove a long-term commitment to them. Naturally my parents will understand."

"But we can't afford the cost of two houses," said Joyce uncertainly.

"I realize that, but it's you who have always wanted to live in Leeds, and this will give you the chance to stop commuting from London every week. After I've done the rounds why don't you stay up, contact a few local estate agents, and see what's on the market?"

"All right, if that's what you really want," said Joyce. "I'll start next week."

Charles and Fiona spent a quiet weekend at their cottage in Sussex. Charles tried to do some gardening while he kept one ear open for the telephone. Fiona began to realize how anxious he was when she looked through the French windows and saw her finest delphinium being taken for a weed.

Charles eventually gave the weeds a reprieve and came in and turned on the television to catch Maudling, Macleod, Thatcher, and Carrington enter No. 10 Downing Street looking pensive, only to leave smiling. The senior appointments had been made: the Cabinet was taking shape. The new Prime Minister came out and waved to the crowds before being whisked away in his official car.

Would he remember who had organized the young vote for him before he was even the party leader?

"When do you want to go back to Eaton Square?" Fiona inquired from the kitchen.

"Depends," said Charles.

"On what?"

"On whether the phone rings."

Simon sat staring at the television. All those hours of work on Housing and Local Government, and the PM had offered the portfolio to someone else. He had left the set on all day but didn't learn who it was, only that the rest of the Housing and Local Government team had remained intact.

"Why do I bother?" he said out loud. "The whole thing's a farce."

"What were you saying, darling?" asked Elizabeth as she came into the room.

The phone rang again. It was the newly appointed Home Secretary, Reginald Maudling.

"Simon?"

"Reggie, many congratulations on your appointment—not that it came as a great surprise."

"That's what I'm calling about, Simon. Would you like to join me at the Home Office as Under-Secretary?"

"Like to? I'd be delighted."

"Thank heavens for that," said Maudling. "It took me a dickens of a time to convince Ted Heath that you should be released from the Housing and Local Government team."

When Andrew and Louise arrived back at Cheyne Walk after the weekend a red box was waiting for him in the drawing room. "Under-Secretary of State for Scotland" was printed in gold on the side.

"They'll be round to collect that later today," he told Louise. He turned the key to find the box was empty, and then he saw the small envelope in one corner. It was addressed to "Andrew Fraser Esquire, MP." He tore it open. It contained a short handwritten note from the Permanent Secretary, the senior civil servant at the Scottish Office.

"In keeping with a long tradition, ministers are presented with the last red box from which they worked. *Au revoir*. No doubt we will meet again."

"I suppose it could be used as a lunch box," said Louise, standing by the door.

"Or perhaps an overnight case," offered Andrew.

"Or a very small cot," added his wife, trying to make her words casual.

Andrew looked up to see Louise looking radiant.

"I let your parents know last night, but I wasn't going to tell you until dinner this evening."

Andrew threw his arms around her.

"By the way," Louise added, "we've already decided on her name."

When Raymond arrived back at Lincoln's Inn he let his clerk know that he wanted to be flooded with work. Over lunch with Sir Nigel Hartwell, the head of chambers, he explained that he thought it unlikely that the Labour party would be in Government again for some considerable time.

"Age is on your side, Raymond. Another full Parliament and you'll be barely forty, so you can still look forward to many years in the Cabinet."

"I wonder," said Raymond, uncharacteristically hesitant.

"Well, you needn't worry about briefs. Solicitors have been calling constantly since it was known you were back on a more permanent basis."

Raymond began to relax.

Joyce phoned him after lunch with the news that she hadn't found anything suitable, but the estate agent had assured her that they were expecting a lot more on the market in the autumn.

"Well, keep looking," said Raymond.

"Don't worry, I will," said Joyce, sounding as if she was enjoying the whole exercise. "If we find something perhaps we can think of starting a family," she added tentatively.

"Perhaps," said Raymond brusquely.

Charles eventually received a call on the Monday night, not from No. 10 Downing Street but from No. 12, the office of the Chief Whip. Because the Chief Whip's is not an official post, he is paid as the Parliamentary Secretary to the Treasury and he works from No. 12. The Prime Minister and the Chancellor of the Exchequer, being the first and second Lords of the Treasury, live at Nos. 10 and 11 Downing Street respectively.

The Chief Whip had phoned to say he hoped that Charles

would be willing to soldier on as a junior Whip. When he heard the disappointment in Charles's voice he added, "For the time being."

"For the time being," repeated Charles and put the phone down.

"At least you're a member of the Government. You haven't been left out in the cold," said Fiona gamely.

"True," he replied.

"People are sure to come and go during the next five years."

Charles had to agree with his wife but it didn't lessen his disappointment. Returning to the Commons as a member of the Government, however, turned out to be far more reward- ing than he had expected. This time it was his party that were making the decisions.

The Queen traveled early that July morning to the House of Lords in the Irish State Coach. An escort of the Household Cavalry accompanied her, preceded by a procession of lesser state carriages in which the Imperial State Crown and other royal trappings were transported. Charles could remember watching the ceremony from the streets when he was a boy. Now he was taking part in it. When the Queen arrived at the Upper House she was accompanied by the Lord Chancellor through the Sovereign's entrance to the robing room, where her ladies-in-waiting began to prepare her for the ceremony.

Charles always considered the State opening of Parliament a special occasion for members of both Houses. As a Whip he watched the members take their seats in the Commons and await the arrival of Black Rod. Once the Queen was seated on the throne the Lord Great Chamberlain commanded the Gen- tleman Usher of Black Rod to inform the Commons that: "It is Her Majesty's pleasure they attend her immediately in this House." Black Rod, wearing his black topcoat, black waist- coat, black knee-breeches, black stockings, and black shoes, resembled the devil's advocate rather than the Queen's mes- senger. He marched alone across the great tiled floor joining the two Chambers until he reached the doors of the House of

Commons which were slammed in his face when he was just two paces away from them.

He struck the door three times with the silver tip of his long thin black rod. In response a little window in the door was flicked back to check on who it was—not unlike a sleazy nightclub, Charles's father had once observed. Black Rod was then allowed admittance to the Lower House. He advanced toward the table and made three obeisances to the chair before saying, "Mr. Speaker, the Queen commands this Honorable House to attend Her Majesty immediately in the House of Peers."

With that, the Serjeant-at-Arms, bearing the mace, led Mr. Speaker, in full court dress, a gold embroidered gown of black satin damask, back toward the Lords. They were followed by the Clerk of the House and the Speaker's chaplain, behind whom came the Prime Minister, accompanied by the leader of the Opposition, then Government ministers with their opposite numbers, and finally as many backbenchers as could squeeze into the rear of the Lords' Chamber.

The Lords themselves were waiting in the Upper House, dressed in red capes with ermine collars, looking somewhat like benevolent Draculas, accompanied by peeresses glittering in diamond tiaras and wearing long evening dresses. The Queen was seated on the throne, in her full Monarchical robes, the Imperial State Crown on her head originally made for George IV. She waited until the procession had filled the Chamber and all was still.

The Lord Chancellor shuffled forward and, bending down on one knee, presented her with a printed document. It was the speech, written by the Government of the day, and although she had read over a copy of the script earlier that morning she had made no personal contribution to its contents, as her role on this occasion was only ceremonial. She looked up at her subjects and began to read.

Charles stood at the back of the cramped gathering, but with his height he had no trouble in following the entire proceedings. Their lordships were all in their places for the Queen's speech, with the law lords seated in their privileged position in the center of the Chamber, an honor bestowed upon them by an Act of 1539. The Lord Chancellor stood to one side of the Woolsack, which was stuffed with wool from the days when it was the staple commodity of England. When the Lords are in session he acts much as the Speaker does for the Commons.

Charles could spot his elderly father, the Earl of Bridgwater, nodding off during the Queen's speech, which promised that Britain would make a determined effort to become a full member of the EEC. "My Government also intends to bring in a bill to enact trade union reform," she declared. Charles, along with everyone else from the Commons, was counting the likely number of bills that would be presented during the coming months and soon worked out that the Whips' office were going to be in for a busy session.

As the Queen finished her speech Charles took one more look at his father, now sound asleep. How Charles dreaded the moment when he would be standing there watching his brother Rupert in ermine. The only compensation would be if he could produce a son who would one day inherit the title, as it was now obvious Rupert would never marry.

It was not as if he and Fiona had not tried. He was beginning to wonder if the time had not come to suggest that she visit a specialist. He dreaded finding out she was unable to bear a child.

The speech delivered, the Sovereign left the Upper House followed by Prince Philip and Prince Charles to a fanfare of trumpets. At the other end of the Chamber the procession of MPs, led again by the Speaker, made their way back in pairs from the red benches of the Lords to the green of the Commons.

The leader of the Opposition, having formed his own team, invited Andrew to cover the Home Office brief as number two. Andrew was delighted by the challenge of this new responsibility, especially when he discovered Simon Kerslake was to be his opposite number in Government.

Louise once again became very large in a short period, but Andrew tried to keep his mind off the pregnancy, as he dreaded her going through that amount of pain and sorrow for a third time. He telephoned Elizabeth Kerslake and they agreed to meet privately.

"That's a hard question to answer without ifs and buts," she told Andrew over coffee in her room the following day.

"But what would your advice be if Louise were to lose the third child?"

Elizabeth took a long time considering her reply. "If that happened I cannot believe it would be wise to put her through the same ordeal again," she said flatly. "The psychological repercussions alone might affect her for the rest of her life."

Andrew sat staring in front of him.

"Enough of this morbid talk," Elizabeth added. "I checked Louise last week and I can see no reason why this shouldn't turn out to be a routine birth."

As the first weeks of the new Tory administration took shape, Simon and Andrew became locked in battle over several issues and were soon known as "the mongoose and the rattlesnake." When either of the names "Kerslake" or "Fraser" was cranked up on the old-fashioned wall machines indicating one of them had risen to speak, members drifted back into the Chamber. Andrew found himself a constant visitor to the table office, a tiny room in the corridor behind the Speaker's chair where members tabled their questions, usually scribbled on yellow sheets, but still acceptable to the omniscient clerks had they been written on postage stamps.

The clerks often helped Andrew reword a question so that it would be acceptable to the chair, a function they carried out for any member, even Tom Carson, who had once accused them of political bias when they suggested one of his questions was out of order. When Carson was finally referred to the Speaker, he was called for and reprimanded, and his question deposited in one of the mock-Gothic wastepaper baskets in the Order office.

Once behind the Speaker's chair, Simon and Andrew would good-humoredly discuss the issues on which they were crossing swords. The opportunity to be out of sight of the Press Gallery above them was often taken by the two opposing members, but once they had both returned to the dispatch box they would tear into each other, looking for any weakness in the other's argument.

On one subject they found themselves in total accord. Ever since August 1969, when the troops had first been sent in, Parliament had been having another of its periodic bouts of trouble with Northern Ireland. In October 1970 the House devoted a full day's business to listen to members' opinions in the never-ending effort to find a solution to the growing clash between the Protestant extremists and the IRA. The motion before the House was to allow emergency powers to be renewed in the province.

Andrew rose from his seat on the front bench to deliver the opening speech for the Opposition. He said he took no side in this unhappy affair, but he felt sure the House was united in condemning violence. Yet however hard he searched for the answer he found neither faction willing to give an inch. "Goodwill" and "trust" were words that might as well have been left out of any dictionary printed in Ulster. It was not long before Andrew came to the conclusion that Gladstone was right when he had said, "Every time I find the solution to the Irish question, they change the question."

When Andrew had finished he surprised members by leaving the Chamber and not returning for several minutes.

Simon had been selected to wind up for the Government and had prepared his speech with meticulous care. Although both sides appeared in agreement on the main issue, the mood as always could change in a moment if an unfortunate view was expressed by a Government minister.

During the debate, much to everyone's surprise, Andrew Fraser kept leaving the Chamber. Simon left only twice between three-thirty and the ten o'clock division, once to take a call from his wife, and then again at seven-thirty for a quick supper.

presenting a bill to curb the trade unions at the same time which may well influence many members of the Labour party from voting with us on Europe. Because of this problem, the Prime Minister requires a regular 'state of play' assessment on Europe even though legislation may not be presented on the floor of the Commons for at least another year. He'll want to know periodically how many of our side are still against entry, and how many from the Opposition we can rely on to break ranks when the crucial vote is taken."

"Perhaps I should become Member of Parliament and then at least I could spend a little more time with you."

"Especially on the European issue if you were a 'don't know.' "

The "Great Debate" was discussed by the media to the point of boredom. Members were nevertheless conscious that they were playing a part in history. And, because of the unusual spectacle of the Whips not being in absolute control of the voting procedure, the Commons sprang to life, and excitement began to build up over the weeks and months of debate.

Charles retained his normal task of watching over fifty members on all normal Government bills, but because of the priority given to the issue of entry into Europe he had been released from all other duties. He knew that this was his chance to atone for his disastrous winding-up speech on the economy which he sensed his colleagues had still not completely forgotten.

"I'm gambling everything on this one," he told Fiona. "And if we lose the final vote I will be sentenced to the back benches for life."

"And if we win?"

"It will be hard to keep me off the front bench," replied Charles.

Robert Fraser was one of those noisy children who after only a few weeks sounded as if he was on the front bench.

"Perhaps he's going to be a politician after all," concluded Louise, staring down at her son.

When Simon came back Andrew was still absent from the Chamber, and he had not returned by the time the Shadow Home Secretary began to sum up. Andrew did eventually take his seat on the front bench but Simon had already begun his speech.

As Andrew entered the Chamber and took his place on the front bench, an elderly Conservative rose from his seat.

"On a point of order, Mr. Speaker."

Simon sat down immediately and turned his head to listen to the point his colleague wanted to make.

"Is it not a tradition of this House, sir," began the elder statesman rather ponderously, "for a front-bench spokesman to have the courtesy to remain in his seat during the debate in order that he may ascertain views other than his own?"

"That is not a point of order," replied the Speaker above the cries of "Hear, hear" from the Conservative benches. Andrew scribbled a quick note and hurriedly passed it over to Simon. On it was written a single sentence.

"I accept the point my Right Honorable friend makes," Simon began, "and would have complained myself had I not known that the Honorable Gentleman, the member for Edinburgh Carlton, has spent most of the afternoon in hospital." Simon paused to let the effect sink in. "Where his wife was in labor. I am not given to accepting as necessarily accurate all the Opposition tells me," he continued, "but I am able to confirm this statement because it was my wife who delivered the baby." The House began to laugh. "I can assure my Honorable friend that my wife has spent her entire afternoon indoctrinating the infant in the value of Conservative policies as understood by his grandfather, which is why the Honorable Gentleman has found it necessary to be absent himself from so much of the debate." Simon waited for the laughter to subside. "For those members of the House who thrive on statistics, it's a boy and he weighs four pounds three ounces."

There are times in the House when affection is displayed on both sides, thought Andrew, who considered it was ironic that during an Irish debate an Englishman had demonstrated such affection for a Scotsman.

There was no challenge when the Speaker "collected the voices" at ten o'clock so the matter was decided "on the nod" and Simon joined Andrew behind the Speaker's chair.

"Just over four pounds doesn't sound very big to me. I thought I'd take a second opinion from the Minister of Health."

"I agree," said Andrew, "the little blighter is stuck in an incubator, but your wife is doing everything she can to fatten him up. I'm off to watch him now."

"Good luck," said Simon.

Andrew sat by the incubator all night, hating the drip, drip, drip of the little plastic tube that passed up the child's nose and down into his stomach. He feared that when he woke his son would be dead and continually went to the washbasin and put a damp, cold cloth over his eyes to ensure he remained awake. He finally lost the battle and dozed off in a "dad's bed" in the corner.

When his father woke, Robert Bruce Fraser was very much alive. The crumpled father rose from his bed to admire his crumpled offspring, who was receiving milk down the plastic tube from a night nurse.

Andrew stared down at the crinkly face. The boy had inherited his square jaw, but he had his mother's nose and hair coloring. Andrew chuckled at the time Louise had wasted over girls' names. Robert it would be.

Robert Bruce Fraser traveled to Cheyne Walk with his mother and father three weeks later, having topped the scales earlier that morning at five pounds ten ounces.

Elizabeth Kerslake had told them to be thankful: the postnatal examination had shown that it would not be possible for Louise to bear another child.

CHAPTER TWELVE

THE CHIEF WHIP looked round at his colleagues, wondering which of them would volunteer for such a thankless task.

A hand went up, and he was pleasantly surprised.

"Thank you, Charles."

Charles had already warned Fiona that he was going to volunteer to be the Whip responsible for the issue that had most dominated the last election: Britain's entry into the EEC. Everyone in that room realized that it would be the most demanding marathon of the entire Parliament, and there was an audible sigh of relief when Charles volunteered.

"Not a job for anyone with a rocky marriage," he heard one Whip whisper. At least that's something I don't have to worry about, thought Charles, but he made a note to take home some flowers that night.

"Why was it the bill everyone wanted to avoid?" asked Fiona as she arranged the daffodils.

"Because many of our side don't necessarily back Edward Heath in his lifelong ambition to take Britain into Europe while quite a few of the Opposition do," said Charles, accepting a large brandy. "Added to that, we have the problem

"What has changed your mind?" asked Andrew.

"He never stops shouting at everyone, he's totally preoccupied with himself, and he falls asleep as soon as someone
else offers an opinion," she replied.

"At last I think I've found it." After Raymond heard the news
he took the train up to Leeds the following Friday. Joyce had
selected four houses for him to consider, but he had to agree
with her that the one in Chapel Allerton was exactly what
they were looking for. It was also by far the most expensive.

"Can we afford it?" asked Joyce anxiously.

"Probably not, but one of the problems of seeing four
houses is that you end up only wanting the best one."

"I could go on looking."

"No, you've found the right house; now I'll have to work out
how we can pay for it, and I think I may have come up with an
idea."

Joyce said nothing, waiting for him to continue.

"We could sell our place in Lansdowne Road."

"But where would we live when you're in London?"

"I could rent a small flat somewhere between the law courts
and the Commons while you set up our real home in Leeds."

"But wouldn't you get lonely?"

"Of course I will," said Raymond, trying to sound convincing. "But almost every member north of Birmingham is parted
from his wife during the week. In any case, you've always
wanted to settle in Yorkshire, and this might be our best
chance. If my practice continues to grow we can buy a second
house in London at a later date."

Joyce looked apprehensive.

"One added bonus," said Raymond, "your being in Leeds
will ensure I never lose the seat."

She smiled, as she always felt reassured whenever Raymond
showed the slightest sign of needing her.

On Monday morning Raymond put in a bid for the house in
Chapel Allerton before returning to London. After a little bargaining over the phone during the week, he and the owner

settled on a price. By Thursday Raymond had put his Lansdowne Road house on the market and was surprised by the amount the estate agent thought it would fetch.

All Raymond had to do now was find himself a flat.

Simon sent a note to Ronnie expressing his thanks for keeping him so well informed about what was happening at Nethercote and Company. It had been eight months since he had resigned from the board because of his appointment as a minister, but Ronnie saw that the minutes of each meeting were posted to him to study in his own time. "His own time": Simon had to laugh at the thought.

His overdraft at the bank now stood at a little over £72,000, but as Ronnie intended the shares should be offered at five pounds each when they went public Simon felt sure there was still a fair leeway, as his personal holding should realize £300,000. Elizabeth warned him not to spend a penny of the profit until the money was safely in the bank. He was thankful she didn't know the full extent of his borrowing.

Over one of their occasional lunches at the Ritz, Ronnie spelled out to Simon his plans for the future of the company.

"Now that the Tories are in I think I'll go public in eighteen months' time. This year's profits are up again and next year's look even better. So 1973 looks a perfect bet."

Simon looked apprehensive and Ronnie responded quickly. "If you're having any problem, Simon, I'll be happy to take the shares off your hands at their market value. At least that way you'd show a small profit."

"No, no," said Simon. "I'll hang in there now that I've waited this long."

"Suit yourself," said Ronnie. "Now tell me—how are you enjoying the Home Office?"

Simon put down his knife and fork. "Of the three great offices of state, it's the one most involved with people, so there's a new challenge at a personal level every day, although it can be depressing too. Locking people up in prisons, banning immigrants and deporting harmless aliens isn't my idea of fun.

The Home Office never seems to want anyone to enjoy too much freedom."

"And what about Ireland?"

"What about Ireland?" said Simon, shrugging his shoulders.

"I'd give the north back to Eire," said Ronnie, "or let them go independent and give them a large cash incentive to do so. At the moment the whole exercise is money down the drain."

"We're discussing people," said Simon, "not money."

"Ninety percent of the voters would back me," said Ronnie, lighting a cigar.

"Everyone imagines ninety percent of the people support their views, until they stand for election," said Simon. "The issue of Ireland is far too important to be glib about. I repeat, we're discussing people, eight million people, all of whom have the same right to justice as you and I. And as long as I work in the Home Office I intend to see that they get it."

Ronnie remained silent.

"I'm sorry, Ronnie," continued Simon. "Too many people have an easy solution to Ireland. If there *was* an easy solution the problem wouldn't have lasted over two hundred years."

"Don't be sorry," said Ronnie. "I'm so stupid, I've only just worked out for the first time why you're in public office."

"You're a typical self-made Fascist," said Simon, teasing his companion once again.

"You may be right, but you won't change my mind on hanging. Your lot should bring back the rope; the streets aren't safe any longer."

"For property developers like you, hoping for a quick killing?"

Both men laughed.

"Andrew, do you want lunch?"

"In a moment, in a moment."

"That's what you said half an hour ago."

"I know, but he's nearly got it. Just give me a few more minutes." Louise waited and watched, but Robert collapsed in a heap again.

"No doubt you're expecting him to play soccer for England by the time he's two."

"No, certainly not," said Andrew, carrying his son back into the house. "Rugby for Scotland."

Louise was touched by the amount of time Andrew spent with Robert. She told her disbelieving friends that he regularly fed and bathed the baby and even changed his nappy.

"Don't you think he's good-looking?" asked Andrew, strapping his son carefully into his chair.

"Yes," said Louise, laughing.

"That's because he looks like me," said Andrew, putting his arms round his wife.

"He most certainly does not," said Louise firmly.

Crash. A bowlful of porridge had been deposited on the floor, leaving just a lump left in the spoon, which Robert was now smearing across his face and hair.

"He looks as if he has just stepped out of a concrete mixer," said Andrew.

Louise stared at her son. "Perhaps you're right. There *are* times when he looks like you."

"How do you feel about rape?" asked Raymond.

"I can't see that it's relevant," Stephanie Arnold replied.

"I think they'll go for me on it," said Raymond.

"But why?"

"They'll be able to pin me in a corner, damage my character."

"But where does it get them? They can't prove lack of consent."

"Maybe, but they will offer it as background to prove the rest of the case."

"Because you raped someone doesn't prove you murdered them."

Raymond and Stephanie Arnold, who was new to chambers, continued discussing their first case together on the way to the Old Bailey, and she left Raymond in no doubt that she was delighted to be led by him. They were to appear together to defend a laborer accused of the rape and murder of his step-daughter.

"Open and shut case unfortunately," said Raymond, "but we're going to make the Crown prove their argument beyond anyone's doubt."

When the case stretched into a second week Raymond began to believe that the jury were so gullible they might even get their client off. Stephanie was sure they would.

The day before the judge's summing up Raymond invited Stephanie to dinner at the House of Commons. That'll make them turn their heads, he thought to himself. They won't have seen anything in a white shirt and black stockings that looks like that for some time, certainly not Mr. Speaker.

Stephanie seemed flattered by the invitation and sat through the stodgy meal served in the Strangers' Dining Room, obviously impressed as former Cabinet ministers flitted in and out, all of them acknowledging him.

"How's the new flat?" asked Stephanie.

"Worked out well," replied Raymond. "The Barbican is so convenient for Parliament and the law courts."

"Does your wife like it?" she asked, lighting a cigarette but not looking at him directly.

"She's not in town that much nowadays. She spends most of her time in Leeds—doesn't care much for London."

The awkward pause that followed was interrupted by a sudden clanging of bells.

"Are we on fire?" said Stephanie, quickly stubbing out her cigarette.

"No," said Raymond, laughing. "Just the ten o'clock division. I have to leave you and vote. I'll be back in about fifteen minutes."

"Shall I order coffee?"

"No, don't bother," said Raymond. "It's foul. Perhaps . . . perhaps you'd like to come back to the Barbican? Then you can give a verdict on my flat."

"Maybe it's an open and shut case." She smiled.

Raymond returned the smile before joining his colleagues as they flooded out of the dining room down the corridor toward the Commons Chamber. He didn't have time to explain to Stephanie that he had only six minutes to get into the right lobby. As Raymond had no idea what they were voting on that night he followed the surge of Labour members into the Noes lobby. The bells stopped and the doors were bolted.

Whenever the vote is called for at the end of the debate the Speaker puts the question and the moment he reaches the words, "I think the Ayes have it," the roar of "No" from those opposed to the motion ensures a vote at ten o'clock. Bells peal out over the Palace of Westminster, and in some nearby restaurants and members' homes in the division-bell area.

Members then scurry into the Ayes or Noes division lobby before the cry of "Lock the doors" is heard. Once the doors have been secured each member then files past two clerks seated at a high desk at the far end of the corridor who tick off his name. As Raymond stepped past the clerks he came toward the exit doors which were angled so as to make a funnel through which only one member at a time could pass. The Whip acting as teller shouted out the mounting vote. "Seventy-three," he called as Raymond passed him. The only particular rule relating to voting was that members could not wear a hat or overcoat while in the lobby. A clerk had once told Raymond that this dated from the days when lazy members sent their driver off in the hansom cab, hats over ears, coat buttoned up to the nose, to march through the corridors and give their masters' names. Some of them would have been a damn sight better MPs than their employers, Raymond had often thought.

While in the corridor he discovered that they were voting on a clause of the Trade Union Bill concerning the validity of closed shops. He was in no doubt that he supported his party on that subject.

When he returned to the Strangers' Dining Room after the vote he found Stephanie checking her face in a compact mirror, a small round face with green eyes and brunette hair. She was replacing the trace of lipstick. He suddenly felt conscious of being a little overweight for a man not yet forty.

"Shall we go?" he suggested, after he had signed the bill.

When Simon came back Andrew was still absent from the Chamber, and he had not returned by the time the Shadow Home Secretary began to sum up. Andrew did eventually take his seat on the front bench but Simon had already begun his speech.

As Andrew entered the Chamber and took his place on the front bench, an elderly Conservative rose from his seat.

"On a point of order, Mr. Speaker."

Simon sat down immediately and turned his head to listen to the point his colleague wanted to make.

"Is it not a tradition of this House, sir," began the elder statesman rather ponderously, "for a front-bench spokesman to have the courtesy to remain in his seat during the debate in order that he may ascertain views other than his own?"

"That is not a point of order," replied the Speaker above the cries of "Hear, hear" from the Conservative benches. Andrew scribbled a quick note and hurriedly passed it over to Simon. On it was written a single sentence.

"I accept the point my Right Honorable friend makes," Simon began, "and would have complained myself had I not known that the Honorable Gentleman, the member for Edinburgh Carlton, has spent most of the afternoon in hospital." Simon paused to let the effect sink in. "Where his wife was in labor. I am not given to accepting as necessarily accurate all the Opposition tells me," he continued, "but I am able to confirm this statement because it was my wife who delivered the baby." The House began to laugh. "I can assure my Honorable friend that my wife has spent her entire afternoon indoctrinating the infant in the value of Conservative policies as understood by his grandfather, which is why the Honorable Gentleman has found it necessary to be absent himself from so much of the debate." Simon waited for the laughter to subside. "For those members of the House who thrive on statistics, it's a boy and he weighs four pounds three ounces."

There are times in the House when affection is displayed on both sides, thought Andrew, who considered it was ironic that during an Irish debate an Englishman had demonstrated such affection for a Scotsman.

There was no challenge when the Speaker "collected the voices" at ten o'clock so the matter was decided "on the nod" and Simon joined Andrew behind the Speaker's chair.

"Just over four pounds doesn't sound very big to me. I thought I'd take a second opinion from the Minister of Health."

"I agree," said Andrew, "the little blighter is stuck in an incubator, but your wife is doing everything she can to fatten him up. I'm off to watch him now."

"Good luck," said Simon.

Andrew sat by the incubator all night, hating the drip, drip, drip of the little plastic tube that passed up the child's nose and down into his stomach. He feared that when he woke his son would be dead and continually went to the washbasin and put a damp, cold cloth over his eyes to ensure he remained awake. He finally lost the battle and dozed off in a "dad's bed" in the corner.

When his father woke, Robert Bruce Fraser was very much alive. The crumpled father rose from his bed to admire his crumpled offspring, who was receiving milk down the plastic tube from a night nurse.

Andrew stared down at the crinkly face. The boy had inherited his square jaw, but he had his mother's nose and hair coloring. Andrew chuckled at the time Louise had wasted over girls' names. Robert it would be.

Robert Bruce Fraser traveled to Cheyne Walk with his mother and father three weeks later, having topped the scales earlier that morning at five pounds ten ounces.

Elizabeth Kerslake had told them to be thankful: the post-natal examination had shown that it would not be possible for Louise to bear another child.

CHAPTER
TWELVE

THE CHIEF WHIP looked round at his colleagues, wondering which of them would volunteer for such a thankless task.

A hand went up, and he was pleasantly surprised.

"Thank you, Charles."

Charles had already warned Fiona that he was going to volunteer to be the Whip responsible for the issue that had most dominated the last election: Britain's entry into the EEC. Everyone in that room realized that it would be the most demanding marathon of the entire Parliament, and there was an audible sigh of relief when Charles volunteered.

"Not a job for anyone with a rocky marriage," he heard one Whip whisper. At least that's something I don't have to worry about, thought Charles, but he made a note to take home some flowers that night.

"Why was it the bill everyone wanted to avoid?" asked Fiona as she arranged the daffodils.

"Because many of our side don't necessarily back Edward Heath in his lifelong ambition to take Britain into Europe, while quite a few of the Opposition do," said Charles, accepting a large brandy. "Added to that, we have the problem of presenting a bill to curb the trade unions at the same time which may well influence many members of the Labour party from voting with us on Europe. Because of this problem, the Prime Minister requires a regular 'state of play' assessment on Europe even though legislation may not be presented on the floor of the Commons for at least another year. He'll want to know periodically how many of our side are still against entry, and how many from the Opposition we can rely on to break ranks when the crucial vote is taken."

"Perhaps I should become Member of Parliament and then at least I could spend a little more time with you."

"Especially on the European issue if you were a 'don't know.' "

The "Great Debate" was discussed by the media to the point of boredom. Members were nevertheless conscious that they were playing a part in history. And, because of the unusual spectacle of the Whips not being in absolute control of the voting procedure, the Commons sprang to life, and excitement began to build up over the weeks and months of debate.

Charles retained his normal task of watching over fifty members on all normal Government bills, but because of the priority given to the issue of entry into Europe he had been released from all other duties. He knew that this was his chance to atone for his disastrous winding-up speech on the economy which he sensed his colleagues had still not completely forgotten.

"I'm gambling everything on this one," he told Fiona. "And if we lose the final vote I will be sentenced to the back benches for life."

"And if we win?"

"It will be hard to keep me off the front bench," replied Charles.

Robert Fraser was one of those noisy children who after only a few weeks sounded as if he was on the front bench.

"Perhaps he's going to be a politician after all," concluded Louise, staring down at her son.

"What has changed your mind?" asked Andrew.

"He never stops shouting at everyone, he's totally preoccupied with himself, and he falls asleep as soon as someone else offers an opinion," she replied.

"At last I think I've found it." After Raymond heard the news he took the train up to Leeds the following Friday. Joyce had selected four houses for him to consider, but he had to agree with her that the one in Chapel Allerton was exactly what they were looking for. It was also by far the most expensive.

"Can we afford it?" asked Joyce anxiously.

"Probably not, but one of the problems of seeing four houses is that you end up only wanting the best one."

"I could go on looking."

"No, you've found the right house; now I'll have to work out how we can pay for it, and I think I may have come up with an idea."

Joyce said nothing, waiting for him to continue.

"We could sell our place in Lansdowne Road."

"But where would we live when you're in London?"

"I could rent a small flat somewhere between the law courts and the Commons while you set up our real home in Leeds."

"But wouldn't you get lonely?"

"Of course I will," said Raymond, trying to sound convincing. "But almost every member north of Birmingham is parted from his wife during the week. In any case, you've always wanted to settle in Yorkshire, and this might be our best chance. If my practice continues to grow we can buy a second house in London at a later date."

Joyce looked apprehensive.

"One added bonus," said Raymond, "your being in Leeds will ensure I never lose the seat."

She smiled, as she always felt reassured whenever Raymond showed the slightest sign of needing her.

On Monday morning Raymond put in a bid for the house in Chapel Allerton before returning to London. After a little bargaining over the phone during the week, he and the owner settled on a price. By Thursday Raymond had put his Lansdowne Road house on the market and was surprised by the amount the estate agent thought it would fetch.

All Raymond had to do now was find himself a flat.

Simon sent a note to Ronnie expressing his thanks for keeping him so well informed about what was happening at Nethercote and Company. It had been eight months since he had resigned from the board because of his appointment as a minister, but Ronnie saw that the minutes of each meeting were posted to him to study in his own time. "His own time": Simon had to laugh at the thought.

His overdraft at the bank now stood at a little over £72,000, but as Ronnie intended the shares should be offered at five pounds each when they went public Simon felt sure there was still a fair leeway, as his personal holding should realize £300,000. Elizabeth warned him not to spend a penny of the profit until the money was safely in the bank. He was thankful she didn't know the full extent of his borrowing.

Over one of their occasional lunches at the Ritz, Ronnie spelled out to Simon his plans for the future of the company.

"Now that the Tories are in I think I'll go public in eighteen months' time. This year's profits are up again and next year's look even better. So 1973 looks a perfect bet."

Simon looked apprehensive and Ronnie responded quickly. "If you're having any problem, Simon, I'll be happy to take the shares off your hands at their market value. At least that way you'd show a small profit."

"No, no," said Simon. "I'll hang in there now that I've waited this long."

"Suit yourself," said Ronnie. "Now tell me—how are you enjoying the Home Office?"

Simon put down his knife and fork. "Of the three great offices of state, it's the one most involved with people, so there's a new challenge at a personal level every day, although it can be depressing too. Locking people up in prisons, banning immigrants and deporting harmless aliens isn't my idea of fun.

The Home Office never seems to want anyone to enjoy too much freedom."

"And what about Ireland?"

"What about Ireland?" said Simon, shrugging his shoulders.

"I'd give the north back to Eire," said Ronnie, "or let them go independent and give them a large cash incentive to do so. At the moment the whole exercise is money down the drain."

"We're discussing people," said Simon, "not money."

"Ninety percent of the voters would back me," said Ronnie, lighting a cigar.

"Everyone imagines ninety percent of the people support their views, until they stand for election," said Simon. "The issue of Ireland is far too important to be glib about. I repeat, we're discussing people, eight million people, all of whom have the same right to justice as you and I. And as long as I work in the Home Office I intend to see that they get it."

Ronnie remained silent.

"I'm sorry, Ronnie," continued Simon. "Too many people have an easy solution to Ireland. If there *was* an easy solution the problem wouldn't have lasted over two hundred years."

"Don't be sorry," said Ronnie. "I'm so stupid, I've only just worked out for the first time why you're in public office."

"You're a typical self-made Fascist," said Simon, teasing his companion once again.

"You may be right, but you won't change my mind on hanging. Your lot should bring back the rope; the streets aren't safe any longer."

"For property developers like you, hoping for a quick killing?"

Both men laughed.

"Andrew, do you want lunch?"

"In a moment, in a moment."

"That's what you said half an hour ago."

"I know, but he's nearly got it. Just give me a few more minutes." Louise waited and watched, but Robert collapsed in a heap again.

"No doubt you're expecting him to play soccer for England by the time he's two."

"No, certainly not," said Andrew, carrying his son back into the house. "Rugby for Scotland."

Louise was touched by the amount of time Andrew spent with Robert. She told her disbelieving friends that he regularly fed and bathed the baby and even changed his nappy.

"Don't you think he's good-looking?" asked Andrew, strapping his son carefully into his chair.

"Yes," said Louise, laughing.

"That's because he looks like me," said Andrew, putting his arms round his wife.

"He most certainly does not," said Louise firmly.

Crash. A bowlful of porridge had been deposited on the floor, leaving just a lump left in the spoon, which Robert was now smearing across his face and hair.

"He looks as if he has just stepped out of a concrete mixer," said Andrew.

Louise stared at her son. "Perhaps you're right. There *are* times when he looks like you."

"How do you feel about rape?" asked Raymond.

"I can't see that it's relevant," Stephanie Arnold replied.

"I think they'll go for me on it," said Raymond.

"But why?"

"They'll be able to pin me in a corner, damage my character."

"But where does it get them? They can't prove lack of consent."

"Maybe, but they will offer it as background to prove the rest of the case."

"Because you raped someone doesn't prove you murdered them."

Raymond and Stephanie Arnold, who was new to chambers, continued discussing their first case together on the way to the Old Bailey, and she left Raymond in no doubt that she was delighted to be led by him. They were to appear together to defend a laborer accused of the rape and murder of his step-daughter.

"Open and shut case unfortunately," said Raymond, "but we're going to make the Crown prove their argument beyond anyone's doubt."

When the case stretched into a second week Raymond began to believe that the jury were so gullible they might even get their client off. Stephanie was sure they would.

The day before the judge's summing up Raymond invited Stephanie to dinner at the House of Commons. That'll make them turn their heads, he thought to himself. They won't have seen anything in a white shirt and black stockings that looks like that for some time, certainly not Mr. Speaker.

Stephanie seemed flattered by the invitation and sat through the stodgy meal served in the Strangers' Dining Room, obviously impressed as former Cabinet ministers flitted in and out, all of them acknowledging him.

"How's the new flat?" asked Stephanie.

"Worked out well," replied Raymond. "The Barbican is so convenient for Parliament and the law courts."

"Does your wife like it?" she asked, lighting a cigarette but not looking at him directly.

"She's not in town that much nowadays. She spends most of her time in Leeds—doesn't care much for London."

The awkward pause that followed was interrupted by a sudden clanging of bells.

"Are we on fire?" said Stephanie, quickly stubbing out her cigarette.

"No," said Raymond, laughing. "Just the ten o'clock division. I have to leave you and vote. I'll be back in about fifteen minutes."

"Shall I order coffee?"

"No, don't bother," said Raymond. "It's foul. Perhaps . . . perhaps you'd like to come back to the Barbican? Then you can give a verdict on my flat."

"Maybe it's an open and shut case." She smiled.

Raymond returned the smile before joining his colleagues as they flooded out of the dining room down the corridor toward the Commons Chamber. He didn't have time to explain to Stephanie that he had only six minutes to get into the right lobby. As Raymond had no idea what they were voting on that night he followed the surge of Labour members into the Noes lobby. The bells stopped and the doors were bolted.

Whenever the vote is called for at the end of the debate the Speaker puts the question and the moment he reaches the words, "I think the Ayes have it," the roar of "No" from those opposed to the motion ensures a vote at ten o'clock. Bells peal out over the Palace of Westminster, and in some nearby restaurants and members' homes in the division-bell area.

Members then scurry into the Ayes or Noes division lobby before the cry of "Lock the doors" is heard. Once the doors have been secured each member then files past two clerks seated at a high desk at the far end of the corridor who tick off his name. As Raymond stepped past the clerks he came toward the exit doors which were angled so as to make a funnel through which only one member at a time could pass. The Whip acting as teller shouted out the mounting vote. "Seventy-three," he called as Raymond passed him. The only particular rule relating to voting was that members could not wear a hat or overcoat while in the lobby. A clerk had once told Raymond that this dated from the days when lazy members sent their driver off in the hansom cab, hats over ears, coat buttoned up to the nose, to march through the corridors and give their masters' names. Some of them would have been a damn sight better MPs than their employers, Raymond had often thought.

While in the corridor he discovered that they were voting on a clause of the Trade Union Bill concerning the validity of closed shops. He was in no doubt that he supported his party on that subject.

When he returned to the Strangers' Dining Room after the vote he found Stephanie checking her face in a compact mirror, a small round face with green eyes and brunette hair. She was replacing the trace of lipstick. He suddenly felt conscious of being a little overweight for a man not yet forty.

"Shall we go?" he suggested, after he had signed the bill.

Once they had reached the flat Raymond put on a Charles Aznavour record and retired to the small kitchen to prepare coffee. He was totally oblivious to the fact that women were beginning to find him attractive. A little extra weight and a few gray hairs had not harmed his appearance, if anything giving him an air of authority.

"There's no doubting this is a bachelor flat," Stephanie remarked as she took in the one comfortable leather chair, the pipe stand, and the Spy cartoons of turn-of-the-century judges and politicians.

"I suppose that's because that's what it is," he mused, setting down a tray laden with coffee and two brandy balloons generously filled with cognac.

"Don't you get lonely?" she asked.

"From time to time," he said, pouring the coffee.

"And between times?"

"Black?" he asked, not looking at her.

"Black," she said.

"Sugar?"

"For a man who has served as a minister of the Crown and who, it's rumored, is about to become the youngest QC in the country, you're still very unsure of yourself with women."

Raymond blushed, but raised his head and stared into her eyes.

In the silence he caught Aznavour's words, "You've let yourself go . . ."

"Would my Honorable friend care to dance?" she said quietly.

Raymond could still remember the last occasion he had danced. This time he was determined it would be different. He held Stephanie so that their bodies touched and they swayed rather than danced to the music of Marcel Stellman. She didn't notice Raymond slipping off his glasses and putting them into his jacket pocket. He bent over and kissed her neck. She gave a long sigh, and when they parted, she said, "Let's hope this is between times."

*   *   *

Charles studied his chart of 330 Conservatives. He felt confident of 217, not sure about fifty-four, and had almost given up on fifty-nine. On the Labour side the best information he could glean was that fifty Socialists were expected to defy the Whip and join the Government's ranks when the great vote took place.

"The main fly in the ointment," Charles reported to the Chief Whip, "is still the Trade Union Reform Bill. The left are trying to convince those Socialists who still support the bill that there is no cause so important for which they should enter the same lobby as those Tory trade union bashers." He went on to explain his fear that unless the Government were willing to modify the Trade Union Bill they might lose Europe on the back of it. "Alec Pimkin doesn't help matters by trying to gather the waverers in our party round him."

"There's no chance of the Prime Minister modifying one sentence of the Trade Union Bill," said the Chief Whip, draining his gin and tonic. "He promised it in his speech at the party conference, and he intends to deliver by the time he goes to Blackpool at the end of this year. I can also tell you he isn't going to like your conclusions on Pimkin, Charles. He cares almost as passionately about trade union reform as he does about Europe." Charles was about to protest. "I'm not complaining, you've done damn well so far. Just keep working on the fifty waverers. Threaten, cajole, bully, bribe. Try anything, but get them in the right lobby come the night, Pimkin included."

"How about sex?" asked Charles.

"You've been seeing too many American films," said the Chief Whip, laughing. "In any case I don't think we've got anyone other than Miss Norse to offer them."

Charles returned to his office and went over the list once again. His forefinger stopped at the letter "P." Charles strolled out into the corridor and looked around; his quarry wasn't there. He checked the Chamber: no sign of him. He passed the library. No need to look in there, he thought, and moved on to the smoking room where he found his man, about to order another gin.

"Alec," said Charles expansively.

The rotund figure of Pimkin looked round.

May as well try bribery first, thought Charles. "Let me get you a drink."

"That's good of you, old fellow," said Pimkin, nervously fingering his bow tie.

"Now, Alec, what's this about your voting against the European Bill?"

Simon was horrified when he read the initial document. Its implications were all too evident.

The report of the new Boundary Commission had been left in the red box for him to study over the weekend. He had agreed at a meeting of Home Office officials that he would steer it through the House as quickly as possible so that it would make the basis for the seats to be contested at the next election. As the Secretary of State reminded him: there must be no hold-ups.

Simon had read the document carefully. In essence the changes made sense and, because of the movement of families from urban to rural areas, it would undoubtedly create more winnable seats for the Conservatives overall. No wonder the party wanted no hold-ups. But what could he do about the decision the Commission had come to on his own constituency, Coventry Central? His hands were tied. If he suggested any change from the Boundary Commission's recommendations he would rightly be accused of gerrymandering.

Because of the city's dwindling population the Commission had recommended that the four constituencies of Coventry become three. Coventry Central was to be the one to disappear, its voters distributed among Coventry West, Coventry East, and Coventry North. Simon realized this would leave one safe seat for his sitting colleague and two safe Labour seats. It had never been far from his mind how marginal a constituency he represented. Now he was on the verge of being without one at all. He would have to traipse around the country all over again looking for a new seat to fight at the next election, while at the same time taking care of his constituents in the moribund one; and at the stroke of a pen—*his* pen— they would pass on their loyalties to someone else. If only he had remained in Housing and Local Government he could have put up a case for keeping all four seats.

Elizabeth was sympathetic when he explained the problem but told him not to concern himself too much until he had spoken to the vice-chairman of the party, who advised candidates which constituencies were likely to become available.

"It may even work out to your advantage," she added.

"What do you mean?" said Simon.

"You could get a safer seat nearer London."

"With my luck I'll end up with a marginal in Newcastle."

Elizabeth prepared his favorite meal and spent the evening trying to keep up his spirits. After three portions of shepherd's pie Simon fell asleep almost as soon as he put his head on the pillow. But she stayed awake long into the night.

The casual conversation with the head of Gynecology at St. Mary's kept running through her mind. Although she hadn't confided in Simon, she could recall her supervisor's every word.

"I notice from the roster that you've had far more days off than you are entitled to, Dr. Kerslake. You must make up your mind if you want to be a doctor or the wife of an MP."

Elizabeth stirred restlessly as she considered the problem, but came to no conclusion except not to bother Simon while he had so much on his mind.

"Do these boundary changes affect you?" Louise asked, looking up from her copy of *The Times*.

Andrew was bouncing a small rubber ball on Robert's head.

"You'll give him brain damage," said Louise.

"I know, but think of the goals he'll score—and it won't be long before I can start him on rugby."

Robert started to cry when his father stopped to answer his mother's question. "No, Edinburgh isn't affected. There's such a small movement in the population that the seven city seats will remain intact. The only real changes in Scotland will be in Glasgow and the Highlands."

"That's a relief," said Louise. "I should hate to have to look for another constituency."

"Poor old Simon Kerslake is losing his seat altogether and he daren't do anything about it."

"Why not?" asked Louise.

"Because he's the minister in charge of the bill, and if he tried anything clever we would crucify him."

"So what will he do?"

"Have to shop around for a new seat, or convince an older colleague to stand down in his favor."

"But surely ministers find it easy to pick up a plum seat?"

"Not necessarily," said Andrew. "Many constituencies don't like to have someone foisted on them and want to choose their own man. And some actually prefer a local man who will never be a minister, because they feel he can devote more time to them."

"Andrew, can you revert to being some use in Opposition?"

"What are you suggesting?" asked Andrew.

"Just keep throwing that ball at your stupid son's head or he'll be crying all day."

"Take no notice of her, Robert. She'll feel differently when you score your first goal against England."

CHAPTER
THIRTEEN

AT EXACTLY THE time Raymond was ready to stop the affair Stephanie began leaving a set of court clothes in the flat. Although the two had gone their separate ways at the conclusion of the case they continued to see one another a couple of evenings a week. Raymond had had a spare key made so that Stephanie didn't have to spend her life checking when he had a three-line whip.

At first he began simply to avoid her, but she would then seek him out. When he did manage to give her the slip he would often find her back in his flat when he returned from the Commons. When he suggested they should be a little more discreet she began to make threats, subtle at first, but after a time more direct.

During the period of their affair Raymond conducted three major cases for the Crown, all of which had successful conclusions and which added to his reputation. On each occasion his clerk made certain Stephanie was not assigned to be with him. Now that his residency problem had been sorted out Raymond's only worry was how to end their relationship. He quickly discovered that getting rid of Stephanie Arnold was going to prove considerably more difficult than picking her up.

Simon was on time for his appointment at Central Office. He explained his dilemma to Sir Edward Mountjoy—vice-chairman of the party responsible for candidates—in graphic detail.

"What bloody bad luck," said Sir Edward. "But perhaps I may be able to help," he added, opening the green folder on the desk in front of him. Simon could see that he was studying a list of names. It made him feel once again like an undergraduate who needed someone to die.

"There seem to be about a dozen safe seats that will fall vacant at the next election, caused either by retirement or redistribution."

"Anywhere in particular you could recommend?"

"I fancy Littlehampton."

"Where's that?" said Simon.

"It will be a new seat, safe as houses. It's in Sussex, on the borders of Hampshire." He studied an attached map. "Runs proud to Charles Seymour's constituency which remains unchanged. Can't think you would have many rivals there," said Sir Edward. "But why don't you have a word with Charles? He's bound to know everyone involved in taking the decision."

"Anything else that looks promising?" asked Simon, only too aware that Seymour might not prove altogether cooperative.

"Let me see. Can't afford to put all your eggs in one basket, can we? Ah, yes—Redcorn, in Northumberland." Again the vice-chairman studied the map. "Three hundred and twenty miles from London and no airport within eighty miles, and their nearest main line station is forty miles. I think that one's only worth trying for if you get desperate. My advice would be to speak to Charles Seymour about Littlehampton. He must know the lay of the land in that neck of the woods."

Two clichés in one sentence, thought Simon. Thank heavens Sir Edward would never have to make a speech from the dispatch box.

"I'm sure you're right, Sir Edward," he said.

"Selection committees are being formed already," continued Sir Edward, "so you shouldn't have to wait too long."

"I appreciate your help," said Simon. "Perhaps you could let me know if anything else comes up in the meantime."

"Of course, delighted. The problem is that if one of our side were to die during the sessions you couldn't desert your present seat because that would cause two by-elections. We certainly don't want a by-election in Coventry Central with you being accused of being a carpetbagger somewhere else."

"Don't remind me," said Simon.

Charles had whittled down the fifty-nine anti-Common Market members to fifty-one, but he was now dealing with the hard kernel who seemed quite immune to future advancement or bullying. When he made his next report to the Chief Whip Charles assured him that the Conservatives who would vote against entry into Europe were outnumbered by the Socialists who had declared they would support the Government. The Chief Whip seemed pleased, but asked if Charles had made any progress with Pimkin's disciples.

"Those twelve mad right-wingers?" said Charles sharply. "They seem to be willing to follow Pimkin even into the valley of death. I've tried everything but they're still determined to vote against Europe whatever the cost."

"The maddening thing is that that bloody nuisance Pimkin has nothing to lose," said the Chief Whip. "His seat disappears at the end of this Parliament in the redistribution. I can't imagine anyone with his extreme views would find a constituency to select him, but by then he'll have done the damage." The Chief Whip paused. "If his twelve would even abstain I would feel confident of advising the PM of victory."

"The problem is to find a way of turning Pimkin into Judas and then urging him to lead the chosen twelve into our camp," said Charles.

"You achieve that, and we'd certainly win."

Charles returned to the Whips' office to find Simon Kerslake waiting by his desk.

"I dropped by on the off-chance, hoping you might be able to spare me a few moments," said Simon.

"Of course," said Charles, trying to sound welcoming. "Take a pew."

Simon sat down opposite him. "You may have heard that I lose my constituency as a result of the Boundary Commission report and Edward Mountjoy suggested I have a word with you about Littlehampton, the new seat that borders your constituency."

"It does indeed," said Charles, masking his surprise. He had not considered the problem as his own seat remained intact. He recovered quickly. "And how wise of Edward to send you to me. I'll do everything I can to help."

"Littlehampton would be ideal," said Simon. "Especially while my wife is still working in Paddington."

Charles raised his eyebrows.

"I don't think you've met Elizabeth. She's a doctor at St. Mary's," Simon explained.

"Yes, I can see how convenient Littlehampton would be. Why don't I start by having a word with Alexander Dalglish, the constituency chairman, and see what I can come up with?"

"That would be extremely helpful."

"Not at all. I'll call him at home this evening and find out what stage they've reached over selection, and then I'll put you in the picture."

"I'd appreciate that."

"While I've got you, let me give you the whip for next week," said Charles, passing over a sheet of paper. Simon folded it up and put it in his pocket. "I'll call you the moment I have some news."

Simon left feeling happier and a little guilty about his past prejudice concerning Charles, whom he watched disappear into the Chamber to carry out his bench duty.

The European issue had been given six days for debate by

back-benchers, the longest period of time allocated to one motion in living memory.

Charles strolled down the aisle leading to the front bench and took a seat on the end to check on another set of speeches. Usually he listened intently to see if he could spot a member wavering in his position, but on this occasion his thoughts were in Littlehampton. Andrew Fraser was on his feet, and Charles was delighted to be able to confirm the tick alongside his name before he drifted into deep thought.

"I for one shall vote for entry into Europe," Andrew was telling the House. "When my party was in power I was a pro-European, and now we are in Opposition I can see no good reason to do a volte-face. The principles that held true two years ago hold true today. Not all of us . . ."

Tom Carson leaped up and asked if his Honorable friend would give way. Andrew resumed his seat immediately.

"Would my Honorable friend really support the peasant farmers of France before the sheep farmers in New Zealand?" asked Carson.

Andrew rose and explained to his colleague that he would certainly expect safeguards for New Zealand, but the initial vote on the floor of the House was on the principle of entry. The details could and should be dealt with in committee. He went on to express the view that had his Honorable friend talked of wogs or Jews in such a context the House would have been in uproar. "Why is it therefore acceptable to the anti-marketeers to describe French farmers as peasants?"

"Perhaps it's you who is the peasant," Carson shouted back, in seven words thus ruining his case for the lamb farmers of New Zealand.

Andrew ignored the jibe and went on to tell the House that he believed in a united Europe as a further insurance against a third world war. He concluded with the words:

"Britain has for a thousand years written history, even the history of the world. Let us decide with our votes whether our children will read that history, or continue to write it." Andrew sat down to acclamation from both sides.

By the time Andrew had resumed his seat Charles had

formed a plan and left the Chamber when one of his own colleagues started what promised to be a long, boring, and predictable speech.

Instead of returning to the Whips' office which afforded no privacy, Charles disappeared into one of the telephone booths near the cloisters above the Members' Cloakroom. He checked the number and dialed it.

"Alexander, it's Charles. Charles Seymour."

"Good to hear from you, Charles, it's been a long time. How are you?"

"Well. And you?"

"Can't complain. What can I do for a busy man like you?"

"Wanted to chew over the new Sussex constituency with you, Littlehampton. How's your selection of a candidate going?"

"They've left me to draw up a short list of six for final selection by the full committee in about ten days' time."

"Have you thought of standing yourself, Alexander?"

"Many times," came back the reply. "But the old lady wouldn't allow it, neither would the bank balance. Do you have any ideas?"

"Might be able to help. Why don't you come and have a quiet dinner at my place early next week?"

"That's kind of you, Charles."

"Not at all, it will be good to see you again. It's been far too long. Next Monday suit you?"

"Absolutely."

"Good, let's say eight o'clock, 27 Eaton Square."

Charles put the phone down, returned to the Whips' Office and, penciled a note in his diary.

Raymond had just finished making his contribution to the European debate when Charles returned to take a seat on a half-empty Treasury bench. Raymond had made a coherent economic case for remaining free of the other six European countries and for building stronger links with the Commonwealth and America. He doubted that Britain could take the financial burden of entering a club that had been in existence for so long. If the country had joined at its inception it might have been different, he argued, but he would have to vote against this risky, unproven venture that he suspected could only lead to higher unemployment. When Raymond sat down he did not receive the acclamation that Andrew had and, worse, what praise he did elicit came from the left wing of the party who had spent so much time in the past criticizing *Full Employment at Any Cost?* Charles put a cross by the name Gould.

A note was being passed along the row to Raymond from one of the House Badge messengers, dressed in white tie and black tails. It read, "Please ring head of chambers as soon as convenient."

Raymond left the floor of the House and went to the nearest telephone in the corner of the Members' Lobby. He was immediately put through to Sir Nigel Hartwell.

"You wanted me to phone?"

"Yes," said Sir Nigel. "Are you free at the moment?"

"I am," said Raymond. "Why? Is it something urgent?"

"I'd rather not talk about it over the phone," said Sir Nigel ominously.

Raymond took a tube from Westminster to Temple and was in chambers fifteen minutes later. He went straight to Sir Nigel's office, sat down in the comfortable chair in the corner of the spacious club-like room, crossed his legs, and watched Sir Nigel pace about in front of him. He was clearly determined to get something off his chest.

"Raymond, I have been asked by those in authority about you taking silk. I've said I think you'd make a damn good QC." A smile came over Raymond's face, but it was soon wiped off. "But I need an undertaking from you."

"An undertaking?"

"Yes," said Sir Nigel. "You must stop having this damn silly er . . . relationship with another member of chambers." He rounded on Raymond and faced him.

Raymond turned scarlet but before he could speak the head of chambers continued.

"Now I want your word on it," said Sir Nigel, "that it will end, and end immediately."

"You have my word," said Raymond quietly.

"I'm not a prig," said Sir Nigel, pulling down on his waistcoat, "but if you are going to have an affair for God's sake make it as far away from the office as possible and, if I may advise you, that should include the House of Commons and Leeds. There's still a lot of the world left over and it's full of women."

Raymond nodded his agreement: he could not fault the head of chambers' logic.

Sir Nigel continued, obviously embarrassed. "There's a nasty fraud case starting in Manchester next Monday. Our client has been accused of setting up a series of companies that specialize in life insurance but avoid paying out on the claims: I expect you remember all the publicity. Miss Arnold has been put on the case as a reserve junior. They tell me it could last several weeks."

"She'll try and get out of it," said Raymond glumly.

"She already has, but I made it quite clear that if she felt unable to take the case on she would have to find other chambers."

Raymond breathed a sigh of relief. "Thank you," he said.

"Sorry about this. I know you've earned your silk, old boy, but I can't have members of chambers going around with egg on their faces. Thank you for your cooperation: I can't pretend I enjoyed that."

"Got time for a quiet word?" asked Charles.

"You're wasting your time, dear thing, if you imagine the disciples will change their minds at this late stage," said Alec Pimkin. "All twelve of them will vote against the Government on Europe. That's final."

"I don't want to discuss Europe this time, Alec. It's far more serious, and on a personal level. Let's go and have a drink on the terrace."

Charles ordered the drinks, and the two men strolled out on

to the quiet end of the terrace toward the Speaker's house. Charles stopped as soon as he was certain there was no longer anyone within earshot.

"If it's not Europe, what is it?" asked Pimkin, staring out at the Thames.

"What's this I hear about you losing your seat?"

Pimkin turned pale and touched his bow tie nervously. "It's this bloody boundary business. My constituency is swallowed up, and no one seems willing to interview me for a new one."

"What's it worth if I secure you a safe seat for the rest of your life?"

Pimkin looked suspiciously up at Charles. "Almost anything up to a pound of flesh," he added with a false laugh.

"No, I won't need to cut that deep."

The color returned to Pimkin's cheeks. "Whatever it is, you can rely on me, old fellow."

"Can you deliver the disciples?" said Charles.

Pimkin turned pale again.

"Not on the small votes in committee," said Charles, before Pimkin could reply. "Not on the clauses even, just on the second reading, the principle itself. Standing by the party in their hour of need, no desire to cause an unnecessary general election, all that stuff—you fill in the details for the disciples. I know you can convince them, Alec."

Pimkin still didn't speak.

"I deliver a copper-bottomed seat, you deliver twelve votes. I think we can call that a fair exchange."

"What if I get them to abstain?" said Pimkin.

Charles waited, as if giving the idea considerable thought. "It's a deal," he said, never having hoped for anything more.

Alexander Dalglish arrived at Eaton Square a little after eight. Fiona met him at the door and explained that Charles had not yet returned from the Commons.

"But I expect him any moment," she added. "May I offer you a drink?"

Another thirty minutes passed before Charles hurried in.

"Sorry I'm late, Alexander," he said, grasping his guest by the hand. "Hoped I might make it just before you." He kissed his wife on the forehead.

"Not at all," said Alexander. "I couldn't have asked for more pleasant company."

"What will you have, darling?" asked Fiona.

"A strong whisky, please, and can we go straight into dinner? I've got to be back at the talkshop by ten."

Charles guided his guest toward the dining room and seated him at the side of the table before taking his place below the Holbein portrait of the first Earl of Bridgwater, an heirloom his grandfather had left him. Fiona took a seat opposite her husband. During the meal of Beef Wellington, Charles spent a great deal of time catching up on what Alexander had been doing since they had last met. Although they had spent three years together in the Guards as brother officers they rarely saw each other outside of regimental reunions since Charles had entered the House. He made no mention of the real purpose behind the meeting until Fiona provided the opportunity when she served coffee.

"I know you two have a lot to talk about, so I'll leave you to get on with it."

"Thank you," said Alexander. He looked up at Fiona and smiled. "For a lovely dinner."

She smiled back and left them alone.

"Now, Charles," said Alexander, picking up the file he had left on the floor by his side. "I need to pick your brains."

"Go ahead, old fellow," said Charles, "only too delighted to be of assistance."

"Sir Edward Mountjoy has sent me a pretty long list for us to consider, among them a Home Office minister and one or two other Members of Parliament who'll be losing their present seats. What do you think of . . . ?"

Dalglish opened the file in front of him as Charles poured him a generous glass of port and offered him a cigar from a gold case that he picked up from the sideboard.

"What a magnificent object," said Alexander, staring in awe at the crested box and the engraved C.G.S. along its top.

"A family heirloom," said Charles. "Should have been left to my brother Rupert, but I was lucky enough to have the same initials as my grandfather."

Alexander handed it back to his host before returning to his notes.

"Here's the man who impresses me," he said at last. "Kerslake, Simon Kerslake."

Charles remained silent.

"You don't have an opinion, Charles?"

"Yes."

"So what do you think of Kerslake?"

"Strictly off the record?"

Dalglish nodded, but said nothing.

Charles sipped his port. "Very good," he said.

"Kerslake?"

"No, the port. Taylor's '35. I'm afraid Kerslake is not the same vintage. Need I say more?"

"Well, no, I follow your drift but it's most disappointing. He looks so good on paper."

"On paper is one thing," said Charles, "but having him as your member for twenty years is quite another. You want a man you can rely on. And his wife—never seen in the constituency, you know." He frowned. "I'm afraid I've gone too far."

"No, no," said Alexander. "I've got the picture. Next one is Norman Lamont."

"First class but he's already been selected for Kingston, I'm afraid," said Charles.

Dalglish looked down at his file once again. "Well, what about Pimkin?"

"We were at Eton together. His looks are against him, as my grandmother used to say, but he's a sound man, and very good in the constituency, so they tell me."

"You would recommend him then?"

"I should snap him up before another constituency adopts him."

"That popular, is he?" said Alexander. "Thanks for the tip. Pity about Kerslake."

"That was strictly off the record," said Charles.

"Of course. Not a word. You can rely on me."

"Cigar to your liking?"

"Excellent," said Alexander, "but your judgment has always been so good. You only have to look at Fiona to realize that."

Charles smiled.

Most of the other names Dalglish produced were either unknown, unsuitable, or easy to dismiss. When Alexander left shortly before ten Fiona asked him if the chat had been worthwhile.

"Yes, I think we've found the right man."

Raymond had the locks on his flat changed that afternoon. It turned out to be more expensive than he had bargained for, and the carpenter had insisted on cash in advance.

The carpenter grinned as he pocketed the money. "I make a fortune doing this job, Guv'nor, I can tell you. At least one gentleman a day, always cash, no receipt. Means the wife and I can spend a month in Ibiza every year, tax free."

Raymond smiled at the thought. He checked his watch; he could just catch the Thursday seven-ten from King's Cross and be in Leeds by ten o'clock for a long weekend.

Alexander Dalglish phoned Charles a week later to tell him Pimkin had made the short list, and that they hadn't considered Kerslake.

"Pimkin didn't go over very well with the committee at the first interview."

"No, he wouldn't," said Charles. "I warned you his looks were agin' him and he may come over a bit right wing at times but he's as sound as a bell and will never let you down, take my word."

"I'll have to, Charles. Because by getting rid of Kerslake we've removed his only real challenger."

Charles put the phone down and dialed the Home Office.

"Simon Kerslake, please."

"Who's calling?"

"Seymour, Whips' office." He was put straight through.

"Simon, it's Charles. I thought I ought to give you an update on Littlehampton."

"That's thoughtful of you," said Simon.

"Not good news, I'm afraid. It turns out the chairman wants the seat for himself. He's making sure the committee only interviews idiots."

"How can you be so certain?"

"I've seen the short list and Pimkin's the only sitting member they're considering."

"I can't believe it."

"No, I was pretty shocked myself. I pressed the case for you, but it fell on deaf ears. Didn't care for your views on hanging or some such words. Still, I can't believe you'll find it hard to pick up a seat."

"I hope you're right, Charles, but in any case thanks for trying."

"Any time. Let me know of any other seats you put your name in for. I have a lot of friends up and down the country."

"Thank you, Charles. Can you pair me for next Thursday?"

Two days later Alec Pimkin was invited by the Littlehampton Conservatives to attend a short-list interview for the selection of a Tory candidate for the new constituency.

"How do I begin to thank you?" he asked Charles when they met up in the bar.

"Keep your word—and I want it in writing," replied Charles.

"What do you mean?"

"A letter to the Chief Whip saying you've changed your mind on the main European vote, and you and the disciples will be abstaining on Thursday."

Pimkin looked cocky. "And if I don't play ball, dear thing?"

"You haven't got the seat yet, Alec, and I might find it necessary to phone Alexander Dalglish and tell him about that

awfully nice little boy you made such a fool of yourself over when you were up at Oxford."

Three days later the Chief Whip received the letter from Pimkin. He immediately summoned his junior Whip.

"*Well done*, Charles. How did you manage to succeed where we've all failed—and the disciples as well?"

"Matter of loyalty," said Charles. "Pimkin saw that in the end."

On the final day of the Great Debate on "the principle of entry" into Europe the Prime Minister delivered the winding-up speech. He rose at nine-thirty to cheers from both sides. At ten o'clock the House divided and voted in favor of "the principle" by a majority of 112. Sixty-nine Labour MPs, led by Roy Jenkins, had helped to swell the Government's majority.

Raymond Gould voted against the motion in accordance with his long-held beliefs. Andrew Fraser joined Simon Kerslake and Charles Seymour in the Ayes lobby. Alec Pimkin and the twelve disciples remained in their places on the Commons benches while the vote took place.

When Charles heard the Speaker read out the final result he felt a moment of triumph, although he realized that he still had the committee stage to go through. Hundreds of clauses, any of which could go wrong and turn the bill into a farce. Nevertheless the first round belonged to him.

Ten days later Alec Pimkin defeated a keen young Conservative just down from Cambridge and a local woman councillor to be selected as prospective candidate for Littlehampton.

CHAPTER
FOURTEEN

ANDREW STUDIED THE case once again and decided to make his own inquiries. Too many constituents had in the past demonstrated that they were willing to lie to him in surgery as happily as they would in the witness box to any judge.

Robert was trying to climb up on to his lap. Andrew hoisted him the remainder of the way in one tug and attempted to return to his papers. "Whose side are you on?" Andrew demanded as his son dribbled all over his freshly written notes. He stopped to pat his bottom. "Ugh," he said, putting the case file by his side on the floor. A few minutes later Robert had been changed and left with his mother.

"I'm afraid your son is not overanxious to help me in my desire to secure the release of an innocent man," Andrew shouted over his shoulder.

He settled down to go over the papers once more, something about the case didn't ring true . . . Andrew dialed the Procurator Fiscal's number. There was one man who could cut his work in half with a sentence.

"Good morning, Mr. Fraser. What can I do for you, sir?"

Andrew had to smile. Angus Sinclair was a contemporary of

his father and had known Andrew all his life, but once he was in his office he treated everyone as a stranger, making no exception.

"He even calls his wife 'Mrs. Sinclair' when she rings the office," Sir Duncan once told him. Andrew was willing to join in the game.

"Good morning, Mr. Sinclair. I need your advice as Procurator Fiscal."

"Always happy to be of service, sir."

"I want to talk to you off the record about the Paddy O'Halloran case. Do you remember it?"

"Of course, everyone in this office remembers that case."

"Good," said Andrew. "Then you'll know what a help you can be to me in cutting through the thicket."

"Thank you, sir," the slight burr came back down the telephone.

"A group of my constituents, whom I wouldn't trust further than I could toss a caber, claim O'Halloran was framed for the Princes Street bank robbery last year. They don't deny he has criminal tendencies"—Andrew would have chuckled if he hadn't been speaking to Angus Sinclair—"but they say he never left a pub called the Sir Walter Scott the entire time the robbery was taking place. All you have to tell me, Mr. Sinclair, is that you have no doubt that O'Halloran was guilty and I'll drop my inquiries. If you say nothing, I shall dig deeper."

Andrew waited, but he received no reply.

"Thank you, Mr. Sinclair." Although he knew it would elicit no response, he couldn't resist adding: "No doubt I'll see you at the golf club some time over the weekend." The silence continued.

"Good-bye, Mr. Sinclair."

"Good day, Mr. Fraser."

Andrew settled back: it was going to be a lengthy exercise. He started by checking with all the people who had confirmed O'Halloran's alibi that night but after interviewing the first eight he came to the reluctant conclusion that none of them could be trusted as a witness. Whenever he came across another of O'Halloran's friends the expression "anyone's for a pint" kept crossing his mind. The time had come to talk with the landlord of the Sir Walter Scott.

"I couldn't be sure, Mr. Fraser, but I think he was here that evening. Trouble is, O'Halloran came almost every night. It's hard to recall."

"Do you know anyone who might remember? Someone you could trust with your cash register?"

"That'd be pushing your luck in this pub, Mr. Fraser." The landlord thought for a moment. "However, there's old Mrs. Bloxham," he said at last, slapping the drying-up cloth over his shoulder. "She sits in that corner every night." He pointed to a small round table that would have been crowded had it seated more than two people. "If she says he was here, he was."

Andrew asked the landlord where Mrs. Bloxham lived and then, hoping she was in, made his way to 43 Mafeking Road, neatly sidestepping a gang of young children playing football in the middle of the street. He climbed some steps that badly needed repairing and knocked on the door of number forty-three.

"Is it another general election already, Mr. Fraser?" asked a disbelieving old lady as she peered through the letterbox.

"No, it's nothing to do with politics, Mrs. Bloxham," said Andrew, bending down. "I came round to seek your advice on a personal matter."

"A personal matter? Better come on in out of the cold then," she said, opening the door to him. "There's a terrible draft rushes through this corridor."

Andrew followed the old lady as she shuffled down the dingy corridor in her carpet slippers to a room that he would have said was colder than it had been outside on the street. There were no ornaments in the room save a crucifix that stood on a narrow mantelpiece below a pastel print of the Virgin Mary. Mrs. Bloxham beckoned Andrew to a wooden seat by a table yet unlaid. She eased her plump frame into an ancient stuffed armchair. It groaned under her weight and a strand of horsehair fell to the floor. Andrew looked more carefully at the old lady. She was wearing a black shawl over a dress she must have worn a thousand times. Once settled in her chair, she kicked off her slippers.

"Feet still giving you trouble, then?" he inquired.

"Doctor doesn't seem to be able to explain the swellings," she said, without bitterness.

Andrew leaned on the table and noticed what a fine piece of furniture it was, and how incongruous it looked in its present surroundings. He was struck by the craftsmanship of the carved Georgian legs. She noticed he was admiring it. "My great-grandfather gave that to my great-grandmother the day they were married, Mr. Fraser."

"It's magnificent," said Andrew.

She didn't seem to hear because all she said was, "What can I do for you, sir?" The second time that day he had been addressed by an elder in that way.

Andrew went over the O'Halloran story again. Mrs. Bloxham listened intently, leaning forward slightly and cupping her hand round her ear to be sure she could hear every word.

"That O'Halloran's an evil one," she said, "not to be trusted. Our Blessed Lady will have to be very forgiving to allow the likes of him to enter the kingdom of heaven." Andrew smiled. "Not that I'm expecting to meet all that many politicians when I get there either," she added, giving Andrew a toothless grin.

"Could O'Halloran possibly have been there that Friday night as all his friends claim?" Andrew asked.

"He was there all right," said Mrs. Bloxham. "No doubt about that—saw him with my own eyes."

"How can you be so sure?"

"Spilled his beer over my best dress, and I knew something bad would happen on the thirteenth, especially with it being a Friday. I won't forgive him for that. I still haven't been able to get the stain out despite what those washing-powder ads tell you on the telly."

"Why didn't you inform the police immediately?"

"Didn't ask," she said simply. "They've been after him for a long time for a lot of things they couldn't pin on him, but for once he was in the clear."

Andrew finished writing his notes and then rose to leave.

Mrs. Bloxham heaved herself out of the chair, dispensing yet more horsehair on to the floor. They walked to the door together. "I'm sorry I couldn't offer you a cup of tea but I'm right out at the moment," she said. "If you had come tomorrow it would have been all right."

Andrew paused on the doorstep.

"I get the pension tomorrow, you see," she replied to his unasked question.

It took Elizabeth some time to find a locum to cover for her so that she could travel to Redcorn for the interview. Once again the children had to be left with a baby-sitter. The local and national press had made him the hot favorite for the new seat. Elizabeth put on what she called her best Conservative outfit, a pale blue suit with a dark blue collar that hid everything on top and reached well below her knees.

The journey from King's Cross to Newcastle took three hours and twenty minutes, on what was described in the timetable as "the express." At least Simon was able to catch up with a great deal of the paperwork that had been stuffed into his red box. Civil servants, he reflected, rarely allowed politicians time to involve themselves in politics. They wouldn't have been pleased to learn that he spent an hour of the journey reading the last four weekly copies of the *Redcorn News*.

At Newcastle they were met by the wife of the Association treasurer, who had volunteered to escort the minister and Mrs. Kerslake to the constituency to be sure they were in time for the interview. "That's very thoughtful of you," said Elizabeth, as she stared at the mode of transport that had been chosen to take them the next forty miles.

The ancient Austin Mini took a further hour and a half through the winding B-roads before they reached their destination, and the treasurer's wife never drew breath once throughout the entire journey. When Simon and Elizabeth piled out of the car at the market town of Redcorn they were physically and mentally exhausted.

The treasurer's wife took them through to the constituency headquarters and introduced them both to the agent.

"Good of you to come," he said. "Hell of a journey, isn't it?"

Elizabeth felt unable to disagree with his judgment. But on this occasion she made no comment, feeling that if this was to be Simon's best chance of returning to Parliament she had already decided to give him every support possible. Nevertheless she dreaded the thought of her husband making the journey to Redcorn twice a month as she feared they would see even less of each other than they did at present, let alone the children.

"Now the form is," began the agent, "that we are interviewing six potential candidates and they'll be seeing you last." He winked knowingly.

Simon and Elizabeth smiled uncertainly.

"I'm afraid they won't be ready for you for at least another hour, so you have time for a stroll round the town."

Simon was glad of the chance to stretch his legs and take a closer look at Redcorn. He and Elizabeth walked slowly round the pretty market town, admiring the Elizabethan architecture that had somehow survived irresponsible or greedy town planners. They even climbed the hill to take a look inside the magnificent perpendicular church which dominated the surrounding area.

As he walked back past the shops in the high street Simon nodded to those locals who appeared to recognize him.

"A lot of people seem to know who you are," said Elizabeth, and then they saw the paper rack outside the local newsagent. They sat on the bench in the market square and read the lead story under a large picture of Simon.

"Redcorn's next MP?" ran the headline.

The story volunteered the fact that although Simon Kerslake had to be considered the favorite, Bill Travers, a local farmer who had been chairman of the county council the previous year, was still thought to have an outside chance.

Simon began to feel a little sick in the stomach. It reminded him of the day he had been interviewed at Coventry Central nearly eight years before. Now that he was a minister of the Crown he wasn't any less nervous.

When he and Elizabeth returned to constituency headquarters they were informed that only two more candidates had been seen and the third was still being interviewed. They walked around the town once again, even more slowly this time, watching the shopkeepers put up their colored shutters and turn "Open" signs to "Closed."

"What a pleasant market town," said Simon, trying to find out how his wife was feeling.

"And the people seem so polite after London," she added.

Simon smiled as they headed back to the party headquarters. As they passed Simon and Elizabeth they bid the strangers "Good evening," courteous people whom Simon felt he would have been proud to represent. But although they walked slowly Elizabeth and he could not make their journey last more than thirty minutes.

When they returned a third time to constituency headquarters the fourth candidate was leaving the interview room. She looked very despondent. "It shouldn't be long now," said the agent, but it was another forty minutes before they heard a ripple of applause, and a man dressed in a Harris tweed jacket and brown trousers left the room. He didn't seem happy either.

The agent ushered Simon and Elizabeth through, and as they entered everyone in the room stood. Ministers of the Crown did not visit Redcorn often.

Simon waited for Elizabeth to be seated before he took the chair in the center of the room facing the committee. He estimated that there were about fifty people present and they were all staring at him, showing no aggression, merely curiosity. He looked around at the weather-beaten faces. Most of them, male and female, were dressed in tweed. In his dark striped London suit Simon felt out of place.

"And now," said the chairman, "we welcome the Right Honorable Simon Kerslake, MP."

Simon had to smile at the mistake so many people made in thinking that all ministers were automatically members of the

Privy Council, and therefore entitled to the prefix "Right Honorable" instead of the plain "Honorable" accorded to all MPs—and then only when they were present in the House.

"Mr. Kerslake will address us for twenty minutes, and he has kindly agreed to answer questions after that," added the chairman.

Simon felt confident he had spoken well, but even his few carefully chosen quips received no more than a smile, and his more serious comments elicited little response. This was not a group of people given to showing their emotions. When he had finished he sat down to respectful clapping and murmurs.

"Now the minister will take questions," said the chairman.

"Where do you stand on hanging?" said a scowling middle-aged woman in a gray suit seated in the front row.

Simon explained his reasons for being a convinced aboli-tionist. The scowl did not move from the questioner's face and Simon thought to himself how much happier she would be with Ronnie Nethercote as her member.

A man in a hacking jacket asked: "How do you feel, Mr. Kerslake, about this year's farm subsidy?"

"Good on eggs, tough on beef, and disastrous for pig farm-ers. Or at least that's what I read on the front page of *Farmers Weekly* yesterday." Some of them laughed for the first time. "It hasn't proved necessary for me to have a great knowledge of farming in Coventry Central, but if I am lucky enough to be selected for Redcorn I shall try to learn quickly, and with your help I shall hope to master the farmers' problems." Several heads nodded their approval.

"Miss Pentecost, chairman of the Women's Advisory," an-nounced a tall, thin spinsterish woman who had stood up to catch the chairman's eye. "May I be permitted to ask Mrs. Ker-slake a question? If your husband were offered this seat, would you be willing to come and live in Northumberland?"

Elizabeth had dreaded the question because she knew that if Simon was offered the constituency she would be expected to resign her post at the hospital. Simon turned and looked toward his wife.

"No," she replied directly. "I am a doctor at St. Mary's Hospital, Paddington, where I practice gynecology. I support my husband in his career but, like Margaret Thatcher, I believe a woman has the right to a good education and then the chance to use her qualifications to their best advantage."

A ripple of applause went round the room and Simon smiled at his wife.

The next question was on Europe, and Simon gave an un-equivocal statement as to his reasons for backing the Prime Minister in his desire to see Britain as part of the Common Market.

Simon continued to answer questions on subjects ranging from trade union reform to violence on television before the chairman asked, "Are there any more questions?"

There was a long silence and just as he was about to thank Simon the scowling lady in the front row, without being rec-ognized by the chair, asked what Mr. Kerslake's views were on abortion.

"Morally, I'm against it," said Simon. "At the time of the Abortion Act many of us believed it would stem the tide of divorce. We have been proved wrong: the rate of divorce has quadrupled. Nevertheless, in the cases of rape or fear of physi-cal or mental injury arising from birth I would have to support the medical advice given at the time. Elizabeth and I have two children and my wife's job is to see that babies are safely deliv-ered," he added.

The lips moved from a scowl to a straight line.

"Thank you," said the chairman. "It was good of you to give us so much of your time. Perhaps you and Mrs. Kerslake would be kind enough to wait outside."

Simon and Elizabeth joined the other hopeful candidates, their wives, and the agent in a small dingy room at the back of the building. When they saw the half-empty trestle table in front of them they both remembered they hadn't had any lunch and devoured what was left of the curling cucumber sandwiches and the cold sausage rolls.

"What happens next?" Simon asked the agent between mouthfuls.

"Nothing out of the ordinary. They'll have a discussion, allowing everyone to express their views, and then vote. It should all be over in twenty minutes."

Elizabeth checked her watch: it was seven o'clock and the last train was at nine-fifteen.

"Ought to make the train comfortably," said Simon.

An hour later when no smoke had emerged from the chimney the agent suggested to all the candidates who had a long journey ahead of them that they might like to check into the Bell Inn just over the road.

When Simon looked around the room it was clear that everyone else had done so in advance.

"You had better stay put in case you're called again," Elizabeth said. "I'll go off and book a room and at the same time call and see how the children are getting on."

"Probably eaten the poor baby-sitter by now," said Simon.

Elizabeth smiled before slipping out and making her way to the small hotel.

Simon opened his red box and tried to complete some work. The man who looked like a farmer came over and introduced himself.

"I'm Bill Travers, the chairman of the new constituency," he began. "I only wanted to say that you'll have my full support as chairman if the committee select you."

"Thank you," said Simon.

"I had hoped to represent this area, as my grandfather did. But I shall understand if Redcorn prefers to choose a man destined for the Cabinet rather than someone who would be happy to spend his life on the back benches."

Simon was touched by his opponent's goodwill, and would have liked to respond in kind but Travers quickly added, "Forgive me, I'll not waste any more of your time. I can see"—he looked down at the red box—"that you have a lot of work to catch up on."

Simon felt guilty as he watched the man walk away. A few minutes later Elizabeth returned and tried to smile. "The only room left is smaller than Peter's and it faces the main road, so it's just about as noisy."

"At least no children to say 'I'm hungry'," he said, touching her hand.

It was a little after nine when a weary chairman came out and asked all the candidates if he could have their attention. Husbands and wives all faced him. "My committee want to thank you for going through this grim procedure. It has been hard for us to decide something that we hope not to have to discuss again for twenty years." He paused. "The committee are going to invite Mr. Bill Travers to fight the Redcorn seat at the next election."

In a sentence it was all over. Simon's throat went dry.

He and Elizabeth didn't get much sleep in their tiny room at the Bell Inn, and it hadn't helped that the agent told them the final vote had been twenty-five—twenty-three.

"I don't think Miss Pentecost liked me," said Elizabeth, feeling guilty. "If I had told her that I would have been willing to live in the constituency I think you'd have been offered the seat."

"I doubt it," said Simon. "In any case it's no use agreeing to their terms at the interview and then imposing your own when you have been offered the constituency. My guess is you'll find Redcorn has chosen the right man."

Elizabeth smiled at her husband, grateful for his support.

"There will be other seats," said Simon, only too aware that time was now running out. "You'll see."

Elizabeth prayed that he would prove right, and that next time the choice of a constituency would not make her have to face the dilemma she had so far managed to avoid.

When Raymond took silk, the second Tuesday after the Easter holiday, and became a Queen's Counsel, Joyce made one of her periodic trips to London. The occasion she decided warranted another visit to Harvey Nichols. She recalled her first trip to the store so many years before when she had accompanied her husband to meet the Prime Minister. Raymond had come so far since then although their relationship seemed to have progressed so little. She had given up hope of being a mother, but still wanted him to believe she was a good wife. She couldn't help thinking how much better-looking Raymond had become in middle age, and feared the same could not be said of her.

She enjoyed watching the legal ceremony as her husband was presented in court before the judges. Latin words spoken but not understood. Suddenly her husband was Raymond Gould, QC, MP.

She and Raymond arrived late in chambers for the celebration party. Everyone seemed to have turned out in her husband's honor. Raymond felt full of bonhomie and was chatting to the chief clerk when Sir Nigel handed him a glass of champagne. Then he saw a familiar figure by the mantelpiece and remembered that the trial in Manchester was over. He managed to circle the room speaking to everyone but Stephanie Arnold. To his horror he turned to see her introducing herself to his wife. Every time he glanced toward them they seemed deeper in conversation.

"Ladies and gentlemen," said Sir Nigel, banging a table. He waited for silence. "We are always proud in chambers when one of our members takes silk. It is a comment not only on the man but also on his chambers. And when it is the youngest silk—still under forty—it adds to that pride. All of you, of course, know that Raymond also serves in another place in which we expect him to rise to even greater glory. May I add finally how pleasant it is to have his wife Joyce among us tonight. Ladies and gentlemen," he concluded. "The toast is Raymond Gould, QC."

"Raymond Gould, QC," said everyone in chorus. Then, "Speech, speech."

"I would like to thank all those people who made this great honor possible," began Raymond. "My producer, my director, the other stars, and not forgetting the criminals, without whom I would have no profession to profess. And finally," he said, "to those of you who want to see the back of me, I direct you all to work tirelessly to ensure the return of a Labour Government at the next election. Thank you."

The applause was sustained and genuine and many of his

colleagues were impressed by how relaxed Raymond had become of late. As they came up to congratulate him Raymond couldn't help noticing that Stephanie and Joyce had resumed their conversation. Raymond was handed another glass of champagne just as an earnest young pupil called Patrick Montague who had recently joined them from chambers in Bristol engaged him in conversation. Although Montague had been with them for some weeks Raymond had never spoken to him at length before. He seemed to have very clear views on criminal law and the changes that were necessary. For the first time in his life Raymond felt he was no longer a young man.

Suddenly both women were at his side.

"Hello, Raymond."

"Hello, Stephanie," he said awkwardly and looked anxiously toward his wife. "Do you know Patrick Montague?" he asked, absentmindedly.

The three of them burst out laughing.

"What's so funny?" asked Raymond.

"You do embarrass me sometimes, Raymond," said Joyce. "Surely you realize Stephanie and Patrick are engaged?"

CHAPTER
FIFTEEN

"WITH OR WITHOUT civil servants?" asked Simon as Andrew entered the minister's office.

"Without, please."

"Fine," said Simon and pressed a switch on the intercom by his desk.

"I don't want to be disturbed while I'm with Mr. Fraser," he said and ushered his colleague toward a comfortable seat in the corner.

"Elizabeth was asking me this morning to find out how Robert was getting on."

"It's his second birthday next month and he's overweight for a scrum-half," replied Andrew. "And how's your search for a seat working out?"

"Not too good. The last three constituencies to come up haven't even asked to see me. I can't put a finger on why, except they all seem to have selected local men."

"It's still a long time to the next election. You're sure to find a seat before then."

"It might not be so long if the Prime Minister decides to go to the country and test his strength against the unions."

"That would be a foolish thing to do," said Andrew. "He might defeat us but he still wouldn't defeat the unions."

A young woman came into the room with two cups of coffee, put them on the low Formica table, and left the two men alone.

"Have you had time to look at the file?" Andrew continued.

"Yes, I went over it last night between checking over Peter's prep and helping Michael to build a model galleon."

"And how do you feel?" Andrew asked.

"Not very good. I can't get to grips with this new maths they're now teaching, and my mast was the only one that fell off when Elizabeth launched the galleon in the bath."

Andrew laughed.

"I think you've got a case," said Simon, sounding serious.

"Good," said Andrew. "Now the reason I wanted to see you privately is because I feel there are no party political points to be made out of this case for either of us. I've no plans to try to embarrass your department, and I consider it's in the best interest of my constituents to cooperate as closely as I can with you."

"Thank you," said Simon. "So where do you want to go from here?"

"I'd like to table a planted question for your department in the hope that you would consider opening an inquiry. If the inquiry comes to the same conclusion as I have, I would expect you to order a retrial."

Simon hesitated. "And if the inquiry goes against you will you agree to no reprisals for the Home Office?"

"You have my word on it."

"Shall I ask the civil servants to come in now?"

"Yes, please do."

Simon returned to his desk and pressed a button. A moment later three men in almost identical suits, white shirts with stiff collars, and discreet ties entered the room. Between them they could have ruined any police identification parade.

"Mr. Fraser," began Simon, "is asking the Home Office to consider . . ."

*   *   *

"Can you explain why Simon Kerslake missed a vote yesterday?"

Charles looked across the table at the Chief Whip.

"No, I can't," he said. "I've been distributing the weekly whip to him the same as every member of my group."

"What's behind it then?"

"I think the poor man has been spending a lot of his time traipsing around the country looking for a seat to fight at the next election."

"That's no excuse," said the Chief Whip. "Duties in the House must come first, every member knows that. He missed a vote on a vital clause during the European Bill last Thursday while everyone else in your group has proved reliable. Despite our majority we seem to be in single figures for almost every clause. Perhaps I should have a word with him?"

"No, no, I'd rather you didn't," said Charles, fearing he sounded a little too insistent. "I consider it my responsibility. I'll speak to him and see that it doesn't happen again."

"All right, Charles, if that's the way you want to play it. Thank God it can't last much longer and the damn thing will soon be law, but we must remain vigilant over every clause. The Labour party know only too well that if they defeat us on certain key clauses they can still scupper the whole bill, and if I lost one of those by a single vote I would cut Kerslake's throat. Or anyone else's who was responsible."

"I'll make sure he gets the message," said Charles.

"How's Fiona reacting to all these late nights?" the Chief Whip asked, finally relaxing.

"Very well, considering. In fact now that you mention it I have never seen her looking better."

"Can't say my wife is enjoying 'the prep school antics,' as she describes our continual late-night sittings. I've had to promise to take her to the West Indies this winter to make up for it. Well, I'll leave you to deal with Kerslake then. Be firm, Charles. Just remember, we can't afford to lose a vote at this late stage."

*   *   *

"Norman Edwards?" repeated Raymond in disbelief. "The General Secretary of the Haulage Union?"

"Yes," said Fred Padgett, getting up from behind his desk.

"But he burned *Full Employment at Any Cost?* on a public bonfire with every journalist he could lay his hands on to witness the conflagration."

"I know," said Fred, returning a letter to the filing cabinet. "I'm only your agent, I'm not here to explain the mysteries of the universe."

"When does he want to see me?" asked Raymond.

"As soon as possible."

"Better ask him if he can come for a drink back at the house round six o'clock."

Raymond had had a heavy Saturday morning surgery and thanks to the still imminent Martians had only found time to grab a sandwich at the pub before going off to pursue his favorite pastime. This week Leeds were playing Liverpool at Elland Road. Sitting in the directors' box every other week in full view of his constituents while he supported his local football team killed 30,000 birds with one stone. Later, when talking to the lads in the dressing room after the match, he found himself lapsing into a pronounced Yorkshire accent that bore no resemblance to the one he used to address high court judges during the week.

Leeds won three-two and after the match Raymond joined the directors for a drink in the boardroom. He became so impassioned about an off-side decision that could have lost them a point that he nearly forgot about his meeting with Norman Edwards.

Joyce was in the garden showing the union leader her early snowdrops when Raymond returned.

"Sorry I'm late," he shouted, as he hung up his yellow and blue scarf. "I've been to the match."

"Who won?" asked Edwards.

"Leeds, of course, three-two."

"Damn," said Norman, his accent leaving the other in no

doubt that he had not spent many nights outside of Liverpool.

"Come on in and have a beer," said Raymond.

"I'd prefer a vodka."

The two men went into the house while Joyce continued with her gardening.

"Well," said Raymond, pouring his guest a Smirnoff. "What brings you all the way from Liverpool if it wasn't to watch the football? Perhaps you want a signed copy of my book for your next union bonfire."

"Don't give me any hassle, Ray. I came all this way because I need your help, simple as that."

"I'm all ears," said Raymond.

"We had a full meeting of the General Purposes Committee yesterday, and one of the brothers has spotted a clause in the European Bill which could put us all out of work."

Norman passed over a copy of the bill to Raymond with the relevant clause marked in red. It gave the minister power to make new haulage and lorry regulations which would come before the House as statutory instruments and thus could not be amended.

"If that gets through the House my boys are in deep trouble."

"Why?" said Raymond.

"Because those bloody Frogs know only too well that there's a Channel between us and them, and if my lads are forced by law to sleep a night each side the only people who'll end up making money on the deal will be the guest-house proprietors."

"What's behind it?" asked Raymond.

"They want us to drop the stuff our end, so they can pick it up on the other side."

"But wouldn't that also be true when they need to deliver goods to us?"

"No. Their journeys are much longer to the coast, and they have to stay overnight anyway, not to mention the fact that there are eight of them to one of us. It's diabolical, nothing less."

Raymond studied the wording in detail while Edwards helped himself to another vodka.

"The clause doesn't stop you from going over the next day."

"And how much do you think that will add to your costs?" asked Raymond.

"I'll tell you, enough to make us uncompetitive, that's how much," replied the trade union leader.

"Point taken," said Raymond. "So what's wrong with asking your own member to put the case?"

"Don't trust him. He's pro-European at any price."

"And what about your sponsored trade union representative in the House?"

"Tom Carson? You must be joking. He's so far to the left that even his own side are suspicious when he supports a cause. We lost the 'tachograph' clause because he championed it. In any case I only put him in the House to get him off my back." Raymond laughed. "Now, all my General Purposes Committee want to know is: would you be willing to fight this clause in the House for us? Not that we can afford the sort of fees you're used to at the bar," he added.

"There would be no fee involved," said Raymond, "but I'm sure you'll be able to repay me in kind sometime in the future."

"Got the picture," said Edwards, touching the side of his nose with a forefinger. "What do I do next?"

"You go back to Liverpool and hope that I am better on an away pitch than your team."

Norman Edwards put on an old raincoat and started to button it up. He smiled at Raymond. "I may have been appalled by your book, Ray. But it doesn't mean I didn't admire it."

The Speaker looked down at the front bench. "Mr. Andrew Fraser."

"Number seventeen, sir," said Andrew.

The Speaker looked down to check over the question, seeking a Home Office answer.

Simon rose to the dispatch box, opened his file, and said, "Yes, sir."

"Mr. Andrew Fraser," called the Speaker again.

Andrew rose from his place on the Opposition front bench to put his supplementary.

"May I thank the minister for agreeing to an inquiry so quickly, and ask him that, if he discovers an injustice has been done to my constituent Mr. Paddy O'Halloran, that the Home Secretary will order a retrial immediately?"

Simon rose again.

"Yes, sir."

"I am grateful to the Honorable Gentleman," said Andrew, half-rising from his place.

All over in less than a minute, but older members who listened to the brief exchange between Fraser and Kerslake in the House that day had no doubt that considerable preparation had gone into that minute from both sides.

"The damn man missed another three-line whip, Charles. It must be the last time. You've been protecting him for far too long."

"It won't happen again," promised Charles convincingly. "I would like to give him one more chance. Allow him that."

"You're very loyal to him," said the Chief Whip. "But next time I'm going to see Kerslake myself and get to the bottom of it."

"It won't happen again," repeated Charles.

"Hm," said the Chief Whip. "Next problem is, are there any clauses on the European Bill that we should be worried about next week?"

"Yes," replied Charles. "This haulage clause that Raymond Gould is fighting. He made a brilliant case on the floor of the House, and got all his own side and half of ours backing him."

"He's not the sponsored MP for the Haulage Union," said the Chief Whip, surprised.

"No, the unions obviously felt Tom Carson wouldn't help the cause and he's hopping mad at the slight."

"Clever of them to pick Gould. He improves as a speaker

every time I hear him, and no one can fault him when it comes to a point of law."

"So we'd better face the fact that we're going to lose the clause?"

"Never. We'll redraft the damn thing so that it's acceptable and *seen* to be compassionate. It's not a bad time to be the defender of the union interests. That way we'll keep Gould from getting all the credit. I'll speak to the PM tonight—and don't forget what I said about Kerslake."

Charles returned to his office and realized that in future he would have to be more careful about telling Simon Kerslake when he was paired for the European Bill. He suspected he had carried this ploy as far as he could for now.

Simon had read the final report prepared by his department on the O'Halloran case while Elizabeth was trying to get to sleep. He only had to go over the details once to realize that he would have to order a retrial and institute a full investigation into the past record of the police officers who had been involved in the case.

When Andrew heard the news, and that the retrial would be held in London, he asked Raymond Gould to represent O'Halloran.

"Praise indeed," said Raymond, who still considered Andrew among the Commons' finest orators. He somehow managed to fit O'Halloran into his busy schedule.

The trial was in its third day when Mr. Justice Comyns, after listening to Mrs. Bloxham's evidence, stopped proceedings and instructed the jury to return a verdict of not guilty.

Andrew received praise from all quarters of the House, but he was quick to acknowledge the support given him by Simon Kerslake and the Home Office. *The Times* even wrote a leader the next day on the proper use of influence by a constituency MP.

Some months later the court awarded O'Halloran £25,000 in compensation. The only drawback Andrew's success caused was that every convict's mother north of Hadrian's wall queued to tell him about her innocent son at his fortnightly surgery. But during the year he took only one seriously and once again began to check into the details.

During the long hot summer of 1972 clause after clause of the European Bill was voted on, often through the night. On some occasions the Government managed majorities of only five or six but somehow the bill remained intact.

Charles would often arrive home at Eaton Square at three in the morning to find Fiona asleep, only to leave again before she had woken. Veterans of the House, both servants and elected, confirmed they had never experienced anything like it since the Second World War.

And, just as suddenly, the last vote was taken and the marathon was over. The European Bill was through the Commons and on its way to the Upper House to receive their lordships' approval. Charles wondered what he would do with all the hours that were suddenly left him in the day.

When the bill finally received the Royal Assent in October the Chief Whip held a celebration lunch at the Carlton Club in St. James's to thank all his team. "And in particular, Charles Seymour," he said, raising his glass during an impromptu speech. When the lunch broke up the Chief Whip offered Charles a lift back to the Commons in his official car. They traveled along Piccadilly, down Haymarket, through Trafalgar Square, and into Whitehall. Just as the Commons came into sight the black Rover turned into Downing Street, as Charles assumed, to drop the Chief Whip at No. 12. But as the car stopped the Chief Whip said, "The Prime Minister is expecting you in five minutes."

"What? Why?" said Charles, as he joined his colleague outside No. 10.

"Timed it rather well, didn't I?" said the Chief Whip—and headed off toward No. 12.

Charles stood alone in front of No. 10. The door was

opened by a man in a long black coat. "Good afternoon, Mr. Seymour."

The Prime Minister saw Charles in his study and, as ever, wasted no time on small talk.

"Thank you for all the hard work you have put in on the European Bill."

"It was a tremendous challenge," said Charles, searching for words.

"As will be your next job," said Mr. Heath. "I want you to take over as one of the Ministers of State at the Department of Trade and Industry."

Charles was speechless.

"With all the problems we are going to encounter with the trade unions during the next few months, that should keep you fully occupied."

"It certainly will," said Charles.

He still hadn't been asked to sit down, but as the Prime Minister was now rising from behind his desk it was clear that the meeting was over.

"You and Fiona must come and have dinner at No. 10 as soon as you've settled into your new department," said the Prime Minister as they walked toward the door.

"Thank you," Charles said.

As he stepped back on to Downing Street a driver opened the back door of a shiny Austin Westminster. It was several moments before Charles realized the car was his.

"The Commons, sir?"

"No, I'd like to return to Eaton Square for a few minutes," he said, sitting back and enjoying the thought of tackling his new job.

The car drove past the Commons, up Victoria Street, and on to Eaton Square. He wanted to tell Fiona that all the hard work had been rewarded. He felt guilty about how little he had seen of her lately, although he could not believe it would be much better now that he was to be involved in trade union legislation. How much he still hoped for a son, perhaps even that would prove possible now. The car came to a halt outside the Georgian house. Charles ran up the steps and into the hall.

He could hear his wife's voice from the first floor. He took the wide staircase in bounds of two and three at a time, and threw open the bedroom door.

"I'm the new Minister of State at the Department of Trade and Industry," he announced to Fiona, who was lying in bed.

Alexander Dalglish looked up. He showed no sign of interest in Charles's elevation.

When Andrew rang Angus Sinclair at the Procurator Fiscal's office to find that nothing was known of Ricky Hodge and that Sinclair was able to confirm that he had no criminal record, Andrew felt he had stumbled on a case with international implications.

As Ricky Hodge was in a Turkish jail any inquiries had to be made through the Foreign Office. Andrew did not have the same relationship with the Foreign Secretary as he did with Simon, so he felt the direct approach would be best and put down a question to be answered in the House. He worded it carefully: "What action does the Foreign Secretary intend to take over the confiscation of a British passport from a constituent of the Honorable member for Edinburgh Carlton, details of which have been supplied to him?"

When the question came in front of the House on the following Wednesday the Foreign Secretary rose to answer the question himself. He stood at the dispatch box and peered over his half-moon spectacles and said:

"Her Majesty's Government are pursuing this matter through the usual diplomatic channels."

Andrew was quickly on his feet. "Does the Right Honorable Gentleman realize that my constituent has been in a Turkish prison for six months and has still not been charged?"

"Yes, sir," replied the Foreign Secretary. "I have asked the Turkish Embassy to supply the Foreign Office with more details of the case."

Andrew leaped up again. "How long will my constituent have to be forgotten in Ankara before the Foreign Secretary does more than ask for the details of his case?"

The Foreign Secretary rose again showing no sign of annoyance. "I will report those findings to the Honorable member as quickly as possible."

"When? Tomorrow, next week, next year?" Andrew shouted angrily.

"When?" joined in a chorus of Labour back-benchers, but the Speaker called for the next question above the uproar.

Within the hour Andrew received a handwritten note from the Foreign Office. It read: "If Mr. Fraser would be kind enough to telephone, the Foreign Secretary would be delighted to make an appointment to see him."

Andrew phoned from the Commons and was invited to join the Foreign Secretary in Whitehall immediately.

The Foreign Office, known as "The Palazzo" by its inmates, has an atmosphere of its own. Although Andrew had worked in a Government department as a minister he was still struck by its grandeur. He was met at the courtyard entrance and guided along yards of marble corridors before climbing a fine double staircase at the top of which he was greeted by the Foreign Secretary's Principal Private Secretary.

"Sir Alec will see you immediately, Mr. Fraser," he said, and led Andrew past the magnificent pictures and tapestries which lined the way. He was taken into a beautifully proportioned room. The Foreign Secretary stood in front of an Adam fireplace over which hung a portrait of Lord Palmerston.

"Fraser, how kind of you to come at such short notice. I do hope it has not caused you any inconvenience." Platitudes, thought Andrew. Next the silly man will be mentioning my father. "I don't think we have met before, but of course I have known your father for many years. Won't you sit down?"

"I realize you are a busy man. Can we get down to the point at issue, Foreign Secretary?" Andrew demanded.

"Of course," Sir Alec said courteously. "Forgive me for taking up so much of your time." Without a further word, he handed Andrew a file marked "Richard M. Hodge—Confidential." "Although Members of Parliament are not subject to the Official Secrets Act I know you will respect the fact that this file is classified."

Another bluff, thought Andrew. He flicked back the cover. It was true: exactly as he had suspected, Ricky Hodge had never been arrested or charged. He turned the page. "Rome, child prostitution; Marseilles, narcotics; Paris, blackmail." Page after page, ending in Turkey, where Hodge had been found in possession of four pounds of heroin which he had been selling in small packets on the black market. In his twenty-nine years Ricky Hodge had spent eleven of the last fourteen in foreign jails.

Andrew closed the file and could feel the sweat on his forehead. It was some moments before he spoke. "I apologize, Foreign Secretary," he said. "I have made a fool of myself."

"When I was a young man," said Sir Alec, "I made a similar mistake on behalf of a constituent. Ernie Bevin was Foreign Secretary at the time. He could have crucified me in the House with the knowledge he had. Instead he revealed everything over a drink in this room. I sometimes wish the public could see members in their quiet moments as well as in their rowdy ones."

Andrew thanked Sir Alec and walked thoughtfully back to the House. The *Evening Standard* poster outside the Commons caught his eye. "O'Halloran arrested again." He bought a copy, stood by the railings, and began reading. Paddy O'Halloran had been detained in a Glasgow police station and charged with robbing the Bank of Scotland in Sauchiehall Street. Andrew wondered if his friends would allege it was another "frame up" by the police until he read the next paragraph. "O'Halloran was arrested leaving the bank in possession of a shotgun and £25,000 in used notes. He said when apprehended by the police, 'I've just been clearing my account.'"

At home, Louise told him that Ricky Hodge had done him a favor.

"How's that possible?" asked Andrew.

"You won't take yourself so seriously in future." She smiled.

When Andrew conducted his next surgery in Edinburgh two weeks later he was surprised to see that Mrs. Bloxham had made an appointment.

As he greeted her at the door he was even more surprised. She was wearing a bright crimplene dress and a new pair of squeaky brown leather shoes. She also looked as if "Our Blessed Lady" might have to wait a few more years to receive her after all. Andrew motioned her to a seat.

"I came to thank you, Mr. Fraser," she said, once she was settled.

"What for?" asked Andrew.

"For sending that nice young man round from Christie's. They auctioned great-grandma's table for me. I couldn't believe my luck—it fetched £1,400." Andrew smiled. "So it don't matter about the stain on the dress any more." She paused. "It even made up for having to eat off the floor for three months."

Simon steered the new Boundary Commission recommendations unspectacularly through the House as an order in Council, and suddenly he had lost his own constituency. His colleagues in Coventry were understanding, and nursed those wards that would become theirs at the next election in order that he might spend more time searching for a new seat.

Seven seats became available during the year but Simon was only interviewed for two of them. Both were almost on the Scottish border and both put him in second place. He began to appreciate what it must feel like for an Olympic favorite to be awarded the silver medal.

Ronnie Nethercote's monthly board reports began to paint an increasingly somber picture, thus reflecting in real life what the politicians were decreeing in Parliament. Ronnie had decided to postpone going public until the climate was more advantageous. Simon couldn't disagree with the judgment, but when he checked his special overdraft facility the interest on his loans had pushed the figure in red to over £90,000.

When unemployment first passed the million mark and Ted Heath ordered a pay and prices freeze strikes broke out all over the country.

* * *

The new parliamentary session in the autumn was dominated by the issue of a Prices and Incomes policy. Charles Seymour became involved in putting the case for the Government. While he didn't always win every argument, he was now so well briefed on his subject that he no longer feared making a fool of himself at the dispatch box. Raymond Gould and Andrew Fraser both made passionate speeches on behalf of the unions, but the Conservative majority beat them again and again.

However, the Prime Minister was moving inexorably toward a head-on clash with the unions and an early general election.

When all three party conferences were over members returned to the Commons aware that it was likely to be their last session before the general election. It was openly being said in the corridors that all the Prime Minister was waiting for was a catalyst. The miners provided it. In the middle of a bleak winter they called an all-out strike for more pay in defiance of the Government's new trade union legislation.

In a television interview the Prime Minister told the nation that with unemployment at an unprecedented 2,294,448 and the country on a three-day week he had to call an election to ensure that the rule of law be maintained. The inner Cabinet advised Heath to plump for 28 February 1974.

"Who runs the country?" became the Tory theme but seemed only to emphasize class differences, rather than uniting the country as Edward Heath had hoped.

Andrew Fraser had his doubts but he faced a different threat in his own constituency, where the Scottish Nationalists were using the quarrel between the two major parties to promote their own cause. He returned to Scotland, to be warned by his father that the Scottish Nationalists were no longer a joke and that he would be facing a hard campaign against the robust local candidate, Jock McPherson.

Raymond Gould traveled back to Leeds, confident that the northeast industrial area would not tolerate Heath's highhandedness.

Charles felt sure that the people would back any party

which had shown the courage to stand up to the unions, although the left wing, led vociferously by Tom Carson, made a great play of the "two nations" issue, insisting that the Government were out to crush the Labour movement once and for all.

Charles drove down to Sussex to find his supporters glad of the chance to put those "lazy trade unionists" in their place.

Simon, with no seat to fight, worked on in the Home Office right up to the day of the election, convinced that his career was facing only a temporary setback.

"I'll fight the first by-election that comes up," he promised Elizabeth.

"Even if it's a mining seat in South Wales?" she replied.

Many months had passed before Charles had found it possible even to sustain a conversation with Fiona for any length of time. Neither wanted a divorce, both citing the ailing Earl of Bridgwater as their reason, although inconvenience and loss of face were nearer the truth. In public it would have been hard to detect the change in their relationship since they had never been given to overt affection.

Charles gradually became aware that it was possible for marriages to have been over for years without outsiders knowing it. Certainly the old earl never found out, because even on his deathbed he told Fiona to hurry up and produce an heir.

"Do you think you'll ever forgive me?" Fiona once asked her husband.

"Never," he replied, with a finality that encouraged no further discourse.

During the three-week election campaign in Sussex they both went about their duties with a professionalism that masked their true feelings.

"How is your husband bearing up?" someone would inquire.

"Much enjoying the campaign and looking forward to returning to Government," was Fiona's stock reply.

"And how is dear Lady Fiona?" Charles was continuously asked.

"Never better than when she's helping in the constituency," was his.

On Sundays, at one church after another, he read the lesson with confidence while she sang "Fight the good fight" in a clear contralto.

The demands of a rural constituency are considerably different from those of a city. Every village, however small, expects the member to visit them and to recall the local chairmen's names. Subtle changes were taking place: Fiona no longer whispered the names in Charles's ear. Charles no longer turned to her for advice.

During the campaign Charles would ring the photographer on the local paper to discover which events his editor had instructed him to cover that day. With the list of places and times in his hand Charles would arrive on each occasion a few minutes before the photographer. The Labour candidate complained officially to the local editor that Mr. Seymour's photograph was never out of the paper.

"If you were present at these functions we would be only too happy to publish your photo," said the editor.

"But they never invite me," cried the Labour candidate.

They don't invite Seymour either, the editor wanted to say, but he somehow manages to be there. It was never far from the editor's mind that his proprietor was a Tory peer so he kept his mouth shut.

All the way up to election day Charles and Fiona opened bazaars, attended dinners, drew raffles, and only just stopped short of kissing babies.

Once, when Fiona asked him, Charles admitted that he hoped to be moved to the Foreign Office as a Minister of State, and perhaps to be made a Privy Councillor.

On the last day of February they dressed in silence and went off to their local polling station to vote. The photographer was there on the steps to take their picture. They stood closer together than they had for some weeks, looking like a smart register office couple. Charles knew it would be the main photograph on the front page of the *Sussex Gazette* the following day, as surely as he knew the Labour candidate would be relegated to a half-column mention on the inside page not far from the obituaries.

The count in a rural seat is always taken the following morning at a more leisurely pace than is customary for its city cousins. So Charles anticipated that by the time he arrived in the town hall the Conservative majority in the House would already be assured. But it was not to be, and the result still hung in the balance that Friday morning.

Edward Heath did not concede when the newscasters predicted he would fail to be given the overall majority he required. Charles spent the day striding around the town hall with an anxious look on his face. The little piles of votes soon became larger and it was obvious that he would hold the seat with at least his usual 21,000—or was it 22,000?—majority. He never could remember the exact figure. But as the day progressed it became more and more difficult to assess the national verdict.

The last result came in from Northern Ireland a little after four o'clock that afternoon and a BBC commentator announced—

Labour	301
Conservative	296
Liberal	14
Ulster Unionists	11
Scottish Nationalists	7
Welsh Nationalists	2
Others	4

Ted Heath invited the Liberal leader to join him at Downing Street for talks in the hope that they could form a coalition. The Liberals demanded a firm commitment to electoral reform and, in particular, to proportional representation by the next election. Heath knew he could never get his backbenchers to deliver. On the Monday morning he told the Queen in her drawing room at Buckingham Palace that he was unable to form a Government. She called for Harold Wilson.

He accepted her commission and drove back to Downing Street to enter the front door. Heath left by the back.

By the Tuesday afternoon every member, having watched the drama unfold, had returned to London. Raymond had increased his majority and now hoped that the Prime Minister had long since forgotten his resignation and would offer him a job.

Andrew had had the hard and unpleasant fight with Jock McPherson, just as his father had predicted, and held on to his seat by only 2,229.

Charles, still unsure of the exact majority by which he had won, drove back to London, resigned to Opposition. The one compensation was that he would be reinstated on the board of Seymour's where the knowledge he had gained as a minister of Trade and Industry could only be of value.

Simon left the Home Office on 1 March 1974 with little more than an empty red box to show for nine years as a parliamentarian.

BOOK THREE

1974–1977

MINISTERS OF STATE

CHAPTER
SIXTEEN

"HIS DIARY LOOKS rather full at the moment, Mr. Charles."

"Well, as soon as it's convenient," Charles replied over the phone. He held on as he heard the pages being turned.

"12 March at ten-thirty, Mr. Charles?"

"But that's nearly a fortnight away," he said, irritated.

"Mr. Spencer has only just returned from the States and—"

"How about a lunch, then—at my club?" Charles interrupted.

"That couldn't be until after 19 March."

"Very well, then," said Charles. "12 March, at ten-thirty."

During the fourteen-day wait Charles had ample time to become frustrated by his seemingly aimless role in Opposition. No car came to pick him up and whisk him away to an office where real work had to be done. Worse, no one sought his opinion any longer on matters that affected the nation. He was going through a sharp bout of what is known as "ex-ministers' blues."

He was relieved when the day for the appointment with Derek Spencer at last came round. But although he arrived on time he was kept waiting for ten minutes before the chairman's secretary took him through.

"Good to see you after so long," said Spencer, coming round his desk to greet him. "It must be nearly six years since you've visited the bank."

"Yes, I suppose it is," said Charles. "But looking around the old place it feels like yesterday. You've been fully occupied, no doubt?"

"Like a Cabinet minister, but I hope with better results."

They both laughed.

"Of course I've kept in touch with what's been happening at the bank."

"Have you?" said Spencer.

"Yes, I've read all the reports you've sent out over the past years, not to mention the *Financial Times*'s coverage."

"I hope you feel we've progressed satisfactorily in your absence."

"Oh. Yes," said Charles, still standing. "Very impressive."

"Well, now what can I do for you?" asked the chairman, returning to his seat.

"Simple enough," said Charles, finally taking an unoffered chair. "I wish to be reinstated on the board."

There was a long silence.

"Well, it's not quite that easy, Charles. I've just recently appointed two new directors and . . ."

"Of course it's that easy," said Charles, his tone changing. "You have only to propose my name at the next meeting and it will go through, especially as you haven't a member of the family on the board at the present time."

"We have, as a matter of fact. Your brother the Earl of Bridgwater has become a non-executive director."

"What? Rupert never told me," said Charles. "Neither did you."

"True, but things have changed since—"

"Nothing has changed except my estimation of the value of your word," said Charles, suddenly realizing that Spencer had never intended he should return to the board. "You gave me your assurance—"

"I won't be spoken to like this in my own office."

"If you're not careful, the next place I shall do it will be in your boardroom. Now, will you honor your undertaking or not?"

"I don't have to listen to threats from you, Seymour. Get out of my office before I have you removed. I can assure you that you will never sit on the board again as long as I'm chairman."

Charles turned and marched out, slamming the door as he left. He wasn't sure with whom to discuss the problem and returned immediately to Eaton Square to consider a plan of campaign.

"What brings you home in the middle of the afternoon?" asked Fiona.

Charles hesitated, considered the question, and then joined his wife in the kitchen and told her everything that had happened at the bank. Fiona continued to grate some cheese as she listened to her husband.

"Well, one thing is certain," she said, not having spoken for several minutes but delighted that Charles had confided in her. "After that fracas, you can't both be on the board."

"So what do you think I ought to do, old girl?"

Fiona smiled; it was the first time he had called her that for nearly two years. "Every man has his secrets," she said. "I wonder what Mr. Spencer's are?"

"He's such a dull middle-class fellow I doubt if—"

"I've just had a letter from Seymour's Bank," interrupted Fiona.

"What about?"

"Only a shareholder's circular. It seems Margaret Trubshaw is retiring after twelve years as the board secretary. Rumor has it she wanted to do five more years, but the chairman has someone else in mind. I think I might have lunch with her."

Charles returned his wife's smile.

Andrew's appointment as Minister of State at the Home Office came as no surprise to anyone except his three-year-old son, who quickly discovered how to empty any red boxes that were left unlocked, refilling them with marbles or sweets, even managing to fit a football into one. As Robert didn't understand "For Your Eyes Only," it didn't seem to make a ... of difference that Cabinet committee papers were sometimes found glued together with old bubble gum.

"Can you remove that latest stain in the red box?"

"Good heavens, what caused it?" asked Louise, staring down at a jelly-like blob.

"Frog spawn," said Andrew, grinning.

"He's a brainwashed Russian spy," warned Louise, "with a mental age about the same as most of your colleagues in the House. Yes, I'll remove the stain if you sit down and write that letter."

Andrew nodded his agreement.

Among the many letters of commiseration Simon received when he did not return to the House was one from Andrew Fraser. Simon could imagine him sitting in his old office and implementing the decisions he had been involved in making just a few weeks before.

There was also a letter from Ronnie Nethercote inviting him to return to the board of Nethercote and Company at £5,000 a year, which even Elizabeth acknowledged as a generous gesture.

It was not long before Ronnie Nethercote had made Simon an executive director of the company. Simon enjoyed negotiating with the trade unions at a level he had not experienced before. Ronnie made it clear how he would have dealt with the "Commie bastards" given half a chance. "Lock them all up until they learn to do a day's work."

"You would have lasted about a week in the House of Commons," Simon told him.

"After a week with those windbags I'd have been only too happy to return to the real world."

Simon smiled. Ronnie, he felt, was like so many others—imagining all Members of Parliament were unemployable except the one they knew.

*   *   *

Raymond waited until the last Government appointment was announced before he finally gave up any hope of a job. Several leading political journalists pointed out that he had been left on the back benches while lesser men had been given Government posts but it was scant comfort. Reluctantly he returned to Lincoln's Inn to continue his practice at the bar.

Harold Wilson, starting his third administration, made it clear that he would govern as long as possible before calling an election. But as he did not have an overall majority in the House few members believed that he could hold out for more than a matter of months.

Fiona returned home after her lunch with Miss Trubshaw with a large Cheshire Cat grin on her face. It remained firmly in place during the hours she had to wait for Charles to get back from the Commons after the last division.

"You look pleased with yourself," said Charles, shaking out his umbrella before closing the front door. His wife stood in the hallway, her arms crossed.

"How has your day been?" she asked.

"So-so," said Charles, wanting to hear the news. "But what about you?"

"Oh, pleasant enough. I had coffee with your mother this morning. She seems very well. A little cold in the head, otherwise—"

"To hell with my mother. How did your lunch with Miss Trubshaw go?"

"I wondered how long it would take you to get round to that."

She continued to wait just as long as it took for them to walk into the drawing room and sit down. "After seventeen years as secretary to your father and twelve years as secretary to the board there isn't much Miss Trubshaw doesn't know about Seymour's or its present chairman," Fiona began.

"So what did you discover?"

"Which do you want to hear about first, the name of his mistress or the number of his Swiss bank account?"

Fiona revealed everything she had learned over her two-hour lunch, explaining that Miss Trubshaw usually only drank fortified wine but on this occasion she had downed most of a vintage bottle of Pommard. Charles's smile grew wider and wider as each fact came pouring out. To Fiona he looked like a boy who has been given a box of chocolates and keeps discovering another layer underneath.

"Well done, old girl," he said when she had come to the end of her tale. "But how do I get all the proof I need?"

"I've made a deal with our Miss Trubshaw."

"You've what?"

"A deal. With Miss Trubshaw. You get the proof if she remains as secretary to the board for a further five years, and no loss of benefit to her pension."

"Is that all she wants?" said Charles, guardedly.

"And the price of another lunch at the Savoy Grill when you're invited back on the board."

Unlike many of his Labour colleagues Raymond now enjoyed dressing up in white tie and tails and mixing with London society. An invitation to the annual bankers' banquet at the Guildhall was no exception. The Prime Minister was the guest of honor and Raymond wondered if he would drop a hint as to how long he expected the parliamentary session to last before he felt he had to call an election.

At the pre-dinner drinks Raymond had a quick word with the Lord Mayor before becoming involved in a conversation with a circuit court judge on the problems of the parity of sentencing.

When dinner was announced Raymond found his seat on one of the long fingers stretching away from the top table. He checked his place card. Raymond Gould QC, MP. On his right was the chairman of Chloride, Michael Edwardes, and on his left an American banker who had just taken up an appointment in the City.

Raymond found Michael Edwardes's views on how the Prime Minister should tackle the nationalized industries fascinating, but he devoted far more of his attention to the Euro Bond manager from Chase Manhattan. She must have been thirty, Raymond decided, if only because of her elevated position at the bank and her claim to have been an undergraduate at Wellesley at the time of Kennedy's death. He would have put Kate Garthwaite at far younger and was not surprised to learn she played tennis in the summer and swam every day during the winter—to keep her weight down, she confided. She had a warm, oval face, and her dark hair was cut in what Raymond thought was a Mary Quant style. Her nose turned up slightly at the end and would have cost a lot of money for a plastic surgeon to reproduce. There was no chance of seeing her legs as they were covered by a long dress, but what he could see left Raymond more than interested.

"I see there's an 'MP' behind your name, Mr. Gould. May I ask which party you represent?" she asked, in an accent heard more often in Boston.

"I'm a Socialist, Mrs. Garthwaite. Where do your sympathies lie on this occasion?"

"I would have voted Labour at the last election if I had been qualified," she declared.

"Should I be surprised?" he teased.

"You certainly should. My ex-husband is a Republican congressman."

He was about to ask his next question when the toastmaster called for silence. For the first time Raymond turned his eyes to the top table and the Prime Minister. Harold Wilson's speech stuck firmly to economic problems and the role of a Labour Government in the City and gave no clue as to the timing of the next election. Nevertheless, Raymond considered it a worthwhile evening. He had made a useful contact with the chairman of a large public company. And he had acquired Kate's telephone number.

*   *   *

The chairman of Seymour's reluctantly agreed to see him a second time, but it was obvious from the moment Charles walked in when no hand was proffered that Derek Spencer intended it to be a short interview.

"I thought I ought to see you personally," said Charles as he settled back in the comfortable leather chair and slowly lit a cigarette, "rather than raise my query at the AGM next month."

The first sign of apprehension began to show on the chairman's face, but he said nothing.

"I'm rather keen to discover why the bank should pay out a monthly check of £400 to an employee called Miss Janet Darrow, whom I have never come across, although it appears she has been on the payroll for over five years. The checks, it seems, have been going to a branch of Lloyds in Kensington."

Derek Spencer's face became flushed.

"What I am at a loss to discover," continued Charles after he had inhaled deeply, "is what services Miss Darrow has been supplying to the bank. They must be quite impressive to have earned her £25,000 over the last five years. I appreciate that this is a small amount when you consider the bank's turnover of 123 million last year, but my grandfather instilled in me at an early age the belief that if one took care of the pennies the pounds would take care of themselves."

Still Derek Spencer said nothing, although beads of sweat had appeared on his forehead. Suddenly Charles's tone changed. "If I find I am not a member of the board by the time of the Annual General Meeting I feel it will be my duty to point out this slight discrepancy in the bank's accounts to the other shareholders present."

"You're a bastard, Seymour," the chairman said quietly.

"Now that is not accurate. I am the second son of the former chairman of this bank and I bear a striking resemblance to my father, although everyone says I have my mother's eyes."

"What's the deal?"

"No deal. You will merely keep to your original agreement and see that I am reinstated on the board before the AGM.

You will also cease any further payments to Miss Janet Darrow immediately."

"If I agree, will you swear never to mention this matter to anyone again?"

"I will. And, unlike you, I am in the habit of keeping my word."

Charles rose from his chair, leaned over the desk, and stubbed out his cigarette in the chairman's ashtray.

Andrew Fraser was surprised when he heard that Jock McPherson wanted to see him. The two men had never been on good terms since McPherson had failed to be elected to the Scottish Labour Party Executive Committee and had then left the party to stand against him at Edinburgh Carlton. Since McPherson had switched his allegiance they had barely been on speaking terms. However, Andrew realized it would be foolish not to see him after the SNP's sweeping successes in the election.

Andrew was even more surprised when McPherson asked if all seven SNP Members of Parliament could also attend the meeting, not in Andrew's office but somewhere private. He agreed, even more mystified.

McPherson and his band of renegade Scots arrived together at Cheyne Walk, looking as though they had already held a meeting between themselves. Andrew offered them a variety of seats, including the dining room chairs, a pouffe, and even the kitchen stool, apologizing that his London flat had never been intended to accommodate nine men in the drawing room.

While the men settled themselves Andrew remained standing by the mantelpiece, facing Jock McPherson who had obviously been chosen to act as their spokesman.

"I'll get straight to the point," McPherson began. "We want you to fight under the SNP banner at the next election."

Andrew tried not to show his disbelief, and began, "I don't feel . . ."

"Hear me out," said McPherson, raising his massive palms.

"We want you to contest the Edinburgh Carlton seat not just as a Scottish Nationalist candidate but as leader of the party."

Andrew still couldn't believe what he was hearing but remained silent.

"We're convinced you'll lose your seat in any case if you stand as a Socialist," McPherson continued, "but we realize that there are many people in Scotland who, whatever their political views, admire what you have achieved in the nine years you have been in the House. After all, man, you were brought up and educated in Edinburgh. With you as leader, we believe we could capture forty to fifty of the seventy-one seats in Scotland. And I may add that your own party is moving inexorably to the left, a state of affairs that I can't believe you are altogether happy about."

Andrew still made no comment. He listened as each one of the MPs put his own view, which became predictable long before the last one had spoken. Every Scottish tone from a Highland lilt to a Glasgow growl was represented in the voices. It became clear that they had given the matter considerable thought and were obviously sincere. "I am very flattered, gentlemen," he began when the last one had said his piece. "And I assure you I will give your offer my serious consideration."

"Thank you," said McPherson. They all stood up like clan leaders in the presence of a new chief.

"We'll wait to hear from you then," said McPherson. One by one they shook hands with their host before filing out.

As soon as they had left Andrew went straight into the kitchen where Robert was still waiting impatiently to play football before going to bed.

"In a moment, in a moment," he said in response to his son's noisy demands. "I'll join you in the garden."

"And what did that lot want?" inquired Louise, as she continued to peel the potatoes.

Andrew went over the details of their proposition.

"And how did you respond?"

"I didn't. I shall wait a week and then decline as gracefully as possible."

"What made you decide against the offer so quickly?"

"I don't like being told by Jock McPherson, or anyone else for that matter, that I will lose my seat at the next election if I don't fall in with their plans." He headed toward the kitchen door. "I'll be back to the red box as soon as I've scored a couple of goals against MacPele." A moment later he had joined Robert in the garden.

"Now listen, clever boots, I'm going to teach you how to feint a pass so that your opponent goes one way while you go the other."

"Sounds just like politics to me," muttered Louise, watching them out of the kitchen window.

27 Eaton Square,
London, SW1
23 April 1974

Dear Derek,

Thank you for your letter of 18 April and your kind invitation to rejoin the board of Seymour's. I am delighted to accept and look forward to working with you again.

Yours sincerely,
Charles Seymour.

Fiona checked the wording and nodded. Short and to the point. "Shall I post it?"

"Yes, please," said Charles as the phone rang.

He picked it up. "730-9712. Charles Seymour speaking."

"Oh, hello, Charles. It's Simon Kerslake."

"Hello, Simon," said Charles, trying to sound pleased to hear from his former colleague. "What's it like out there in the real world?"

"Not much fun, which is exactly why I'm phoning. I've been short-listed for Pucklebridge, Sir Michael Harbour-Baker's seat. He's nearly seventy and has decided not to stand again at the next election. As his constituency touches the south border of yours, I thought you might be able to put in a word for me again."

"Delighted," said Charles. "I'll speak to the chairman tonight. You can rely on me, and good luck. It would be nice to have you back in the House."

Simon gave him his home number which Charles repeated slowly, as if he were writing it down.

"I'll be in touch," said Charles.

"I really appreciate your help."

Simon put down the phone.

Elizabeth looked up from her copy of *The Lancet*.

"I don't trust that man," she said.

"A woman's intuition again?" said Simon, smiling. "You were wrong about Ronnie Nethercote."

"That's yet to be proved."

It was several days before Kate Garthwaite agreed to see Raymond again. And when she eventually joined him for dinner at the House she was not overwhelmed or flattered and she certainly didn't hang on his every word.

She was lively, fun, intelligent, and well informed and they began to see each other regularly. As the months passed Raymond found himself missing her at weekends when he was in Leeds with Joyce. Kate enjoyed her independence and made none of the demands on him that Stephanie had, never once suggesting he spend more time with her or that she might leave clothes behind in the flat.

Raymond sipped his coffee. "That was a memorable meal," he said, falling back into the sofa.

"Only by the standards of the House of Commons," replied Kate.

Raymond put an arm round her shoulder before kissing her gently on the lips.

"What! Rampant sex as well as cheap Beaujolais?" she exclaimed, stretching over and pouring herself some more coffee.

"I wish you wouldn't always make a joke of our relationship," said Raymond, stroking the back of her hair.

"I have to," said Kate quietly.

"Why?" Raymond turned to face her.

"Because I'm frightened of what might happen if I take it seriously."

Raymond leaned over and kissed her again. "Don't be frightened. You're the best thing that's happened to me in my whole life."

"That's what I'm worried about," said Kate, turning away.

Charles sat through the Annual General Meeting in silence. The chairman made his report for the year ending March 1974 before welcoming two new directors to the board and the return of Charles Seymour.

There were several questions from the floor which Derek Spencer had no trouble in handling. As Charles had promised, there was not even a hint of Miss Janet Darrow. Miss Trubshaw had let Fiona know that the payment had been stopped and also mentioned that she was still worried that her contract was coming to an end on 1 July.

When the chairman brought the AGM to a close Charles asked courteously if he could spare him a moment.

"Of course," said Spencer, looking relieved that the meeting had gone through without a hitch. "What can I do for you?"

"I think it might be wiser to talk in the privacy of your office."

The chairman glanced at him sharply but led him back to his room.

Charles settled himself comfortably in the leather chair once more and removed some papers from his inside pocket. Peering down at them he asked, "What does BX41207122, Bank Rombert, Zurich, mean to you?"

"You said you would never mention—"

"Miss Darrow," said Charles. "And I shall keep my word. But now, as a director of the bank, I am trying to find out what BX41207122 means to you?"

"You know damn well what it means," said the chairman, banging his clenched fist on the desk.

"I know it's your *private*"—Charles emphasized the last word—"account in Zurich."

"You could never prove anything," said Derek Spencer defiantly.

"I agree with you, but what I am able to prove," said Charles, shuffling through the papers that were resting on his lap, "is that you have been using Seymour's money to do private deals, leaving the profit in your Zurich account without informing the board."

"I've done nothing that will harm the bank, and you know it."

"I know the money has been returned with interest, and I could never prove the bank had suffered any loss. Nevertheless, the board might take a dim view of your activities remembering they pay you £40,000 a year to make profits for the bank, not for yourself."

"When they saw all the figures they would at worst rap me over the knuckles."

"I doubt if the Director of Public Prosecutions would take the same lenient attitude if he saw these documents," said Charles, holding up the papers that had been resting on his lap.

"You'd ruin the bank's name."

"And you would probably spend the next ten years in jail. If, however, you did get away with it you would be finished in the City, and by the time your legal fees had been paid there wouldn't be much left of that nest-egg in Zurich."

"So what do you want this time?" demanded Spencer, sounding exasperated.

"Your job," said Charles.

"My job?" said Spencer in disbelief. "Do you imagine because you've been a junior minister you're capable of running a successful merchant bank?" he added scornfully.

"I didn't say I would run it. I can buy a competent chief executive to do that."

"Then what will you be doing?"

"I shall be the chairman of Seymour's which will convince

City institutions that we wish to continue in the traditions of generations of my family."

"You're bluffing," stammered Spencer.

"If you are still in this building in twenty-four hours' time," said Charles, "I shall send these to the DPP."

There was a long silence.

"If I agreed," said Spencer at last, "I would expect two years' salary as compensation."

"One year," said Charles. Spencer hesitated, then nodded slowly. Charles rose to his feet and put the papers resting on his lap back into his inside pocket.

They consisted of nothing more than the morning mail from Sussex Downs.

Simon felt the interview had gone well but Elizabeth was not so sure. They sat huddled in a room with five other candidates and their wives, patiently waiting.

He thought back to his answers, and to the eight men and four women on the committee.

"You must admit it's the most ideal seat I've been considered for," said Simon.

"Yes, but the chairman kept eyeing you suspiciously."

"But Millburn mentioned that he had been at Eton with Charles Seymour."

"That's what worries me," whispered Elizabeth.

"A 15,000 majority at the last election and only forty minutes from London. We could even buy a little cottage . . ."

"If they invite you to represent them."

"At least this time you were able to tell them you would be willing to live in the constituency."

"So would anyone in their right mind," said Elizabeth.

·The chairman came out and asked if Mr. and Mrs. Kerslake would be kind enough to return once more to see the committee.

Oh, God, thought Simon. What else can they want to know?

"It's too near London to be my fault this time," chuckled Elizabeth.

The committee sat and stared at them with long faces.

"Ladies and gentlemen," said the chairman. "After our lengthy deliberations, I formally propose that Mr. Simon Kerslake be invited to contest Pucklebridge at the next election. Those in favor . . .?"

All twelve hands went up.

"Those against . . .?"

"Carried unanimously," said the chairman. He then turned to Simon. "Do you wish to address your committee?"

The prospective Conservative Member of Parliament for Pucklebridge rose. They all waited expectantly.

"I don't know what to say, except that I'm very happy and honored and I can't wait for a general election."

They all laughed and came forward and surrounded them. Elizabeth dried her eyes before anyone reached her.

About an hour later the chairman accompanied Simon and Elizabeth back to their car and bade them good night. Simon wound down his window.

"I knew you were the right man," Millburn said, "as soon as Charles Seymour phoned"—Simon smiled—"and warned me to avoid you like the plague."

"Could you tell Miss Trubshaw to come in?" Charles asked his secretary.

Margaret Trubshaw arrived a few moments later and remained standing in front of his desk. She couldn't help but notice the change of furniture in the room. The modern Conran suite had been replaced by a leather clublike sofa. Only the picture of the eleventh Earl of Bridgwater remained in place.

"Miss Trubshaw," began Charles, "since Mr. Spencer has felt it necessary to resign so suddenly I think it important for the bank to keep some continuity now that I'm taking over as chairman."

Miss Trubshaw stood like a Greek statue, her hands hidden in the sleeves of her dress.

"With that in mind, the board has decided to extend your contract with the bank for a further five years. Naturally, there will be no loss in your pension rights."

"Thank you, Mr. Charles."

"Thank you, Miss Trubshaw."

Miss Trubshaw almost bowed as she left the room.

"And Miss Trubshaw?"

"Yes, Mr. Charles," she said, holding on to the door knob.

"I believe my wife is expecting a call from you. Something about inviting you to lunch at the Savoy Grill."

CHAPTER
SEVENTEEN

"A BLUE SHIRT," said Raymond, looking at the Turnbull and Asser label with suspicion. "A *blue* shirt," he repeated.

"A fortieth-birthday present," shouted Kate from the kitchen.

I shall never wear it, he thought, and smiled to himself.

"And what's more, you'll wear it," she said, her Boston accent carrying a slight edge.

"You even know what I'm thinking," he complained as she came in from the kitchen. He always thought how elegant she looked in her tailored office suit.

"It's because you're so predictable, Carrot Top."

"Anyway, how did you know it was my birthday?"

"A massive piece of detective work," said Kate, "with the help of an outside agent and a small payment."

"An outside agent. Who?"

"The local paper shop, my darling. In the *Sunday Times* they tell you the name of every distinguished person celebrating a birthday in the following seven days. In a week during which only the mediocre were born, you made it."

Raymond had to laugh.

"Now listen, Carrot Top."

Raymond pretended to hate his new nickname. "Do you have to call me by that revolting name?"

"Yes. I can't stand Raymond."

He scowled. "In any case, carrot tops are green."

"No comment. Try on your shirt."

"Now?"

"Now."

He took off his black coat and waistcoat, removed his white shirt, and eased the stud on his stiff collar, leaving a small circle above his Adam's apple. Curly red hairs stuck up all over his chest. He quickly put on the new gift. The fabric had a pleasant soft feel about it. He started to do up the buttons, but Kate walked over and undid the top two.

"You know what? You've brought a whole new meaning to the word 'uptight.'"

Raymond scowled again.

"But in the right clothes you could even pass for good looking. Now. Where shall we go to celebrate your birthday?"

"The House of Commons?" suggested Raymond.

"Good God," said Kate. "I said celebrate, not hold a wake. What about Annabel's?"

"I can't afford to be seen in Annabel's."

"With me, you mean?"

"No, no, you silly woman, because I'm a Socialist."

"If members of the Labour party are not allowed to indulge in a good meal then perhaps it's time for you to change parties. In my country one only sees the Democrats in the best restaurants."

"Oh, do be serious, Kate."

"I intend to be. Now what have you been up to in the House lately?"

"Not a lot," said Raymond sheepishly. "I've been snowed under in court and . . ."

"Precisely. It's time you did something positive before your colleagues in Parliament forget you exist."

"Have you anything particular in mind?" asked Raymond, folding his arms across his chest.

"As a matter of fact, I have," said Kate. "I read in the same Sunday paper as the one in which I discovered your best-kept secret that it is proving difficult for the Labour party to repeal the Tories' trade union legislation. It appears there are long-term legal implications which the front bench are still trying to find a way round. Why don't you set that so-called 'first class' mind of yours to working out the legal niceties?"

"Not such a stupid idea." Raymond had become used to Kate's political sense, and when he had remarked on it she had only said, "Just another bad habit I picked up from my ex-husband."

"Now, where do we celebrate?" she asked.

"Compromise," said Raymond.

"I'm all ears."

"The Dorchester."

"If you insist," said Kate, not sounding over-enthusiastic.

Raymond started to change his shirt.

"No, no, no, Carrot Top, people have been known to wear blue shirts at the Dorchester."

"But I haven't got a tie to match," said Raymond triumphantly.

Kate thrust her hand into the Turnbull and Asser bag and drew out a dark blue silk tie.

"But it's got a pattern on it," said Raymond in disgust. "What will you expect next?"

"Contact lenses," said Kate.

Raymond stared at her, and blinked.

On the way out of the door Raymond's gaze fell upon the brightly wrapped package that Joyce had posted from Leeds earlier in the week. He had completely forgotten to open it.

"Damn," said Charles, putting down *The Times* and draining his coffee.

"What's the problem?" asked Fiona as she poured out another cup.

"Kerslake's been selected for Pucklebridge, which means

he's back in the House for life. Obviously my chat to Archie Millburn had no effect."

"Why have you got it in for Kerslake?" asked Fiona.

Charles folded the paper and considered the question. "It's quite simple really, old girl. I think he's the only one of my contemporaries who could stop me leading the party."

"Why him in particular?"

"I first came across him when he was President of the Union at Oxford. He was damn good then, and now he's better. He had rivals, but he brushed them aside like flies. No, despite his background, Kerslake's the one man left who frightens me."

"It's a long race yet, my darling, and he could still stumble."

"So could I, but what he doesn't realize is that I shall be putting out some of his hurdles."

Andrew worded the letter very carefully. He assured Jock McPherson and his colleagues that he had been flattered by their approach, but explained that he had decided his loyalties were still firmly based in the Labour party.

He accepted the point Jock had made about the left trying to gain control, but felt that every democratic party was bound to have a maverick element within its ranks, which was not necessarily unhealthy. He added that he considered the offer to have been confidential on both sides.

"Why add that postscript?" asked Louise when she had read the letter through.

"It's only fair to Jock," said Andrew. "If it gets around I turned him down it will have the opposite effect to the one they were trying to create."

"I'm not so sure they will act in the same magnanimous way when the next election comes round."

"Ah, Jock will make a lot of noise, but he's all right underneath . . ."

"That isn't what your father says about him," said Louise. "He's sure they'll want revenge."

"Father always sees grubs under even the greenest leaf."

"So if we're not about to celebrate your leadership of the

Scottish Nationalists we'll have to be satisfied with celebrating your fortieth birthday."

"But that's not for at least—"

"—another month, a week before Robert's fourth birthday."

"How would you like to commemorate the occasion, darling?"

"I thought we might have a week in the Algarve on our own."

"Why don't we have two weeks? Then we can celebrate your fortieth birthday as well?"

"Andrew Fraser, you just lost yourself one vote in Edinburgh Carlton."

Simon listened intently to Ronnie's report at the monthly board meeting. Two tenants had not paid their quarterly rent, and another quarter date was fast approaching. Ronnie's solicitors had sent firm reminders, followed a month later by writs, but this action had also failed to elicit any money.

"It only proves what I feared most," said Ronnie.

"What's that?" asked Simon.

"They just haven't got the cash."

"So we will have to replace them with new tenants."

"Simon, when you next travel from Beaufort Street to Whitechapel start counting the 'To Let' signs on office blocks along the way. When you've passed a hundred you'll find you still haven't reached the City."

"So what do you think we should do about it?"

"Try and sell one of our larger properties to secure cash flow. We can at least be thankful that even at these prices they are still worth a lot more than our borrowings. It's the companies who are the other way around that have to call in the receiver."

Simon thought about his overdraft, now approaching £100,000, and was beginning to wish he had accepted Ronnie's generous offer to buy back his shares. He accepted reluctantly that the opportunity had now passed.

When the board meeting was over he drove to St. Mary's to

pick up Elizabeth. It was to be one of their three-times-a-week journeys to Pucklebridge as Simon tried to get round all the villages before Wilson called an election.

Archie Millburn was turning out to be a conscientious chairman who had accompanied them on nearly every trip.

"He's been very kind to us," said Elizabeth, on their way down.

"He certainly has," said Simon. "Remember he also has to run Millburn Electronics. But, as he reminds us so often, once he's introduced us to every village chairman we'll be on our own."

"Have you ever discovered why he and Charles Seymour didn't see eye to eye?"

"No, he hasn't mentioned his name since that night. All I know for certain is that they were at school together."

"So what do you intend to do about Seymour?"

"Not a lot I can do," said Simon. "Except keep my eyes very wide open."

"The man who has deserted Edinburgh once too often"—Andrew read the Scottish Nationalist leaflet that had been sent to him that morning by his father. It was full of half-truths and innuendos.

"Andrew Fraser, the man who has forgotten Edinburgh, should no longer be allowed to represent a Scottish seat." It went on to declare: "He now lives far away from the problems of his constituents in a smart apartment building in fashionable Chelsea among his Tory friends. He visits the City of Edinburgh only a few times a year to make well-publicized appearances . . . Has being a minister gone to his head?"

"How dare they?" cried Louise in a rage. Andrew had never seen his wife so angry. "How dare they come to my home, offer you the leadership of their dreadful little party, and then write such a pack of lies? And did you read this?" she added, pointing to the last paragraph, " 'His wife Louise, née Forsyth'," she read out aloud, " 'comes from one of the wealthiest families in Scotland. She is a close relation of the owners of

Forsyth's in Princes Street.' I'm a second cousin once removed, and they don't even give me a discount in the main store."

Andrew started to laugh.

"What's so funny?"

He took her in his arms. "I always suffered under the illusion that you would inherit the Forsyth empire and I would never have to work again," he mocked. "Now we shall have to live off Robert's earnings as a star football player."

"Don't joke, Andrew. It won't seem funny when the election comes round."

"I'm far more concerned about the extreme left trying to infiltrate my General Management Committee," he said, his voice changing, "than I am by Jock McPherson's band of mad little islanders. But at this moment of time my red box is too full to worry about either of them."

Raymond made such a penetrating speech during the second reading of the new Trade Union Bill that the Whips put him on the standing committee, the perfect medium for him to display his skills as the committee debated each clause, point by point. He was able to show his colleagues where the legal pitfalls were and how to find a way round them. The rest of the committee soon learned from Raymond the meaning of "mastering a brief," and it was not long before trade union leaders were calling him at the House and even at his flat to learn his views on how their members should react to a host of different legal problems. Raymond showed patience with each of them and, more important, gave them excellent professional advice for the price of a phone call. He found it ironic how quickly they chose to forget that he was the author of *Full Employment at Any Cost?* Snippets began to appear in the national press, ranging from laudatory comments from those involved with the bill to a pointed suggestion in the *Guardian* that, whatever had happened in the past, it would be insupportable if Raymond Gould were not made a member of the Government in the near future.

"If they were to offer you a job, would it make any difference to our relationship?" Kate asked.

"Certainly," said Raymond. "I shall have found the perfect excuse not to wear your blue shirts."

Harold Wilson held the crumbling edifice together for a further six months before finally having to call a general election. He chose 10 October 1974.

Raymond immediately returned to his constituency to fight his fifth campaign. When he met Joyce at Leeds City station he couldn't help remembering that his dumpy wife was only four years older than Kate. He kissed her on the cheek as one might a distant relative, then she drove him back to their Chapel Allerton home.

Joyce chatted away on the journey home and it became clear that the constituency was under control and that this time Fred Padgett was well prepared for a general election. "He hasn't really stopped since the last one," she said. As for Joyce, she was undoubtedly better organized than the agent and the secretary put together. What was more, Raymond thought, she enjoyed it. He glanced over at her and couldn't help thinking she even looked prettier at election time.

Unlike his colleagues in rural seats, Raymond did not have to make speech after speech in little village halls. His votes were to be found in the high street where he addressed the midday shoppers through a megaphone, and walked around supermarkets, pubs, and clubs, grasping hands before repeating the whole process a few streets away.

Joyce set her husband a schedule that allowed few people in the Leeds community to escape him. Some saw him a dozen times during the three-week campaign—most of them at the football match on the Saturday afternoon before the election.

Once the game was over Raymond was back trooping round the working men's clubs, drinking pint after pint of John Smith's bitter. He accepted it was inevitable that he would put on half a stone during any election campaign. He dreaded what Kate's comments would be when she saw him.

Somehow he always found a few minutes in each day to steal away and phone her. She seemed so busy and full of news it only made Raymond feel downcast; she couldn't possibly be missing him.

The local trade unionists backed Raymond to the hilt. They may have found him stuck up and distant in the past, but they knew "where his heart was," as they confided to anyone who would listen. They banged on doors, delivered leaflets, drove cars to polling booths. They rose before he did in the morning and could still be found preaching to the converted after the pubs had thrown them out at night.

Raymond and Joyce cast their votes in the local secondary school on the Thursday of election day, looking forward to a large Labour victory. The Labour party duly gained a working majority in the House of forty-three over the Conservatives, but only three over all the parties combined. Nevertheless Harold Wilson looked set for another five years when the Queen invited him to form his fourth administration. The count in Leeds that night gave Raymond his biggest majority ever: 12,207 votes.

He spent the whole of Friday and Saturday thanking his constituents, then set out for London on the Sunday evening.

"He must invite you to join the Government this time," said Joyce, as she walked down the platform of Leeds City station with her husband.

"I wonder," said Raymond, kissing his wife on the other cheek. He waved at her as the train pulled out of the station. She waved back enthusiastically.

"I do like your new blue shirt, it really suits you," were the last words he heard her say.

During the election campaign Charles had had to spend a lot of time at the bank because of a run on the pound. Fiona seemed to be everywhere in the constituency at once, assuring voters that her husband was just a few yards behind.

After the little slips were counted the swing against Charles to the Labour candidate didn't amount to more than one percent in his 22,000 majority. When he heard the overall result he returned to London resigned to a long spell in Opposition. As he began to catch up with his colleagues in the House, he found many of them already saying openly that Heath had to go after two election defeats in a row.

Charles knew then that he would have to make up his mind once again on where he stood over the election of a new party leader, and that once again he must pick the right man.

Andrew Fraser returned to London after a grueling and unhappy campaign. The Scottish Nationalists had concentrated their attack on him, Jock McPherson sailing close to libel and slander. Sir Duncan advised his son against any legal action. "Only plays into their hands," he warned. "Small parties always benefit from the publicity."

Louise wanted him to inform the press that he had been offered the leadership of the SNP but Andrew felt it would serve no purpose, and might even rebound against him: and he also reminded her that he had given his word. In the last week of the campaign he spent most of his time trying—and failing—to stop Frank Boyle, a Communist, who had recently moved from Glasgow, from being elected to his General Management Committee. On polling day he scraped home by 1,656, Jock McPherson taking second place. At least he looked secure for another five years; but it didn't help that the Scottish Nationalists had increased their overall seats in the House to eleven.

Andrew, Louise, and Robert took the plane to London on the Sunday night to find the red box awaiting them and a message that the Prime Minister wanted Andrew to continue as Minister of State at the Home Office.

Simon had a glorious campaign. He and Elizabeth had started moving into their new cottage the day the election was announced, thankful that, now she had to commute, her salary at the hospital had made it possible for them to employ a nanny.

A double bed and a couple of chairs sufficed as Elizabeth cooked on an old Aga from provisions still packed in tea chests. They seemed to use the same two forks for everything. During the campaign Simon covered the 200-square-mile constituency for a second time and assured his wife that she need only take the final week off from from her duties at St. Mary's.

The voters of Pucklebridge sent Simon Kerslake back to Parliament with a majority of 18,419, the largest in the constituency's history. The local people had quickly come to the conclusion that they now had a member who was destined to have a Cabinet career.

Kate kept her remarks very gentle as it became obvious by the Monday night that the Prime Minister was not going to offer Raymond a job in the new administration. She cooked his favorite meal of roast beef—overdone—and Yorkshire pudding in the flat that night, but he didn't comment on it and hardly spoke.

CHAPTER
EIGHTEEN

AFTER SIMON HAD been back at the Commons for a week he felt a sense of déjà vu, a feeling that most members returning to the House for a second or even third time often experience. The sense was heightened by finding everything unchanged, even the policeman who greeted him at the Members' Entrance. When Edward Heath announced his Shadow team Simon was not surprised that he wasn't included, as he never had been a known supporter of the Tory leader. He was, however, mystified but not displeased to discover Charles Seymour was not among the names to be found in the Shadow Cabinet.

"Do you regret turning him down now the full team has been published?" asked Fiona, looking up from her copy of the *Daily Mail.*

"It wasn't an easy decision but I think it'll prove right in the long run," replied Charles, buttering another piece of toast.

"What did he offer in the end?"

"Shadow Minister of Industry."

"That sounds rather interesting," said Fiona.

"Everything about it was interesting except the salary, which would have been nothing. Don't forget the bank pays me £40,000 a year while I'm chairman."

Fiona folded her paper. "But you've just appointed a full-time chief executive, so your responsibilities at the bank should be only part-time compared with when you took the chair over. So what's your real reason?"

Charles accepted that he could rarely fool Fiona. "The truth is that I'm far from certain Ted will be leading the party at the next election."

"Then who will if he doesn't?" asked Fiona.

"Whoever's got the guts to oppose him."

"I'm not sure I understand," said Fiona, beginning to clear away the plates.

"Everyone accepts that he has to allow his name to go forward for reelection now that he's lost twice in a row."

"That's fair enough," agreed Fiona.

"But as he has appointed all possible contenders to the Cabinet or Shadow Cabinet over the last ten years, someone he has selected in the past will have to oppose him. No one of lesser stature would stand a chance."

"Is there a member of the Shadow Cabinet willing to stand?" asked Fiona, returning to her seat at the end of the table.

"One or two are considering it, but the problem is that if they lose it could easily end their political career," said Charles, folding his napkin.

"But if they win?"

"They will undoubtedly be the next Prime Minister."

"Interesting dilemma. And what are you going to do about it?"

"I'm not supporting anyone at the moment, but I've got my eyes wide open," said Charles, folding his copy of *The Times* and rising from the table.

"Is there a front runner?" asked Fiona, looking up at her husband.

"No, not really. Although Kerslake is trying to rally support for Margaret Thatcher, but that idea is doomed from the start."

"A woman leading the Tory party? Your lot haven't got the imagination to risk it," said Elizabeth, tasting the sauce. "The day that happens I shall eat my one and only Tory hat in full view of all the delegates at the party conference."

"Don't be so cynical, Elizabeth. She's the best bet we've got at the moment."

"But what are the chances of Ted Heath standing down? I always thought the leader of the party stayed on until he was hit by the mythical bus. I don't know Heath very well, but I can never imagine him resigning."

"I agree," said Simon. "So the 1922 Committee will have to change the rules."

"You mean the back-benchers will put pressure on him to go?"

"No, but a lot of the committee in their present mood would be willing to volunteer as driver for that bus."

"If that's true, he must realize that his chances of holding on are slim?"

"I wonder if any leader ever knows that," said Simon.

"You ought to be in Blackpool next week," said Kate, resting her elbow on the pillow.

"Why Blackpool?" Raymond asked, staring up at the ceiling.

"Because, Carrot Top, that's where they are holding this year's Labour party conference."

"What do you imagine I could hope to accomplish there?"

"You'd be seen to be alive. At present you're just a rumor in trade union circles."

"But if you're not a minister or a trade union leader all you do at a party conference is spend four days eating foul food, sleeping in seedy guest houses, and applauding second-rate speeches."

"I've no interest in where you put your weary head at night

but I do want you to revive your contacts with the unions during the day."

"Why?" said Raymond. "That lot can't influence my career."

"Not at the moment," said Kate. "But I predict that, like my fellow Americans at their conventions, the Labour party will one day select their leader at the party conference."

"Never," said Raymond. "That is and will always remain the prerogative of elected members of the House of Commons."

"That's the sort of crass, short-sighted, pompous statement I would expect a Republican to make," she said, before plonking a pillow over his head. Raymond feigned death, so she lifted up a corner and whispered in his ear, "Have you read any of the resolutions to be debated at this year's conference?"

"A few," came back Raymond's muffled reply.

"Then it might serve you well to note Mr. Anthony Wedgwood Benn's contribution," she said, removing the pillow.

"What's he up to this year?"

"He's calling on 'conference,' as he insists on describing your gathering of the brothers, to demand that the next leader be chosen by a full vote of the delegates, making up an electoral college from all the constituencies, the trade union movement, and Parliament—I suspect in that order."

"Madness. But what do you expect? He's married to an American."

"Today's extremist is tomorrow's moderate," said Kate blithely.

"A typical American generalization."

"Benjamin Disraeli, actually."

Raymond placed the pillow back over his head.

Andrew always attended the party conference, although he would never have voted for Tony Benn's resolution on the method of selecting a leader. He feared that if the trade unions were given that sort of power a leader who was totally unacceptable to his colleagues in the House of Commons could be selected. He was relieved when the motion was defeated but he noted that the majority against was far from overwhelming.

Despite being a minister Andrew could only get a small room at Blackpool in a guest house masquerading as a hotel, and that some two miles from the conference center. Such were the problems created by 4,000 self-important people converging on a seaside resort for a week that many had to forgo the Presidential Suite.

Andrew still had to carry on his job as Minister of State, with red boxes being delivered and taken every morning and afternoon, while making his presence felt at the conference. He spent half his time on a phone in the hotel lobby putting through transfer-charge calls to the Home Office. No one in the Soviet Union would have believed it, especially if they had realized that the Minister of State for Defense, who had the room next to Andrew's, was pacing up and down the corridor waiting for the phone to be free.

Andrew had never addressed the 3,000 delegates at a party conference. Even Cabinet ministers are only allowed a maximum of ten minutes at the rostrum unless they are members of the National Executive. Over half the Labour Cabinet had failed to be elected to this body, which consisted mainly of the leaders of the larger trade unions.

As he left the morning session Andrew was surprised to find Raymond Gould roaming around looking lost. They fell on each other like sane men locked in an asylum and decided to lunch together at the River House, Andrew's favorite restaurant a few miles outside of Blackpool.

Although they had both been in the House for nearly ten years it was the first time they discovered how much they had in common. Andrew had never considered himself a close friend of Raymond's but he had always admired his stand on devaluation.

"You must have been disappointed when the PM didn't ask you to rejoin the Government," Andrew began.

Raymond stared down at the menu. "Very," he finally admitted, as a girl joined them in the bar to take their order.

"Nevertheless, you were wise to come to Blackpool. This is where your strength lies."

"Come on. Everybody knows you're the trade unions' pin-up boy, and they still have a lot of influence as to who sits in the Cabinet."

"I haven't noticed," said Raymond mournfully.

"You will when they eventually choose the leader."

"That's funny, that's exactly what . . . Joyce said last week."

"Sensible girl, Joyce. I fear it will happen in our time as members."

Bill Scott, the proprietor, told them their table was ready and they went through to the small dining room.

"Why fear?" asked Raymond, as he took his seat.

"Middle-of-the-road democrats like myself will end up as so many leaves on a bonfire."

"But I'm middle-of-the-road myself, practically right wing on some issues."

"Perhaps. But every party needs a man like you, and at this moment union leaders wouldn't mind if you were a card-carrying Fascist; they'd still back you."

"Then what makes you attend the conference?"

"Thank God it still gives one a chance to keep in touch with the grass roots, and I live in hope that the extreme left will never be much more than an unruly child that the grown-ups have to learn to live with."

"Let's hope you're right," said Raymond, "because they're never going to grow up." Andrew laughed as Raymond continued in a different mood. "I still envy you your job at the Home Office. I didn't go into politics to spend my life on the back benches."

"There may well come a day when I sit and envy you from those same back benches," said Andrew.

As he spoke, the chairman of the Boilermakers' Union shouted across as he passed their table, "Good to see you, Ray." He showed no recognition of Andrew. Raymond turned and smiled at the man and waved back as Caesar might have done to Cassius.

When they had both rejected the choice of date and walnut pudding or Pavlova, Andrew suggested a brandy.

Raymond hesitated.

"You'll see more double brandies drunk here than you will at the Conservative party conference next week. Ask any waitress."

"Have you decided how you're going to vote in the leadership battle?" asked Fiona over breakfast.

"Yes," said Charles, "and at this point in my career I can't afford to make the wrong choice."

"So who have you decided on?" asked Fiona.

"While there isn't a serious contender to oppose Ted Heath it remains in my best interest to continue backing him."

"Isn't there one Shadow Cabinet minister who has the guts to stand against him?"

"The rumor grows that Margaret Thatcher will act as whipping girl. If she gets close enough to force a second ballot the serious contenders will then join in."

"What if she won the first round?"

"Don't be silly, Fiona," said Charles, taking more interest in his scrambled egg. "The Tory party would never elect a woman to lead them. We're far too traditional. That's the sort of immature mistake the Labour party would make to prove how much they believe in equality."

Simon was still pushing Margaret Thatcher to throw her hat in the ring.

"She certainly has enough of them," said Elizabeth.

It amused Andrew and Raymond to watch the Tory party leadership struggle while they got on with their respective jobs. Raymond would have dismissed Thatcher's chances if Kate hadn't reminded him that the Tories had been the first party to choose a Jewish leader, and also the first to select a bachelor.

"So why shouldn't they be the first to elect a woman?" she demanded. He would have continued to argue with her but the damn woman had proved to be right so often in the past. "Let's wait and see," was all he said.

The 1922 Committee announced that the election for leader would take place on 4 February 1975.

At a press conference in early January at the House of Commons Margaret Thatcher announced she would allow her name to go forward to contest the leadership. Simon immediately spent his time exhorting his colleagues to support "The Lady" and joined a small committee under Airey Neave that was formed for the purpose. Charles Seymour warned his friends that the party could never hope to win a general election with a woman leading them. As the days passed, nothing became clearer than the uncertainty of the outcome.

At four o'clock on a particularly wet and windy day the chairman of the 1922 Committee announced the figures:

Margaret Thatcher	130
Edward Heath	119
Hugh Fraser	16

According to the 1922 Committee rules, the winner needed a fifteen percent majority and so a second round was necessary. "It will be held in seven days' time," the Chief Whip announced. Three former Cabinet ministers immediately declared they were candidates, while Ted Heath, having been warned that he would get fewer votes a second time round, withdrew from the ballot.

They were the longest days in Simon's life. He did everything in his power to hold Thatcher's supporters together. Charles meanwhile decided to play the second round very low-key. When the time came to vote he put his cross on the ballot paper next to the former Secretary of State he had served under at Trade and Industry. "A man we can all trust," he told Fiona.

When the votes had been counted and confirmed the chairman of the 1922 Committee announced that Margaret

Thatcher was the outright winner with a vote of 146 to 79 from her nearest challenger.

Simon was delighted while Elizabeth hoped he had forgotten about the promise to eat her hat. Charles was dumbfounded. They both wrote to their new leader immediately.

11 February 1975

Dear Margaret,

Many congratulations on your victory as the first woman leader of our party. I was proud to have played a small part in your triumph and will continue to work for your success at the next election.

Yours,
Simon.

27 Eaton Square,
London, SW1
11 February 1975

Dear Margaret,

I made no secret of backing Ted Heath in the first round of the leadership contest having had the privilege of serving in his administration. I was delighted to have supported you on the second ballot. It illustrates how progressive our party is that we have chosen a woman who will undoubtedly be Britain's next Prime Minister.

Be assured of my loyalty.

Yours,
Charles.

Margaret Thatcher answered all her colleagues' letters within the week. Simon received a handwritten letter inviting him to join the new Shadow team as number two in the Education Department. Charles received a typed note thanking him for his letter of support.

CHAPTER
NINETEEN

SEYMOUR'S BANK HAD weathered the Great War, the thirties' crash, and then the Second World War. Charles had no intention of being the chairman who presided over its demise in the seventies. Soon after taking over from Derek Spencer—at the board's unanimous insistence—he had discovered that being chairman wasn't quite the relaxed job he expected, and while he remained confident that the bank could ride the storm he still wasn't taking any risks. The business sections of the newspapers were full of stories of the Bank of England acting as a "lifeboat" and having to step in to assist ailing financial institutions, along with daily reports of the collapse of yet another property company. The time when property values and rents automatically increased each year had become a thing of the past.

When he had accepted the board's offer, Charles insisted that a chief executive be appointed to carry out the day-to-day business while he remained the man with whom other City chairmen dealt. He interviewed several people for the position but he did not find anyone suitable. Head-hunting seemed to be the next move, the expense of which was saved when he overheard a conversation at the next table at White's that the newly appointed chief executive of the 1st Bank of America was sick of having to report to the board in Chicago every time he wanted to use a first-class stamp.

Charles immediately invited the chief executive to lunch at the House of Commons. Clive Reynolds had come from a similar background to Derek Spencer: London School of Economics, followed by the Harvard Business School and a series of successful appointments which had culminated in his becoming chief executive of the 1st Bank of America. This similarity did not worry Charles, as he made it clear to Mr. Reynolds that the appointee would be the chairman's man.

When Reynolds was offered the appointment he drove a hard bargain and Charles looked forward to his doing the same on behalf of Seymour's. Reynolds ended up with £50,000 a year and enough of a profit incentive to ensure that he didn't deal for himself or encourage any other headhunters to invite him to join their particular jungle.

"He's not the sort of fellow we could invite to dinner," Charles told Fiona, "but his appointment will enable me to sleep at night knowing the bank is in safe hands."

Charles's choice was rubber-stamped by the board at their next meeting, and as the months passed it became obvious that the 1st Bank of America had lost one of its prime assets well below the market value.

Clive Reynolds was a conservative by nature, but when he did take what Charles described as a risk—and Reynolds called a "hunch"—over fifty percent of them paid off. While Seymour's kept its reputation for caution and good husbandry, they managed a few quite spectacular coups thanks to their new chief executive.

Reynolds had enough sense to treat his new chairman with respect without ever showing deference while their relationship remained at all times strictly professional.

One of Reynolds's first innovations had been to suggest they check on every customer account over £250,000 and Charles had approved.

"When you've handled the account of a company for many

years," Reynolds pointed out, "it sometimes is not apparent when one of your traditional customers is heading for trouble as it would be to a newcomer. If there are any 'lame ducks' let's discover them before they hit the ground"—a simile that Charles repeated at several weekend parties.

Charles enjoyed his morning meetings with Clive Reynolds as he picked up a great deal about a profession to which he had previously only brought gut feeling and common sense. In a very short time he learned enough from his new tutor to make him sound like David Rockefeller when he rose to speak in a finance debate on the floor of the House, an unexpected bonus.

Charles knew little of Reynolds's private life except what was on file. He was forty-one, unmarried, and lived in Esher, wherever that was. All Charles cared about was that Reynolds arrived each morning at least an hour before him, and left after him every night, even when the House was in recess.

Charles had studied fourteen of the confidential reports on customers with loans over £250,000. Clive Reynolds had already picked out two companies with whom he felt the bank should revise their current position.

Charles still had three more reports to consider before he presented a full assessment to the board.

The quiet knock on the door, however, meant that it was ten o'clock and Reynolds had arrived to make his daily report. Rumors were circulating in the City that the bank rate would go up on Thursday, so Reynolds wanted to go short on dollars and long on gold. Charles nodded. As soon as the announcement had been made about the bank rate, Reynolds continued: "It will be wiser to return to dollars as the new round of pay negotiations with the unions is about to take place. This in turn will undoubtedly start a fresh run on the pound." Charles nodded again.

"I think the dollar is far too weak at two-ten," Reynolds added. "With the unions settling at around twelve percent the dollar must strengthen, say, to nearer one-ninety." He added that he was not happy about the bank's large holding in Slater Walker and wanted to liquidate half the stock over the next month. He proposed to do so in small amounts over irregular periods. "We also have three other major accounts to consider before we make known our findings to the board. I'm concerned about the spending policy of one of the companies, but the other two appear stable. I think we should go over them together when you have time to consider my reports. Perhaps tomorrow morning, if you could manage that. The companies concerned are Speyward Laboratories, Blackies Limited, and Nethercote and Company. It's Speyward I'm worried about."

"I'll take the files home tonight," said Charles, "and give you an opinion in the morning."

"Thank you, Chairman."

Charles had never suggested that Reynolds should call him by his first name.

Archie Millburn held a small dinner party to celebrate Simon's first anniversary as the member for Pucklebridge. Although these occasions had originally been to introduce the party hierarchy to their new member, Simon now knew more about the constituency and its flock than he did, as Archie was the first to admit.

Elizabeth, Peter, and Michael had settled comfortably into their small cottage, while Simon, as a member of the Shadow Education team, had visited schools—nursery, primary, public, and secondary; universities—red brick, plate glass, and Oxbridge; technical colleges, art institutes, and even borstals. He had read Butler, Robbins, and Plowden and listened to children and to professors of psychology alike. He felt that after a year he was beginning to understand the subject, and only longed for a general election so that he could once again turn rehearsal into performance.

"Opposition must be frustrating," observed Archie when the ladies had retired after dinner.

"Yes, but it's an excellent way to prepare yourself for Government and do some basic thinking about the subject. I never found time for such luxury as a minister."

"But it must be very different from holding office?" said Archie, clipping a cigar.

"True. In Government," said Simon, "you're surrounded by civil servants who don't allow you to lift a finger or give you a moment to ponder, while in Opposition you can think policy through even if you do often end up having to type your own letters."

Archie pushed the port down to Simon's end of the table. "I'm glad the girls are out," said Archie conspiratorially, "because I wanted you to know I've decided to give up being chairman at the end of the year."

"Why?" said Simon, taken aback.

"I've seen you elected and settled in. It's time for a younger man to have a go."

"But you're only my age."

"I can't deny that, but the truth is that I'm not giving enough time to my electronics company, and the board are continually reminding me of it. No one has to tell you that these are not easy times."

"It's sad," said Simon. "Just as you get to know someone in politics you or they always seem to move on."

"Fear not," said Archie. "I don't intend to leave the area, and I feel confident that you will be my member for at least another twenty years, by which time I will be happy to accept an invitation to dine with you in Downing Street."

"You may find that it's Charles Seymour who is residing at No. 10," said Simon, striking a match to light his cigar.

"Then I won't be getting an invitation," said Archie with a smile.

Charles couldn't sleep that night after his discovery, and his tossing and turning kept Fiona awake. He had opened the Nethercote file when he was waiting for dinner to be served. His first act with any company was to glance down the names of the directors to see if he knew anyone on the board. He recognized no one until his eye stopped at "S. J. Kerslake, MP."

The cook felt sure that Mr. Seymour had not enjoyed his dinner, because he hardly touched the main course.

On his arrival at Seymour's, only moments after Clive Reynolds, he called for his chief executive. He appeared a few minutes later without his usual armful of files, surprised to see the chairman so early. Once Reynolds was seated Charles opened the file in front of him. "What do you know about Nethercote and Company?"

"Private company. Net asset value approaching £10,000,000, running a current overdraft of £7,000,000 of which we service half. Efficiently managed with a good board of directors, will ride out the current problems in my view, and should be well oversubscribed when they eventually go public."

"How much of the company do we own?"

"Seven and a half percent. As you know, the bank never take eight percent of any company because then we would have to declare an interest under section twenty-three of the Finance Act. It has always been a policy of this bank to invest in a major client without becoming too involved with the running of the company."

"Who are their principal bankers?"

"The Midland."

"What would happen if we put our seven and a half percent up for sale and did not renew the overdraft facility at the end of the quarter, but called it in instead?"

"They would have to seek finance elsewhere."

"And if they couldn't?"

"They would have to start selling their assets, which under that sort of forced-sale position would be very damaging for any company, if not impossible, in the present climate."

"And then?"

"I would have to check my file and . . ."

Charles passed over the file and Reynolds studied it carefully, frowning. "They already have a cash-flow problem because of bad debts. With a sudden increased demand they might go under. I would strongly advise against such a move, Chairman. Nethercote have proved a reliable risk over the years, and I think we stand to make a handsome profit when they are quoted on the Stock Exchange."

"For reasons I cannot disclose to you," said Charles, looking up from his chair, "I fear that remaining involved with this company may turn out to be a financial embarrassment for Seymour's." Reynolds looked at him, puzzled. "You will inform the Midland Bank that we will not be renewing this loan at the next quarter."

"Then they would have to look for support from another bank. The Midland would never agree to shoulder the entire amount on their own."

"And try to dispose of our seven and a half percent immediately."

"But that could lead to a crisis of confidence in the company."

"So be it," said Charles, as he closed the file.

"But I do feel—"

"That will be all, Mr. Reynolds."

"Yes, Chairman," said the mystified chief executive, who had never thought of his boss as an irrational man. He turned to leave. Had he looked back he would have been even more mystified by the smile that was spread across Charles Seymour's face.

"They've pulled the rug out from under our feet," said Ronnie Nethercote angrily.

"Who?" said Simon, who had just come into the room.

"The Midland Bank."

"Why would they do that?"

"An outside shareholder put all his stock on the market without warning, and the Midland got worried about their position. They wouldn't be prepared to continue such a large overdraft position on their own."

"Have you been to see the manager?" asked Simon, unable to disguise his anxiety.

"Yes, but he can't do anything. His hands are tied by a main board directive," said Ronnie, slumping deeper into his seat.

"How bad is it?"

"They've given me a month to find another bank. Otherwise I'll have to start selling some of our assets."

"What will happen if we don't manage to come up with another bank?" asked Simon desperately.

"The company could be bankrupt within weeks. Do you know any bankers who are looking for a good investment?"

"Only one, and I can assure you he wouldn't help."

Charles put the phone down satisfied. He wondered if there was anything that could still be regarded as secret. It had taken him less than an hour to find out the size of Kerslake's overdraft. "Banker to banker confidentiality," he had assured them. He was still smiling when Reynolds knocked on the door.

"The Midland weren't pleased," he immediately briefed Charles.

"They'll get over it," his chairman replied. "What's the latest on Nethercote?"

"Only a rumor, but everyone now knows they're in trouble and the chairman is searching around for a new backer," said Reynolds impassively. "His biggest problem is that no one is touching property companies at the moment."

"Once they've collapsed, what's to stop us picking up the pieces and making a killing?"

"A clause that was slipped through in the Finance Act which your Government passed three years ago. The penalties range from a heavy fine to having your banking license taken away."

"Oh, yes, I remember," said Charles. "Pity. So how long do you expect them to last?"

"Once the month is up," said Reynolds stroking a clean-shaven chin, "if they fail to find a backer the creditors will swarm in like locusts."

"Aren't the shares worth anything?" asked Charles innocently.

"Not the paper they are written on at the moment," said Reynolds, watching his chairman carefully.

This time the chief executive couldn't miss the chairman's smile as Charles thought of Simon Kerslake and his overdraft of £108,000 now backed by worthless shares. Pucklebridge would soon be looking for a new member.

At the end of a month during which no bank came to his rescue Ronnie Nethercote caved in and agreed to call in the receiver and file a bankruptcy notice. He still hoped that he could pay off all his creditors even if the shares he and his fellow directors held remained worthless. He felt as worried for Simon and his career as he did for himself, but he knew there was nothing the receiver would allow him to do to help one individual.

When Simon told Elizabeth she didn't complain. She had always feared this could be the eventual outcome of her husband joining the board of Nethercote.

"Can't Ronnie help?" she asked. "After all, you've supported him enough in the past."

"No, he can't," replied Simon, avoiding telling her where the real responsibility for his downfall lay.

"But do bankrupts automatically have to leave Parliament?" was Elizabeth's next question.

"No, but I shall because I could never be considered for further promotion—I'd always be rightly tainted with 'lack of judgment.' "

"It seems so unfair when you weren't personally to blame."

"There are different rules for those who wish to live in the spotlight," Simon said simply.

"But in time, surely—" began Elizabeth.

"I'm not willing to remain on the back benches for another twenty years only to hear whispered in the corner of the smoking room—Would have made the Cabinet if it hadn't been for . . ."

"Does that mean the children will have to be taken away from school?"

"I'm afraid so," said Simon, his hands shaking. "As a bankrupt I can hardly expect the receiver to view the fees for my sons' education as a dire necessity even if I could find the money."

"So we'll have to get rid of the nanny, too?"

"Not necessarily, but we may both have to make sacrifices in order that she can be part-time."

"But my work at the hospital . . ." began Elizabeth but didn't complete the sentence. "What happens next?"

"I'll have to tell Archie Millburn tonight. I've already written my letter of resignation to hand to him. I shall make an appointment to see the Chief Whip on Monday to explain why I am going to apply for the Chiltern Hundreds."

"What does that mean?"

"It's one of the only ways of leaving the House in mid-session—other than dying. Officially it's a nominal office under the Crown which therefore debars you from membership of the House."

"It all sounds rather formal to me."

"I'm afraid it will cause an embarrassing by-election in Pucklebridge," Simon admitted.

"Can nobody help?"

"There aren't a lot of people around who have a spare £108,000 for a worthless bunch of shares."

"Would you like me to come with you when you go to see Archie?" Elizabeth asked, rising from her seat.

"No, darling. It's kind of you to ask, but I'm the one who made such a fool of myself."

Elizabeth leaned over and pushed back the hair that had fallen over his forehead. She couldn't help noticing some gray strands that must have appeared in the last few weeks. "We'll just have to live off my salary while you look for a job."

Simon drove slowly down to Pucklebridge to keep his impromptu appointment with the chairman. Archie Millburn, standing hands on hips in his garden, listened to the tale with a sad face. "It's been happening to a lot of good people in the City lately, but what I can't understand is: if the company owns such prime properties, why has no one made a takeover bid? Sounds as if it's an asset-stripper's dream."

"It appears to be a matter of confidence," said Simon.

"A sacred word in the City," agreed Archie, while he continued to prune his Roosevelts and Red Mistresses.

Simon handed him the prepared letter of resignation, which Millburn read over and reluctantly accepted.

"I won't mention this to anyone until you've seen the Chief Whip on Monday. I'll call a special meeting of the full committee on Tuesday evening and inform them of your decision then. You had better be prepared for an unfriendly barrage from the press on Tuesday night."

The two men shook hands. "Your misfortune is our misfortune," said Archie. "In a very short time you've gained the respect and the affection of the local people. You'll be missed."

Simon drove back to London and, although the car radio was on low, he did not take in the news flash that they kept repeating every thirty minutes.

CHAPTER TWENTY

RAYMOND WAS AMONG the first to hear the announcement, and was stunned by it. Harold Wilson was going to resign less than halfway through the five-year Parliament, and for no apparent reason other than that he had just passed his sixtieth birthday. He proposed to remain Prime Minister only so long as the Labour party took to select its new leader. Raymond and Kate sat glued to the television, picking up every scrap of information they could. They discussed the implications far into the night.

"Well, Carrot Top, could this mean rehabilitation for our forgotten hero?"

"Who can say?"

"Well, if you can't, who can?"

"The next leader," said Raymond.

The fight for the leadership was a straight battle between the left and right wings of the party, James Callaghan on the right and Michael Foot on the left. Andrew and Raymond both wanted the same man and it was with some relief that they saw

Callaghan, despite losing the first ballot, come through to be elected leader. The Queen duly called for Callaghan and asked him to form a new administration.

As tradition demands Andrew sent his resignation to Downing Street, as did every other member of the Government, to allow the new Prime Minister to select his own team.

Raymond was in court listening to the judge's summing up when his junior passed him a note: "Please call 10 Downing Street as soon as possible." The judge took a further thirty minutes, meticulously explaining to the jury the legal definition of manslaughter, before Raymond could escape. He ran down the corridor and stopped at one of the clerks' private boxes to make the call. The plastic dial rotating back into place after each number seemed to take forever.

After he had been passed through three people a voice said, "Good afternoon, Ray"—the unmistakable gravelly tones of the new Prime Minister. "I think it's time you rejoined the Government"—Raymond held his breath—"as Minister of State at the Department of Trade." Minister of State: only one place away from the Cabinet.

"You still there, Ray?"

"Yes, Prime Minister, and I'd be delighted to accept."

He put the phone down, immediately picked it up again, and dialed the City office of the Chase Manhattan Bank. They put him through to the Euro Bond manager.

Andrew had left his desk at the Home Office and returned to Cheyne Walk. He stayed away from the House of Commons where the lobby correspondents were hanging about like hyenas, scampering off to phone their papers with even the rumor of a rumor. The new Cabinet had been selected, and now it was the turn of the Ministers of State. All Andrew knew for certain was that his old job at the Home Office had been given to someone else.

"Why don't you go and play football with Robert?" Louise suggested. "And stop moping around under my feet?"

"Yes, Dad, yes, Dad, yes, Dad," demanded his son, running

upstairs to reappear a few minutes later dressed in the Liverpool kit that he had bought himself from eleven weeks' hard-saved pocket money.

"Go on, Andrew. I can always call you if the phone goes."

Andrew smiled, took off his jacket, and put on the pair of old gym shoes Robert was holding out for him. He followed his five-year-old son into the garden to find him already dribbling up and down the thin strip between the flower beds. The little goal he had bought for Robert—or was it for himself?—at Christmas was already set up at the far end of the grass and they took turns defending it. Andrew always had to start in goal. He rubbed his hands together to keep warm as Robert dribbled toward him. He came out of the goal ready to stifle a shot, but Robert kicked the ball to the right and ran to the left, leaving his father spread-eagled on the ground before he pushed the ball gently into the goal. "That's called a feint," he shouted triumphantly, as he ran back past his prostrate father.

Andrew picked himself up. "I know what it's called," he said, laughing. "You seem to have forgotten who taught you the feint in the first place. Let's see if you can do it twice running," he added, returning to defend the goal.

Robert dribbled away from his father until he reached the end of the garden, then turned to face him again. He had begun advancing toward the goal for a second time when there was the sound of the phone ringing. Andrew looked toward the house just as Robert kicked the ball, which rising sharply, struck him in the face. He and the ball fell back into the goal mouth.

Louise opened the kitchen window and shouted, "It's only my mother."

"Wake up, Dad," demanded Robert simultaneously.

Andrew's face was still stinging from the blow. "I'm going to get you for that," he said. "Your turn to defend the goal."

Robert rushed forward to take his place between the posts, jumping up and down trying to touch the crossbar with the tips of his fingers. Andrew took his time as he moved toward his son. When he was about a yard in front of Robert he feinted to the right and ran to the left but Robert had seen the move coming and leaped on the ball shouting, "No goal."

Once again Andrew returned to the end of the garden, thinking over what move he could try next. He suddenly ran straight at Robert and kicked the ball firmly toward the right-hand corner of the goal mouth. But again Robert anticipated the move and caught the ball above his head before pulling it to his chest and shouting, "No goal, Dad, no goal!" He tossed the ball confidently back along the ground to his father's feet.

"Right, the fooling around is over," said Andrew, not quite convinced. He kicked the ball from one foot to the other, trying to look skillful.

"Come on, Dad," Robert complained.

This time Andrew advanced with a look of determination on his face. He tried a change of pace to make his son leave the goal mouth too early. Robert duly came out of the goal; Andrew kicked the ball a little harder and higher than his previous attempt. As he did so he heard the phone ring again and turned his head toward the house. He didn't see his shot cannon against the left-hand corner of the goal post and bounce away.

"It's the Prime Minister," shouted Louise from the window. Andrew turned to walk quickly back toward the house. Out of the corner of his eye he saw the ball bounce on to the path, on its way toward the gate and into the road.

Robert was already running toward the open gate. "I'll save it, Dad, I'll save it."

"No," screamed Andrew at the top of his voice and turned back to run as fast as he could after his son.

Louise froze as she stared out of the window, still holding on to the phone with her rubber gloves. She watched as Andrew turned his back and tore toward the pavement until he was only a yard behind his son. The ball bounced on into the road and Robert dived for it a split second before his father threw himself on his son.

Louise was the only one who saw the driver of the massive Shell tanker slam on its brakes and swerve—too late—to avoid them. Andrew and Robert collided with the corner of the wide metal mudguard and were thrown back together before rolling over and over several times, ending up in the gutter.

"Are you there, Andrew?" asked the Prime Minister.

Louise dropped the phone and ran out of the kitchen toward the open gate. Her husband lay motionless beside the curb with their son in his arms, the ball still clutched against his chest. She tried to hold on to both of them as Andrew's blood poured down over Robert's red shirt and on to her rubber gloves.

She fell on to her knees by the curbside. "Let them live, let them live," was all she said.

Robert was crying softly as he held firmly on to the ball and stared at his unconscious father. She had to lean over to hear him repeating, "No goal, Dad, no goal."

When the complete list of ministers was published in *The Times* two days later the only unfilled post left was that of Minister of State for Defense. *The Times*'s political editor, David Wood, surmised that the position was being held open for Mr. Andrew Fraser, who was expected to be out of hospital by the end of the week. Wood's final paragraph read:

> Politicians from all parties joined forces in praising Mr. Fraser's remarkable courage in diving in front of a moving lorry to rescue his only son, Robert, who was chasing a football. Both father and son were rushed to St. Thomas's Hospital with internal injuries, where surgeons operated through the night to save Mr. Fraser's life.
>
> As was reported in the final edition of yesterday's paper, his five-year-old son Robert died during the night before Mr. Fraser regained consciousness.

"My God," exclaimed Elizabeth, "how dreadful."

"What's dreadful?" asked Simon, as he took his seat at the

breakfast table. She passed the paper to her husband and pointed to the picture of Robert.

"Poor kid," said Simon before he had finished the article.

"Certainly puts our own problems into perspective. If Peter or Michael were killed we really would have something to worry about."

Neither of them spoke for several minutes. Then Elizabeth asked, "Are you dreading it?"

"Yes, I am," said Simon. "I feel like a condemned man eating his last breakfast, and the worst part of it is that I have to drive myself to the gallows."

"I wonder if we will ever laugh about today?"

"No doubt—when I collect my parliamentary pension."

"Can we live off that?"

"Hardly. I don't get the first payment until I'm sixty-five, so we have a twenty-five-year wait to find out." He got up. "Can I give you a lift to the hospital?"

"No thanks. I intend to savor the joys of being a two-car family for at least another week. Just let's hope the new Marina holds its price as well as Sir Michael Edwardes claimed it would."

Simon laughed, kissed his wife, and left for his appointment with the Chief Whip at the House of Commons. As he started the car Elizabeth rushed out. "I forgot to tell you, Ronnie phoned while you were in the bath."

"I'll call him as soon as I reach the House."

Simon made his way to the Commons. He felt sick as he passed Cheyne Walk and thought of Andrew Fraser and all he must be going through. He made a mental note to write to him immediately. At the Commons the policeman on the gate saluted as he drove in. "Good morning, sir," he said.

"Good morning," said Simon. He parked his car on the second level of the new underground car park and took the escalator up to the Members' Entrance. He couldn't help reflecting that ten years ago he would have taken the stairs. He continued through the Members' Cloakroom, up the marble staircase to the Members' Lobby. Habit made him turn left into the little post office to check whether he had any mail.

"Mr. Kerslake," the man behind the counter called into an intercom, and a few seconds later a parcel and a packet of letters held together by a thick elastic band thudded into an office basket. Simon left the parcel marked "London School of Economics" and the letters on the desk in his room and checked his watch: over forty minutes before his appointment with the Chief Whip. He went to the nearest phone and dialed Nethercote and Company. Ronnie answered the phone himself.

"Sacked the telephone operator last Friday," he explained. "Only me and my secretary left."

"You called, Ronnie," a millimeter of hope in Simon's voice.

"Yes, I wanted to express how I felt. I tried to write you a letter over the weekend but I'm not very good with words." He paused. "Nor it seems with figures. I just wanted to say how desperately sorry I am. Elizabeth told me you were going to see the Chief Whip this morning. I'll be thinking of you."

"That's kind, Ronnie, but I went into it with my eyes wide open. As an advocate of free enterprise, I can hardly complain when I turn out to be one of its victims."

"A very philosophical attitude for this time of the morning."

"How are things your end?"

"The receiver's checking the books. I still believe we can get out with all our creditors fully paid. At least that way I'll avoid the stigma of bankruptcy." There was a longer pause. "Oh Christ, that was tactless."

"Don't worry about it, Ronnie, the overdraft was my decision."

Simon already wished he had been as frank with his wife.

"Let's have lunch one day next week."

"It will have to be somewhere that takes luncheon vouchers," said Simon wryly.

"Good luck, mate," said Ronnie.

Simon decided to fill up the remaining thirty minutes at the House by going to the library and glancing over the rest of the morning press. He settled himself in a corner of the "B" Room, next to the fireplace over which hung a notice reminding members not to have overloud or prolonged conversations.

He leafed through the papers, which all carried photographs of Andrew Fraser and his wife and son. The same portrait of five-year-old Robert appeared on almost every front page. Elizabeth was right: in so many respects they were lucky.

The story of the probable break-up of Nethercote and Company was detailed on the financial pages. They quoted approvingly Ronnie's view that all creditors ought to be paid in full. Not one of the articles mentioned Simon's name, but he could already anticipate the headlines in tomorrow's paper with another picture of a young MP and his happy family. "The Rise and Fall of Simon Kerslake." Over ten years' work quickly forgotten: he would be old news within a week.

The library clock inched toward the hour that he could no longer put off. Simon heaved himself out of the deep leather chair like an old man and walked slowly toward the Chief Whip's office.

Miss Norse, the Chief's ancient secretary, smiled benignly as he came in.

"Good morning, Mr. Kerslake," she said brightly. "I'm afraid the Chief is still with Mrs. Thatcher but I did remind him of your appointment so I don't expect him to be long. Would you care to have a seat?"

"Thank you," he said.

Alec Pimkin always claimed that Miss Norse had a set patter for every occasion. His imitation of her saying, "I hope I find you in rude health, Mr. Pimkin," had brought chuckles to the Members' Dining Room on many occasions. He must have exaggerated, thought Simon.

"I hope I find you in rude health, Mr. Kerslake," said Miss Norse, not looking up from her typing. Simon choked back a laugh.

"Very rude, thank you," he said, wondering how many tragic stories or tales of lost opportunities Miss Norse had had to listen to over the years. She stopped suddenly and looked at her note pad.

"I should have mentioned it to you before, Mr. Kerslake, a Mr. Nethercote rang."

"Thank you, I've spoken to him already."

Simon was leafing through an out-of-date copy of *Punch* when the Chief Whip strode in.

"I can spare you one minute, Simon, one and a half if you are going to resign," he said, laughing, and marched off toward his office. As Simon followed him down the corridor the phone by Miss Norse's side rang. "It's for you, Mr. Kerslake," she shouted to their retreating backs.

Simon turned and said, "Can you take the number?"

"He says it's urgent."

Simon stopped, hesitating. "With you in a moment," he said to the Chief Whip, who disappeared into his office. Simon walked back and took the phone from Miss Norse's outstretched hand.

"Simon Kerslake here. Who is it?"

"It's Ronnie."

"Ronnie," said Simon flatly.

"I've just had a call from Morgan Grenfell. One of their clients has made an offer of one pound twenty-five a share for the company and they're willing to take over the current liabilities."

Simon was trying to do the sums in his head.

"Don't bother working it out," Ronnie said. "At one pound twenty-five your shares would be worth £75,000."

"It won't be enough," said Simon, as he recalled his overdraft of £108,712, a figure etched in his memory.

"Don't panic. I've told them I won't settle for anything less than one pound fifty a share and it has to be within seven days, which will give them ample time to check the books. That would bring you in £90,000 but you would still be £18,000 down the Swanee, which you'll have to learn to live with. If you sell the wife as well as the second car you should just about survive."

Simon could tell by the way his friend was speaking that Ronnie already had a cigar between his lips.

"You're a genius."

"Not me—Morgan Grenfell. And I bet they'll make a handsome profit in the long run for their unnamed client who seemed to have all the inside information. If you're still on for lunch next Tuesday, don't bring your luncheon vouchers. It's on me."

Simon put the phone down and kissed Miss Norse on the forehead. She was completely taken aback by a situation for which she had no set reply. She remained silent as the Chief Whip put his head round the door. "An orgy in the Chief Whip's office? You'll be on page three of the *Sun* next, Miss Norse." Simon laughed. "I've got a crisis on over tonight's vote. The Government are reneging on our agreement for pairing, and I have to get a delegation back from Brussels in time for the ten o'clock division. Whatever it is, can it wait, Simon?"

"Yes, of course."

"Can you come to my office, Miss Norse—if I can drag you away from James Double-O-Seven Kerslake?"

Simon left and almost bounced to the nearest phone. First he called Elizabeth and then Archie Millburn at his office. Archie didn't sound all that surprised.

"Don't you think it might be wise for us to stop seeing each other?"

"Why?" said Raymond. "Palmerston had a mistress when he was seventy, and he still beat Disraeli come the election."

"Yes, but that was before the days of a dozen national newspapers *and* investigative journalism. Frankly it wouldn't take a Woodward or Bernstein more than a few hours to discover our little secret."

"We'll be all right. I've destroyed all the tapes."

"Do be serious."

"You're always telling me I'm far too serious."

"Well, I want you to be now. Very."

Raymond turned to face Kate. "I love you, Kate, and I know I always will. Why don't we stop this charade and get married?"

She sighed. "We've been over this a hundred times. I'll want to return to America eventually, and in any case I wouldn't make a very good Prime Minister's wife."

"Three American women have in the past," said Raymond sulkily.

"To hell with your historical precedents—and what's more, I hate Leeds."

"You've never been there."

"I don't need to if it's colder than London."

"Then you'll have to be satisfied with being my mistress." Raymond took Kate in his arms. "You know, I used to think being Prime Minister was worth every sacrifice, but now I'm not so sure."

"It's still worth the sacrifice," said Kate, "as you'll discover when you live at No. 10. Come on, or my dinner will be burned to a cinder."

"You haven't noticed these," said Raymond smugly, pointing down at his feet.

Kate stared at the fashionable new slip-ons.

"I never thought the day would come," she said. "Pity you're starting to go bald."

When Simon returned home his first words were "We'll survive."

"Thank God for that," Elizabeth said. "But what have you done about your resignation letter?"

"Archie said he would return it the day I became Prime Minister."

"If that's ever to be true I want you to promise me just one thing."

"Anything," said Simon.

"You'll never speak to Ronnie Nethercote again."

For a moment Simon hesitated before saying, "That's not completely fair, Elizabeth, because I haven't been totally straight with you from the beginning." He then sat his wife down on the sofa and told her the whole truth.

It was Elizabeth's turn to remain silent.

"Oh, hell," she said, looking up at Simon. "I do hope Ronnie can forgive me."

"What are you talking about?"

"I phoned him back soon after you had left for the Commons and I spent at least ten minutes telling him why he was the biggest two-faced bastard I'd ever come across, and I didn't want to hear from him again in my life."

It was Simon's turn to collapse on to the sofa. "How did he respond?" he asked anxiously. Elizabeth faced her husband. "That's the strange thing, he didn't even protest. He just apologized."

"Do you think she will ever speak again?"

"God knows, I hope so," said his father, staring at the picture of his grandchild on the mantelpiece. "She's still young enough to have another child."

Andrew shook his head. "No, that's out of the question. The doctor warned me a long time ago that could be dangerous."

He had returned home from hospital ten days after the accident. The first thing he and Louise did was to attend Robert's funeral. With Andrew on crutches, Sir Duncan had to support Louise during the short service. As soon as the burial was over Andrew took his wife back to Cheyne Walk and put her to bed, before returning downstairs to join his parents.

Andrew's mother bowed her head. "Whatever happens, you must move from this place as soon as possible. Every time Louise looks out of that kitchen window she'll relive the tragedy."

"I hadn't thought of that," said Andrew. "I'll start looking for a new house immediately."

"And what do you plan to do about the Prime Minister's offer?" inquired Sir Duncan.

"I haven't finally made up my mind," he said sharply. "He's given me until Monday to come to a decision."

"You must take it, Andrew. If you don't your political career will be finished. You can't sit at home and mourn Robert's death for the rest of your life."

Andrew looked up at his father. "No goal, Dad, no goal," he murmured and left them to go and sit with Louise in the bedroom. Her eyes were open but there was no expression on her face. Little white hairs had appeared at either side of her head that he had not noticed the week before. "Feeling any better, my darling?" he asked.

There was still no reply.

He undressed and climbed into bed beside her, holding her close, but she did not respond. She felt detached and distant. He watched his tears fall on her shoulder and run down on to the pillow. He fell asleep and woke again at three in the morning. No one had closed the curtains and the moon shone in through the windows, lighting the room. He looked at his wife. She had not moved.

Charles paced up and down the room angrily.

"Give me the figures again."

"Nethercote has accepted a bid of £7,500,000, which works out at one pound fifty a share," said Clive Reynolds.

Charles stopped at his desk and scribbled the figures down on a piece of paper. £90,000, leaving a shortfall of only £18,000. It wouldn't be enough. "Damn," he said.

"I agree," said Reynolds, "I always thought we were premature to lose our position in the company in the first place."

"An opinion you will not voice outside this room," said Charles.

Clive Reynolds did not reply.

"What's happened to Nethercote himself?" asked Charles, searching for any scrap of information he could find about Simon Kerslake.

"I'm told he's starting up again in a smaller way. Morgan Grenfell were delighted by the deal and the manner in which he handled the company during the takeover. I must say we let it fall into their laps."

"Can we get any stock in the new company?" asked Charles, ignoring his comment.

"I doubt it. It's only capitalized at one million although Morgan Grenfell are giving Nethercote a large overdraft facility as part of the deal."

"Then all that remains necessary is to see the matter is never referred to again."

Andrew spent the weekend reading over the letters of condolence sent to him and Louise. There were over a thousand, many from people he didn't even know. He selected a few to take into the bedroom and read to Louise; not that he was sure she could even hear him. The doctor had told him not to disturb her unless it was really necessary. After such a severe shock she was now suffering from acute depression and must be nursed slowly back to health. Louise had walked a few paces the previous day but needed to rest today, the doctor explained to him.

He sat by the side of their bed, and quietly read the letters from the Prime Minister, from a contrite Jock McPherson, from Simon Kerslake, from Raymond Gould, and from Mrs. Bloxham. There was no sign that Louise had taken in anything he had said.

"What shall I do about the PM's offer?" he asked. "Shall I accept it?"

She made no response of any kind.

"He's asked me to be the Minister of State for Defense, but I need to know how you would feel." After sitting with her for a few more minutes and eliciting no response he left her to rest.

Each night he slept with her and tried to infuse her with his love, but he only felt more alone.

On the Monday morning he called his father and told him he had decided to turn down the Prime Minister's offer. He couldn't leave Louise alone for long periods while she was still in this state.

Andrew returned to the bedroom and sat by her side.

He said in a whisper, as if to himself, "Should I have taken the job?"

Louise gave such a slight nod that Andrew nearly missed it but her fingers were moving. He placed his hand between her fingers and palm and she squeezed gently and repeated the nod, then fell asleep.

Andrew phoned the Prime Minister.

*   *   *

Raymond dug deeper into the red box.

"You enjoying yourself, Carrot Top?"

"It's fascinating," said Raymond. "Do you know—"

"No, I don't. You haven't spoken to me in the last three hours, and when you do it's to tell me how you spend the day with your new mistress."

"My new mistress?"

"The Secretary of State for Trade."

"Oh, him."

"Yes, him."

"What sort of day did you have at the bank?" asked Raymond, not looking up from his papers.

"I had a most fascinating day," replied Kate.

"Why, what happened?"

"One of our customers required a loan," said Kate.

"A loan," repeated Raymond, still concentrating on the file in front of him. "How much?"

" 'How much do you want?' I said. 'How much have you got?' they asked. 'Four hundred and seventeen billion at the last count,' I told them. 'That will do fine to start with,' they said. 'Sign here,' I said. But I couldn't close the deal because the lady concerned was only in possession of a £50 banking card."

Raymond burst out laughing and slammed down the lid of the red box. "Do you know why I love you?"

"My taste in men's clothes?" suggested Kate.

"No, no. Just your taste in men."

"I always thought that mistresses were supposed to get fur coats, trips to the Bahamas, the odd solitaire diamond, yet all I ever get is to share you with your red box."

Raymond opened the box once more, took out a small package, and handed it to Kate.

"What's this?"

"Why don't you open it and find out?"

Kate slipped off the purple Asprey paper and found inside an exquisitely made miniature, a solid gold replica of a red box on a gold chain. The neat lettering on the side of the lid read, "For Your Eyes Only."

"Although they don't announce the birthdays of ministers' mistresses in the *Sunday Times*, I can still remember the day we met."

Andrew made a bid for the house in Pelham Crescent the day he was shown over it, and Louise's mother came down to London immediately to organize the move.

"Let's hope this does the trick," she said.

Andrew prayed for nothing more. The move from Cheyne Walk took about a fortnight, and Louise could still walk only a few paces before she had to sit down. Louise's mother rarely left the house and Andrew began to feel guilty about how much he was enjoying his new job at the Ministry of Defense. Each night and then again in the morning he would try a few words to Louise. She nodded occasionally, touched him once in a while and even began writing notes to him, but never spoke and never cried. The doctor became even more pessimistic. "The crucial time has passed," he explained.

Andrew would sit with her for hours while he worked through the red boxes. Harrier jump jets for the RAF, Polaris missiles for the Royal Navy, Chieftain tanks for the Army, what should Labour's attitude be to Trident when Polaris was phased out? Should we allow Cruise to be based on British soil? There was so much to learn before he could face the civil servants on their own ground or the members from the dispatch box. As the months passed Andrew was always asking questions; a year had gone by and he was beginning to know some of the answers.

He looked up at his wife once again. She was gazing at the portrait of Robert on the mantelpiece.

On the anniversary of his son's sixth birthday Andrew stayed at Pelham Crescent all day with Louise. For the first time a tear lodged in her eye. As he held her, he kept remembering the lorry. He could see it so clearly now as if in slow motion. If only the phone hadn't gone, if only the gate had been closed, if only he had turned earlier, if only he had run a little faster. "No goal, Dad, no goal."

If only he had scored that goal.

CHAPTER
TWENTY-ONE

RAYMOND ENTERED A Washington ablaze with red, white, and blue as the Americans prepared for their bicentennial. He was among the three ministers chosen to represent the United Kingdom when they presented a copy of Magna Carta to the United States Congress. He was making his first trip to America on Concorde only a few weeks after its inaugural flight. Tom Carson had complained to the House about the expense of the trip but his words had fallen upon a silent Chamber.

As the plane taxied to a halt at Dulles airport three limousines drew up. The three ministers were given a car each and motorcycle outriders rushed them to the grounds of the British Embassy on Massachusetts Avenue in less than thirty minutes.

Raymond had an immediate love affair with America, perhaps because it reminded him so much of Kate with its bubbling enthusiasm, its spirit, and sense of perpetual innovation. During the ten-day visit he managed to forge several useful contacts in the Senate and House, and over the weekend became an unrepentant sightseer of the beautiful Virginia countryside. He concentrated on getting to know those contemporaries whom he felt would be on the American political stage for the next twenty years, while his more senior colleagues dealt with President Ford and his immediate entourage.

Raymond enjoyed starting each day with the *Washington Post* and the *New York Times*. He quickly learned how to reject those sections that seemed full of endless advertisements for non-essentials he couldn't believe anyone really bought. Once he had finished reading both papers he found he had to wash his hands as they were always black with newsprint. The one occasion he kept the Outlook section of the *Washington Post* was when it did profiles on the three ministers from London. He tucked the paper away as he wanted to show Kate the paragraph that read: "The two Secretaries of State are interesting men at the end of their careers, but it is Raymond Gould we should keep our eyes on because he has the look of a future Prime Minister."

As Raymond flew out of Washington on his way back to London he presumed, like any lover, that the affair with America could be continued whenever he chose to return.

Simon was in Manchester as a guest of the Business School when he received Elizabeth's message to call her. It was most unusual for Elizabeth to phone in the middle of the day and Simon assumed the worst: something must have happened to the children. The Principal of the Business School accompanied him to his private office, then left him alone.

Dr. Kerslake was not at the hospital, he was told, which made him even more anxious. He dialed the Beaufort Street number.

Elizabeth picked up the receiver so quickly that she must have been sitting by the phone waiting for him to call.

"I've been sacked," she said.

"What?" said Simon, unable to comprehend.

"I've been made redundant—isn't that the modern term meant to lessen the blow? The hospital governors have been instructed by the Department of Health and Social Security to make cutbacks and three of us in gynecology have lost our jobs. I go at the end of the month."

"Darling, I'm sorry," he said, knowing how inadequate his words must have sounded.

"I didn't mean to bother you, but I just wanted someone to talk to," she said. "Everyone else is allowed to complain to their MP, so I thought it was my turn."

"Normally what I do in these circumstances is to put the blame on the Labour party." Simon was relieved to hear Elizabeth laugh.

"Thanks for ringing me back so quickly, darling. See you tomorrow," she said and put the phone down.

Simon returned to his group and explained that he had to leave for London immediately. He took a taxi to the airport and caught the next shuttle to Heathrow. He was back at Beaufort Street within three hours.

"I didn't mean you to come home," Elizabeth said contritely when she saw him on the doorstep.

"I've come back to celebrate," Simon said. "Let's open the bottle of champagne that Ronnie gave us when he closed the deal with Morgan Grenfell."

"Why?"

"Because Ronnie taught me one thing. You should always celebrate disasters, not successes."

Simon hung up his coat and went off in search of the champagne. When he returned with the bottle and two glasses Elizabeth asked, "What's your overdraft looking like nowadays?"

"Down to £16,000, give or take a pound."

"Well, that's another problem then, I won't be giving any pounds in the future, only taking."

"Don't be silly. Someone will snap you up," he said, embracing her.

"It won't be quite that easy," said Elizabeth.

"Why not?" asked Simon, trying to sound cheerful.

"Because I had already been warned about whether I wanted to be a politician's wife or a doctor."

Simon was stunned. "I had no idea," he said. "I'm so sorry."

"It was my choice, darling, but I will have to make one or

two decisions if I want to remain in medicine, especially if you're going to become a minister."

Simon remained silent: he had always wanted Elizabeth to make this decision herself and he was determined not to try to influence her.

"If only we weren't so short of money."

"Don't worry about the money," said Simon.

"I do worry, but it may just be an excuse because I worry more about becoming bored when the children have grown up. I just wasn't cut out to be a politician's wife," she added. "You should have married someone like Fiona Seymour and you'd be Prime Minister by now."

"If that's the only way I can be sure of getting the job I'll stick with you," said Simon, taking Elizabeth in his arms. Simon couldn't help thinking of all the support his wife had given him during their marriage and even more so since his financial crisis. He knew exactly what his wife must do.

"You mustn't be allowed to give up being a doctor," he said. "It's every bit as important as wanting to be a minister. Shall I have a word with Gerry Vaughan? As Shadow spokesman for Health he might—"

"Certainly not, Simon. If I am to get another job, it'll be without anyone doing you or me a favor."

Louise was now coping on her own, and had almost returned to a normal life except she still couldn't speak. She seemed to be self-sufficient within her own world and the doctor agreed that she no longer needed a full-time nurse.

The day the nurse left Andrew decided to take Louise off for a week's holiday abroad. He wanted to return to the South of France and the Colombe d'Or, but the specialist had advised against it, explaining that any past association might trigger off a memory that in itself could cause a further relapse.

"Witch doctors' mumbo jumbo," Andrew complained but nevertheless took her to Venice, not Colombe d'Or. Once there, he was delighted by the interest Louise showed in the beautiful and ancient city. Her eyes lit up at the sight of Torcello and she appeared to revel in the trip on a gondola down the twisting waterways past irreplaceable Italian architecture. Again and again she squeezed his hand. As they sat on a piazza for an evening drink, she inclined her head and listened to a quintet playing on St. Mark's Square. Andrew was confident that she could now hear everything he told her. The night before they flew back to England he woke to find her reading James Morris's *Venice* which he had left by his side of the bed. It was the first time she had opened a book since the accident. When he smiled at her she grinned back. He laughed, wanting to hear her laugh.

Andrew returned to the Ministry of Defense on Monday. On his desk there was a general directive from the Chancellor of the Exchequer, requiring the budget estimates for all the big-spending Departments of State. Andrew fought hard to keep the Polaris missile after being convinced by the Joint Chiefs of its strategic importance to the nation's defense. He was, however, continually reminded by his colleagues in the House that it was party policy to rid themselves of "the warmongers' toy."

When the Secretary of State returned from Cabinet he told Andrew, "We've had our way: the Cabinet were impressed by the case. But I can promise you one thing—you won't be the golden boy at this year's party conference."

"It will make a change for them even to notice me," replied Andrew.

He breathed a sigh of relief while the Joint Chiefs were delighted, but a week later he lost—by default—the same argument with his own General Purposes Committee in Edinburgh. In his absence, they passed a resolution deploring the retention of the Polaris missile and demanded that all the ministers involved should reconsider their decision. They stopped short of naming Andrew, but everyone knew whose scalp they were after. His case was not helped by Tom Carson making yet another inflammatory speech in the House, claiming that Andrew had been browbeaten by the Joint Chiefs and was nothing more than a Polaris puppet.

Andrew's trips to Edinburgh had become less frequent over

the past year because of his commitments to Louise and the Defense Department. During the year three members of his General Management Committee had been replaced with a new group calling themselves "Militant Tendency" led by Frank Boyle. It wasn't just Edinburgh Carlton that was facing the problem of a left-wing insurgence—as Andrew learned from colleague after colleague who was beginning to work out why the left were pushing a resolution at the party conference proposing that members should be re-selected for each election. Some of his more right-wing colleagues had already been replaced, and it didn't take a Wrangler to work out that once a majority of the Trotskyites had secured places on his Management Committee Andrew could be removed at their whim, whatever his past experience or record.

Whenever Andrew was in Edinburgh the local people continually assured him of their support and their confidence in him, but he could not forget, despite their avowals, that it would still take only a handful of votes to remove him. Andrew feared what the outcome would be if many other members were facing the same problem as he faced in Edinburgh.

"Dad, can I have a new cricket bat, please?"

"What's wrong with the old one?" asked Simon, as they came out of the house.

"It's too small," he said, waving it around as if it was an extension to his arm.

"It will have to do, I'm afraid."

"But Martin Henderson's dad has given him a new bat to start the season."

"I'm sorry, Peter, the truth is that Martin's father is far better off than I am."

"I'll tell you one thing," said Peter with feeling. "I'm sure not going to be an MP when I grow up." Simon smiled as his son removed an old cricket ball from his trouser pocket and tossed it over to his father. "Anyway, I bet you can't get me out even though I've only got a small bat."

"Don't forget we still have the junior size stumps left over from last year," said Simon, "so it will be just as hard to hit them."

"Stop making excuses, Dad. Just admit you're past it."

Simon burst out laughing. "We'll see," he said, with more bravado than conviction. Simon always enjoyed a few overs in the garden against his elder son although at the age of thirteen Peter was already able to play his best deliveries with a confidence that was beginning to look ominous.

It was several overs before Simon removed Peter's middle stump and took his turn at the crease.

Michael ran out of the house to join them in the field and Simon couldn't help noticing that he was wearing a pair of jeans that were far too short and had once belonged to Peter.

"Get behind the wicket, nipper," shouted Peter at his eleven-year-old brother. "Because that's where most of the balls will be going." Michael happily obeyed without comment.

A colleague in the House had recently warned Simon that by fourteen they began to beat you and by sixteen they hoped not to show they weren't trying their hardest any longer.

Simon gritted his teeth as he watched his elder son's fastest ball safely on to the middle of the bat. The way he was going Peter wouldn't have to wait much longer before he could clean bowl him.

He managed to keep his wicket intact for a further five minutes before he was rescued by Elizabeth who came out to tell them that supper was ready.

"What, hamburgers and chips again?" said Michael as his mother put a plate in front of him.

"You're lucky to get anything," Elizabeth snapped back.

Simon cursed again at the damage his own selfish greed had brought upon his family, and marveled at how little they all complained. He said nothing, only too aware that the previous day Elizabeth had completed her last week at the hospital and was already missing St. Mary's.

"How did you all get on?" she asked cheerily.

"I'll survive," said Simon, still thinking about his overdraft.

Once the Chancellor had presented his minibudget, in November 1976, the long process of the Finance Bill, confirming all the new measures proposed, fully occupied the House. Charles, although not a member of the front-bench finance team, regularly took the lead among back-benchers on clauses on which he had specialist knowledge.

He and Clive Reynolds studied the new Finance Bill meticulously and between them picked out the seven clauses that would have an adverse effect on banking.

Reynolds guided Charles through each clause, suggesting changes, rewording, and on some occasions presenting an argument for deleting whole sections of the bill. Charles learned quickly and was soon adding his own ideas; one or two even made Clive Reynolds reconsider. After Charles had put forward amendments to the House on three of the clauses both front benches became respectfully attentive whenever he rose to present a case. One morning, after the Government's defeat on a clause relating to banking loans, he received a note of congratulation from Margaret Thatcher.

The clause Charles most wanted to see removed from the bill concerned a client's right to privacy when dealing with a merchant bank. The Shadow Chancellor was aware of Charles's specialized knowledge on this subject and invited him to oppose clause 110 from the front bench. Charles realized that if he could defeat the Government on this clause he might be invited to join the Shadow finance team in the runup to the general election.

Judging by the chairman of Ways and Means' selection of amendments the Whips estimated that clause 110 on banking privacy would be reached some time on Thursday afternoon.

On Thursday morning Charles rehearsed his arguments thoroughly with Clive Reynolds, who only had one or two minor amendments to add before Charles set off for the House. When he arrived at the Commons there was a note on the message board asking him to phone the Shadow Chancellor urgently.

"The Government are going to accept a Liberal amendment tabled late last night," the Shadow Chancellor told him.

"Why?" said Charles.

"Minimum change is what they're really after, but it gets them off the hook and at the same time keeps the Liberal vote intact. In essence nothing of substance has changed, but you'll need to study the wording carefully. Can I leave you to handle the problem?"

"Certainly," said Charles, pleased with the responsibility with which they were now entrusting him.

He walked down the long corridor to the vote office and picked up the sheet with clause 110 on it and the proposed Liberal amendment. He read them both through half a dozen times before he started to make notes. Parliamentary counsel, with their usual expertise, had produced an ingenious amendment. Charles ducked into a nearby phone booth and rang Clive Reynolds at the bank. Charles dictated the amendment over the phone to him and then remained silent while Reynolds considered its implications.

"Clever bunch of sharpies. It's a cosmetic job, but it won't change the power it invests in the Government one iota. Were you thinking of returning to the bank? That would give me time to work on it."

"No," said Charles. "Are you free for lunch?"

Clive Reynolds checked his diary: a Belgian banker would be lunching in the boardroom but his colleagues could handle that. "Yes, I'm free."

"Good," said Charles. "Why don't you join me at White's around one o'clock?"

"Thank you," said Reynolds. "By then I should have had enough time to come up with some credible alternatives."

Charles spent the rest of the morning rewriting his speech which he hoped would counter the Liberal argument and make them reconsider their position. If it met with Reynolds's imprimatur the day could still be his. He read through the clause once more, convinced he had found a way through the loophole the civil servants couldn't block. He placed his speech and the amended clause in his inside pocket and went down to the Members' Entrance and jumped into a waiting taxi.

As the cab drove up St. James's Charles thought he saw his wife coming down the opposite side of the road. He pushed down the window to be sure but she had disappeared into Prunier's. He wondered with which of her girlfriends she was lunching.

The cab traveled on up St. James's and came to a halt outside White's. Charles found he was a few minutes early so he decided to walk down to Prunier's and ask Fiona if she would like to come to the House after lunch and hear him oppose the clause. Reaching the restaurant he glanced through the pane-glass window. He froze on the spot. Fiona was chatting at the bar with a man whose back was to Charles but he thought he recognized his profile although he couldn't be certain. He noticed that his wife was wearing a dress he had never seen before. He didn't move as he watched a waiter bow, then guide the pair toward a corner table where they were conveniently out of sight. Charles's first instinct was to march straight in and confront them; but he remained outside. For what seemed an interminable time he stood alone, uncertain what to do next. Finally he crossed back over St. James's Street and stood in the doorway of the Economist building going over several plans. In the end he decided to do nothing but wait. He stood there so cold and so incensed that he did not consider returning for his lunch appointment with Clive Reynolds a few hundred yards up the road.

An hour and twenty minutes later the man came out of Prunier's alone and headed up St. James's. Charles felt a sense of relief until he saw him turn into St. James's Place. He checked his watch: Reynolds would have left by now but he would still be well in time for clause number 110. A few minutes later Fiona stepped out of the restaurant and followed in the man's footsteps. Charles crossed the road, causing a cab to swerve while another motorist slammed on her brakes. He didn't notice. He shadowed his wife, careful to keep a safe dis tance. When she reached the far end of the passage he watched Fiona enter the Stafford Hotel. Once she was through the swing doors Fiona stepped into an empty lift.

Charles came up to the swing doors and stared at the little numbers above the lift, watching them light up in succession until they stopped at four.

Charles marched through the swing doors and up to the reception desk.

"Can I help you, sir?" the hall porter asked.

"Er—is the dining room in this hotel on the fourth floor?" asked Charles.

"No, sir," replied the hall porter, surprised. "The dining room is on the ground floor to your left"—he indicated the way with a sweep of his hand—"there are only bedrooms on the fourth floor."

"Thank you," said Charles and marched back outside.

He returned slowly to the Economist building, incensed, where he waited for nearly two hours pacing up and down St. James's before the man emerged from the Stafford Hotel; Alexander Dalglish hailed a taxi and disappeared in the direction of Piccadilly.

Fiona left the hotel about twenty minutes later, and took the path through to the park before setting off toward Eaton Square. On three occasions Charles had to fall back to be certain Fiona didn't spot him; once he was so close he thought he saw a smile of satisfaction come over her face.

He had followed his wife most of the way across St. James's Park when he suddenly remembered. He checked his watch, then dashed back to the roadside, hailed a taxi, and shouted, "The House of Commons, as fast as you can." The cabbie took seven minutes and Charles passed him two pound notes before running up the steps into the Members' Lobby and through to the Chamber out of breath. He stopped by the Serjeant-at-Arms's chair.

From the table where he sat during Committee of the whole House, the Mace lowered on its supports in front of the table, the chairman of Ways and Means faced a packed House. He read from the division list.

"The Ayes to the right 294.
The Noes to the left 293.
The Ayes have it, the Ayes have it."

The Government benches cheered and the Conservatives looked distinctly glum. "What clause were they debating?" a still out of breath Charles asked the Serjeant-at-Arms.

"Clause 110, Mr. Seymour."

BOOK FOUR

1977–1989
THE CABINET

CHAPTER
TWENTY-TWO

RAYMOND'S SECOND TRIP to the States was at the behest of the Secretary of State for Trade: he was asked to present the country's export and import assessment to the International Monetary Fund, following up a loan granted to Britain the previous November. His civil servants went over the prepared speech with him again and again, emphasizing to their minister the responsibility that had been placed on his shoulders. Even the Governor of the Bank of England's private office had been consulted.

"A chance to impress a few people beyond the boundaries of Leeds," Kate assured him.

Raymond's speech was scheduled for the Wednesday morning. He flew into Washington on the Sunday and spent Monday and Tuesday listening to the problems of other nations' trade ministers while trying to get used to the dreadful earphones and the female interpreter.

The conference was attended by most of the leading industrial nations and the British Ambassador, Sir Peter Ramsbotham, told Raymond over dinner at the Embassy that this was a real chance to convince the hard-headed international bankers that Britain cared about economic realities and was still worth their financial backing.

Raymond soon realized that convincing such a gathering required a very different technique from shouting from a soap box on a street corner in Leeds or even addressing the House from the dispatch box. He was glad he had not been scheduled to present his case on the opening day. Over leisurely lunches he re-established his existing contacts in Congress and made some new ones.

The night before he was to deliver his speech Raymond hardly slept. He continued to rehearse each crucial phrase and repeated the salient points that needed to be emphasized until he almost knew them by heart. At three o'clock in the morning he dropped his speech on the floor beside his bed and phoned Kate to have a chat before she went to work.

"I'd enjoy hearing your speech at the conference," she told him. "Although I don't suppose it would be much different from the thirty times I've listened to it in the bedroom."

Once he had said good-bye to Kate he fell into a deep sleep. He woke early that morning and went over the speech one last time before leaving for the conference center.

All the homework and preparation proved worthwhile. By the time he turned the last page Raymond couldn't be certain how convincing his case had been, but he knew it was the best speech he had ever delivered. When he looked up the smiles all around the oval table assured him that his contribution had been well received. As the ambassador pointed out to him as he rose to leave, any signs of emotion at these gatherings were almost unknown. He felt confident that the IMF loan would be renewed.

There followed two further speeches before they broke for lunch. At the end of the afternoon session Raymond walked out into the clear Washington air and decided to make his way back to the Embassy on foot. He was exhilarated by the experience of dominating an international conference and picked up an evening paper: an article covering the conference suggested that Raymond would be Britain's next Labor Chancellor. He smiled at the spelling. Just the closing day to

go, followed by the official banquet and he would be back home by the weekend.

When he reached the Embassy the guard had to double-check: they weren't used to ministers arriving on foot and without a bodyguard. Raymond was allowed to proceed down the tree-lined drive toward the massive Lutyens building. He looked up to see the British flag was flying at half mast and wondered which distinguished American had died.

"Who has died?" he asked the tail-coated butler who opened the door for him.

"The Foreign Secretary, sir."

"Anthony Crosland? I knew he had gone into hospital, but . . ." said Raymond almost to himself. He hurried into the Embassy to find it abuzz with telexes and coded messages. Raymond sat alone in his private sitting room for several hours and later, to the horror of the security staff, slipped out for a quiet dinner at the Mayflower Hotel with Senator Hart.

Raymond returned to the conference table at nine o'clock the next morning to listen to the French Minister of Commerce put his case for renewed funds. He was savoring the thought of the official banquet at the White House to be held that evening when he was tapped on the shoulder by Sir Peter Ramsbotham, who indicated by touching his lips with his forefinger and pointing that they must have a word in private.

"The Prime Minister wants you to return on the midmorning Concorde," said Sir Peter. "It leaves in an hour. On arrival in Britain you're to go straight to Downing Street."

"What's this all about?"

"I have no idea, that was the only instruction I received from No. 10," confided the ambassador.

Raymond returned to the conference table and made his apologies to the chairman, left the room, and was driven immediately to the waiting plane. "Your bags will follow, sir," he was assured.

He was back on English soil three hours and forty-one minutes later, a little after seven-thirty. The purser ensured that he was the first to disembark. A car waiting by the side of the plane whisked him to Downing Street. He arrived just as the Prime Minister was going to dinner, accompanied by an elderly African statesman who was waving his trademark fan back and forth.

"Welcome home, Ray," said the Prime Minister, leaving the African leader. "I'd ask you to join us, but as you can see I'm entertaining the President of Malawi. Let's have a word in my study."

Once Raymond had settled into a chair Mr. Callaghan wasted no time.

"Because of Tony's tragic death I have had to make a few changes which will include moving the Secretary of State for Trade. I was hoping you would be willing to take over from him."

Raymond sat up straighter. "I should be honored, Prime Minister."

"Good. You've earned your promotion, Raymond. I also hear you did us proud in America, very proud."

"Thank you."

"You'll be appointed to the Privy Council immediately and your first Cabinet meeting will be at ten o'clock tomorrow. Now, if you'll excuse me, I must catch up with Dr. Banda."

Raymond was left standing in the hall.

He asked his driver to take him back to the flat. All he wanted to do was to tell Kate the news. When he arrived the flat was empty: then he remembered she wasn't expecting him back until the next day. He phoned her home but after twenty continuous rings he resigned himself to the fact that she was out. "Damn," he said out loud, and after pacing around phoned Joyce to let her know the news. Once again there was no reply.

He went into the kitchen and checked to see what was in the fridge: a piece of curled-up bacon, some half-eaten Brie, three eggs. He couldn't help thinking about the banquet he was missing at the White House.

The Right Honorable Raymond Gould QC, MP, Her Britannic Majesty's Principal Secretary of State for Trade, sat on the kitchen stool, opened a tin of baked beans, and devoured them with a fork.

*   *   *

Charles closed the file. It had taken him a month to gather all the proof he needed. Albert Cruddick, the private investigator Charles had selected from the Yellow Pages, had been expensive but discreet. Dates, times, places were all fully chronicled. The only name was that of Alexander Dalglish, the same rendezvous, lunch at Prunier's followed by the Stafford Hotel. They hadn't stretched Mr. Cruddick's imagination but at least the detective had spared Charles the necessity of standing in the entrance of the Economist building once, sometimes twice a week for hours on end.

Somehow he had managed to get through that month without giving himself away. He had also made his own notes of the dates and times Fiona claimed she was going to be in the constituency. He had then called his agent in Sussex Downs and, after veiled questioning, elicited answers that corroborated Mr. Cruddick's findings.

Charles saw as little of Fiona as possible during this time, explaining that the Finance Bill was occupying his every moment. His lie had at least a semblance of credibility for he had worked tirelessly on the remaining clauses left for debate, and by the time the watered-down bill had become law he had just about recovered from the disaster of the Government's successful retention of clause 110.

Charles placed the file on the table by the side of his chair and waited patiently for the call. He knew exactly where she was at that moment and just the thought of it made him sick to his stomach. The phone rang.

"The subject left five minutes ago," said a voice.

"Thank you," said Charles and replaced the receiver. He knew it would take her about twenty minutes to reach home.

"Why do you think she walks home instead of taking a taxi?" he had once asked Mr. Cruddick.

"Gets rid of any smells," Mr. Cruddick had replied quite matter-of-factly.

Charles shuddered. "And what about him? What does he

do?" He never could refer to him as Alexander, or even Dalglish, or as anything but "him."

"He goes to the Lansdowne Club, swims ten lengths or plays a game of squash before returning home. Swimming and squash both solve the problem," Mr. Cruddick explained cheerily.

The key turned in the lock. Charles braced himself and picked up the file. Fiona came straight into the drawing room and was visibly shaken to discover her husband sitting in an armchair with a small suitcase by his side.

She recovered quickly, walked over, and kissed him on the cheek. "What brings you home so early, darling? The Socialists taken the day off?" She laughed nervously at her joke.

"This," he said, standing up and holding the file out to her.

She took off her coat and dropped it over the sofa. Then she opened the buff folder and started to read. He watched her carefully. First the color drained from her cheeks, then her legs gave way and she collapsed onto the sofa. Finally she started to sob.

"It's not true, none of it," she protested.

"You know very well that every detail is accurate."

"Charles, it's you I love, I don't care about him, you must believe that."

"I believe nothing of the sort," said Charles. "You're no longer someone I could live with."

"Live with? I've been living on my own since the day you entered Parliament."

"Perhaps I might have come home more often if you had showed some interest in starting a family."

"And do you imagine I am to blame for that inadequacy?" she said.

Charles ignored the innuendo and continued. "In a few moments I am going to my club where I shall spend the night. I expect you to be out of this house within seven days. When I return I want there to be no sign of you or any of your goods or chattels, to quote the original agreement."

"Where will I go?" she cried.

"You could try your lover first, but no doubt his wife might object. Failing that, you can camp down at your father's place."

"What if I refuse to go?" said Fiona, turning to defiance.

"Then I shall throw you out, as one should a whore, and cite Alexander Dalglish in a very messy divorce case."

"Give me another chance. I'll never look at him again," begged Fiona, starting to cry once more.

"I seem to remember your telling me that once before, and indeed I did give you another chance. The results have been all too plain to see." He pointed to the file where it had fallen to the floor.

Fiona stopped weeping when she realized that Charles remained unmoved.

"I shall not see you again. We shall be separated for at least two years, when we will carry through as quiet a divorce as possible in the circumstances. If you cause me a moment of embarrassment I shall drag you both through the mire. Believe me."

"You'll regret your decision, Charles. I promise you. I'll not be pushed aside quite that easily."

"They've done *what?*" said Joyce.

"Two Communists have put their names forward for election to the General Purposes Committee," repeated Fred Padgett.

"Over my dead body." Joyce's voice was unusually sharp.

"I thought that would be your attitude," said Fred.

Joyce searched for the pencil and paper that were normally on the table by the phone.

"When's the meeting?" she asked.

"Next Thursday."

"Have we got reliable people to stand against them?"

"Of course," said Fred. "Councillor Reg Illingworth and Jenny Simpkins from the Co-op."

"They're both sensible enough but between them they couldn't knock the skin off a rice pudding."

"Shall I phone Raymond at the House and get him to come up for the meeting?"

"No," said Joyce. "He's got enough to worry about now that he's in the Cabinet without piling up trouble for him in Leeds. Leave it to me."

She replaced the receiver and sat down to compose her thoughts. A few minutes later she went over to her desk and rummaged about for the full list of the G.P. Committee. She checked the sixteen names carefully, realizing that if two Communists were to get themselves elected this time within five years they could control the committee—and then even remove Raymond. She knew how these people worked. With any luck, if they got bloody noses now they might slink off to another constituency.

She checked the sixteen names once more before putting on a pair of sensible walking shoes. During the next four days she visited several homes in the area. "I was just passing," she explained to nine of the wives who had husbands on the committee. The four men who never listened to a word their wives said were visited by Joyce after work. The three who had never cared for Raymond were left well alone.

By Thursday afternoon thirteen people knew only too well what was expected of them. Joyce sat alone hoping he would call that evening. She cooked herself a Lancashire hotpot but only picked at it, then later fell asleep in front of the television when she tried to watch the final episode of *Roots*. The phone woke her at five past eleven.

"Raymond?"

"Hope I didn't wake you," said Fred.

"No, no," said Joyce, now impatient to learn the outcome of the meeting. "What happened?"

"Reg and Jenny walked it. Those two Communist bastards only managed three votes between them."

"Well done," said Joyce.

"I did nothing," said Fred, "except count the votes. Shall I tell Raymond what's been happening?"

"No," said Joyce. "No need to let him think we've had any trouble."

Joyce fell back into the chair by the phone, kicked off her walking shoes, and went back to sleep.

She knew she had to plan the whole operation so that her husband would never find out. She sat alone in the house considering the several alternative ways in which she could deceive him. After hours of unproductive thought the idea finally came in a flash. She went over the problems and repercussions again and again until she was convinced that nothing could go wrong. She leafed through the Yellow Pages and made an appointment for the following morning.

The saleslady helped her to try on several wigs, but only one was bearable.

"I think it makes Modom look most elegant, I must say."

She knew that it didn't—it made Modom look awful—but she hoped it would serve its purpose.

She then applied the eye makeup and lipstick she had acquired at Harrods, and pulled out from the back of her cupboard a floral dress she had never liked. She stood in front of the mirror and checked herself. Surely no one would recognize her in Sussex and she prayed that if he found out he would be forgiving.

She left and drove slowly toward the outskirts of London. How would she explain herself if she was caught? Would he remain understanding when he discovered the truth? When she reached the constituency she parked the car in a side road and walked up and down the high street. No one showed any sign of recognition which gave her the confidence to go through with it. And then she saw him.

She had hoped he'd be in the City that morning. She held her breath as he walked toward her. As he passed she said, "Good morning." He turned and smiled, replying with a casual "Good morning," as he might to any constituent. Her heartbeat returned to normal and she went back to find her car.

She drove off completely reassured she could now get away

with it. She went over once again what she was going to say, then all too suddenly she had arrived. She parked the car outside the house opposite, got out, and bravely walked up the path.

As Raymond stood outside the Cabinet room several of his colleagues came over to congratulate him. At exactly ten o'clock the Prime Minister walked in, bade everyone "Good morning," and took his place at the center of the oblong table, while the other twenty-one members of the Cabinet filed in behind him and took their places. The Leader of the House, Michael Foot, sat on his left, while the Foreign Secretary and Chancellor were placed opposite him. Raymond was directed to a seat at the end of the table between the Secretary of State for Wales and the Secretary of State for Education.

"I would like to start the meeting," said the Prime Minister, "by welcoming David Owen as Foreign Secretary and Raymond Gould as Secretary of State for Trade." The other nineteen Cabinet members murmured, "Hear, hear" in a discreetly conservative way. David Owen smiled slightly while Raymond could feel himself going red.

"The first item we must discuss in detail is the proposed pact with the Liberals . . ."

Raymond sat back and decided that today he would only listen.

Andrew sat in the small office and listened carefully to the specialist's opinion. Louise was restored to almost perfect health in every way except for her speech. She was reading regularly and had even begun to write short messages in reply to Andrew's questions. The specialist now felt that she needed some other outside interest to take her mind off Robert. Over a year had passed and she could still spend hours simply staring at his photograph.

"I managed to reach Dr. Kerslake at home," the specialist said, "and I must concur with her opinion that it would be unwise for your wife to contemplate another pregnancy. But Dr. Kerslake does accept my judgment that you should both consider adoption."

"I've already given the idea a lot of thought, even discussed it with my father," Andrew replied. "But both of us felt that Louise would never agree to it."

"It's a calculated risk in the circumstances," said the specialist. "We mustn't forget it's been a whole year. We know to our cost that Mrs. Fraser loves children, and if she is set against such a course she is now well capable of letting you know."

"If Louise shows any response I'd be only too willing to give it a try. But in the end it will all depend on her."

"Good. Find out how she feels," said the specialist, "and if you both decide to go ahead I'll arrange a meeting with the local authority." He rose from behind his desk. "I'm sure it won't be hard to find you a suitable child."

"If it were possible for him to come from a Scottish orphans' home, I would appreciate it."

The specialist nodded. "I'll be in touch with you as soon as I have any news."

When Charles returned home he knew at once Fiona had left. He felt an immediate relief. After a week at his club, he was glad the charade was over, a clean, irrevocable break. He strolled into the drawing room and stopped: something was wrong. It took him a few moments before he realized what she had done.

Fiona had removed every one of the family paintings.

No Wellington above the fireplace, no Victoria behind the sofa. Where the two Landseers and the Constable had hung there was nothing more than thin dusty outlines indicating the size of each picture she had removed. He walked to the library: the Van Dyck, the Murillo, and the two small Rembrandts were also missing. Charles ran down the hall. It couldn't be possible, he thought, as he threw open the dining room door. It was. He stared at the blank wall where only the previous week the Holbein portrait of the first Earl of Bridg-water had hung.

Charles scrabbled in the back of his pocket diary for the number and dialed it frantically. Mr. Cruddick listened to the story in silence.

"Remembering how sensitive you are about publicity, Mr. Seymour, there are two avenues of approach," he began in his normal level tone and sounding unperturbed. "You can grin and bear it, or the alternative is one I have used often in the past."

Because of the demands of his new job Raymond saw less of Kate and almost nothing of Joyce apart from his fortnightly visits to Leeds. He worked from eight in the morning until he fell asleep at night.

"And you love every minute of it," Kate reminded him whenever he complained. Raymond had also become aware of the subtle changes that had taken place in his life since he had become a member of the Cabinet, the way he was treated by other people, how quickly his slightest whim was granted, how flattery fell from almost every tongue. He began to enjoy the change in status although Kate reminded him that only the Queen could afford to get used to it.

At the Labour party conference that year he allowed his name to be put forward for a place on the National Executive. Although he failed to be elected he managed to finish ahead of several other Cabinet ministers and polled only a few votes less than Neil Kinnock, the darling of the constituency section.

Andrew Fraser, who now looked upon Raymond as some-one he could confide in, joined Raymond for what was becoming their traditional conference lunch together on the third day. Andrew told him of his distress at the party's continued drift to the left.

"If some of those resolutions on defense are passed my life will be made impossible," he said, trying to cut into a very tough steak.

"The hotheads always put up resolutions that are never allowed more than a token discussion."

"Token discussion be damned. Some of their mad ideas are beginning to gain credence which, translated, could become party policy."

"Any particular resolution worrying you?" asked Raymond.

"Yes, Tony Benn's latest proposal that members must be reselected before every election. His idea of democracy and accountability."

"Why should you fear that?"

"If your management committee is taken over by half a dozen Trots they can reverse a decision 50,000 voters have previously agreed on."

"You're overreacting, Andrew."

"Raymond, if we lose the next election I can see a split in the party that will be so great we may never recover."

"They've been saying that in the Labour party since the day it was founded."

"I hope you're right, but I fear times have changed," said Andrew. "Not so long ago it was you who envied me."

"That can change again." Raymond abandoned the steak, waved his hand, and asked the waitress to bring two large brandies.

Charles picked up the phone and dialed a number he had not needed to look up. The new young Portuguese maid answered.

"Is Lady Fiona at home?"

"Lady no home, sir."

"Do you know where she is?" asked Charles, speaking slowly and clearly.

"Go down to country, expect back six o'clock. Take message please?"

"No, thank you," said Charles. "I'll call this evening." He replaced the receiver.

As always the reliable Mr. Cruddick was proved right about

his wife's movements. Charles called him immediately. They agreed to meet as planned in twenty minutes.

He drove into the Boltons, parked on the far side of the road a few yards from his father-in-law's house, and settled down to wait.

A few minutes later a large anonymous pantechnicon van came round the corner and stopped outside No. 24. Mr. Cruddick jumped out from the driver's seat. He was dressed in long brown overalls and a flat cap. He was joined by a young assistant who unlocked the back of the van. Mr. Cruddick nodded to Charles before proceeding up the steps to the front door.

The Portuguese maid answered when he pressed the bell.

"We have come to collect the goods for Lady Seymour."

"No understand," said the maid.

Mr. Cruddick removed from an inside pocket a long typewritten letter on Lady Seymour's personal stationery. The Portuguese maid was unable to read the words of a letter her mistress had addressed to Hurlingham Croquet Club agreeing to be their Ladies' President, but she immediately recognized the letterhead and the signature. She nodded and opened the door wider. All Mr. Cruddick's carefully laid plans were falling into place.

Mr. Cruddick tipped his hat, the sign for Mr. Seymour to join them. Charles got out of the car cautiously, checking both ways before he crossed the road. He felt uncomfortable in brown overalls and hated the cap with which Mr. Cruddick had supplied him. It was a little small and Charles was acutely conscious how strange he must look but the Portuguese maid apparently didn't notice the incongruity between his aristocratic mien and the working overalls. It did not take long to discover the whereabouts of most of the pictures. Many were just stacked up in the hall, and only one or two had already been hung.

Forty minutes later the three men had located and loaded into the van all but one of them. The Holbein of the first Earl of Bridgwater was nowhere to be found.

"We ought to be on our way," suggested Mr. Cruddick a little nervously, but Charles refused to give up the search. For another thirty-five minutes Mr. Cruddick sat tapping the wheel of the van before Charles finally conceded that the painting must have been taken elsewhere. Mr. Cruddick tipped his hat to the maid while his partner locked up the back of the van.

"A valuable picture, Mr. Seymour?" he inquired.

"A family heirloom that would fetch two million at auction," said Charles matter-of-factly before returning to his car.

"Silly question, Albert Cruddick," said Mr. Cruddick to himself as he pulled out from the curb and drove toward Eaton Square. When they arrived the locksmith had replaced all three locks on the front door and was waiting on the top step impatiently.

"Strictly cash, guv'nor. No receipt. Makes it possible for the missus and me to go to Ibiza each year, tax free."

By the time Fiona had returned to the Boltons from her trip to Sussex every picture was back in its place at Eaton Square with the exception of Holbein's first Earl of Bridgwater. Mr. Cruddick was left clutching a large check and uttering the unpalatable view that Mr. Seymour would probably have to grin and bear it.

"I'm delighted," said Simon, when he heard the news. "And at Pucklebridge General Hospital?"

"Yes, I answered an advertisement in *The Lancet* for the post of general consultant in the maternity section."

"But your name must have helped there?"

"Certainly not," said Elizabeth vehemently.

"How come?"

"I didn't apply as Dr. Kerslake. I filled out the application form in my maiden name of Drummond."

Simon was momentarily silenced. "But they would have recognized you," he protested.

"I had the full frontal treatment from Estée Lauder to ensure they didn't. The final effect fooled even you."

"Don't exaggerate," said Simon.

"I walked straight past you in Pucklebridge High Street, and said 'Good morning,' and you returned the greeting."

Simon stared at her in disbelief. "But what will happen when they find out?"

"They already have," replied Elizabeth sheepishly. "As soon as they offered me the post I went down to see the senior consultant and told him the truth. He hasn't stopped telling everyone since."

"He wasn't cross?"

"Far from it. In fact he said I nearly failed to be offered the post because he felt I wouldn't be safe let loose on the unmarried doctors."

Andrew held Louise's hand as they approached the door of Grunechan Children's Home on the outskirts of Edinburgh. The matron was waiting on the freshly scrubbed doorstep to greet them.

"Good morning, Minister," she said. "We are honored that you have chosen our little home."

Andrew and Louise smiled.

"Will you be kind enough to follow me?" She led them down a dimly lit corridor to her room, her starched blue uniform crackling as she walked.

"All the children are in the playground at the moment but you will be able to see them from my window." Andrew had already gone over all the orphans' histories and photographs; he couldn't help noticing how one of them bore a striking resemblance to Robert.

They both looked out of the window for several minutes but Louise showed no interest in any of the children. When the boy who resembled Robert ran toward the window, she turned away and took a seat in the corner.

Andrew shook his head. The matron's lips turned down at the corners.

Coffee and biscuits arrived and while they were eating them Andrew tried once more. "Did you want Matron to bring anyone in to meet you, darling?" Louise shook her head. Andrew cursed himself as he feared the experience might only have done her more harm.

"Have we seen everyone?" he asked, looking for an excuse to leave quickly.

"Yes, sir," said the matron, putting down her cup of coffee. "Well," she hesitated, "there was one girl we didn't bother you with."

"Why not?" asked Andrew out of curiosity.

"Well, you see, she's black."

Andrew stiffened.

"And what's more," continued the matron, "we have absolutely no idea who her parents were. She was left on the doorstep. Not at all the sort of girl to be brought up in a minister's home."

Andrew was so incensed that he quite forgot about consulting Louise who was still resting silently in the corner.

"I should like to see her," he said.

"If you insist," said the matron, a little taken aback. "I'm afraid she hasn't got her best clothes on," she added before she left the room.

Andrew paced up and down, conscious that if Louise hadn't been there he might well have lost his temper with the woman. The matron returned a few moments later with a little girl aged four, perhaps five, and so thin that her dress hung on her like a coathanger. Andrew couldn't see her face because she kept her head bowed.

"Look up, child," commanded the matron. The girl raised her head slowly. She had the most perfect oval face and olive skin, piercing black eyes, and a smile that immediately captivated Andrew.

"What's your name?" he asked quietly.

"Clarissa," she said, and dropped her head again. He wanted to help her so much, and it made him feel guilty that he had put the poor child through such a pointless ordeal.

The matron still looked affronted and with a sniff she said, "You can leave us now, child." Clarissa turned and walked toward the door. Looking at Louise the matron added, "I am sure you agree with me, Mrs. Fraser, the girl's not at all suitable."

They both turned to Louise. Her face was alight, her eyes shining in a way Andrew had not seen since Robert's death. She stood up, walked quickly toward the child before she could reach the door, and stared into her black eyes.

"I think you're beautiful," Louise said, "and I do hope you will want to come and live with us."

CHAPTER
TWENTY-THREE

"ORDER, ORDER" HAD meant nothing to the British electorate until 1978 when the House passed a resolution allowing the proceedings in the Commons to be broadcast on radio. Simon had supported the motion on broadcasting, putting forward the argument that radio was a further extension of democracy as it showed the House at work and allowed the voters to know exactly what their elected representatives were up to. Simon listened carefully to a number of his supplementaries, and realized for the first time that he spoke a little too quickly when he had a minister on the run.

Raymond, on the other hand, did not support the motion as he feared that the cries of "Hear, hear" or "Shame" and the heckling of the Prime Minister would sound to listeners like schoolchildren in a playground squabble. Overhearing the words with only one's imagination to set the scene would, he believed, create a false impression about the many aspects of a member's daily duties. When one evening Raymond heard a parliamentary debate in which he had taken part he was delighted to discover his arguments carried so much conviction.

When Andrew heard his own voice on Radio Four one

morning answering questions on defense issues he was suddenly aware that what he had always considered was a faint trace of a Scottish accent was in fact—when he was angry or excited—quite pronounced.

Charles found the morning program an excellent way of catching up with any proceedings he had missed the previous day. As he now woke each morning alone, "Yesterday in Parliament" became his constant companion. He hadn't been aware of how upper class he sounded until the occasion on which he followed Tom Carson. He had no intention of changing his voice for the radio.

When the Queen opened the new underground extension to Heathrow airport on 16 December 1977 Raymond was the minister commanded to be present. Joyce made one of her rare trips down to London as they were invited to join the Queen for lunch after the ceremony. When Joyce selected her new dress from Harvey Nichols, she stood in the little cubicle behind a drawn curtain to make sure it was possible for her to curtsy properly. "Good morning, Your Majesty," she practiced with a slight wobble, to the bemusement of the shop assistant waiting patiently outside.

By the time she had returned to the flat Joyce was confident that she could carry out her part in the proceedings as well as any courtier. As she prepared for Raymond's return from the morning Cabinet meeting she hoped he would be pleased with her efforts. She had long given up hope of being a mother, but still liked to believe she could be a good wife. Raymond had forewarned her that he would have to change as soon as he arrived at the flat to be sure of being at Green Park before the Queen arrived. After they had accompanied an entourage to Heathrow on the new extension, a journey that would take thirty minutes, they were to return to Buckingham Palace for lunch. Raymond had already come in contact with his monarch on several occasions in his official capacity as a Cabinet minister, but for Joyce it was to be the first time she had been presented.

Once she had had her bath and dressed—she knew Raymond would never forgive her if she were the reason he was late—she began to lay out his clothes. Tail coat, gray pinstriped trousers, white shirt, stiff collar, and a silver-gray tie, all hired that morning from Moss Bros. All that he still needed was a clean white handkerchief for his top pocket, just showing in a straight line, as the Duke of Edinburgh always wore his.

Joyce rummaged around in Raymond's chest of drawers, admiring the new shirts as she searched for a handkerchief. When she first saw the scribbled note peeking out underneath the collar of a pink shirt lying near the bottom of the pile, she assumed it must be an old laundry bill. Then she spotted the word "Darling." She felt suddenly sick as she looked more closely.

> Darling Carrot Top,
>   If you ever wear this one I might even agree to marry you.
>
> Kate.

Joyce sank on the end of the bed as the tears trickled down her face. Her perfect day was shattered. She knew at once what course of action she must take. She replaced the unworn shirt and closed the drawer, after first removing the note, and then sat alone in the drawing room waiting for Raymond to return.

He arrived back at the flat with only a few minutes to spare and was delighted to find his wife changed and ready.

"I'm running it a bit close," he said, going straight into the bedroom.

Joyce followed and watched him don his morning dress suit. When he had straightened his tie in the mirror, she faced him.

"What do you think?" he asked, not noticing the slight paleness in her cheeks.

She hesitated. "You look fantastic, Raymond. Now come along or we'll be late, and that would never do."

*   *   *

When Ronnie Nethercote invited him to lunch at the Ritz, Simon knew things must be looking up again. After a drink in the lounge they were ushered to a corner table overlooking the park in the most palatial dining room in London. Scattered around the other tables were men who were household names in Ronnie's world as well as in Simon's.

When the head waiter offered them menus Ronnie waved his hand and said, "Order the country vegetable soup, followed by beef off the trolley, take my word for it."

"Sounds like a safe bet," said Simon.

"Unlike our last little venture," Ronnie grunted. "How much are you still in hock because of the collapse of Nethercote and Company?"

"Fourteen thousand three hundred pounds when I last looked but I'm making inroads slowly. It's paying the interest before you can cut down on the capital that really hurts."

"How do you imagine I felt when we were overdrawn seven mill and then the bank decided to pull the rug from under my feet without any warning?"

"As two of the buttons on your waistcoat can no longer reach the holes they were originally tailored for, Ronnie, I must assume those problems are now a thing of the past."

"You're right." He laughed. "Which is why I invited you to lunch. The only person who ended up losing money on that deal was you. If you'd stayed on as the other directors did, at five grand a year, the company would still owe you £11,100 of earned income."

Simon groaned.

The carver wheeled the trolley of beef up to their table.

"Wait a moment, my boy, I haven't even begun. Morgan Grenfell want me to change the structure of the new company and will be injecting a large amount of cash. At the moment Whitechapel Properties—I hope you approve of the name—is still a one-hundred-pound off-the-shelf company. I own sixty percent and the bank's got forty. Now before the new agreement is signed, I'm going to offer you—"

"Would you like it well done, as usual, Mr. Nethercote?"

"Yes, Sam," said Ronnie, slipping the carver a pound note.

"I am going to offer you—"

"And your guest, sir?" the carver said, glancing at Simon.

"Medium, please."

"Yes, sir."

"I am going to offer you one percent of the new company, in other words one share."

Simon didn't comment, feeling confident Ronnie still hadn't finished.

"Aren't you going to ask?" said Ronnie.

"Ask what?" said Simon.

"You politicians get dumber by the minute. If I am going to offer you a one-pound share, how much do you think I am going to demand in return?"

"Well, I can't believe it's going to be one pound," said Simon, grinning.

"Wrong," said Ronnie. "One percent of the company is yours for one pound."

"Will that be sufficient, sir?" said the carver, putting a plate of beef in front of Simon.

"Hold it, Sam," said Ronnie before Simon could reply. "I repeat I'm offering you one percent of the company for one pound; now ask your question again, Sam."

"Will that be sufficient, sir?" repeated the carver.

"It's most generous," said Simon.

"Did you hear that, Sam?"

"I certainly did, sir."

"Right, Simon, you owe me a pound."

Simon laughed, removed his wallet from his inside pocket, took out a pound note, and handed it over.

"Now the purpose of that little exercise," said Ronnie, turning back to the carver and pocketing the note, "was to prove that Sam here isn't the only person who could make a quid for himself this afternoon." Sam smiled, having no idea what Mr. Nethercote was talking about, and placed a large plate of well-done beef in front of him.

Ronnie took out an envelope from his inside pocket and passed it to Simon.

"Do I open it now?" asked Simon.

"Yes—I want to see your reaction."

Simon opened the envelope and studied its contents. A certificate for one share in the new company with a true value of over £10,000.

"Well, well, what do you say?" said Ronnie.

"I'm speechless," said Simon.

"First politician I've known who's ever suffered from that problem."

Simon laughed. "Thank you, Ronnie. It's an incredibly generous gesture."

"No it's not. You were loyal to the old company, so why shouldn't you prosper with the new one?"

"That reminds me, does the name 'Archie Millburn' mean anything to you?" asked Simon.

Ronnie hesitated. "No, no, should it?"

"Only that I thought he might be the man who convinced Morgan Grenfell that you were worth bailing out."

"No, that name doesn't ring any bells. Mind you, Morgan Grenfell have never admitted where they obtained their information from but they knew every last detail about the old company. But if I come across the name Millburn I'll let you know. Enough of business. Fill me in on what's happening in your world. How's your lady wife?"

"Deceiving me."

"Deceiving you?"

"Yes, she's been putting on wigs and dressing up in strange clothes."

Clarissa wet her bed every night for the first month at Pelham Crescent but Louise never complained. Day by day Andrew watched as mother and daughter grew in mutual confidence. Clarissa assumed from her first meeting with Louise that she could talk as normally as any grown-up and chatted away to her night and day. Half the time Louise didn't reply, only because she couldn't get a word in.

Just when Andrew felt everything was getting back on a normal footing at home trouble erupted in Edinburgh. His General Management Committee, which now included five members of Militant Tendency, tabled a motion of no confidence in their member. Their leader, Frank Boyle, had been building up a power base with the sole intention, Andrew suspected, of ousting the member and taking over himself. He didn't discuss the problem with Louise, as the specialist had advised him to avoid any undue stress while Clarissa was settling in.

The five men who wanted Andrew removed had chosen the following Thursday to hold the meeting because they knew the annual Defense Review was due for a full debate in the House that day. If Andrew was unable to attend their meeting Frank Boyle knew they would have a better chance of winning their motion. If he did turn up to defend himself they were also aware that an embarrassing explanation would have to be made for his absence during the debate. When the Prime Minister was informed of the dilemma by the Chief Whip he had no hesitation in telling Andrew to forget the defense debate and go to Edinburgh.

Andrew took the shuttle up on Thursday afternoon and was met at the airport by his chairman, Hamish Ramsey.

"I apologize about you being put through this ordeal, Andrew," he said at once. "I can assure you it's none of my doing, but I must also warn you it's not the same Labour party that I joined over twenty years ago."

"How do you think the vote will go tonight?" asked Andrew.

"You'll win this time. The votes have been decided before the meeting takes place. There's only one waverer and he's so gutless that your very presence will stop him siding with the Trotskies."

When Andrew arrived at his Edinburgh headquarters he was left alone outside the committee room in a cold corridor for over an hour. He knew his opponents were holding things up in the hope he would become frustrated before he eventually had to face them. At last they invited him to join them and he immediately sensed what the Spanish Inquisition must have felt like: question after question from sour-faced men who had never helped him win the seat in the first place and were now alleging that he had shown scant interest in the constituency. Andrew stood his ground and became angry only when Frank Boyle referred to him as "that son of a Tory."

"When did you last see your father?" flashed through his mind.

"My father has done more for this city than you could ever hope to do in your lifetime," he told Boyle.

"Then why don't you join his party?" came back Boyle's retort.

Andrew was about to answer when Hamish Ramsey banged the table with his gavel and said, "Enough, enough. It's time to stop this squabbling and vote."

Andrew felt a stab of anxiety as the little slips were passed up to the chairman to be counted. The outcome was five-all and Hamish Ramsey immediately cast his vote in favor of Andrew.

"At least you'll be safe for the coming election, laddie," said Hamish as they drove to the Airport Hotel. "But I wouldn't like to account for much beyond that."

When Andrew arrived back in Pelham Crescent the next morning Louise greeted him at the door.

"Everything all right in Edinburgh?" she asked.

"Fine," said Andrew, taking her in his arms.

"Do you want to hear the good news?"

"Yes," said Andrew, smiling.

"Clarissa didn't wet her bed last night. Perhaps you should stay away more often."

Finally Charles knew he had to discuss what could be done about the stolen Holbein with his solicitor, Sir David Napley. Sir David instructed leading counsel and six weeks later

Charles was told that if he sued the Holbein might eventually be returned but not before the story had been on the front page of every national paper. Charles had Albert Cruddick's opinion confirmed: "Grin and bear it."

Fiona had been out of touch for well over a year when the letter came. Charles immediately recognized her handwriting and ripped open the envelope. Only one glance at the writing was enough to make him tear up the missive and deposit the little pieces in the wastepaper basket by his desk. He left for the Commons in a rage.

All through the day he thought of the one word he had taken in from the scrawled hand. Holbein. When he returned from the Commons after the ten o'clock division Charles searched for the remains of the letter, which the daily had conscientiously deposited in the dustbin. After rummaging among potato peelings, eggshells, and empty tins Charles spent over an hour Sellotaping the little pieces of paper together. Then he read the letter carefully.

> 24 The Boltons,
> London, SW 10
> 11 October 1978

Dear Charles,

Enough time has now passed for us to try and treat each other in a civilized way. Alexander and I wish to marry and Veronica Dalglish has agreed to an immediate divorce and has not insisted we wait the necessary two years to establish separation.

"You'll have to wait every day of the two years, you bitch," he said out loud. Then he came to the one sentence for which he was searching.

I realize this might not immediately appeal to you but if you felt able to fall in with our plans I would be happy to return the Holbein immediately.

> Yours ever,
> Fiona.

He crumpled up the paper in the ball of his hand before dropping it on the fire.

Charles remained awake into the early hours considering his reply.

At a Thursday morning Cabinet meeting James Callaghan informed his colleagues that the Liberal leader, David Steel, was not willing to continue the Lib/Lab pact after the end of the current session.

"That can only mean one thing," the Prime Minister continued. "We must all be prepared for a general election at any time from now on. I am confident we can hold out until Christmas, but not for much longer after that."

Raymond was saddened by the news. He felt after two years in the Cabinet that he was just beginning to be of some use to the Department of Trade: the changes he was implementing were starting to take effect. But he knew he needed considerably more time if he hoped to leave a permanent impression on his ministry.

Kate's enthusiasm spurred him on to work even longer hours and to push through as many of his innovations before the next election as possible.

"I'm trying my damnedest," he told her. "But do remember that the speed of the bureaucratic machine makes British Rail look like Concorde."

The Labour Government struggled on through a session dubbed by the press as "the winter of discontent": trying to push bills through the House, losing a clause here and a clause there, Raymond was only too delighted to have reached the recess in one piece.

Raymond spent a cold Christmas in Leeds with Joyce. He returned to London early in the New Year aware it could not be long before the Conservatives felt assured enough to put down a motion of no confidence. When it eventually was tabled no one in Parliament was surprised.

The debate caused a day of intense excitement, not least because a strike had caused the Commons bars to run dry and thirsty members were huddled together in the lobbies, the tea room, the smoking room, and the dining rooms. Harassed Whips rushed hither and thither checking lists, ringing up hospitals, boardrooms, and even great-aunts in their efforts to track down the last few elusive members.

When Mrs. Thatcher rose on 6 April to address a packed House the tension was so electric that the Speaker had considerable difficulty keeping control of the overcharged conductors. She addressed the House in firm, strident tones which brought her own side to their feet when she resumed her place. The atmosphere was no different when it was the turn of the Prime Minister to reply. Both leaders made a gallant effort to rise above the petulance of their adversaries but it was the Speaker who had the last word:

> "The Ayes to the right 311,
> The Noes to the left 310.
> The Ayes have it, the Ayes have it."

Pandemonium broke out. Opposition members waved their order papers in triumph, knowing the Prime Minister would now have to call a general election. James Callaghan immediately announced the dissolution of Parliament and after an audience with the Queen election day was set for 3 May 1979.

At the end of that momentous week those few members left at Westminster were stunned by an explosion in the Members' Car Park. Airey Neave, the Shadow spokesman on Northern Ireland, had been blown up by Irish terrorists as he was driving up the exit ramp to leave the Commons. He died on his way to hospital.

Members hurried back to their constituencies. Both Raymond and Andrew found it hard to escape from their departments at such short notice, but Charles and Simon were out in their respective high streets shaking hands with the voters by the morning following the Queen's proclamation.

For three weeks the arguments about who was competent to govern went back and forth, but on 3 May the British people elected their first woman Prime Minister and gave her party a majority of forty-three in the Commons.

Andrew's sixth election turned out to be his most unpleasant to date and he was only glad that he had left Louise and Clarissa in London. Jock McPherson, still the SNP candidate, called him every name under the sun and added one or two new ones in the evening, while the Trotskyites who had voted against him on the committee proved no help when it came to gathering in the votes on election day. But the citizens of Edinburgh, knowing nothing of the committee's opinions, sent Andrew back to Parliament with a majority of 3,738. The Scottish Nationalist vote crumbled, leaving only two members in the House—and Jock McPherson back in Scotland.

Raymond's vote in Leeds was slightly reduced, while Joyce won the office pool for predicting most accurately what her husband's majority would be. He was beginning to accept that she knew more about the constituency than he ever would.

A few days later when Raymond returned to London Kate had never seen him so depressed and decided to hold off telling him her own news when he said, "God knows how many years it will be before I can be of some use again."

"You can spend your time in Opposition making sure the Government doesn't dismantle all your achievements."

"With a majority of forty-three they could dismantle me if they wanted to," he told her. He placed the red leather box marked "Secretary of State for Trade" in the corner, next to the ones marked "Minister of State at the Department of Trade" and "Parliamentary Under-Secretary at the Department of Employment."

"They're only your first three," Kate tried to reassure him.

*   *   *

Simon increased his majority at Pucklebridge to 19,461, notching up another record after which he and Elizabeth spent the weekend in their cottage with the boys waiting for Mrs. Thatcher to select her team.

Simon was surprised when the Prime Minister phoned personally and asked if he could come up to see her in Downing Street: that was an honor usually afforded only to Cabinet ministers. He tried not to anticipate what she might have in mind.

He duly traveled up from the country and spent thirty minutes alone with the new Prime Minister. When he heard what Mrs. Thatcher wanted him to do he was touched that she had taken the trouble to see him in person. She knew that no member ever found it easy to accede to such a request but Simon accepted without hesitation. Mrs. Thatcher added that no announcement would be made until he had had time to talk his decision over with Elizabeth.

Simon thanked her and traveled back to his cottage in Pucklebridge. Elizabeth sat in silence as she listened to Simon's account of his conversation with the Prime Minister.

"Oh, my God," she said, when he had finished. "She's offered you the chance to be a Minister of State, but in return we have no certainty of peace for the rest of our lives."

"I can still say no," Simon assured her.

"That would be the act of a coward," said Elizabeth, "and you've never been that."

"Then I'll phone the Prime Minister and tell her I accept."

"I ought to congratulate you," she said. "But it never crossed my mind for one moment . . ."

Charles's was one of the few Tory seats in which the majority went down. A missing wife is hard to explain especially when it is common knowledge that she is living with the former chairman of the adjoining constituency. Charles had faced a certain degree of embarrassment with his local committee and he made sure that the one woman who couldn't keep her mouth shut was told his version of the story "in strictest confidence." Any talk of removing him had died when it was rumored that Charles would stand as an independent candidate if replaced. When the vote was counted Sussex Downs still returned Charles to Westminster with a majority of 20,176. He sat alone in Eaton Square over the weekend, but no one contacted him. He read in the Monday *Telegraph*—how he missed *The Times*—the full composition of the new Tory team.

The only surprise was Simon Kerslake's appointment as Minister of State for Northern Ireland.

CHAPTER
TWENTY-FOUR

"WELL, SAY SOMETHING."

"Very flattering, Kate. What reason did you give for turning the offer down?" asked Raymond, who had been surprised to find her waiting for him at the flat.

"I didn't need a reason."

"How did they feel about that?"

"You don't seem to understand. I accepted their offer."

Raymond removed his glasses and tried to take in what Kate was saying. He steadied himself by holding on to the mantelpiece.

Kate continued. "I had to, darling."

"Because the offer was too tempting?"

"No, you silly man. It had nothing to do with the offer as such, but it gives me the chance to stop letting my life drift. Can't you see it was *because* of you?"

"Because of me you're going to leave London and go back to New York."

"To work in New York and start getting my life in perspective. Raymond, don't you realize it's been five years?"

"I know how long it is and how many times I've asked you to marry me."

"We both know that isn't the answer; Joyce can't be brushed aside that easily. And it could even end up being the single reason you fail in your career."

"We can overcome that problem, given time," Raymond reasoned.

"That sounds fine now, until the party wins the next election and lesser men than you are offered the chance to shape future policy."

"Can't I do anything to make you change your mind?"

"Nothing, my darling. I've handed Chase my resignation and begin my new job with Chemical Bank in a month."

"Only four weeks," said Raymond.

"Yes, four weeks. I had to hold off telling you until I had severed all the bonds, had resigned, and could be sure of not letting you talk me out of it."

"Do you know how much I love you?"

"I hope enough to let me go, before it's too late."

Charles would not have normally accepted the invitation. Lately he had found cocktail parties to consist of nothing but silly little bits of food, never being able to get the right drink, and rarely enjoying the trivial conversation. But when he glanced on his mantelpiece and saw an "At Home" from Lady Carrington he felt it might be an amusing break from the routine he had fallen into since Fiona had left. He was also keen to discover more about the rumored squabbles in Cabinet over expenditure cuts. He checked his tie in the mirror, removed an umbrella from the hat stand, and left Eaton Square for Ovington Square.

He and Fiona had been apart for nearly two years. Charles had heard from several sources that his wife had now moved in with Dalglish on a permanent basis despite his unwillingness to cooperate over a divorce. He had remained discreetly silent on his wife's new life except for one or two selected tidbits dropped selectively in the ears of well-chosen gossips.

That way he had elicited for himself sympathy from every quarter while remaining the magnanimous loyal husband.

Charles had spent most of his spare time in the Commons, and his most recent budget speech had been well received both by the House and the national press. During the committee stage of the Finance Bill he had allowed himself to be burdened with a lot of the donkey work. Clive Reynolds had been able to point out discrepancies in some clauses of the bill, which Charles passed on to a grateful Chancellor. Thus Charles received praise for saving the Government from any unnecessary embarrassment. At the same time he disassociated himself from the "wets" as the Prime Minister referred to those of her colleagues who did not unreservedly support her monetarist policies. If he could keep up his work output he was confident he would be preferred in the first reshuffle.

By spending his mornings at the bank and afternoons and evenings in the Commons Charles managed to combine both worlds with the minimum of interruption from his almost non-existent private life.

He arrived at Lord Carrington's front door a little after six-forty-five. A maid answered his knock, and he walked straight through to a drawing room that could have held fifty guests and very nearly did.

He even managed to be served with the right blend of whisky before joining his colleagues from both the Upper and Lower Houses. He saw her first over the top of Alec Pimkin's balding head.

"Who is she?" asked Charles, not expecting Pimkin to know.

"Amanda Wallace," said Pimkin, glancing over his shoulder. "I could tell you a thing or two . . ." but Charles had already left his colleague in midsentence. The sexual aura of the woman was attested to by the fact that she spent the entire evening surrounded by attentive men, like moths around a candle. If Charles had not been one of the tallest men in the room he might never have seen the flame. It took him another ten minutes to reach her side of the room where Julian Ridsdale, a colleague of Charles's in the Commons, introduced them only to find himself dragged away moments later by his wife.

Charles was left staring at a woman who would have looked beautiful in anything from a ballgown to a towel. Her slim body was encased in a white silk dress, and her fair hair touched her bare shoulders. But what struck Charles most was the translucent texture of her skin. It had been years since he had found it so hard to make conversation.

"I expect you already have a dinner engagement?" Charles asked her in the brief intervals before the vultures closed in again.

"No," she replied and smiled encouragingly. She agreed to meet him at Walton's in an hour's time. Charles dutifully began to circulate round the room but it was not long before he found his eyes drawn back to her. Every time she smiled he found himself responding but Amanda didn't notice because she was always being flattered by someone else. When he left an hour later he smiled directly at her, and this time did win a knowing grin.

Charles sat alone at a corner table in Walton's for another hour. He was just about to admit defeat and return home when she was ushered to the table. The anger that had developed from being kept waiting was forgotten the moment she smiled and said, "Hello, Charlie."

He was not surprised to learn that his tall, elegant companion earned her living as a model. As far as Charles could see she could have modeled anything from toothpaste to stockings.

"Shall we have coffee at my place?" Charles asked after an unhurried dinner. She nodded her assent and he called for the bill, not checking the addition for the first time in many years.

He was delighted, if somewhat surprised, when she rested her head on his shoulder in the cab on the way back to Eaton Square. By the time they had been dropped off at Eaton Square most of Amanda's lipstick had been removed. The cabbie thanked Charles for his excessive tip and couldn't resist adding, "Good luck, sir."

Charles never did get round to making the coffee. When he

woke in the morning, to his surprise he found her even more captivating, and for the first time in weeks quite forgot "Yesterday in Parliament."

Elizabeth listened carefully as the man from Special Branch explained how the safety devices worked. She tried to make Peter and Michael concentrate on not pressing the red buttons that were in every room and would bring the police at a moment's notice. The electricians had already wired the rooms in Beaufort Street and now they had nearly finished at the cottage.

At Beaufort Street a uniformed policeman stood watch by the front door night and day. In Pucklebridge, because the cottage was so isolated, they had to be surrounded by arc lamps that could be switched on at a moment's notice.

"It must be damned inconvenient," suggested Archie Millburn during dinner. After his arrival at the cottage he had been checked by security patrols with dogs before he was able to shake hands with his host.

"Inconvenient is putting it mildly," said Elizabeth. "Last week Peter broke a window with a cricket ball and we were immediately lit up like a Christmas tree."

"Do you get any privacy?" asked Archie.

"Only when we're in bed. Even then you can wake up to find you're being licked; you sigh and it turns out to be an Alsatian."

Archie laughed. "Lucky Alsatian."

Every morning when Simon was driven to work he was accompanied by two detectives, a car in front and another to the rear. He had always thought there were only two ways from Beaufort Street to Westminster. For the first twenty-one days as minister he never traveled the same route twice.

Whenever he was due to fly to Belfast he was not informed of either his departure time or from which airport he would be leaving. While the inconvenience drove Elizabeth mad the tension had the opposite effect on Simon. Despite everything, it was the first time in his life he didn't feel it was necessary to explain to anyone why he had chosen to be a politician.

Inch by inch he worked to try to bring the Catholics and Protestants together. Often after a month of inches he would lose a yard in one day, but he never displayed any anger or prejudice except perhaps as he told Elizabeth, "a prejudice for common sense." Given time, Simon believed, a breakthrough would be possible—if only he could find on both sides a handful of men of goodwill.

During the all-party meetings both factions began to treat him with respect and—privately—with affection. Even the Opposition spokesman at Westminster openly acknowledged that Simon Kerslake was turning out to be an excellent choice for the "dangerous and thankless ministry."

Andrew also knew he would require a handful of men of good-will when Hamish Ramsey resigned as chairman of Edinburgh Carlton.

"I don't need the hassle any longer," Hamish told him. "I'm not in politics for the same reason as that bunch of trouble-makers." Andrew reluctantly let him go and had to work hard to convince Hamish's deputy, David Connaught, that he should stand in his place. When David finally agreed to allow his name to go forward he was immediately opposed by Frank Boyle, who had already made his opinion of the sitting member abundantly clear. Andrew canvassed every person on the committee during the run up to election for the new chairman. He estimated the voting was going to be seven-all, which would still allow Hamish to give his casting vote in favor of Connaught.

Andrew phoned Hamish at home an hour before the meeting was due to begin. "I'll call and leave a message for you at the House when it's all over," Ramsey told him. "Don't worry, you're safe this time. At least I'll leave you with the right chairman."

Andrew left Pelham Crescent after he had tucked Clarissa up in bed and read her another chapter of *Jacob Two Two*. He told Louise he would return from Westminster straight after the ten o'clock vote. He sat in the Chamber and listened to Charles Seymour deliver a well-argued discourse on monetarist policy. Andrew didn't always agree with the logic of Seymour's case and he had never cared much for the man himself; but he had to admit that such talent was wasted on the back benches.

During the speech a note was passed to Andrew by an attendant. He unfolded the little white slip. Stuart Gray, the lobby correspondent for *The Scotsman*, needed to speak to him urgently. Andrew slipped from his place on the front bench, stepping over the feet of Shadow ministers still intent on Seymour's speech. He felt like a small boy leaving a cinema in the middle of a film in pursuit of an ice lolly. He found Gray waiting for him in the Members' Lobby.

Andrew had known Stuart since he had first entered the House, when the journalist had told him, "You and I are each other's bread and butter, so we'd better make a sandwich." Andrew had laughed, and they had had few differences of opinion in the fifteen years since. Stuart suggested that they go down to Annie's Bar for a drink. They strolled along the corridor and took the stairway near the tea room to the basement bar, named after a former barlady.

Andrew settled down on a couch at the side of a pillar while Stuart went up to the bar to order two whiskies.

"Cheers," said the journalist, putting Andrew's glass down on the table in front of him.

Andrew took a long gulp. "Now, what can I do for you?" he asked. "Is my father being tiresome again?"

"I'd call him a supporter compared with your new chairman."

"What do you mean? I've always found David Connaught to be a sound fellow myself," said Andrew, a little pompously.

"I'm not interested in your views of David Connaught," said Stuart. "I want an opinion on your new chairman, Frank Boyle." The journalist sounded very much on the record.

"What?"

"He won the vote tonight seven to six."

"But . . ." Andrew fell silent.

"Come on, Andrew. We both know the bloody man's a Commie troublemaker, and my editor is screaming for a quote."

"I can't say anything, Stuart, not until I know all the facts."

"I've just told you all the facts: now, are you going to give me a quote?"

"Yes." Andrew paused. "I am sure Mr. Boyle will continue to serve in the best traditions of the Labour party, and I look forward to working in close cooperation with him."

"Balls," said Stuart. "They will only print that in Pseuds Corner in *Private Eye.*"

"It's the only quote you're going to get out of me tonight," said Andrew.

Stuart looked at his friend and could see lines on his face that he had never noticed before. "I'm sorry," he said. "I went too far. Please get in touch when the time's right. With that bastard Boyle in charge you might be in need of my help."

Andrew thanked him absentmindedly, downed his whisky in one gulp, then walked out of Annie's Bar and along the terrace corridor to the phone booths at the foot of the stairs. He dialed Ramsey's home number.

"What in heaven's name happened?" was all he could ask.

"One of our voters didn't show," said Hamish Ramsey. "Claimed he was held up in Glasgow and couldn't get back in time. I was just about to ring you."

"Bloody irresponsible of him," said Andrew. "Why didn't you postpone the vote?"

"I tried to, but Frank Boyle produced the rule book. 'Any motion proposed fourteen days before a meeting cannot be postponed without the agreement of the proposer and seconder.' I'm sorry, Andrew; my hands were tied."

"It's not your fault, Hamish. I couldn't have had a better chairman than you. I'm only sorry you didn't leave in a blaze of glory."

Hamish chuckled. "Don't you ever forget, Andrew, the voters have the last word in a democracy. In Edinburgh you're the man who has served them for more than fifteen years and they won't forget that quickly."

"You can get dressed now, Miss Wallace," said the gynecologist returning to her desk.

Amanda started to slip back into her latest Dior outfit—a light blue denim suit bought the previous day in Conduit Street in an attempt to cheer herself up.

"It's the third time in five years," said Elizabeth Kerslake, leafing through the confidential file and trying not to sound accusing.

"I may as well book into the same clinic as before," said Amanda, matter-of-factly.

Elizabeth was determined to make her reconsider the consequences. "Is there any chance that the father would want you to have this child?"

"I can't be certain who the father is," said Amanda, looking shame-faced for the first time. "You see, it was the end of one relationship and the beginning of another."

Elizabeth made no comment other than to say, "I estimate that you are at least eight weeks pregnant, but it could be as much as twelve." She looked back down at the file. "Have you considered giving birth to the child and then bringing it up yourself?"

"Good heavens, no," said Amanda. "I make my living as a model, not as a mother."

"So be it," Elizabeth sighed, closing the file. "I'll make all the"—she avoided saying usual—"necessary arrangements. You must see your GP immediately and ask him to sign the required clearance forms. Then phone me in about a week, rather than make the trip down to Pucklebridge again."

Amanda nodded her agreement. "Could you let me know what the clinic is going to charge this time? I'm sure they are suffering from inflation like the rest of us."

"Yes, I will look into that, Miss Wallace," said Elizabeth, just managing to keep her temper as she showed Amanda to the door. Once her patient had left Elizabeth picked up the confidential file from her desk, walked over to the cabinet, and flicked through S, T, U, until she found the right slot. Perhaps she should have been sterner with her but she was convinced that it would have made little difference. She paused, wondering if having the child might change the woman's cavalier attitude to life.

Charles returned home after the debate feeling pleased with himself. He had received praise for his latest speech from every wing of the party, and the Chief Whip had made it quite clear that his efforts on the Finance Bill had not gone unnoticed.

As he drove back to Eaton Square he wound down the car window and let the fresh air rush in and the cigarette smoke out. His smile widened at the thought of Amanda sitting at home waiting for him. It had been a glorious couple of months. At forty-eight he was experiencing realities he had never even dreamed of in fantasy. As each day passed he expected the infatuation to wear off, but instead it only grew more intense. Even the memory the day after was better than anything he had experienced in the past.

Once the Holbein had been restored to his dining room wall Charles planned to talk to Amanda about their future; if she said "Yes" he would even be willing to grant Fiona a divorce. He parked the car and took out his latch key, but she was already there opening the front door to throw her arms around him.

"Why don't we go straight to bed?" she greeted him.

Charles would have been shocked had Fiona uttered such feelings even once in their fifteen years of married life, but Amanda made it appear quite natural. She was already lying naked on the bed before Charles could get his waistcoat off. After they had made love and she was settled in his arms Amanda told him she would have to go away for a few days.

"Why?" said Charles, puzzled.

"I'm pregnant," she said matter-of-factly. "I've already

booked myself into a clinic. Don't worry. I'll be as right as rain in no time."

"But why don't we have the baby?" said a delighted Charles, looking down into her gray eyes. "I've always wanted a son."

"Don't be silly, Charlie. There's years ahead of me for that."

"But if we were married?"

"You're already married. Besides, I'm only twenty-six."

"I can get a divorce in a moment and life wouldn't be so bad with me, would it?"

"Of course not, Charlie. You're the first man I've ever really cared for."

Charles smiled hopefully. "So you'll think about the idea?"

Amanda looked into Charles's eyes anxiously. "If I *were* to have a child I do hope he'd have blue eyes like yours."

"Will you marry me?" he asked.

"I'll think about it. In any case, you may have changed your mind by morning."

Raymond drove Kate to Heathrow. He was wearing the pink shirt she had chosen for him; she was wearing the little red box. He had so much to tell her on the way to the airport that she hardly spoke at all. The last four weeks had gone by in a flash. It was the first time he had been grateful for being in Opposition.

"It's all right, Carrot Top. Don't fuss. We'll see each other whenever you come to New York."

"I've only been to America twice in my life," he said. She tried to smile.

Once she had checked her eleven bags in at the counter, a process that seemed to take forever, she was allocated a seat.

"Flight BA 107, gate number fourteen, boarding in ten minutes," she was informed.

"Thank you," she said and rejoined Raymond, who was sitting on the end of an already crowded tubular settee. He had bought two plastic cups of coffee while Kate had been checking in. They were both already cold. They sat and held hands like children who had met on a summer holiday and had now to return to separate schools.

"Promise me you won't start wearing contact lenses the moment I've gone."

"Yes, I can promise you that," said Raymond, touching the bridge of his glasses.

"I've so much I still want to tell you," she said.

He turned toward her. "Vice-presidents of banks shouldn't cry," he said, brushing a tear from her cheek. "The customers will realize you're a soft touch."

"Neither should Cabinet ministers," she replied. "All I wanted to say, is that if you really feel . . ." she began.

"Hello, Mr. Gould."

They both looked up to see a broad smile spread across the face of someone whose tan proved that he had just arrived from a sunnier climate.

"I'm Bert Cox," he said, thrusting out his hand, "I don't suppose you remember me." Raymond let go of Kate's hand and shook Mr. Cox's.

"We were at the same primary school in Leeds, Ray. Mind you, that was a million light years ago. You've come a long way since then."

How can I get rid of him? wondered Raymond desperately.

"This is the missus," Bert Cox continued obliviously, gesturing at the silent woman in a flowery dress by his side. She smiled but didn't speak. "She sits on some committee with Joyce, don't you, love?" he said, not waiting for her reply.

"This is the final call for Flight BA 107, now boarding at gate number fourteen."

"We always vote for you, of course," continued Bert Cox. "The missus"—he pointed to the lady in the flowered dress again—"thinks you'll be Prime Minister. I always say—"

"I must go, Raymond," said Kate, "or I'll miss my flight."

"Can you excuse me for a moment, Mr. Cox?" said Raymond.

"Delighted. I'll wait. I don't often get a chance to have a word with my MP."

Raymond walked with Kate toward the barrier. "I am sorry

about this. I'm afraid they're all like that in Leeds—hearts of gold, but never stop talking. What were you going to say?"

"Only that I would have been happy to live in Leeds, however cold it is. I never envied anyone in my life, but I do envy Joyce." She kissed him gently on the cheek and walked toward the barrier before he could reply. She didn't look back.

"Are you feeling all right, madam?" asked an airport official as she went through the security barrier.

"I'm fine," said Kate, brushing aside her tears. She walked slowly toward gate fourteen, happy that he had worn the pink shirt for the first time. She wondered if he had found the note she had left underneath the collar. If he had asked her just one more time . . .

Raymond stood alone and then turned to walk aimlessly toward the exit.

"An American lady, I would have guessed," said Mr. Cox rejoining him. "I'm good on accents."

"Yes," said Raymond, still alone.

"A friend of yours?" he asked.

"My best friend," said Raymond.

When ten days had passed and Elizabeth had not yet heard from Miss Wallace she decided she had no choice but to contact her direct. She flicked through her personal file and noted the latest number Amanda had given.

Elizabeth picked up the phone and dialed. It was some time before anybody answered.

"730-9712. Charles Seymour speaking." There was a long silence. "Is anyone there?"

Elizabeth couldn't reply. She replaced the receiver and felt her whole body come out in a cold sweat. She closed Amanda Wallace's file and returned it to the cabinet.

CHAPTER
TWENTY-FIVE

SIMON HAD SPENT nearly a year preparing a White Paper entitled "A Genuine Partnership for Ireland" for consideration by the House. The Government's aim was to bring north and south together for a period of ten years at the end of which a more permanent arrangement could be considered. During those ten years both sides would remain under the direct rule of Westminster and Dublin. Both Protestants and Catholics had contributed to "the Charter," as the press had dubbed the complex agreement. With considerable skill, patience, and fortitude Simon had convinced the political leaders of Northern Ireland to append their names to the final draft when and if it was approved by the House.

He admitted to Elizabeth that the agreement was only a piece of paper, but he felt it was a foundation stone on which the House could base an eventual settlement. On both sides of the Irish Sea politicians and journalists alike were describing the Charter as a genuine breakthrough.

The Secretary of State for Northern Ireland was to present the White Paper to the Commons when Irish business was next scheduled on the parliamentary calendar. Simon, as the architect of the Charter, had been asked to deliver the winding-up speech on behalf of the Government. He knew that if the House backed the concept of the document he might then be allowed to prepare a parliamentary bill and thus overcome a problem so many other politicians had failed to solve before him. If he succeeded Simon felt that all the sacrifices he had made in the past would prove worthwhile.

When Elizabeth sat down to read through the final draft in Simon's study that evening even she admitted for the first time that she was pleased he had accepted the Irish appointment.

"Now, embryonic statesman," she continued, "are you ready for your dinner like every normal human being at this time in the evening?"

"I certainly am." Simon moved his copy of the 129-page Charter from the dining room table to the sideboard, planning to go over it yet again once he had finished dinner.

"Damn," he heard Elizabeth say from the kitchen.

"What is it?" he asked, not looking up from his toy, like a child studying a jigsaw and wondering where a colorless piece fitted in.

"I'm out of Bisto."

"I'll go and buy some," Simon volunteered. The two policemen on the door were chatting when the minister came out.

"Come on, my wife needs a packet of Bisto, so affairs of state must be held up for the time being."

"I'm very sorry, sir," said the sergeant. "When I was told you would be in for the rest of the evening I allowed the official car to go off duty. But Constable Barker can accompany you."

"That's no problem," said Simon. "We can take my wife's car. I'll just find out where she's parked the damn thing."

He slipped back into the house but returned a moment later. "Been in the force long?" he asked Constable Barker as they walked down the road together.

"Not that long, sir. Started on the beat just over a year ago."

"Are you married, Constable?"

"Fine chance on my salary, sir."

"Then you won't have encountered the problem of being Bisto-less."

"They've never heard of gravy in the police canteen, sir."

"You should try the House of Commons sometime," said Simon. "I don't think you'd find it any better—the food, that is, not to mention the salary."

The two men laughed as they headed off toward the car.

"What does your wife think of the Mini Metro?" the constable asked as Simon put the key in the door.

Like everyone else in Beaufort Street, Elizabeth heard the explosion, but she was the first to realize what it had to be. She ran out of the front door in search of the duty policeman. She saw him running down the road and quickly followed.

The little red Metro was scattered all over the side street, the glass from its windows making the pavement look as though there had been a sudden hailstorm.

When the sergeant saw the severed head he pulled Elizabeth back. Two other bodies lay motionless in the road, one of them an old lady with the contents of her shopping bag spread around her.

Within minutes, six police cars had arrived and Special Branch officers had cordoned off the area with white ribbon. An ambulance rushed the bodies to Westminster Hospital. The job of picking up the remains of the police constable needed a very resolute man.

Elizabeth was taken to the hospital in a police car, where she learned that the old lady had died before arrival while her husband was on the critical list. When she told the surgeon in charge that she was a doctor he was more forthcoming and answered her questions candidly. Simon was suffering from multiple fractures, a dislocated hip, and a severe loss of blood. The only question he was not willing to be drawn on was when she asked about his chances.

She sat alone outside the operating theater waiting for any scrap of news. Hour after hour went by, and Elizabeth kept recalling Simon's words: "Be tolerant. Always remember there are still men of goodwill in Northern Ireland." She found it almost impossible not to scream, to think of the whole lot of them as evil murderers. Her husband had worked tirelessly on their behalf. He wasn't a Catholic or a Protestant, just a man trying to do an impossible task. Although she couldn't help thinking that it was she who had been the intended target.

Another hour passed.

A tired, gray-faced man came out into the corridor through the flapping rubber doors. "He's still hanging on, Dr. Kerslake. Your husband has the constitution of an ox; most people would have let go by now." He smiled. "Can I find you a room so that you can get some sleep?"

"No, thank you," Elizabeth replied. "I'd prefer to be near him."

She rang home to check the children were coping and her mother answered the phone. She had rushed over the moment she had heard the news and was keeping them away from the radio and television.

"How is he?" she asked.

Elizabeth told her mother all she knew, then spoke to the children.

"We're taking care of Grandmother," Peter told her.

Elizabeth couldn't hold back the tears. "Thank you, darling," she said, and quickly replaced the receiver. She returned to the bench outside the operating theater, kicked off her shoes, curled her legs under her body, and tried to snatch some sleep.

She woke with a start in the early morning. Her back hurt and her neck was stiff. She walked slowly up and down the corridor in her bare feet stretching her aching limbs, searching for anyone who could tell her some news. Finally a nurse brought her a cup of tea and assured her that her husband was still alive. But what did "still alive" mean? She stood and watched the grim faces coming out of the operating theater and tried not to recognize the telltale signs of despair. The surgeon told her she ought to go home and rest: they would have nothing to tell her for several hours. A policeman kept all journalists—who were arriving by the minute—in an anteroom off the main corridor.

Elizabeth didn't move from the corridor for another day and another night, and she didn't return home until the surgeon told her it was all over.

When she heard the news she fell on her knees and wept.

"God must want the Irish problem solved as well," he added. "Your husband will live, Dr. Kerslake, but it's a miracle."

"Got time for a quick one?" asked Alexander Dalglish.

"If you press me," said Pimkin.

"Fiona," shouted Alexander. "It's Alec Pimkin, he's dropped in for a drink."

She came through to join them. She was dressed in a bright yellow frock and had allowed her hair to grow down past her shoulders.

"It suits you," said Pimkin, tapping his bald head.

"Thank you," said Fiona. "Why don't we all go through to the drawing room?"

Pimkin happily obeyed and had soon settled himself into Alexander's favorite chair.

"What will you have?" asked Fiona, as she stood by the drinks cabinet.

"A large gin with just a rumor of tonic."

"Well, how's the constituency faring since my resignation?"

"It ticks along, trying hard to survive the biggest sex scandal since Profumo," chuckled Pimkin.

"I only hope it hasn't harmed your election chances," said Alexander.

"Not a bit of it, old fellow," said Pimkin, accepting the large Beefeaters and tonic Fiona handed him. "On the contrary, it's taken their minds off me for a change."

Alexander laughed.

"In fact," continued Pimkin, "interest in the date of your wedding has only been eclipsed by Charles and Lady Di. Gossips tell me," he continued, clearly enjoying himself, "that my Honorable friend, the member for Sussex Downs, made you wait the full two years before you could place an announcement in *The Times*."

"Yes, that's true," said Fiona. "Charles didn't even answer my letters during that period, but lately when any problem's arisen he's been almost friendly."

"Could that be because he also wants to place an announcement in *The Times*?" said Pimkin, downing his gin quickly in the hope of being offered a second.

"What do you mean?"

"The fact that he has lost his heart to another."

"Another?" said Alexander Dalglish.

"No less—" Pimkin paused as he sipped pointedly at his empty glass "—than Miss Amanda Wallace, only daughter of the late and little-lamented Brigadier Boozer Wallace."

"Amanda Wallace?" said Fiona in disbelief. "Surely he's got more sense than that."

"I don't think it has a lot to do with sense," said Pimkin holding out his glass. "More to do with sex."

"But he's old enough to be her father."

"If that is the case," said Pimkin, "Charles can always adopt her."

Alexander laughed.

"But I am informed by a reliable source," continued Pimkin, "that marriage is being proposed."

"You can't be serious," said Fiona flatly.

"The subject has most certainly been broached for she is undoubtedly pregnant and Charles is hoping for a son," said Pimkin in triumph as he accepted his second double gin.

"That's not possible," said Fiona under her breath.

"And I am also informed," continued Pimkin, "that some of the more ungenerous of our brethren are already suggesting the name of several candidates for the role of father."

"Alec, you're incorrigible."

"My dear, it is common knowledge that Amanda has slept with half the Cabinet and a considerable cross section of back-benchers."

"Stop exaggerating," said Fiona.

"And what's more," continued Pimkin as if he hadn't heard her, "she has only stopped short of the Labour front bench because her mother told her they were common and she might catch something from them."

Alexander laughed again. "But surely Charles hasn't fallen for the pregnancy trick?"

"Hook, line, and sinker. He's like an Irishman who's been locked into a Guinness brewery over the weekend. Dear Amanda has my Honorable friend uncorking her at every opportunity."

"But she's plain stupid," said Alexander. "The only time I met her she assured me that Michael Parkinson was turning out to be an excellent chairman of the party."

"Stupid she may well be," said Pimkin, "but plain she is not and together, I'm told, they are updating the *Kama Sutra.*"

"Enough, Alec, enough," said Fiona, laughing.

"You're right," said Pimkin, aware that his glass was nearly empty once again. "A man of my impeccable reputation cannot afford to be seen associating with people living in sin. I must leave immediately, darlings," he said, rising to his feet. Pimkin put his glass down and Alexander accompanied him to the front door.

As it closed Alexander turned to Fiona. "Never short of useful information, our former member," he said.

"I agree," said Fiona. "So much gleaned for such a small investment in Beefeaters."

As Alexander walked back into the drawing room he added, "Does it change your plans for the return of the Holbein?"

"Not in any way," said Fiona.

"So you'll still be at Sotheby's next week for their Old Masters sale?"

Fiona smiled. "Certainly. And if the price is right we won't have to worry about what we give Charles for a wedding present."

Three weeks after the bombing Simon left the Westminster Hospital on crutches, Elizabeth by his side. His right leg had been so shattered that he had been told he would never walk properly again. As he stepped out on to Horseferry Road a hundred cameras flashed to meet their editors' demand to capture the instant hero. He smiled as if there were no pain. "Don't let those murderers think they got to you," he was warned by both sides. Elizabeth's smile showed only relief that her husband was still alive.

After three weeks of complete rest Simon returned to his Irish Charter against doctor's orders, knowing the document was still due to be debated in the House in less than a fortnight. The Secretary of State and the other Minister of State for Northern Ireland visited him at home on several occasions and it was agreed that the Minister of State would take over Simon's responsibilities temporarily and deliver the winding-up speech. During his absence the whole Northern Ireland office grew to realize just how much work Simon had put into the Charter, and no one was at all complacent about taking his place.

The attempt on Simon's life and the build up to the special debate on the Charter became of such national interest that the BBC decided to broadcast the entire proceedings on Radio Four from three-thirty to the vote at ten o'clock.

On the afternoon of the debate Simon sat up in bed listening to every word on the radio as if it were the final episode in his favorite serial and he was desperate to know the outcome. The speeches opened with a clear and concise presentation of the Charter by the Secretary of State for Northern Ireland, which left Simon feeling confident that the whole House would support him. The Opposition spokesman followed with a fair-minded speech, raising one or two queries he had over the controversial Patriots' Clause with its special rights for Protestants in the south and Catholics in the north, and also how it would affect the Catholics unwilling to register in Northern Ireland. Otherwise he reassured the House that the Opposition supported the Charter and would not be calling for a division.

Simon began to relax for the first time as the debate continued, but his mood changed as some back-bench members started to express more and more anxiety over the Patriots' Provision. One or two back-benchers were even insisting that the Charter should not be sanctioned by the House until the need for the Patriots' Provision was fully explained by the Government. Simon realized that a few narrow-minded men were simply playing for time in the hope the Charter would be held up and later forgotten. For generations such men had succeeded in stifling the hopes and aspirations of the Irish people while they allowed bigotry to undermine any real desire for peace.

Elizabeth came in and sat on the end of the bed. "How's it going?" she asked.

"Not well," said Simon, "it will all depend on the Opposition spokesman."

They both sat and listened. But no sooner had the Opposition spokesman risen that Simon realized that he too had misunderstood the real purpose of the Patriots' Provision and that what Simon had agreed to with both sides in Dublin and Belfast was not being accurately explained to the House. There was no malice in the speech and he was clearly following what had been agreed through the usual channels but Simon could sense that his lack of conviction was sowing doubts in the minds of his fellow members. He feared a division might be called after all.

After one or two members had interrupted to voice further doubts about the Patriots' Clause the Shadow minister suggested: "Perhaps we should wait until the Minister of State is fully recovered and able to report to the House himself." A few "hear, hears" could be heard around the Chamber.

Simon felt sick. He was going to lose the Charter if it didn't get through the House tonight. All the hard work and goodwill would count for nothing. He made a decision.

"I'd love a hot cup of cocoa," he said, trying to sound casual.

"Of course, darling. I'll just go and turn the kettle on. Would you like a biscuit while I'm up?"

Simon nodded. Once the bedroom door was closed, he slipped quietly out of bed and dressed as quickly as possible. He picked up his blackthorn stick, a gift from Dr. Fitzgerald, the Irish Prime Minister, which had been among the dozens of presents awaiting his return from hospital. Then he hobbled silently down the stairs and across the hall, hoping Elizabeth would not hear him. He eased the front door open. When the policeman on duty saw him Simon put a finger to his lips and closed the door very slowly behind him. He made his way laboriously up to the police car, lurched into the back, and said, "Switch on the radio, please, and drive me to the House as quickly as possible."

Simon continued to listen to the Opposition spokesman as the police car weaved in and out of the traffic on a route he hadn't traveled before. They arrived at the St. Stephen's entrance to the Commons at nine-twenty-five.

Visitors stood to one side as they might for royalty but Simon didn't notice. He hobbled on through the Central Lobby, oblivious to the awkwardness of his gait, turning left past the policeman and on toward the entrance of the House. He prayed he would reach the Chamber before the Government spokesman rose to deliver his winding-up speech. Simon passed an astonished chief doorkeeper and arrived at the bar of the House as the new digital clock showed nine-twenty-nine.

The Opposition spokesman was resuming his place on the front bench to muffled cries of "Hear, hear." The Speaker rose but before he had time to call upon the Minister of State to reply Simon stepped slowly forward on to the green carpet of the Commons. For a moment there was a stunned silence; then the cheering began. It had reached a crescendo by the time Simon arrived at the front bench. His blackthorn stick fell to the floor as he clutched the dispatch box. The Speaker called out his name sotto voce.

Simon waited for the House to come to complete silence.

"Mr. Speaker, I must thank the House for its generous welcome. I return this evening because having listened to every word of the debate on the radio I feel it necessary to explain to Honorable members what was behind my thinking with the Patriots' Provision. This was not some superficial formula for solving an intractable problem, but an act of good faith to which the representatives from all sides felt able to put their names. It may not be perfect, since words can mean different things to different people—as lawyers continually demonstrate to us."

The laughter broke the tension that had been building up in the House.

"But if we allow this opportunity to pass today it will be another victory for those who revel in the mayhem of Northern Ireland whatever their reason, and a defeat for all men of goodwill."

The House was silent as Simon went on to explain in detail the thinking behind the Patriots' Provision and the effect it would have on both Protestants and Catholics in north and south. He also covered the other salient clauses in the Charter, answering the points that had been raised during the debate until, in glancing up at the clock above the Speaker's chair, he realized he had less than a minute left.

"Mr. Speaker, we in this great House, who have in the past decided the fate of nations, are now given an opportunity to succeed today where our predecessors have failed. I ask you to support this Charter—not unreservedly, but to show the bombers and the murderers that here in Westminster we can cast a vote for the children of tomorrow's Ireland. Let the twenty-first century be one in which the Irish problem is only a part of history. Mr. Speaker, I seek the support of the whole House."

The motion on the Charter was agreed without division.

Simon immediately returned home and on arrival silently crept upstairs. He closed the bedroom door behind him and fumbled for the switch. The light by the side of the bed went on and Elizabeth sat up.

"Your cocoa's gone cold and I've eaten all the biscuits," she said, grinning, "but thank you for leaving the radio on, at least I knew where you were."

CHAPTER
TWENTY-SIX

CHARLES AND AMANDA were married at the most inconspicuous register office in Hammersmith. They then departed for a long weekend in Paris. Charles had told his bride that he preferred her not to let anyone learn of the marriage for at least another week. He didn't want Fiona to find yet a further excuse for not returning the Holbein. Amanda readily agreed, and then remembered—but surely Alec Pimkin didn't count.

Paris turned out to be fun, even though Charles was sensitive about Amanda's obvious pregnancy—never more so than when they arrived on the Friday night at the Plaza Athenée and were escorted to a suite overlooking the courtyard. Later, over dinner, Amanda astonished the waiters with her appetite as well as the cut of her dress.

Over breakfast in bed the next day Charles read in the *Herald Tribune* that Mrs. Thatcher was considering a reshuffle that very weekend. He cut the honeymoon short and returned to London on the Saturday, two days earlier than planned. Amanda was not overjoyed. Her husband spent the whole of Sunday at Eaton Square alongside a phone that never rang.

That same Sunday evening the Prime Minister called for

Simon Kerslake and told him that he was to be made a Privy Councillor and would be moved from the Northern Ireland Office to Defense as Minister of State.

He had started to protest, but Mrs. Thatcher forestalled any discussion. "I don't want any more dead heroes, Simon," she said sharply.

Elizabeth was relieved when she heard the news, although it took her some time to get used to her husband being referred to as "the Right Honorable Simon Kerslake." For some weeks the old joke of "rarely right and never honorable" had to be suffered by both of them from countless well-meaning constituents who imagined they were the only people who had thought of the quip.

Mrs. Thatcher called Charles Seymour on the Monday morning while he was waiting in Eaton Square for the return of the Holbein. Both sides' solicitors had agreed that the first Earl of Bridgwater should be back at Charles's home by eleven that morning. Only the Queen or Mrs. Thatcher could have kept Charles from being there to receive it.

The Prime Minister's call came long after he thought the reshuffle was over, but then Mrs. Thatcher had been informed that Charles was in Paris on his honeymoon and wouldn't be back until the Monday morning.

Charles took a taxi to Downing Street and was quickly ushered into the Prime Minister's study. Mrs. Thatcher began by complimenting him on the work he had carried out on successive Finance Bills in Opposition and in Government. She then invited him to join the front-bench team as the Financial Secretary to the Treasury.

Charles accepted gracefully, and after a short policy discussion with the Prime Minister drove back to Eaton Square to celebrate both his triumphs. Amanda met him at the door to tell him the Holbein had been returned. Fiona had kept her part of the bargain: the painting had been delivered at eleven o'clock sharp.

Charles strode confidently into his drawing room and was delighted to find the bulky package awaiting him. He was by no means so pleased to be followed by Amanda, a cigarette in one hand and a glass of gin in the other; but this was not a day for quarrels, he decided. He told her of his appointment, but she didn't seem to take in its significance until her husband opened a bottle of champagne.

Charles poured out two glasses and handed one to his bride.

"A double celebration. What fun," she said, first draining the gin.

Charles took a quick sip of the champagne before he began to untie the knots and tear away the smart red wrapping paper that covered his masterpiece. Once the paper had been removed he pulled back the final cardboard covers. Charles stared with delight at the portrait.

The first Earl of Bridgwater was back home. Charles picked up the gold frame he knew so well to return it to its place in his study but he noticed that the picture had come a little loose. "Damn," he said.

"What's the matter?" asked Amanda, still leaning against the door.

"Nothing important, only I shall have to get the frame fixed. I'll drop it into Oliver Swann on the way to the bank. I've waited nearly three years; another couple of days won't make any difference."

Now that Charles had accepted the post of Financial Secretary to the Treasury he knew there was one little arrangement he had to clear up before the appointment became public knowledge. With that in mind, he left Eaton Square and dropped the Holbein off at the framer. He then went on to the bank and summoned Clive Reynolds to his office. It was clear from Reynolds's manner that the news of Charles's ministerial appointment had not yet leaked out.

"Clive," Charles called him for the first time. "I have a proposition to put to you."

Clive Reynolds remained silent.

"The Prime Minister has offered me a post in the Government."

"Congratulations," said Reynolds, "and well deserved, if I may say so."

"Thank you," said Charles. "Now: I'm considering offering you the chance to stand in for me as chairman during my absence."

Clive Reynolds looked surprised.

"On the clear understanding that if the Conservatives were to return to Opposition or I were to lose my appointment in Government I would be reinstated as chairman immediately."

"Naturally," said Reynolds. "I should be delighted to fill the appointment for the interim period."

"Good man," said Charles. "It can't have escaped your notice what happened to the last chairman in the same situation."

"I shall make certain that will not happen again."

"Thank you," said Charles. "I shall not forget your loyalty when I return."

"And I shall also endeavor to carry on the traditions of the bank in your absence," said Reynolds, his head slightly bowed.

"I feel sure you will," said Charles.

The board accepted the recommendation that Clive Reynolds be appointed as temporary chairman and Charles vacated his office happily to take up his new post at the Treasury.

Charles considered it had been the most successful week of his life and on the Friday evening on the way back to Eaton Square he dropped into Oliver Swann's gallery to pick up the Holbein.

"I'm afraid the picture didn't quite fit the frame," said Mr. Swann.

"Oh, I expect it's worked loose over the years," Charles said noncommittally.

"No, Mr. Seymour, this frame was put on the portrait quite recently," said Swann.

"That's not possible," said Charles. "I remember the frame as well as I remember the picture. The portrait of the first Earl of Bridgwater has been in my family for over 400 years."

"Not this picture," said Swann.

"What do you mean?" said Charles, beginning to sound anxious.

"This picture came up for sale at Sotheby's about three weeks ago."

Charles went cold as Swann continued.

"It's the school of Holbein, of course," he said, "probably painted by one of his pupils around the time of his death. I should think there are a dozen or so in existence."

"A dozen or so," repeated Charles, the blood drained from his face.

"Yes, perhaps even more. At least it's solved one mystery for me," said Swann, chuckling.

"What's that?" asked Charles, choking out the words.

"I couldn't work out why Lady Fiona was bidding for the picture, and then I remembered that your family name is Bridgwater."

"At least *this* wedding has some style," Pimkin assured Fiona between mouthfuls of sandwich at the reception after her marriage to Alexander Dalglish. Pimkin always accepted wedding invitations as it allowed him to devour mounds of smoked salmon sandwiches and consume unlimited quantities of champagne. "I particularly enjoyed that *short* service of blessing in the Guards' Chapel; and Claridges can always be relied on to understand my little proclivities." He peered round the vast room and only stopped to stare at his reflection in a chandelier.

Fiona laughed. "Did you go to Charles's wedding?"

"My darling, the only Etonians who have ever been seen in Hammersmith pass through it as quickly as possible on a boat, representing either Oxford or Cambridge."

"So you weren't invited," said Fiona.

"I'm told that only Amanda was invited, and even she nearly found she had another engagement. With her doctor, I believe."

"Well, Charles certainly can't afford another divorce."

"No, not in his present position as Her Majesty's. Financial

Secretary. One divorce might go unnoticed but two would be considered habit-forming, and all diligent readers of Nigel Dempster have been able to observe that consummation has taken place."

"But how long will Charles be able to tolerate her behavior?"

"As long as he still believes she has given him a son who will inherit the family title. Not that a marriage ceremony will necessarily prove legitimacy," added Pimkin.

"Perhaps Amanda won't produce a son."

"Perhaps whatever she produces it will be obvious that it's not Charles's offspring," said Pimkin, falling into a chair that had been momentarily left by a large buxom lady.

"Even if it was I can't see Amanda as a housewife."

"No, but it suits Amanda's current circumstances to be thought of as the loving spouse."

"Time may change that, too," said Fiona.

"I doubt it," said Pimkin. "Amanda is stupid, that has been proven beyond reasonable doubt, but she has a survival instinct second only to a mongoose. So while Charles is spending all the hours of the day advancing his glittering career she would be foolish to search publicly for greener pastures. Especially when she can always lie in them privately."

"You're a wicked old gossip," said Fiona.

"I cannot deny it," said Pimkin, "for it is an art at which women have never been as accomplished as men."

"Thank you for such a sensible wedding present," said Alexander, joining his wife of two hours. "You selected my favorite claret."

"Giving a dozen bottles of the finest claret serves two purposes," said Pimkin, his hands resting lightly on his stomach. "First, you can always be assured of a decent wine when you invite yourself to dine."

"And second?" asked Alexander.

"When the happy couple split up you can feel relieved that they will no longer have your present to quarrel over."

"Did you give Charles and Amanda a present?" asked Fiona.

"No," said Pimkin, deftly removing another glass of champagne from a passing waiter. "I felt your return of the bogus Earl of Bridgwater was quite enough for both of us."

"I wonder where he is now?" said Alexander.

"He no longer resides in Eaton Square," said Pimkin with the air of one who has divulged a piece of information which can only guarantee further rapt attention.

"Who would want the phony earl?"

"We are not aware of the provenance of the buyer, as he emanates from one of Her Majesty's former colonies, but the seller . . ."

"Stop teasing, Alec. Who?"

"None other than Mrs. Amanda Seymour."

"Amanda?"

"Yes. Amanda, no less. The dear, silly creature retrieved the false earl from the cellar where Charles had buried him with full military honors."

"But she must have realized it was a fake."

"My dear Amanda wouldn't know the difference between a Holbein and an Andy Warhol but she still happily accepted £10,000 for the impersonation. I am assured that the dealer who purchased this fabricated masterpiece made what I think vulgar people in the City describe as 'a quick turn.'"

"Good God," said Alexander. "I only paid £8,000 for it myself."

"Perhaps you should get Amanda to advise you on these matters in future," said Pimkin. "In exchange for my invaluable piece of information I'm bound to inquire if the real Earl of Bridgwater is to remain in hiding."

"Certainly not, Alec. He is merely awaiting the right moment to make a public appearance," said Fiona, unable to hide a smile.

"And where is Amanda now?" asked Alexander, obviously wanting to change the subject.

"In Switzerland producing a baby, which we can but hope will bear sufficient resemblance to a white Caucasian to convince one of Charles's limited imagination that he is the father."

"Where *do* you get all your information from?" asked Alexander.

Pimkin sighed dramatically. "Women have a habit of pouring their hearts out to me, Amanda included."

"Why should she do that?" asked Alexander.

"She lives safe in the knowledge that I am the one man she knows who has no interest in her body." Pimkin drew breath, but only to devour another smoked salmon sandwich.

Charles phoned Amanda every day while she was in Geneva. She kept assuring him all was well, and that the baby was expected on time. He had considered it prudent for Amanda not to remain in England advertising her pregnancy, a less than recent occurrence to even the most casual observer. She for her part did not complain. With £10,000 safely tucked away in a private Swiss account there were few little necessities she could not have brought to her, even in Geneva.

It had taken a few weeks for Charles to become accustomed to Government after such a long break. He enjoyed the challenge of the Treasury and quickly fell in with its strange traditions. He was constantly reminded that his was the department on which the Prime Minister kept the closest eye, making the challenge even greater. The civil servants, when asked their opinion of the new Financial Secretary, would reply variously: able, competent, efficient, hardworking—but without any hint of affection in their voices. When someone asked his driver, whose name Charles could never remember, the same question he proffered the view, "He's the sort of minister who always sits in the back of a car. But I'd still put a week's wages on Mr. Seymour becoming Prime Minister."

Amanda produced her child in the middle of the ninth month. After a week's recuperation she was allowed to return to England. She discovered traveling with her offspring was a nuisance and by the time she arrived at Heathrow she was more than happy to turn the child over to the nanny Charles had selected.

Charles had sent a car to pick her up from the airport. He

had an unavoidable conference with a delegation of Japanese businessmen, he explained, all of them busy complaining about the new Government tariffs on imports. At the first opportunity to be rid of his oriental guests he bolted back to Eaton Square.

Amanda was there to meet him at the door. Charles had almost forgotten how beautiful his wife was, and how long she had been away.

"Where's my child?" he asked, after he had given her a long kiss.

"In a nursery that's more expensively furnished than our bedroom," she replied a little sharply.

Charles ran up the wide staircase and along the passage. Amanda followed. He entered the nursery and stopped in his tracks as he stared at the future Earl of Bridgwater. The little black curls and deep brown eyes came as something of a shock.

"Good heavens," said Charles, stepping forward for a closer examination. Amanda remained by the door, her hand clutching its handle.

She had a hundred answers ready for his question.

"He's the spitting image of my great-grandfather. You skipped a couple of generations, Harry," said Charles, lifting the boy high into the air, "but there's no doubt you're a real Seymour."

Amanda sighed with inaudible relief. The hundred answers she could now keep to herself.

"It's more than a couple of generations the little bastard has skipped," said Pimkin. "It's an entire continent." He took another sip of christening champagne before continuing. "This poor creature, on the other hand," he said, staring at Fiona's firstborn, "bears a striking resemblance to Alexander. Dear little girl should have been given a kinder legacy with which to start her life."

"She's beautiful," said Fiona, picking Lucy up from the cradle to check her nappy.

"Now we know why you needed to be married so quickly," added Pimkin between gulps. "At least this child made wedlock, even if it was a close-run thing."

Fiona continued as if she had not heard his remark. "Have you actually seen Charles's son?"

"I think we should refer to young Harry as Amanda's child," said Pimkin. "We don't want to be had up under the Trade Descriptions Act."

"Come on, Alec, have you seen Harry?" she asked, refusing to fill his empty glass.

"Yes, I have. And I am afraid he also bears too striking a resemblance to his father for it to go unnoticed in later life."

"Anyone we know?" asked Fiona, probing.

"I am not a scandalmonger," said Pimkin, removing a crumb from his waistcoat. "As you well know. But a certain Brazilian *fazendeiro* who frequents Cowdray Park and Ascot during the summer months has obviously maintained his interest in English fillies."

Pimkin confidently held out his glass.

CHAPTER
TWENTY-SEVEN

JAMES CALLAGHAN'S RESIGNATION as Labour party leader in October 1980 took none of the political analysts by surprise. Unlike his predecessor he was over sixty-five, the age at which his party had recommended retirement.

Those same analysts were surprised, however, when Michael Foot, the veteran left-winger, defeated Denis Healey by 139 votes to 129 to become the new leader of the Labour party. The analysts immediately predicted a long spell of opposition for the socialists.

The Conservatives took much pleasure in watching a leadership struggle from the sidelines for a change. When Charles Seymour heard the result it amused him that the Labour party had ended up replacing a sixty-year-old with a sixty-four-year-old, who in turn was being replaced by a sixty-seven-year-old. Lord Shinwell, who at the age of ninety-six was the oldest living former Labour Cabinet minister, declared that he would be a candidate for party leadership when Foot retired.

When the election for the Shadow Cabinet came a week later Andrew decided not to submit his name. Like many of his colleagues he liked the new leader personally but had rarely been able to agree with him on domestic issues and was totally opposed to his defense and European policies. Instead he took on the chairmanship of the Select Committee on Scottish Affairs. Raymond for his part considered that Foot was destined to be no more than an interim leader and was therefore quite happy to serve under him. When the election to the Shadow Cabinet was announced Raymond came eighth. Michael Foot invited him to continue shadowing the Trade portfolio.

When Andrew entered the Commons Chamber the day after the election he walked up the gangway and took a seat on the back benches for the first time in fourteen years. He looked down at Raymond lounging on the front bench and recalled his own words: "There may well come a day when I sit and envy you from the same back benches."

Andrew was not surprised when he heard from his local committee in Edinburgh that he would once again have to submit himself to reselection as their candidate some time during 1981. When the Labour conference the previous October had approved the mandatory reselection of Labour MPs he had realized his biggest battle would be internal. Frank Boyle had even managed to replace another of Andrew's supporters with one of his own henchmen.

Roy Jenkins, the former deputy leader of the Labour party, was returning from Brussels as soon as his term as President of the European Commission came to an end. After delivering the Dimbleby lecture on television Jenkins made no secret of the fact that he was considering founding a new party that would take in those moderate radicals who felt the Labour party had swung too far to the left. The party conference had removed the power of selection of the leaders from Members of Parliament; for many this was the final straw, and several Labour MPs told Jenkins they were ready to defect. Andrew would have preferred to remain loyal to the party and try to change it from the inside, but he was fast coming to the conclusion that that hour had passed.

In his morning mail was a curt note from the constituency

secretary informing him that Frank Boyle was going to oppose him for the nomination. Andrew flew up to Edinburgh on the day of the meeting, fearing the worst. No one met him at the airport, and at party headquarters David Connaught greeted him with a glum face.

, Andrew stood in front of the committee in a cold, cheerless room and answered the same questions that had been put to him only three years before. He gave exactly the same answers: where he stood on nuclear disarmament, why he was in favor of a close association with the United States, his attitude to a wealth tax—on and on, predictable question after predictable question, but he never once allowed them to exasperate him.

He ended with the words: "I have been proud to serve the people of Edinburgh Carlton for almost twenty years as the Labour member and hope to do so for at least another twenty. If you now feel unable to reselect me I would have to consider standing as an independent candidate." For the first time, one or two members of the committee looked anxious.

"We are not intimidated by your threats, Mr. Fraser," said Frank Boyle. "The Labour party has always been bigger than any individual. Now we know where Mr. Fraser's real interests lie I suggest we move to a vote."

Twelve little slips of paper were passed out. "Fraser" or "Boyle" were scribbled on them before they were sent back to the chairman.

Frank Boyle slowly gathered up the slips, clearly relishing Andrew's discomfort. He unfolded the first slip of paper. "Boyle," he said, glancing at the others round the table.

He opened a second—"Fraser"—then a third, "Boyle," followed by "Fraser, Fraser, Fraser."

Andrew kept count in his head: four-two in his favor.

"Fraser," followed by "Boyle, Boyle, Fraser."

ιSix-four in Andrew's favor, with two still unopened: he only needed one more vote. "Boyle." Six-five. The chairman took some considerable time opening the last slip.

"Boyle," he announced in triumph.

He paused for effect. "Six votes all," he declared. "Under

standing order forty-two of the Party Constitution," he said, as if he had learned the words off by heart before the meeting, "in the result of a tie the chairman shall have the casting vote." He paused once again.

"Boyle," he said, lingering for a moment. "I therefore declare that Frank Boyle is selected as the official Labour party candidate for the constituency of Edinburgh Carlton at the next general election." He turned to Andrew and said, "We shall no longer be requiring your services, Mr. Fraser."

"I would like to thank those of you who supported me," Andrew said quietly and left without another word.

The next day the *Scotsman* came out with a lengthy article on the dangers of a small group of willful people having the power to remove a member who had served his constituents honorably over a long period of time. Andrew phoned Stuart Gray to thank him. "I only wish the article had come out the day before," he said.

"It was set up for yesterday," Stuart told him, "but the announcement from Buckingham Palace of Prince Charles's engagement to Lady Diana Spencer moved everything else out—even the Rangers–Celtic report. By the way, doesn't Boyle's nomination have to be confirmed by his General Management Committee?"

"Yes, but they are putty in his hands. That would be like trying to explain to your mother-in-law about your wife's nagging."

"Then why don't you appeal to the National Executive and ask for the decision to be put to a full meeting of the constituency party?"

"Because it would take weeks to get the decision overturned and more importantly I'm no longer certain that I want to fight the seat as a Labour candidate."

Andrew listened to the reporter's question and said, "Yes, you may quote me."

As the date for an election drew nearer Charles decided it might be wise to introduce Amanda to the constituency. He had explained to those who inquired that his wife had had rather a bad time of it after the birth, and had been told by her doctors not to participate in anything that might raise her blood pressure—though one or two constituents considered that the Sussex Downs' Conservatives would find it hard to raise the blood pressure of a ninety-year-old with a pacemaker. Charles had also decided to leave Harry at home, explaining that it was he who had chosen a public life, not his son.

The annual Garden Party held in the grounds of Lord Cuckfield's country home seemed to Charles to be the ideal opportunity to show off Amanda and he asked her to be certain to wear something appropriate.

He was aware that designer jeans had come into fashion, and that his clothes-conscious wife never seemed to dress in the same thing twice. He also knew that liberated women didn't wear bras. But he was nevertheless shocked when he saw Amanda in a near see-through blouse and jeans so tight it looked as if she had been poured into them. Charles was genuinely horrified.

"Can't you find something a little more . . . conservative?" he suggested.

"Like the things that old frump Fiona used to wear?"

Charles couldn't think of a suitable reply. "The Garden Party will be frightfully dull," said Charles desperately. "Perhaps I should go on my own."

Amanda turned and looked him in the eye. "Are you ashamed of me, Charlie?"

He drove his wife silently down to the constituency and every time he glanced over at her he wanted to make an excuse to turn back. When they arrived at Lord Cuckfield's home his worst fears were confirmed. Neither the men nor the women could take their eyes off Amanda as she strolled around the lawns devouring strawberries. Many of them would have used the word "hussy" if she hadn't been the member's wife.

Charles might have escaped lightly had it only been the one risqué joke Amanda told—to the bishop's wife—or even her curt refusals to judge the baby contest or to draw the raffle; but he was not to be so lucky. The chairman of the Women's Advisory Committee had met her match when she was introduced to the member's wife.

"Darling," said Charles. "I don't think you've met Mrs. Blenkinsop."

"No, I haven't," said Amanda, ignoring Mrs. Blenkinsop's outstretched hand.

"Mrs. Blenkinsop," continued Charles, "was awarded the OBE for her services to the constituency."

"OBE?" Amanda asked innocently.

Mrs. Blenkinsop drew herself up to her full height.

"Order of the British Empire," she said.

"I've always wondered," said Amanda, smiling. "My dad used to tell me it stood for 'other buggers' efforts.' "

"Seen the Persil anywhere?" asked Louise.

"No, I stopped washing my own pants some time ago," replied Andrew.

"Ha, ha," said Louise. "But if you haven't taken them who has—two giant packets are missing?"

"The phantom Persil thief strikes again. Whatever next?" said Andrew. "The Bovril perhaps?"

"Stop making a fool of yourself and go and fish Clarissa out of the bath."

Andrew pulled himself out of the armchair, dropped *The Economist* on the carpet, and ran upstairs. "Time to get out, young lady," he said even before he reached the bathroom door. First he heard the sobbing, then when he opened the door he found Clarissa covered from head to toe in soap flakes. Her thick black curly hair was matted with them. Andrew burst out laughing but he stopped when he saw Clarissa's knees and shins were bleeding. She held a large scrubbing brush in one hand which was covered in a mixture of soap powder and blood.

"What's the matter, darling?" asked Andrew, kneeling on the bath mat.

"It isn't true," said Clarissa, not looking at him.

"What isn't true?" asked Andrew gently.

"Look on the box," she said, pointing at the two empty packets which were standing on the end of the bath. Andrew glanced at the familiar picture on the box of a little fair-haired girl in a white party dress.

"What isn't true?" he repeated, still uncertain what Clarissa meant.

"It isn't true that Persil washes whiter and can remove even the blackest spots. Two large packets and I'm still black," she said.

Andrew had to smile which only made Clarissa cry even more. After he had washed off all the suds and gently dried her he put antiseptic ointment on the cuts and bruises.

"Why am I so black?" she asked.

"Because your mother and father were black," replied Andrew, guiding his daughter through to her bedroom.

"Why can't you be my father? Then I'd be white."

"I am your father now so you don't need to be."

"Yes, I do."

"Why?"

"Because the children at school laugh at me," Clarissa said, clutching firmly on to Andrew's hand.

"When I was at school they used to laugh at me because I was small," said Andrew. "They called me puny."

"What did you do about it?" asked Clarissa.

"I trained hard and ended up as captain of the school rugby team and that made them stop laughing."

"But by then you were big. I can't train to be white."

"No, I was still small, and you won't need to train."

"Why?" asked Clarissa, still not letting go of his hand.

"Because you're going to be beautiful, and then all those ugly white girls will be oh so jealous."

Clarissa was silent for some time before she spoke again. "Promise, Daddy?"

"I promise," he said, remaining on the edge of the bed.

"Like Frank Boyle is jealous of you?"

Andrew was startled. "What do you know about him?"

"Only what I heard Mummy say, that he's going to be the Labour man for Edinburgh, but you'll still beat him."

Andrew was speechless.

"Is he going to be the Labour man, Daddy?" she asked.

"Yes, he is."

"And will you beat him?"

"I'll try."

"Can I help?" Clarissa asked, a tiny smile appearing on her face.

"Of course. Now off you go to sleep," said Andrew, getting up and drawing the curtains.

"Is he black?"

"Who?" asked Andrew.

"The nasty Frank Boyle."

"No," said Andrew, laughing, "he's white."

"Then he ought to be made to have my skin then I could have his."

Andrew turned off the light, relieved Clarissa could no longer see his face.

Harry's second birthday party was attended by all those two-year-olds in the vicinity of Eaton Square whom his nanny considered acceptable. Charles managed to escape from a departmental meeting accompanied by a large paint board and a red tricycle. As he parked his car in Eaton Square he spotted Fiona's old Volvo driving away toward Sloane Square. He dismissed the coincidence although he still had plans for regaining the priceless Holbein. Harry naturally wanted to ride the tricycle round and round the dining room table. Charles sat watching his son and couldn't help noticing that he was smaller than most of his friends. Then he remembered that great grandfather had only been five feet eight inches tall.

It was the moment after the candles had been blown out, and nanny switched the light back on, that Charles was first aware that something was missing. It was like the game children play with objects on a tray: everyone shuts his eyes, nanny takes one away, and then you all have to guess which piece it was.

It took Charles some time to realize that the missing object was his gold cigar box. He walked over to the sideboard and studied the empty space. He continued to stare at the spot where the small gold box left to him by his great-grandfather had been the previous night. Now all that was left in its place was the matching lighter.

He immediately asked Amanda if she knew where the heirloom was, but his wife seemed totally absorbed in lining up the children for a game of musical chairs. After checking carefully in the other rooms Charles went into his study and phoned the Chelsea police.

An inspector from the Crime Squad came round immediately and took down all the details. Charles was able to supply the police officer with a photograph of the box which carried the initials C.G.S. He stopped just short of mentioning Fiona by name. The inspector assured Charles that he would deal with the investigation personally. Charles returned to the party to find nannies arriving to gather their wards.

When the Edinburgh Carlton Labour party issued a press statement after their AGM announcing that Frank Boyle had been selected to fight the seat as their candidate, Andrew was surprised and touched by the flood of letters and calls of goodwill he received, many from people he didn't even know. Most of the messages begged him to stand at the next general election as an Independent.

Twenty Labour MPs and one Conservative had joined the newly formed Social Democratic Party and many others were expected to follow. Andrew knew he would have to make an announcement soon if he didn't want his supporters to drift away. He spent agonizing hours discussing with Louise the problem of severing the final bonds with the party.

"What shall I do?" he asked, yet again.

"I can't tell you that; I just hope you make up your mind fairly quickly."

"Why quickly?"

"Because I'm going to vote for the Social Democrats at the next election, so you had better be my local candidate."

A few days later Roy Jenkins, Andrew's old chief at the Home Office, phoned to say he was fighting a by-election in Glasgow as the SDP candidate.

"I do hope you will feel able to join us," said Jenkins.

Andrew had always admired Jenkins's firm stand against the left and felt he was the one man who might break the two-party system.

"I need a little more time," he replied.

A week later Andrew made up his mind and informed the Chief Whip that he was leaving the party and would be joining the SDP. Then he packed a bag and traveled to Glasgow.

Roy Jenkins won the seat at Glasgow Hillhead with a large enough swing to worry both main parties. By Easter, a total of twenty-nine Members of Parliament had broken away to join him, while the alliance of SDP and Liberal MPs together could muster more than forty votes on the floor of the House.

With opinion polls putting them in second place, it began to look possible that the Social Democrats might hold the balance of power after the next election. The Conservatives were now running a poor third in all the national opinion polls.

Charles heard nothing for three weeks about the missing gold box and was beginning to despair when the inspector phoned to say that the family heirloom had been found.

"Excellent news," said Charles. "Are you able to bring the box round to Eaton Square?"

"It's not quite as simple as that, sir," said the policeman.

"What do you mean?"

"I would prefer not to discuss the matter over the phone. May I come and see you, sir?"

"By all means," said Charles, slightly mystified.

He waited impatiently for the inspector to arrive, although the policeman was at the front door barely ten minutes later. His first question took Charles by surprise.

"Are we alone, sir?"

"Yes," said Charles. "My wife and son are away visiting my mother-in-law in Wales. You say you've found the gold box," he continued, impatient to hear the inspector's news.

. "Yes, sir."

"Well done, Inspector. I shall speak to the Commissioner personally," he added, guiding the officer toward the drawing room.

"I'm afraid there's a complication, sir."

"How can there be when you've found the box?"

"We cannot be sure there was anything illegal about its disappearance in the first place."

"What do you mean, Inspector?"

"The gold case was offered to a dealer in Grafton Street for £2,500."

"And who was doing the selling?" asked Charles impatiently.

"That's the problem, sir. The check was made out to Amanda Seymour and the description fits your wife," said the inspector. Charles was speechless. "And the dealer has a receipt to prove the transaction." The inspector passed over a copy of the receipt. Charles was unable to steady his shaking hand as he recognized Amanda's signature.

"Now, as this matter has already been referred to the Director of Public Prosecutions I thought I ought to have a word with you in private, as I am sure you would not want us to prefer charges."

"Yes, no, of course, thank you for your consideration, Inspector," said Charles flatly.

"Not at all, sir. The dealer has made his position clear: he would be only too happy to return the cigar box for the exact sum he paid for it. I don't think that could be fairer."

Charles made no comment other than to thank the inspector again before showing him out.

He returned to his study, phoned Amanda at her mother's house, and told her to return immediately. She started to protest, but he had already hung up.

Charles remained at home until they all arrived back at

Eaton Square late that night. The nanny and Harry were immediately sent upstairs.

It took Charles about five minutes to discover that only a few hundred pounds of the money was left. When his wife burst into tears he struck her across the face with such force that she fell to the ground. "If anything else goes missing from this house," he said, "you will go with it and I will also make sure you spend a very long time in jail." Amanda ran out of the room sobbing uncontrollably.

The next day Charles advertised for a full-time governess. He also moved his own bedroom to the top floor so that he could be close to his son. Amanda made no protest.

Once the governess had settled in Amanda quickly became bored with the child and began disappearing for long periods. Charles couldn't be sure where she was most of the time, and didn't care.

After Pimkin had recounted the latest state of affairs to Alexander Dalglish in well-embroidered detail Fiona remarked to her husband, "I never thought the day would come when I would feel sorry for Charles."

On a sleepy Thursday in April 1982 Argentina attacked and occupied two small islands whose 1,800 British citizens were forced to lower the Union Jack for the first time in over a hundred years. Few members returned to their constituency that Friday and the House met unusually on a Saturday morning to debate the crisis while the nation followed every word on the radio.

The same day Mrs. Thatcher immediately dispatched a task force halfway around the globe to recapture the islands. Her fellow countrymen followed every scrap of news so intently that the London theaters found themselves empty at the height of the season.

Simon felt exhilarated to be a member of the Defense team at such an historic moment, and Elizabeth didn't begrudge him those days when he left before she had woken and arrived home after she had fallen asleep.

Under less public scrutiny but almost equal pressure, Charles beavered away at the Treasury addressing the economic problems that had been presented. He spent day after day in the House helping to put the Government's case. Like Simon he found he could only snatch moments to be at home but, unlike Elizabeth, his wife remained in bed until midday. When Charles did manage to slip away from the department he spent all his spare time with Harry, whose progress he followed with delighted concern.

At the time when the Union Jack was raised once again in the Falklands, the budget became an Act.

CHAPTER
TWENTY-EIGHT

"PM TO GO in Nov" and "Will Maggie wait till June?" were two of the headlines Andrew read on the first day of the new Parliamentary session.

Anyone who is defending a marginal seat is always on edge as the statutory five years draws to a close, and the new SDP members all treated their seats as marginal. Andrew was no exception.

He had worked hard to prove he was worth his place in the group the leader of the Social Democrats was beginning to form in the Commons. When Roy Jenkins had announced the make-up of his Shadow team Andrew was appointed Defense spokesman and enjoyed the challenge of pitting himself against the two main parties in the Commons in the run-up to the election. But once the Falklands crisis was over he knew his real problems were not going to be in Westminster but in Edinburgh, where he spent an increasing amount of his time. Hamish Ramsey phoned to ask him if there was anything he could do to help.

"Be my chairman for the election campaign," said Andrew simply.

Ramsey agreed without hesitation and within a fortnight four members of Andrew's old Labour party committee had defected to join him. Support for Andrew came from the most surprising quarters, including Jock McPherson, who pledged that the Scottish Nationalists would not be contesting the Edinburgh Carlton seat as they had no desire to see Frank Boyle in Parliament. Sir Duncan Fraser kept very quiet about what the Conservatives were up to until they announced that Jamie Lomax would be their standardbearer.

"Lomax. Lomax," repeated Andrew. "He and I were at school together," he told his father. "He was known as Loopy Lomax. You've selected the biggest idiot of his generation."

"That's a disgraceful slur on an able man," said Sir Duncan, trying to keep a straight face. "I can assure you it took a lot of convincing the committee to make certain Lomax was selected."

"How did you fix it?"

"I must admit it wasn't easy. We had some very good applicants, but I managed to undermine every one of them and point out how blemish-free Lomax's political past was," said Sir Duncan, winking.

"Nonexistent careers make for the best blemish-free pasts," said Andrew, and burst out laughing.

"Yes, I'm afraid one or two of the committee noticed that. But you must admit Lomax is a fine figure of a man," added his father.

"What's that got to do with it?" asked Andrew. "You weren't looking for a male model as candidate."

"I know, but it did help me to swing the ladies on the Women's Advisory Committee round to my way of thinking."

"You're a rogue, Father."

"No, I'm not. There isn't a Conservative in Scotland who would rather see Frank Boyle in the House than you, and as we have no chance of winning the seat, why let *him* in?"

Louise and Clarissa spent the Christmas recess in Edinburgh. Sir Duncan warned Louise that if Andrew lost this election he could never hope to return to the House of Commons again.

*   *   *

During 1983 Margaret Thatcher stuck firm to her monetarist policies and brought inflation below four percent, while in parts of Scotland unemployment rose to fifteen percent. She had gradually stifled any opposition from the "wets" and by the end of her first administration they were totally outmaneuvered. But it was the outcome of the Falklands crisis that had kept her ahead in the opinion polls for over a year. The press speculated on the date of the general election all through the month of April, and after the Conservatives' success in the local elections on 5 May the Prime Minister sought an audience with the Queen. Shortly afterward Margaret Thatcher told the nation that she needed another five years to continue her policies and prove that they worked. The election date was set for 9 June.

Once the election campaign had begun in earnest Stuart Gray interviewed all three candidates on behalf of the *Scotsman* and told Andrew he had a plan to help him.

"You can't," said Andrew. "You're bound to remain neutral and give all three candidates equal column inches during the campaign."

"Agreed," said Stuart. "But on the one hand we know Frank Boyle is sharp and has the looks of an escaped convict, while Jamie Lomax looks like a film star but makes crass statements every time he opens his mouth."

"So?" said Andrew.

"So I'm going to cover the political pages with the worst shots I can find of Boyle and fill up inch after inch with the sayings of Lomax. They'll both get equal coverage while at the same time they'll lose votes."

"They'll suss it out and complain to the editor."

"I doubt it," said Stuart. "I have yet to meet a politician who complained about having his photo in the paper, or one who was angered by seeing his mad views aired to a larger audience than he could have hoped to influence in the past."

"And what do you propose to do about me?"

"That's a problem," admitted Stuart, laughing. "Perhaps I'll leave the columns blank. That's one way you can't lose votes."

Whenever Andrew carried out a door-to-door canvass he found a clear division between those who still backed him and those who thought he had been disloyal to the Labour party. As the canvass returns came in and the colors were put out on the trestle tables in the new party headquarters it became clear from even a cursory glance that it was going to be his toughest election yet.

Andrew had experienced some dirty campaigns over the years, especially when he had been up against the Scottish Nationalists, but after only a few days he had sweet memories of Jock McPherson who was Little Red Riding Hood compared with Boyle. Andrew could just about tolerate hearing that he had been thrown out of the Labour party because he was such a lazy member, even that he had left them in the lurch because he had been told he could never hope to be a minister again, but when it was repeated to him that the Boyle camp were spreading a rumor that Louise had lost her voice because, when she had her baby, it turned out to be black he was furious.

If Andrew had seen Boyle that day he would undoubtedly have hit him. Sir Duncan counseled restraint, pointing out that any other action could only harm Louise and Clarissa. Andrew took a deep breath and said nothing.

With a week to go a local opinion poll in the *Scotsman* showed Boyle leading by thirty-five percent to Andrew's thirty-two. The Conservatives had nineteen percent but fourteen percent remained undecided. Jock McPherson had kept his word: no Scottish Nationalist candidate had entered the lists.

On the Friday before the election McPherson went one better by issuing a statement advising his supporters to back Andrew Fraser.

When Andrew phoned to thank him, he said, "I'm returning a favor."

"I don't remember ever doing you a favor," said Andrew.

"You certainly did, remembering you're an Edinburgh man. One mention to the press of my offer of the leadership of the Scottish Nationalists and I'd have been sunk down the nearest pothole."

With five days to go Alliance supporters from the two Edinburgh constituencies which were not fielding an SDP candidate swarmed in to help Andrew, and he began to believe the canvass returns that were now showing he could win. With two days to go the *Scotsman* proclaimed it was thirty-nine percent to thirty-eight percent in Boyle's favor, but also went on to point out that the Labour party would have a better-oiled machine to depend on when it came to polling day.

In his eve-of-poll message Andrew issued a clear statement on why his views differed from those of his opponent in the Labour party, and how he saw the future of Britain if the Alliance gained enough seats to hold the balance of power. He reminded voters that without exception the national opinion polls showed the SDP now running neck and neck with Labour.

Frank Boyle also put out an eve-of-poll message, delivered to every house in the constituency, showing a picture of Andrew holding Clarissa in his arms under the caption "Does your member tell you the whole truth?" There was no mention of Louise or Clarissa in the text but the innuendo could not have been clearer. Andrew didn't see the sheet until the morning of polling day by which time he knew there was nothing effective he could do to refute Boyle's implied slur. Issuing a writ that could not be dealt with until weeks after the election was over could only prove impotent. He either won the day or he lost it.

To that end, he and Louise never stopped working from seven that morning until ten at night. Helpers arrived from the most unexpected places, as if to prove the *Scotsman* wrong about the Labour party machine, but Andrew couldn't help noticing that there were red rosettes everywhere he went.

Toward the end of the day even Sir Duncan joined him and began chauffeuring SDP voters to the polls in his Rolls Royce.

"We've faced the fact that our candidate has lost so now I've come to help you," he told Andrew bluntly.

As the city hall clock struck ten Andrew sat down on the steps of the last polling station. He knew there was nothing he could do now. He had done everything possible, only avoiding members of the House of Lords and lunatics—neither of which group was entitled to vote.

An old lady was coming out of the polling station with a smile on her face.

"Hello, Mrs. Bloxham," said Andrew. "How are you?"

"I'm fine, Andrew." She smiled. "I nearly forgot to vote and that would never have done."

He raised his tired head.

"Now don't fret yourself, laddie," she continued, "I never failed to vote for the winner in fifty-two years and that's longer than you've lived." She chuckled and left him sitting on the steps.

Andrew somehow picked himself up and made his way through the dark cobbled streets to his election headquarters. They cheered him as he entered the room, and the chairman offered him a "wee dram of whisky."

"To hell with a wee dram," said Andrew. "Just keep pouring."

He tried to get round the room to thank everyone before Hamish Ramsey told him it was time to go over to the city hall for the count. A small band of supporters accompanied the Frasers to the city hall to witness the proceedings. As he entered the hall the first person he saw was Boyle, who had a big smile on his face. Andrew was not discouraged by the smile as he watched the little slips of paper pour out of the boxes. Boyle had yet to learn that the first boxes to be counted were always from the inner wards, where most of the committed Socialists lived.

As both men walked round the tables, the little piles began to be checked—first in tens, then hundreds, until they were finally placed in thousands and handed over to the Sheriff. As the night drew on Boyle's smile turned to a grin, from a grin to a poker face, and finally to a look of anxiety as the piles grew closer and closer in size.

For over three hours the process of emptying the boxes continued and the scrutineers checked each little white slip before handing in their own records. At one twenty-two in the morning the Sheriff added up the list of numbers in front of him and asked the three candidates to join him.

He told them the result.

Frank Boyle smiled once again. Andrew showed no emotion, but called for a recount.

For over an hour, he paced nervously around the room as the scrutineers checked and double-checked each pile: a change here, a mistake there, a lost vote discovered and, on one occasion, the name on the top of a pile of one hundred votes was not the same as the ninety-nine beneath it. At last the scrutineers handed back their figures. Once again the Sheriff added up the columns of numbers and asked the candidates to join him.

This time Andrew smiled while Boyle looked surprised and demanded another recount. The Sheriff acquiesced, but said it must be the last time. Both candidates agreed in the absence of their Conservative rival, who was sleeping soundly in a corner, secure in the knowledge that no amount of recounting would alter his position in the contest.

Once again the piles were checked and double-checked and five mistakes were discovered in the 42,588 votes cast. At three-twenty a.m., with counters and checkers falling asleep at their tables, the Sheriff once more asked the two candidates to join him. They were both stunned when they heard the result and the Sheriff informed them that there would be a further recount in the morning after his staff had managed to get some sleep.

All the voting papers were then placed carefully back in the black boxes, locked, and left in the safekeeping of the local constabulary while the candidates crept away to their beds.

Andrew slept in fits and starts through the remainder of the night. Louise, pale with exhaustion but still grinning, brought him a cup of tea at eight in the morning. He took a cold shower, shaved slowly, and was back at the city hall a few minutes before the count was due to recommence. As he walked up the steps he was greeted by a battery of television cameras and journalists who had heard rumors as to why the count had been held up overnight and knew they couldn't afford to be absent as the final drama unfolded.

The counters looked eager and ready when the Sheriff checked his watch and nodded. The boxes were unlocked and placed in front of the staff for the fourth time. Once again the little piles grew from tens into hundreds and then into thousands. Andrew paced around the tables, more to burn up his nervous energy than out of a desire to keep checking. He had thirty witnesses registered as his counting agents to make sure he didn't lose by sleight of hand or genuine mistake.

Once the counters and scrutineers had finished they sat in front of their piles and waited for the slips to be collected and taken to the Sheriff. When the Sheriff had added up his little columns of figures for the final time he found that no votes had changed hands.

He explained to Andrew and Frank Boyle the procedure he intended to adopt in view of the outcome. He told both candidates that he had spoken to Lord Wylie at nine that morning and the Lord Advocate had read out the relevant statute in election law that was to be followed in such circumstances. Both candidates agreed on which of the two choices they preferred.

The Sheriff walked up onto the stage with Andrew Fraser and Frank Boyle in his wake, both looking anxious.

Everyone in the room stood to be sure of a better view of the proceedings. When the pushing back of chairs, the coughing, and the nervous chattering had stopped, the Sheriff began. First he tapped the microphone that stood in front of him to be sure it was working. The metallic scratch was audible throughout the silent room. Satisfied, he began to speak.

"I, the returning officer for the district of Edinburgh Carlton, hereby declare the total number of votes cast for each candidate to be as follows:

Frank Boyle 18,437
Jamie Lomax 5,714
Andrew Fraser 18,437."

The supporters of both the leading candidates erupted into a noisy frenzy. It was several minutes before the Sheriff's voice could be heard above the babble of Scottish burrs.

"In accordance with section sixteen of the Representation of the People Act 1949 and rule fifty of the Parliamentary Election Rules in the second schedule to that Act, I am obliged to decide between tied candidates by lot," he announced. "I have spoken with the Lord Advocate of Scotland, and have confirmed that the drawing of straws or the toss of a coin may constitute decision by lot for this purpose. Both candidates have agreed to the latter course of action."

Pandemonium broke out again as Andrew and Boyle stood motionless on each side of the Sheriff waiting for their fate to be determined.

"I have borrowed from the Royal Bank of Scotland," continued the Sheriff, aware that twenty million people were watching him on television for the first and probably the last time in his life, "a golden sovereign. On one side is the head of King George III, on the other Britannia. I shall invite the sitting member, Mr. Fraser, to call his preference." Boyle curtly nodded his agreement. Both men inspected the coin.

The Sheriff rested the golden sovereign on his thumb, Andrew and Boyle still standing on either side of him. He turned to Andrew and said, "You will call, Mr. Fraser, while the coin is in the air."

The silence was such that they might have been the only three people in the room. Andrew could feel his heart thumping in his chest as the Sheriff spun the coin high above him.

"Tails," he said clearly when the coin was at its zenith. The sovereign hit the floor and bounced, turning over several times before settling at the feet of the Sheriff.

Andrew stared down at the lady and sighed audibly. The Sheriff cleared his throat before declaring, "Following the decision by lot, I declare the aforementioned Mr. Andrew Fraser

to be the duly elected Member of Parliament for Edinburgh Carlton."

Andrew's supporters charged forward and onto the stage and carried him on their shoulders out of the city hall and through the streets of Edinburgh. Andrew searched for Louise and Clarissa, but they were lost in the crush.

The Royal Bank of Scotland presented the golden sovereign to the member the next day, and the editor of the *Scotsman* rang to ask if there had been any particular reason why he had selected tails.

"Naturally," Andrew replied. "George III lost America for us. I wasn't going to let him lose Edinburgh for me."

CHAPTER
TWENTY-NINE

RAYMOND READ THE *Daily Mail* caption again and smiled: "On the toss of a coin."

It saddened Raymond that Andrew had felt it necessary to leave the Labour party, although he was delighted that he had been returned to the Commons. Raymond was only thankful that there had been no Frank Boyles in his constituency. He often wondered if it was because Joyce kept such a watchful eye on all the committees.

Margaret Thatcher's second victory had come as a bitter blow to him although he couldn't have pretended it was a surprise. Her overall majority of 144 was even larger than had been predicted, while the SDP managed only six seats—although the Alliance were only two percentage points behind Labour in actual votes cast. Raymond was enough of a realist to know that now nothing was going to stop the Tories from governing for another five-year term.

Once again Raymond returned to his practice at the bar and a new round of time-consuming briefs. When the Lord Chancellor, Lord Hailsham, offered him the chance to become a High Court judge, with a place in the House of Lords, Raymond gave the matter considerable thought before finally asking Joyce for her opinion.

"You'd be bored to tears in a week," she told him.

"No more bored than I am now."

"Your turn will come."

"Joyce, I'm nearly fifty, and all I have to show for it is the chairmanship of the Select Committee on Trade and Industry. If the party fails to win next time I may never hold office again. Don't forget that the last occasion we lost this badly we were in Opposition for thirteen years."

"Once Michael Foot has been replaced the party will take on a new look, and I bet you'll be offered one of the senior Shadow jobs."

"That'll depend on who's our next leader," said Raymond. "And I can't see a great deal of difference between Neil Kinnock who looks unbeatable, and Michael Foot— except that Kinnock's ten years younger than I am."

"Then why not stand yourself?" asked Joyce.

"It's too early for me," said Raymond.

"Then why don't you at least wait until we know who's going to be the leader of the party," said Joyce. "You can be a judge at any time—they die off just as quickly as Cabinet ministers."

When Raymond returned to his chambers the following Monday he followed Joyce's advice and let Lord Hailsham know that he was not interested in being a judge in the foreseeable future, and settled down to keep a watchful eye on Cecil Parkinson, the new Secretary of State for Trade and Industry.

Only a few days later Michael Foot announced that he would not be standing for leader when the party's annual conference took place. When he informed the Shadow Cabinet several faces lit up at the thought of the forthcoming battle at Brighton in October. Neil Kinnock and Roy Hattersley became the front runners, while during the weeks leading up to the conference several trade unionists and MPs approached Raymond and asked him to stand; but he told them all "next time."

The vote for the new leader took place on the Sunday before the conference began: as Raymond predicted Kinnock won easily and Hattersley, his closest rival, was elected as his deputy.

After the conference Raymond returned to Leeds for the weekend, still confident that he would be offered a major post in the Shadow Cabinet despite the fact he hadn't supported the winner. Having completed his morning surgery he hung around the house waiting for the new leader to call him, even missing the match against Chelsea. He didn't like being in the second division.

When Neil Kinnock eventually phoned late that evening Raymond was shocked by his offer and replied without hesitation that he was not interested. It was a short conversation.

Joyce came into the drawing room as he sank back into his favorite armchair.

"Well, what did he offer you?" she asked, facing him.

"Transport. Virtually a demotion."

"What did you say?"

"I turned him down, of course."

"Who has he given the main jobs to?"

"I didn't ask and he didn't volunteer, but I suspect we'll only have to wait for the morning papers to find out. Not that I'm that interested," he continued, staring at the floor, "as I intend to take the first place that comes free on the bench. I've wasted too many years already."

"So have I," said Joyce quietly.

"What do you mean?" asked Raymond, looking up at his wife for the first time since she had come into the room.

"If you're going to make a complete break, I think it's time for me to do so as well."

"I don't understand," said Raymond.

"We haven't been close for a long time, Ray," said Joyce, looking straight into her husband's eyes. "If you're thinking of giving up the constituency and spending even more time in London I think we should part." She turned away.

"Is there someone else?" asked Raymond, his voice cracking.

"No one special."

"But someone?"

"There is a man who wants to marry me," said Joyce, "if that's what you mean. We were at school in Bradford together. He's an accountant now and has never married."

"But do you love him?"

Joyce considered the question. "No, I can't pretend I do. But we're good friends, he's very kind and understanding and, more important, he's there."

Raymond couldn't move.

"And the break would at least give you the chance to ask Kate Garthwaite to give up her job in New York and return to London." Raymond gasped. "Think about it and let me know what you decide." She left the room quickly so that he could not see her tears.

Raymond sat alone in the room and thought back over his years with Joyce—and Kate—and knew exactly what he wanted to do now that the whole affair was out in the open.

He caught the last train to London the same evening because he had to be in court by ten o'clock the next morning to attend a judge's summing up. In the flat that night he slept intermittently as he thought about how he would spend the rest of his new life. Before he went into court the next morning he ordered a dozen red roses via Interflora. He phoned the Attorney General. If he was going to change his life he must change it in every way.

When the summing up was over and the judge had passed sentence Raymond checked the plane schedules. Nowadays you could be there in such a short time. He booked his flight and took a taxi to Heathrow. He sat on the plane praying it wasn't too late and that too much time hadn't passed. The flight seemed endless and he took another taxi from the airport.

When he arrived at her front door she was astonished. "What are you doing here on a Monday afternoon?"

"I've come to try and win you back," said Raymond. "Christ, that sounds corny," he added.

"It's the nicest thing you've said in years," she said as he held her in his arms; over Joyce's shoulder Raymond could see the roses brightening up the drawing room.

"Let's go and have a quiet dinner."

Over dinner Raymond told Joyce of his plans to accept the Attorney General's offer to join the bench, but only if she would agree to live in London. After a second bottle of champagne which Joyce had been reluctant to open they finally returned home.

When they arrived back a little after one the phone was ringing. Raymond opened the door and stumbled toward it while Joyce groped for the light switch.

"Ray, I've been trying to get you all night," a lilting Welsh voice said.

"Have you now?" Raymond said thickly, trying to keep his eyes open.

"You sound as if you've been to a good party."

"I've been celebrating with my wife."

"Celebrating before you've heard the news?"

"What news?" said Raymond, collapsing into the armchair.

"I've been juggling the new team around all day and I was hoping you would agree to join the Shadow Cabinet as . . ."

Raymond sobered up very quickly and listened carefully to the new leader. "Can you hold the line?"

"Of course," said the surprised voice on the other end.

"Joyce," said Raymond, as she came out of the kitchen clutching two mugs of very black coffee. "Would you agree to live with me in London if I don't become a judge?"

A broad smile spread across Joyce's face with the realization that he was seeking her approval.

She nodded several times.

"I'd be delighted to accept," he said.

"Thank you, Raymond. Perhaps we could meet at my room in the Commons tomorrow and talk over policy in your new field."

"Yes, of course," said Raymond. "See you tomorrow." He dropped the phone on the floor and fell asleep in the chair.

Joyce replaced the phone and didn't discover until the following morning that her husband was the new Shadow Secretary of State for Social Services.

Raymond sold his flat in the Barbican, and he and Joyce moved into a small Georgian house in Cowley Street, only a few hundred yards from the House of Commons.

Raymond watched Joyce decorate his study first, then she set about the rest of the house with the energy and enthusiasm of a newlywed. Once she had completed the guest bedroom Raymond's parents came down to spend the weekend. He burst out laughing when he greeted his father at the door clutching on to a bag, marked "Gould, the family butcher."

"They do have meat in London, you know," said Raymond.

"Not like mine, son," his father replied.

Over the finest beef Raymond could remember he watched Joyce and his mother chatting away. "Thank God I woke up in time," he said out loud.

"What did you say?" asked Joyce.

"Nothing, my dear, nothing."

Although Raymond spent most of his time on the overall strategy for a future Labour Government, like all politicians he had pet anomalies that particularly upset him. His had always been war widows' pensions, a preoccupation which dated back to his living with his grandmother in Leeds. He remembered the shock when he first realized shortly after leaving university that his grandmother had eked out an existence for thirty years on a weekly widow's pension that wouldn't have covered the cost of a decent meal in a London restaurant.

From the back benches, he had always pressed for the redeeming of war bonds and higher pensions for war widows. His weekly mail showed unequivocally just how major a problem war widows' pensions had become. During his years in Opposition he had worked doggedly to achieve ever-increasing, smaller rises, but he vowed that were he to become Secretary of State he would enact something more radical.

Joyce left a cutting from the *Standard* for him to read when he returned from the Commons that night. She had scribbled across it: "This could end up on the front page of every national paper."

Raymond agreed with her, and the following day he tried to press his view on to a reluctant Shadow Cabinet who seemed more concerned with the planned series of picketing by the Yorkshire miners' union than the case of Mrs. Dora Benson.

Raymond researched the story carefully and discovered that the case didn't differ greatly from the many others he had looked into over the years, except for the added ingredient of a Victoria Cross. By any standards, Mrs. Dora Benson highlighted Raymond's cause. She was one of the handful of surviving widows of the First World War and her husband, Private Albert Benson, had been killed at the Somme leading an attack on a German trench. Nine Germans had been killed before Albert Benson died, which was why he had been awarded the VC. His widow had continued working as a cleaner in the King's Head at Barking for over fifty years. Her only possessions of any value were her war bonds, but with no redemption date they were still passing hands at twenty-five pounds each. Mrs. Benson's case might have gone unnoticed if in desperation she had not asked Sotheby's to auction her husband's medal.

Once Raymond had armed himself with all the facts he put down a question to the minister concerned asking if he would at last honor the Government's long-promised pledges in such cases. A sleepy but packed House heard Simon Kerslake, as Minister of State for Defense, reply that his department was once again considering the problem and he would make known their findings in the near future. Simon settled back on to the green benches satisfied that would pacify Gould. But Raymond's supplementary stunned him and woke up the House.

"Does the Right Honorable Gentleman realize that this eighty-four-year-old widow, whose husband was killed in action and won the Victoria Cross, has a lower income than a sixteen-year-old cadet on his first day in the armed forces?"

Simon rose once more, determined to put a stop to the issue until he had had more time to study the details of this particular case.

"I was not aware of this fact, Mr. Speaker, and I can assure the Right Honorable Gentleman that I shall take into consideration all the points he has mentioned."

Simon felt confident the Speaker would now move on to the next question. But Raymond rose again, the Opposition benches spurring him on.

"Is the Right Honorable Gentleman also aware that an admiral, on an index-linked income, can hope to end his career with a pension of over £500 a week while Mrs. Dora Benson's weekly income remains fixed at £47.32?"

There was a gasp even from the Conservative benches as Raymond sat down.

Simon rose again, painfully aware that he was unprepared for Gould's attack and that he had to stifle it as quickly as he could. "I was not aware of that particular comparison either, but once again I can assure the Right Honorable Gentleman I will give the case my immediate consideration."

To Simon's horror Raymond rose from the benches for yet a third time. He could see that Labour members opposite were enjoying the rare spectacle of watching him up against the ropes. "Is the Right Honorable Gentleman also aware that the annuity for a Victoria Cross is £100 with no extra pension benefits? We pay our fourth-division footballers more, while keeping Mrs. Benson in the bottom league of the national income bracket."

Simon looked distinctly harassed when he in turn rose for a fourth time and made an uncharacteristic remark that he regretted the moment he said it.

"I take the Right Honorable Gentleman's point," he began, his words coming out a little too quickly. "And I am fascinated by his sudden interest in Mrs. Benson. Would it be cynical of me to suggest that it has been prompted by the wide publicity this case has enjoyed in the national press?"

Raymond made no attempt to answer but sat motionless with his arms folded and his feet up on the table in front of him while his own back-benchers screamed their abuse at Simon.

The national papers the next day were covered with pictures of the arthritic Dora Benson with her bucket and mop alongside photos of her handsome young husband in private's uniform. Many of the papers went on to describe how Albert Benson had won his VC, and some of the tabloids used considerable license. But all of them picked up Raymond's point that Mrs. Benson was in the bottom one percent of the income bracket and that the annuity for a Victoria Cross was a pathetic £100.

It was an enterprising and unusually thorough journalist from the *Guardian* who led her story on a different angle which the rest of the national press had to turn to in their second edition. It transpired that Raymond Gould had put down forty-seven questions concerning war widows' pension rights during his time in the House and spoken on the subject in three budgets and five social service debates from the back benches. He had also made the subject the thrust of his maiden speech over twenty years before. But when the journalist revealed that Raymond gave £500 a year to the Erskine Hospital for wounded soldiers every member knew that Simon Kerslake would have to retract his attack and make an apology to the House.

At three-thirty the Speaker rose from his chair and told a packed house that the Minister of State for Defense wished to make a personal statement.

Simon Kerslake rose warily from the front bench and stood nervously at the dispatch box.

"Mr. Speaker," he began. "With your permission and that of the House I would like to make a personal statement. During a question put to me yesterday I impugned the integrity of the Right Honorable Gentleman, the member for Leeds North. It has since been brought to my attention that I did him a gross injustice and I offer the House my sincere apologies, and the

Right Honorable Gentleman the assurances that I will not question his integrity a third time."

While younger members were puzzled by the reference, Raymond smiled to himself.

Aware of how rare personal statements were in anyone's parliamentary career, members looked on eagerly to see how he would respond.

He moved slowly to the dispatch box.

"Mr. Speaker, I accept the gracious manner in which the Right Honorable Gentleman has apologized and hope that he will not lose sight of the greater issue, namely that of war widows' benefits, and in particular the plight of Mrs. Dora Benson."

Simon looked relieved and nodded courteously.

Many Opposition members told Raymond he should have gone for Simon when he had him on the run, while Tom Carson continued shouting at Simon long after the House had proceeded to the next business. *The Times* leader writer proved them wrong when he wrote the next morning: "In an age of militant demands from the left, Parliament and the Labour party have found a new Clement Attlee on their front bench. Britain need have no fear for human dignity or the rights of man should Raymond Gould ever accede to the high office which that gentleman held."

When Raymond returned home from the Commons that night he found Joyce had cut out all the press comments for him to study and had also somehow managed to make inroads into his overflowing correspondence.

Joyce turned out to have a better feel for gut politics than the entire Shadow Cabinet put together.

Alec Pimkin threw a party for all his Tory colleagues who had entered the House in 1964, "To celebrate the first twenty years in the Commons," as he described the occasion in an impromptu after-dinner speech.

Over brandy and cigars the corpulent, balding figure sat back and surveyed his fellow members. Many had fallen by the wayside over the years, but of those that were left, he believed only two men now dominated the intake.

Pimkin's eyes first settled on his old friend Charles Seymour. Despite studying him closely he was still unable to spot a gray hair on the Treasury minister's head. From time to time Pimkin still saw Amanda, who had returned to being a full-time model and was rarely to be found in England nowadays. Charles, he suspected, saw more of her on the covers of magazines than he ever did in his home at Eaton Square. Pimkin had been surprised by how much time Charles was willing to put aside for little Harry. Charles was the last man he would have suspected of ending up a doting father. Certainly there was no sign of his ambitions diminishing, and Pimkin suspected that only one man remained a worthy rival for the party leadership.

His eyes moved on to someone for whom in 1984 Orwell's big brother seemed to hold no fears. Simon Kerslake was deep in animated conversation about his work on the proposed disarmament talks between Thatcher, Gorbachev, and Reagan. Pimkin studied the Defense minister intently. He considered that had *he* been graced with such looks he would not have had to fear for his dwindling majority. Rumors of some financial crisis had long since died away, and Kerslake now seemed well set for a formidable future.

The party began to break up, as one by one his contemporaries came over to thank him for such a "splendid," "memorable," "worthwhile" evening. When the last one had departed and Pimkin found himself alone he drained the drop of brandy that remained in his balloon and stubbed out the dying cigar. He sighed as he speculated on the fact that he could now never hope to be made a minister. He therefore determined to become a kingmaker, for in another twenty years there would be nothing left on which to speculate.

Raymond celebrated his twenty years in the House by taking Joyce to the Guinea Restaurant off Berkeley Square for dinner.

He admired the long burgundy dress his wife had chosen for the occasion and even noticed that one or two women gave it more than a casual glance throughout their meal.

He too reflected on his twenty years in the Commons, and he told Joyce over a brandy that he hoped he would spend more of the next twenty years in Government. 1984 had not turned out to be a good year for the Conservatives, and Raymond was already forming plans to make 1985 as uncomfortable for the Government as possible.

A few weeks later Tony Benn, who had lost his seat at the general election, returned to the House of Commons as the member for Chesterfield. The Conservatives came a poor third and went on to lose two more by-elections early in 1985. Even the press began to acknowledge that the Labour party was once again looking like a serious alternative Government.

The winter of 1985 brought a further rise in the unemployment figures which only increased the Labour party's lead in the polls. And then after the resignation of two cabinet ministers over a small helicopter company in the West Country and the loss of two further by-elections, the Conservatives fell into third place for the first time in five years.

A drop in the price of oil from $22 to $10 a barrel in the space of six weeks did not help the Chancellor's budget judgment. After a long, hot summer Mrs. Thatcher decided on a further cabinet reshuffle bringing in those who would be formulating policy in the run-up to the general election. The average age of the cabinet fell by seven years and the press dubbed it, "Mrs. Thatcher's new lamps for old reshuffle."

CHAPTER THIRTY

ANDREW WAS ON his way to the House of Commons when he heard the first reports on his car radio. There had been no mention of the news in the morning papers so it must have happened overnight. It began with a news flash: just the bare details. HMS *Broadsword*, one of the Navy's destroyers, had been passing through the Gulf of Surt between Tunis and Benghazi when she was boarded by a group of mercenaries, posing as coast guard officials, who took over the ship in the name of Colonel Gaddafi. The newscaster went on to say that there would be a more detailed report in their ten o'clock bulletin.

Andrew had reached his room in the House of Commons by nine-thirty, and he immediately phoned the SDP leader David Owen to discuss the political implications of the news. Once a course of action had been agreed on Andrew took a handwritten letter round to the Speaker's office before the noon deadline, requesting an emergency debate following question time that afternoon. He also sent a copy of the letter by messenger to the Foreign Secretary and the Secretary of State for Defense.

By staying near a radio most of the morning Andrew was able to learn that HMS *Broadsword* was now in the hands of over a hundred guerillas. They were demanding the freedom of all Libyan prisoners in British jails in exchange for the 217-strong crew of the *Broadsword*, who were being held hostage in the engine room.

By twelve o'clock the ticker-tape machine in the Members' Corridor was hovered over by craning necks, and the dining rooms were so full that many members had to go without lunch.

Question time that day had been allocated to Welsh Affairs, so the Chamber itself did not start filling up until nearly three-fifteen although the Palace of Westminster was already packed and buzzing with each new snippet of information. Political correspondents waited hawklike in the Members' Lobby seeking opinions on the crisis from any senior politicians as they passed to and from the Chamber. Few were rash enough to say anything that might be reinterpreted the next day.

When Andrew came into the Chamber he took his seat next to David Owen on the Opposition front bench below the gangway. Since Andrew had the overall responsibility for the Alliance Defense portfolio he was expected to represent the other twenty-two Alliance members. At three-twenty-seven the Prime Minister, followed by the Foreign Secretary and the Secretary of State for Defense, filed into the House and took their places on the Treasury bench. All three looked suitably somber. The last two questions on Welsh Affairs had the largest audience of members since the Aberfan disaster of 1966.

At three-thirty Mr. Speaker Weatherill rose and called for order.

"Statements to the House," he announced in his crisp, military style. "There will be two statements on HMS *Broadsword* before the House debates Welsh Affairs." The Speaker then called the Secretary of State for Defense.

Simon Kerslake rose from the front bench and placed a prepared statement on the dispatch box in front of him.

"Mr. Speaker, with your permission and that of the House, I would like to make a statement concerning Her Majesty's frigate *Broadsword*. At seven-forty GMT this morning HMS *Broadsword* was passing through the Gulf of Surt between Tunis and Benghazi when a group of guerillas, posing as official coast guards, boarded the ship and seized the officer in command, Captain Lawrence Packard, and placed the crew under arrest. The captain and his company did everything possible to resist but were outnumbered three to one. The guerillas, claiming to represent the People's Liberation Army, have since placed Captain Packard and the crew in the engine room of the ship. As far as it is possible to ascertain from our Embassy in Tripoli no lives have been lost, although Captain Packard sustained severe injuries during the battle, and we cannot be certain of his fate. There is no suggestion that *Broadsword* was doing anything other than going about her lawful business. This barbaric act must be looked upon as piracy under the 1958 Geneva Convention on the High Seas. The guerillas are demanding the release of all Libyan prisoners in British prisons in exchange for the return of HMS *Broadsword* and her crew. My Right Honorable friend, the Home Secretary, informs me there are only nine known Libyans in British jails at the present time, two of whom have been sentenced to three months for persistent shoplifting, two who were convicted on more serious drug charges, and the five who tried to hijack a British Airways 747 last year. Her Majesty's Government cannot and will not interfere with the due process of law and has no intention of releasing any of these men."

Loud "Hear, hears," came from all sections of the House.

"My Right Honorable friend, the Foreign Secretary, has made Her Majesty's Government's position clear to the Libyan Ambassador, in particular that Her Majesty's Government cannot be expected to tolerate this sort of treatment of British subjects or of British property. We have demanded and expect immediate action from the Libyan Government."

Simon sat down to loud and prolonged cheers before the leader of the Opposition rose from his place to say that he would wish it to be known that the Opposition gave the Government their full backing. He asked if any plans had been formulated at this early stage for the recovery of *Broadsword*.

Simon rose again. "We are, Mr. Speaker, at present seeking a diplomatic solution, but I have already chaired a meeting of the Joint Chiefs and I anticipate making a further statement to the House tomorrow."

"Mr. Andrew Fraser," said the Speaker.

Andrew rose from his place. "May I inform the Right Honorable Gentleman that we in the Alliance also concur with his views that this is an act of piracy. But can he tell the House how long he will allow negotiations to continue when it is well known throughout the diplomatic world that Gaddafi is a master of procrastination, especially if we were to rely on the United Nations to adjudicate on this issue?" From the noise that greeted Andrew's question it seemed that his views were shared by the majority of the House.

Simon rose to answer the question. "I accept the point the Honorable Gentleman is making but he will know, having been a Minister of State for Defense himself, that I am not in a position to divulge any information which might imperil the safety of *Broadsword*."

Question after question came at Simon. He handled them with such confidence that visitors to the Strangers' Gallery would have found it hard to believe that he had been invited to join the Cabinet only five weeks before.

At four-fifteen, after Simon had answered the last question the Speaker was going to allow, he sank back on the front bench to listen to the statement from the Foreign Office. The House fell silent once again as the Foreign Secretary rose from his place and checked the large double-spaced sheets in front of him. All eyes were now on the tall, elegant man who was making his first official statement since his appointment.

"Mr. Speaker, with your permission and that of the House, I too would like to make a statement concerning HMS *Broadsword*. Once news had reached the Foreign Office this morning of the plight of Her Majesty's ship *Broadsword* my office immediately issued a strongly worded statement to the Government of Libya. The Libyan Ambassador has been called to the Foreign Office and I shall be seeing him again immediately this statement and the questions arising from it has been completed."

Raymond looked up at the Strangers' Gallery from his place on the Opposition front bench. It was one of the ironies of modern diplomacy that the Libyan Ambassador was sitting in the gallery making notes while the Foreign Secretary delivered his statement. He couldn't imagine Colonel Gaddafi inviting the British Ambassador to take notes while he sat in his tent addressing his followers. Raymond was pleased to see an attendant ask the ambassador to stop writing; the prohibition dated from the time when the House had jealously guarded its privacy. Raymond's eyes dropped back to the front bench, and he continued to listen to Charles Seymour.

"Our ambassador to the United Nations has tabled a resolution to be debated by the General Assembly this afternoon, asking representatives to back Britain against this flagrant violation of the 1958 Geneva Convention on the High Seas. I confidently expect the support of the free world over this act of piracy against Her Majesty's ship *Broadsword*. Her Majesty's Government will do everything in its power to ensure a diplomatic solution bearing in mind that the lives of 217 British servicemen are still at risk."

The leader of the Opposition rose for a second time and asked at what point the Foreign Secretary would consider once again breaking off diplomatic relations with Libya.

"I naturally hope it will not come to that, Mr. Speaker, and I expect the Libyan Government to deal quickly with their own mercenaries."

Charles continued to answer questions from all sections of the House but could only repeat that there was little new intelligence to offer the House at the present time. Raymond watched his two contemporaries as they displayed over twenty years of parliamentary skill in presenting their case. He wondered if this episode would make one of them Mrs. Thatcher's obvious successor.

At four-thirty, the Speaker, realizing nothing original had been said for some time, announced that he would allow one further question from each side before returning to the business of the day. He shrewdly called Alec Pimkin who sounded to Raymond like "the very model of a modern major-general" and then Tom Carson who suggested that Colonel Gaddafi was often grossly misrepresented by the British press. Once Carson had sat down, Mr. Speaker found it easy to move on to other business.

The Speaker rose again and thanked the Honorable Gentleman, the member for Edinburgh Carlton, for his courtesy in informing him that he would be making an application under standing order number ten for an emergency debate. The Speaker said he had given the matter careful thought but he reminded the House that, under the terms of the standing order, he did not need to divulge the reasons for his decision, merely decide whether the matter should have precedence over the orders of the day. He ruled that the matter was not proper for discussion within the terms of standing order number ten.

Andrew rose to protest but as the Speaker remained standing he had to resume his seat.

"This does not mean, however," continued Mr. Speaker, "that I would not reconsider such a request at a later date."

Andrew realized that Charles Seymour and Simon Kerslake must have pleaded for more time, but he was only going to allow them twenty-four hours. The clerk at the table rose and bellowed above the noise of members leaving the Chamber, "Adjournment." The Speaker called the Secretary of State for Wales to move the adjournment motion on the problems facing the Welsh mining industry. The Chamber emptied of all but the thirty-eight Welsh MPs who had been waiting weeks for a full debate on the Principality's affairs.

Andrew went straight to his office and tried to piece together the latest information from news bulletins before preparing himself for a full debate the following day. Simon made his way back to the Ministry of Defense to continue discussions with the Joint Chiefs of Staff, while Charles was driven quickly to the Foreign Office.

When Charles reached his room, he was told by the Permanent Under-Secretary that the Libyan Ambassador awaited him.

"Does he have anything new to tell us?" asked Charles.

"Frankly, nothing; it seems that we're not the only people who are unable to make any contact with Colonel Gaddafi."

"Send him in then."

Charles stubbed out his cigarette and stood by the mantelpiece below a portrait of Palmerston. Charles had never met the ambassador before, largely because he had taken over at the Foreign Office only five weeks previously.

When Mr. Kadir, the five-foot-one, dark-haired, immaculately dressed Ambassador for Libya entered the room, the office resembled nothing so much as a study in which a headmaster was about to tick off an unruly boy from the lower fifth.

Charles was momentarily taken aback when he noticed the ambassador's old Etonian tie. He recovered quickly.

"Foreign Secretary?" began Mr. Kadir.

"Her Majesty's Government wishes to make it abundantly clear to your Government," began Charles, not allowing the ambassador to complete his sentiments, "that we consider the act of boarding and holding Her Majesty's ship *Broadsword* against her will as one of piracy on the high seas."

"May I say—?" began Mr. Kadir.

"No, you may not," said Charles, "and until our ship has been released, we shall do everything in our power to bring pressure, both diplomatic and economic, on your Government."

"But may I just say—?" Mr. Kadir tried again.

"My Prime Minister also wants you to know that she wishes to speak to your Head of State at the soonest possible opportunity, so I shall expect to hear back from you within the hour."

"Yes, Foreign Secretary, but may I—"

"And you may further report that we will reserve our right to take any action we deem appropriate if you fail to secure the release into safe custody of HMS *Broadsword* and her crew by twelve noon tomorrow, GMT. Do I make myself clear?"

"Yes, Foreign Secretary, but I would like to ask—"

"Good day, Mr. Kadir."

After the Libyan Ambassador was shown out Charles couldn't help wondering what it was he had wanted to know.

"What do we do now?" he asked when the Permanent Under-Secretary returned, having deposited Mr. Kadir in the lift.

"We act out the oldest diplomatic game in the world."

"What do you mean?" said Charles.

"Our sit-and-wait policy. We're awfully good at it," said the Permanent Under-Secretary, "but then we've been at it for nearly a thousand years."

"Well, while we sit let's at least make some phone calls. I'll start with Secretary of State Kirkpatrick in Washington and then I'd like to speak to Gromyko in Moscow."

When Simon arrived back at the Ministry of Defense from the Commons he was told that the Joint Chiefs were assembled in his office waiting for him to chair the next strategy meeting. As he entered the room to take his place at the head of the table the Joint Chiefs rose.

"Good afternoon, gentlemen," Simon said. "Please be seated. Can you bring me up to date on the latest situation, Sir John?"

Admiral Sir John Fieldhouse, Chief of the Defense Staff, pushed up the half-moon glasses from the end of his nose and checked the notes in front of him.

"Very little has changed in the last hour, sir," he began. "The Prime Minister's office has still had no success in contacting Colonel Gaddafi. I fear we must now treat the capture of *Broadsword* as a blatant act of terrorism, rather similar to the occupation seven years ago of the American Embassy in Iran by students who backed the late Ayatollah Khomeini. In such circumstances we can either 'jaw-jaw or war-war,' to quote Churchill. With that in mind, this committee will have formed a detailed plan by the early evening for the recapture of HMS *Broadsword*, as we assume the Foreign Office are better qualified to prepare for jaw-jaw." Sir John replaced his glasses and looked toward his minister.

"Are you in a position to give me a provisional plan which I could place in front of the Cabinet for their consideration?"

"Certainly, Minister," said Sir John, removing his glasses again before opening a large blue file in front of him.

Simon listened intently as Sir John went over his provisional strategy. Around the table sat eight of the senior ranking staff officers of the Army, Navy, and Air Force, and even the first draft plan bore the stamp of their 300 years of military experience. He couldn't help remembering that his call-up status was still that of a Second Lieutenant. For an hour he asked the Joint Chiefs questions that ranged from the elementary to ones that demonstrated a clear insight into their problems. By the time Simon left the room to attend the Cabinet meeting at No. 10 the Joint Chiefs were already updating their plan.

Simon walked slowly across Whitehall from the Department of Defense to Downing Street, his private detective by his side. Downing Street was thronged with people curious to see the comings and goings of ministers involved in the crisis. Simon was touched that the crowd applauded him all the way to the front door of No. 10, where the journalists and TV crews awaited each arrival. The great television arc lights were switched on as he reached the door and a microphone was thrust in front of him, but he made no comment. Simon was surprised by how many of the normally cynical journalists called out, "Good luck" and "Bring our boys home."

The front door opened and he went straight through to the corridor outside the Cabinet room, where twenty-two of his colleagues were already waiting. A moment later the Prime Minister walked into the Cabinet room and took her seat in the center of the table with Charles and Simon opposite her.

Mrs. Thatcher began by telling her colleagues that she had been unable to make any contact with Colonel Gaddafi and that they must therefore decide on a course of action that did not involve his acquiescence. She invited the Foreign Secretary to brief the Cabinet first.

Charles went over the actions in which the Foreign Office

was involved at the diplomatic level. He reported his meeting with Ambassador Kadir, and the resolution which had been tabled at the UN and was already being debated at an emergency session of the General Assembly. The purpose of asking the United Nations to back Britain on Resolution 12/40, he said, was to gain the diplomatic initiative and virtually guarantee international sympathy. Charles went on to tell the Cabinet that he expected a vote to take place in the General Assembly in New York that evening which would demonstrate overwhelming support for the United Kingdom's resolution, and which would be regarded as a moral victory by the whole world. He was delighted to be able to report to the Cabinet that the Foreign Ministers of both the United States and Russia had agreed to back the UK in her diplomatic endeavors as long as she launched no retaliatory action. Charles ended by reminding his colleagues of the importance of treating the whole affair as an act of piracy, rather than an injury at the hands of the Libyan Government itself.

A legal nicety, thought Simon as he watched the faces of his colleagues round the table. They were obviously impressed that Charles had brought the two super powers together in support of Britain. The Prime Minister's face remained inscrutable. She called upon Simon to air his views.

He was able to report that *Broadsword* had, since the last meeting of the Cabinet, been towed into the Bay of Surt and moored; there was no hope of boarding her except by sea. Captain Packard and his crew of 216 remained under close arrest in the engine room on the lower deck of the ship. From confirmed reports Simon had received in the last hour it appeared that the ship's company were bound, gagged, and that the ventilation systems had been turned off. "Captain Packard," he informed the House, "had refused to cooperate with the guerillas in any way, and we remain unsure of his fate." He paused. "I therefore suggest," Simon continued, "that we have no choice but to mount a rescue operation in order to avoid a protracted negotiation that can only end in grave loss of morale for the entire armed forces. The longer we put off such a decision the harder our task will become. The Joint Chiefs are putting the final touches to a plan code-named 'Shoplifter' which they feel must be carried out in the next forty-eight hours, if the men and the ship are to be saved." Simon added that he hoped diplomatic channels would be kept open while the operation was being worked out, in order that the rescue team could be assured of the greatest element of surprise.

"But what if your plan fails?" interrupted Charles. "We would risk losing not only *Broadsword* and her crew but also the goodwill of the free world."

"There is no serving officer in the British Navy who will thank us for leaving *Broadsword* in Libyan waters while we negotiate a settlement in which, at best, our ship will be returned when it suits the guerillas—to say nothing of the humiliation of our Navy. Gaddafi can laugh at the United Nations while he has captured not only one of our most modern frigates but also the headlines of the world's press. As Ayatollah Khomeini did, he will want to keep them both for as long as he can. These headlines can only demoralize our countrymen and invite the sort of election defeat Carter suffered at the hands of the American people after the Iranian Embassy debacle."

"We would be foolish to take such an unnecessary risk while we have world opinion on our side," protested Charles. "Let us at least wait a few more days."

"I fear that if we wait," said Simon, "the crew will be transferred from the ship to a military prison, which would only result in our having two targets to concentrate on, and then Gaddafi can sit around in the desert taking whatever amount of time suits him."

Simon and Charles weighed argument against counterargument while the Prime Minister listened, taking note of the views of her other colleagues round the table to see if she had a majority for one course or the other. Three hours later, when everyone had given his opinion, she had "fourteen-nine" written on the pad in front of her.

"I think we have exhausted the arguments, gentlemen," she said, "and having listened to the collective views around this table I feel we must on balance allow the Secretary of State for Defense to proceed with Operation Shoplifter. I therefore propose that the Foreign Secretary, the Defense Secretary, the Attorney General, and myself make up a sub-committee, backed up by a professional staff, to consider the Joint Chiefs' plan. The utmost secrecy will be required from us at all times, so the subject will not be raised again until the plan is ready for presentation to a full meeting of the Cabinet. Therefore, with the exception of the sub-committee, all ministers will return to their departments and carry on with their normal duties. We must not lose sight of the fact that the country still has to be governed. Thank you, gentlemen." The Prime Minister asked Charles and Simon to join her in the study.

As soon as the door was closed she said to Charles, "Please let me know the moment you hear the result of the vote in the General Assembly. Now that the Cabinet has favored a military initiative, it is important that you are seen to be pressing for a diplomatic solution."

"Yes, Prime Minister," said Charles without emotion.

Mrs. Thatcher then turned to Simon. "When can I have a rundown on the details of the Joint Chiefs' plan?"

"We anticipate working on the strategy through the night, Prime Minister, and I should be able to make a full presentation to you by ten tomorrow."

"No later, Simon," said the Prime Minister. "Now our next problem is tomorrow's proposed emergency debate. Andrew Fraser will undoubtedly put in a second request for a full debate under standing order number ten and the Speaker gave a clear hint today he will allow it. Anyway, we can't avoid making a policy statement without an outcry from the Opposition benches—and I suspect our own—so I've decided that we will grasp the nettle and no doubt get stung."

The two men looked at each other, exasperated at the thought of having to waste precious hours in the Commons.

"Charles, you must be prepared to open the debate for the Government, and Simon, you will wind up. At least the debate will be on Thursday afternoon; that way some of our colleagues may have gone home for the weekend, though frankly I doubt it. But with any luck we will have secured a moral victory at the United Nations, and we can keep the Opposition minds concentrating on that. When you sum up, Simon, just answer the questions put during the debate without offering any new initiative."

She then added, "Report any news you hear direct to me. I shan't be sleeping tonight."

Charles walked back to the Foreign Office, at least thankful that Amanda was somewhere in South America.

Simon returned to the Joint Chiefs to find a large map of Libyan territorial waters pinned to a blackboard. Generals, admirals, and air marshals were studying the contours and ocean depths like children preparing for a geography test.

They all stood again when Simon entered the room. They looked at him in anticipation, men of action who were suspicious of talk. When Simon told them the Cabinet's decision was to back the Ministry of Defense the suggestion of a smile came over the face of Sir John. "Perhaps that battle will turn out to be our hardest," he said, just loud enough for everyone to hear.

"Take me through the plan again," said Simon, ignoring Sir John's comment. "I have to present it to the Prime Minister by ten o'clock tomorrow."

Sir John placed the tip of a long wooden pointer on a model of HMS *Broadsword* in the middle of a stretch of water in a well-protected bay.

When Charles reached his office the international telegrams and telexes of support for a diplomatic solution were piled high on his desk. The Permanent Under-Secretary reported that the debate in the United Nations had been so one-sided that he anticipated an overwhelming majority when they came to vote. Charles feared his hands were tied; he had to be seen to go through the motions, even by his own staff, although he had not yet given up hopes of undermining Simon's plan. He intended the whole episode to end up as a triumph for the Foreign Office and not for "those warmongers" at the Ministry of Defense. After consulting the Permanent Under-Secretary Charles appointed a small Libyan task force consisting of some older Foreign Office mandarins with experience of Gaddafi and four of the department's most promising high fliers.

Mr. Oliver Miles, the former Ambassador to Libya, had his leave canceled and was deposited in a tiny room in the upper reaches of the Foreign Office so that Charles could call on his local knowledge at any time, day or night, throughout the crisis.

Charles asked the Permanent Under-Secretary to link him up with Britain's ambassador at the United Nations.

"And keep trying to raise Gaddafi."

Simon listened to Sir John go over the latest version of Operation Shoplifter. Thirty-seven men from the crack Special Boat Service, the Marine equivalent of the SAS regiment which had been involved in the St. James's Square siege in April 1984, were now in Rosyth on the Scottish coast, preparing to board HMS *Brilliant*, the sister ship to *Broadsword*.

The men were to be dropped from a submarine a mile outside Rosyth harbor and to swim the last mile and a half under water until they reached the ship. They would then board *Brilliant* and expect to recapture her from a mock Libyan crew in an estimated twelve minutes. *Brilliant* would then be sailed to a distance of one nautical mile off the Scottish coast. The operation was to be completed in sixty-five minutes. The SBS planned to rehearse the procedure on *Brilliant* three times before first light the following morning, when they hoped to have the entire exercise down to one hour.

Simon had already confirmed the order to send two submarines from the Mediterranean full steam in the direction of the Libyan coast. The rest of the fleet was to be seen to be conspicuously going about its normal business while the Foreign Office appeared to be searching for a diplomatic solution.

Simon's request to the Joint Chiefs came as no surprise and was granted immediately. He phoned Elizabeth to explain why he wouldn't be home that night. An hour later the Secretary of State for Defense was strapped into a helicopter and on his way to Rosyth.

Charles followed the proceedings at the United Nations live in his office on a satellite link-up. At the end of a brief debate a vote was called for. The Secretary General announced 147–3 in Great Britain's favor, with twenty-two abstentions. Charles wondered if such an overwhelming vote would be enough to get the Prime Minister to change her mind over Kerslake's plan. He checked over the voting list carefully. The Russians, along with the Warsaw Pact countries and the Americans, had kept their word and voted with the UK. Only Libya, South Yemen, and Djibouti had voted against. Charles was put through to Downing Street and passed on the news. The Prime Minister, although delighted with the diplomatic triumph, refused to change course until she had heard from Gaddafi. Charles put the phone down and asked his Permanent Under-Secretary to call Ambassador Kadir to the Foreign Office once more.

"But it's two o'clock in the morning, Foreign Secretary."

"I am quite aware what time it is but I can see no reason why, when we are all awake, he should be having a peaceful night's sleep."

When Mr. Kadir was shown into his room it annoyed Charles to see the little man still looking fresh and dapper. It was obvious that he had just shaved and put on a clean shirt.

"You called for me, Foreign Secretary?" asked Mr. Kadir politely, as if he had been invited to afternoon tea.

"Yes," said Charles. "We wished to be certain that you are aware of the vote taken at the United Nations an hour ago supporting the United Kingdom's Resolution 12/40."

"Yes, Foreign Secretary."

"In which your Government was condemned by the leaders of ninety percent of the people on the globe"—a fact the Per-

manent Under-Secretary had fed to Charles a few minutes
before Mr. Kadir had arrived.

"Yes, Foreign Secretary."

"My Prime Minister is still waiting to hear from your Head
of State."

"Yes, Foreign Secretary."

"Have you yet made contact with Colonel Gaddafi?"

"No, Foreign Secretary."

"But you have a direct telephone link to his headquarters."

"Then you will be only too aware, Foreign Secretary, that I
have been unable to speak to him," said Mr. Kadir with a wry
smile.

Charles saw the Permanent Under-Secretary lower his eyes.
"I shall speak to you on the hour every hour, Mr. Kadir, but do
not press my country's hospitality too far."

"No, Foreign Secretary."

"Good night, Ambassador," said Charles.

"Good night, Foreign Secretary."

Kadir turned and left the Foreign Office to be driven back
to his Embassy. He cursed the Right Honorable Charles Seymour. Didn't the man realize that he hadn't been back to
Libya, except to visit his mother, since the age of four? Colonel Gaddafi was ignoring his ambassador every bit as much as
he was the British Prime Minister. He checked his watch: it
was two forty-four.

Simon's helicopter landed in Scotland at two forty-five. He
and Sir John were immediately driven to the dockside, then
ferried out to HMS *Brilliant* through the misty night.

"The first Secretary of State not to be piped on board in
living memory," said Sir John as Simon made his way with difficulty, his blackthorn stick tapping up the gangplank. The
captain of the *Brilliant* couldn't disguise his surprise when he
saw his uninvited guests and took them quickly to the bridge.
Sir John whispered something in the captain's ear which
Simon missed.

"When is the next raid due?" asked Simon, staring out from

the bridge but unable to see more than a few yards in front of him.

"They leave the sub at 0300, sir," said the captain, "and should reach *Brilliant* at approximately three-twenty. They hope to have taken command of the ship in eleven minutes and be a mile beyond territorial waters in under the hour."

Simon checked his watch: it was five to three. He thought of the SBS preparing for their task, unaware that the Secretary of State and the Chief of the Defense Staff were on board *Brilliant* waiting for them. He pulled his coat collar up.

Suddenly he was thrown to the deck, a black and oily hand clamped over his mouth before he could protest. He felt his arms whipped up and tied behind his back as his eyes were blindfolded and he was gagged. He tried to retaliate and received a sharp elbow in the ribs. Then he was dragged down a narrow staircase and dumped onto a wooden floor. He lay trussed up like a chicken for what he thought was about ten minutes before he heard the ship's engines revving up and felt the movement of the ship below him. The Secretary of State could not move for another fifteen minutes.

"Release them," Simon heard a voice say in distinctly Oxford English. The rope around his arms was untied and the blindfold and gag removed. Standing over the Secretary of State was an SBS frogman, black from head to toe, his white teeth gleaming. Simon was still slightly stunned as he turned to see the Services Chief also being untied.

"I must apologize, Minister," said Sir John, as soon as his gag was removed, "but I told the captain not to inform the submarine commander we were on board. If I am going to risk 217 of my men's lives I wanted to be sure this rabble from the SBS knew what they were up to." Simon backed away from the six-foot-two giant who towered over him, still grinning.

"Good thing we didn't bring the Prime Minister along for the ride," said Sir John.

"I agree," said Simon, looking up at the SBS commando. "She would have broken his neck." Everyone laughed except the frogman who pursed his lips.

"What's wrong with him?" said Simon.

"If he utters the slightest sound during the first sixty minutes he has no hope of being selected for the final team."

"The Conservative party could do with some back-bench Members of Parliament like that," said Simon, "especially when I have to address the House tomorrow and explain why I'm doing nothing."

By three-forty-nine *Brilliant* was a mile beyond territorial waters. The newspaper headlines that morning ranged from "Diplomatic Victory" in *The Times* to "Gaddafi the Pirate" in the *Mirror*.

At a meeting of the inner Cabinet held at ten in the morning Simon reported his first-hand experience of Shoplifter to the Prime Minister. Charles was quick to follow him. "But after the overwhelming vote in our favor at the UN it must be sensible for us to postpone anything that might be construed as an outright act of aggression."

"If the SBS don't go tomorrow morning we will have to wait another month, Prime Minister," said Simon, interrupting him. All eyes at the meeting of the inner Cabinet turned to Kerslake.

"Why?" asked Mrs. Thatcher.

"Because Ramadan, when Moslems fast and cannot take drink during daylight hours, will be coming to an end tomorrow. Traditionally the heaviest eating and drinking takes place the following day, which means tomorrow night will be our best chance to catch the guerillas off guard. I have been over the entire operation in Rosyth and by now the SBS are well on their way to the submarines and preparing for the assault. It's all so finely tuned, Prime Minister, that obviously we can't throw away such a strategic advantage."

"That's good reasoning," she concurred. "With the weekend ahead of us we must pray that this mess will be all over by Monday morning. Let's put on our negotiating faces for the Commons this afternoon. I expect a very convincing performance from you, Charles."

*　　*　　*

When Andrew rose at three-thirty that Thursday afternoon to ask for a second time for an emergency debate under standing order number ten the Speaker granted his request, directing that the urgency of the matter warranted a debate to commence at seven o'clock that evening.

The Chamber emptied quickly as the members scuttled off to prepare their speeches, although they all knew that less than two percent of them could hope to be called. The Speaker departed the Chamber and did not return until five to seven when he took over the chair from his deputy.

By seven o'clock, when Charles and Simon had entered the House, all thirty-seven SBS men were aboard Her Majesty's submarine *Conqueror*, lying on the ocean bed about sixty nautical miles off the Libyan coast. A second submarine, *Courageous*, was ten miles to her rear. Neither had broken radio silence for the past twelve hours.

The Prime Minister had still not heard from Colonel Gaddafi and they were now only eight hours away from Operation Shoplifter. Simon looked around him. The atmosphere resembled Budget Day and an eerie silence fell as the Speaker called Andrew Fraser to address the House.

He began by explaining, under standing order number ten, why the matter he had raised was specific, important, and needed urgent consideration. He quickly moved on to demand that the Foreign Secretary confirm that if negotiations with Gaddafi failed or dragged on the Secretary of State for Defense would not hesitate to take the necessary action to recover HMS *Broadsword*. Simon sat on the front bench looking glum and shaking his head.

"Gaddafi's nothing more than a pirate," said Andrew. "Why talk of diplomatic solutions?"

The House cheered as each well-rehearsed phrase rolled off Andrew's tongue. When he sat down the cheers came from all parts of the Chamber and it was several minutes before the Speaker could bring the House back to order. Mr. Kadir sat in the Distinguished Strangers' Gallery staring impassively down, trying to memorize the salient points that had been made and the House's reaction to them, so that—if he were ever given the chance—he could pass them on to Colonel Gaddafi.

"The Foreign Secretary," called the Speaker and Charles rose from his place on the Treasury bench. He placed his speech on the dispatch box in front of him and waited. Once again the House fell silent.

Charles opened his case by emphasizing the significance of the United Nations' vote as the foundation for a genuine negotiated settlement. He went on to say that his first priority was to secure the lives of the 217 men on board HMS *Broadsword* and that he intended to work tirelessly to that end. The Secretary General was hoping to contact Gaddafi personally and brief him on the strong feelings of his colleagues in the General Assembly. Charles stressed that taking any other course at the present time could only lose the support and goodwill of the free world. When Charles sat down he realized that the rowdy House was not convinced.

The contribution from the back benches confirmed the Prime Minister's and Simon's beliefs that they had gauged the feelings of the nation correctly, but neither of them allowed the slightest show of emotion to cross their faces and give hope to those who were demanding military action.

By the time Simon rose to wind up for the Government at nine-thirty that night he had spent two and a half hours in the Chamber listening to men and women tell him to get on with exactly what he was already doing. Blandly, he backed the Foreign Secretary in his pursuit of a diplomatic solution. The House became restive, and when the clock reached ten Simon sat down to cries of "Resign" from some of his own colleagues and the more right-wing of the Labour benches.

Andrew watched carefully as Kerslake and Seymour left the Chamber. He wondered what was really going on in his old department.

He arrived home after the debate. Louise congratulated him on his speech and added, "But it didn't evoke much of a response from Simon Kerslake."

"He's up to something," said Andrew. "I only wish I was sitting in his office tonight and could find out what it is."

When Simon arrived in that office he phoned Elizabeth and explained that he would be spending another night at the ministry.

"Some women do lose their men to the strangest mistresses," said Elizabeth. "By the way, your younger son wants to know if you will have time to watch him play hockey in his cuppers' match at Oxford on Saturday."

"What's today?"

"It's still Thursday," she said, "and you're the one in charge of the nation's defenses."

Simon knew the rescue attempt would be all over one way or the other by lunchtime the next day. Why shouldn't he watch his son play hockey?

"Tell him I'll be there," he said.

Although nothing could be achieved between midnight and six o'clock now the submarines were in place, none of the Joint Chiefs left the operations room. Radio silence was not broken once through the night as Simon tried to occupy himself with the bulging red boxes containing other pressing matters which still demanded his attention. He took advantage of the presence of the Joint Chiefs and had a hundred queries answered in minutes that would normally have taken him a month.

At midnight the first editions of the morning papers were brought to him. Simon pinned up the *Telegraph*'s headline on the operations board. "Kerslake's in his Hammock till the great Armada comes." The article demanded to know how the hero of Northern Ireland could be so indecisive while our sailors lay bound and gagged in foreign waters, and ended with the words "Captain, art thou sleeping there below?" "Not a wink," muttered Simon. "Resign" was the single-word headline in the *Daily Express*. Sir John looked over the minister's shoulder and read the opening paragraph.

"I shall never understand why anyone wants to be a politician," he said before reporting: "We have just heard from reconnaissance in the area that both submarines *Conqueror* and *Courageous* have moved up into place."

Simon picked up his stick from the side of his desk and left the Joint Chiefs to go to Downing Street. He took the private lift to the basement and then walked through the tunnel which runs under Whitehall direct to the Cabinet room, thus avoiding the press and any curious onlookers.

He found the Prime Minister sitting alone in the Cabinet room.

Simon went over the final plan with her in great detail, explaining that everything was ready and would be over by the time most people were having their breakfasts.

"Let me know the moment you hear anything, however trivial," she concluded, before returning to the latest gloomy study of the economy from the Wynne Godley team, who were suggesting the pound and the dollar would be on an equal parity by 1988. "One day you may have all these problems on *your* shoulders," she said.

Simon smiled and left her to walk back through the private tunnel to his office on the other side of Whitehall.

He took the lift back up to his room on the sixth floor and joined the Joint Chiefs. Although it was past midnight none of them looked tired despite their all having shared the lonely vigil with their comrades 2,000 miles away. They told stories of Suez and the Falklands, and there was frequently laughter. But it was never long before their eyes returned to the clock.

As Big Ben struck two chimes, Simon thought: four o'clock in Libya. He could visualize the men falling backward over the side of the boat and deep into the water before starting the long, slow swim toward *Broadsword*.

When the phone rang, breaking the eerie silence like a fire alarm, Simon picked it up to hear Charles Seymour's voice.

"Simon," he began, "I've finally got through to Gaddafi and he wants to negotiate." Simon looked at his watch; the SBS men could only be a few hundred yards from *Broadsword*.

"It's too late," he said. "I can't stop them now."

"Don't be such a bloody fool—order them to turn back. Don't you understand we've won a diplomatic coup?"

"Gaddafi could negotiate for months and still end up humiliating us. No, I won't turn back."

"We shall see how the Prime Minister reacts to your arrogance," said Charles and slammed down the receiver.

Simon sat at his desk and waited for the telephone to ring. He wondered if he could get away with taking the damn thing off the hook—the modern equivalent of Nelson placing the telescope to his blind eye, he considered. He needed a few minutes, but the phone rang again only seconds later. He picked it up and heard Margaret Thatcher's unmistakable voice.

"Can you stop them if I order you to, Simon?"

He considered lying. "Yes, Prime Minister," he said.

"But you would still like to carry it through, wouldn't you?"

"I only need a few minutes, Prime Minister."

"Do you understand the consequences if you fail, with Charles already claiming a diplomatic victory?"

"You would have my resignation within the hour."

"I suspect mine would have to go with it," she said. "In which case Charles would undoubtedly be Prime Minister by this time tomorrow." There was a moment's pause before she continued. "Gaddafi is on the other line and I am going to tell him that I *am* willing to negotiate." Simon felt defeated. "Perhaps that will give you enough time, and let's hope it's Gaddafi who has to worry about resignations at breakfast."

Simon nearly cheered.

"Do you know the hardest thing I have had to do in this entire operation?"

"No, Prime Minister."

"When Gaddafi rang in the middle of the night, I had to pretend to be asleep so that he didn't know I was sitting by the phone."

He laughed.

"Good luck, Simon. I'll phone and explain my decision to Charles."

The clock read three-thirty.

On his return the bevy of admirals were variously clenching their fists, tapping the table, or walking around it, and Simon began to sense what the Israelis must have felt like as they waited for news from Entebbe.

The phone rang again. He knew it couldn't be the Prime Minister this time as she was the one woman in England who never changed her mind. It was Charles Seymour.

"I want it clearly understood, Simon, that I gave you the news concerning Gaddafi's desire to negotiate at three-twenty. That is on the record, so there will be only one minister handing in his resignation later this morning."

"I know exactly where you stand, Charles, and I feel confident that whatever happens you'll come through your own mound of manure smelling of roses." He slammed down the phone just as four o'clock struck. For no fathomable reason everyone in the room stood up, but as the minutes passed again one by one they sat back down.

At seven minutes past four radio silence was broken with the five words, "Shoplifter apprehended, repeat Shoplifter apprehended."

Simon watched the Joint Chiefs cheer like schoolchildren reacting to the winning goal at a football match. *Broadsword* was on the high seas in neutral waters. He sat down at his desk and asked to be put through to No. 10. The Prime Minister came on the line. "Shoplifter apprehended," he told her.

"Congratulations, continue as agreed," was all she said.

The next move was to be sure that all the Libyan prisoners who had been taken aboard *Broadsword* would be discharged at Malta and sent home unharmed. Simon waited impatiently for radio silence to be broken again, as agreed, at five o'clock.

Captain Lawrence Packard came on the line as Big Ben struck five. He gave Simon a full report on the operation: one Libyan guerilla had been killed and eleven injured. There had been no, repeat no, British deaths and only a few minor injuries sustained. The thirty-seven SBS men were back on board the submarines *Conqueror* and *Courageous*. HMS *Broadsword* had two engines out of action and currently resembled an Arab bazaar, but was sailing the high seas on her way home. God Save the Queen.

"Congratulations, Captain," said Simon. He returned to Downing Street, no longer bothering to use the secret tunnel. As he limped up the road journalists with no idea of the news that was about to be announced were already gathering outside No. 10. Once again he answered none of their shouted questions. When he was shown into the Cabinet room he found Charles already there with the Prime Minister. He told them both the latest news.

"Well done, Simon," said Mrs. Thatcher.

Charles made no comment.

It was agreed that the Prime Minister would make a statement to the House at three-thirty that afternoon.

"I must admit that my opinion of Charles Seymour has gone up," said Elizabeth in the car on the way to Oxford to watch Peter play in his hockey match.

"What do you mean?" asked Simon.

"He's just been interviewed on television. He said he had backed your judgment all along while having to pretend to carry out pointless negotiations. He had a very good line to the effect that it was the first time in his life that he had felt honorable about lying."

"Smelling like roses," Simon said sharply. Elizabeth didn't understand her husband's response.

He went on to tell his wife everything that had gone on between them during the last few hours.

"Why didn't you say something?"

"And admit that the Foreign Secretary and I were quarrelling throughout the entire operation? It would only show up the Government in a bad light and give the Opposition something to latch on to."

"I'll never understand politics," said Elizabeth resignedly.

It amused Simon to watch his son massacred in the mud while he stood on the touchline in the rain only hours after he had feared Gaddafi might have done the same to him. "It's a walkover," he told the Principal when Peter's college were four goals down by half-time.

"Perhaps he'll be like you and surprise us all in the second half," came back the reply.

At eight o'clock on the following Saturday morning Simon sat in his office and heard the news that *Broadsword* had all engines on full speed and was expected to reach Portsmouth by three o'clock, exactly one week after his son had lost his college match eight-nil: they hadn't had a good second half. Simon had tried to console his downcast son but it didn't help that he had been the goalkeeper.

He was smiling when his secretary interrupted his thoughts to remind him that he was due in Portsmouth in an hour. As Simon reached the door the phone rang. "Explain to whoever it is I'm already late," he said.

His secretary replied, "I don't think I can, sir."

Simon turned round, puzzled. "Who is it?" he asked.

"Her Majesty the Queen."

Simon returned to his desk, picked up the receiver, and listened to the sovereign. When she had finished Simon thanked her and said he would pass on her message to Captain Packard as soon as he reached Portsmouth. During the flight down Simon looked out of the helicopter and stared at a traffic jam that stretched from the coast to London with people who were going to welcome *Broadsword* home. The helicopter landed an hour later.

The Secretary of State for Defense stood on the pier and was able to pick out the destroyer through a pair of binoculars. She was about an hour away but was already so surrounded by a flotilla of small craft that it was hard to identify her.

Sir John told him that Captain Packard had signaled to ask if the Secretary of State wished to join him on the bridge as they sailed into port. "No, thank you," said Simon. "It's his day, not mine."

"Good thing the Foreign Secretary isn't with us," said Sir John. A squad of Tornadoes flew over, drowning Simon's reply. As *Broadsword* sailed into port, the ship's company were all on deck standing to attention in full dress uniform. The ship itself shone like a Rolls-Royce that had just come off the production line.

By the time the captain descended the gangplank a crowd of some 500,000 were cheering so loudly that Simon could not hear himself speak. Captain Packard saluted as the Secretary of State leaned forward and whispered the Queen's message in his ear:

"Welcome home, Rear-Admiral Sir Lawrence Packard."

CHAPTER
THIRTY-ONE

THE *BROADSWORD* FACTOR remained in the memories of the electorate for a far shorter time than had the Falklands victory and the Conservative cause was not helped by the breakdown in Geneva of the disarmament talks between Reagan, Gorbachev, and Thatcher.

The Russians put the blame for the breakdown on Mrs. Thatcher's "aggressive stance" over *Broadsword* after they had backed her for a diplomatic solution at the UN. Within six months the Conservative lead in the opinion polls had dropped to three percent.

"The truth is," noted Raymond at a Shadow Cabinet meeting, "Mrs. Thatcher has had nearly eight years at No. 10 and no Prime Minister has served two full terms in succession—let alone three—since Lord Liverpool in 1812."

At that time of the year when referees leave the field to be replaced by umpires Raymond watched his predictions become history. Once the Christmas recess had ended he felt sure the Prime Minister would go to the country in late May or some time in June rather than face another winter. When the Conservatives held on to the marginal seat in Birmingham and fared better than expected at the local elections in May no one believed the Prime Minister would delay the announcement much longer.

Margaret Thatcher seemed to care nothing for Lord Liverpool or historical precedent, because she called an election for late June, believing that the month that had been a winner for her in the past would prove to be good for her again.

"It's time to let the nation choose who is to govern for the next five years," she declared on "Panorama."

"Of course, it's got nothing to do with the fact she's regained a slight lead in the opinion polls," said Joyce tartly.

"A lead that could well disappear during the next few weeks," Raymond added.

He returned to Yorkshire for only three days of the campaign. As one of the party's leading spokesmen he had to travel around the country addressing meeting after meeting in marginal seats. Many journalists went as far as to suggest that were Raymond leading the party they would be in a far stronger position to win the election. On the few occasions he was back in Leeds he enjoyed the electioneering and felt completely relaxed with his constituents for the first time in his life. He also felt his age when he discovered that the new Tory candidate for Leeds North had been born in 1964, the year he had first entered Parliament. When they met the only insult Raymond suffered at his young rival's hands was being called "sir."

"Please call me by my Christian name," said Raymond.

"Raymond—" began the young man.

"No, Ray will do just fine."

Charles and Simon also saw little of their constituencies as they too toured the marginal seats, adding more and more to their schedules as the polling day became closer. Halfway through the campaign the Conservatives mounted a massive attack on the Alliance, as opinion polls were continuing to show that they were making considerable inroads into the

Conservative vote, while traditional Labour supporters were returning to their old allegiance.

Andrew had to remain in Edinburgh for the entire campaign, to face Frank Boyle once again. But this time, as Stuart Gray informed the constituents of Edinburgh Carlton through his columns in the *Scotsman*, it was a Frank Boyle without teeth. Andrew felt what was left of those teeth a few times during the final three weeks but at least the Royal Bank of Scotland did not find it necessary to part with a second golden sovereign in their 300-year history. Andrew retained his seat by over 2,000 votes, to be returned to Parliament for the eighth time. Louise claimed that her husband's majority were the 2,000 people who had fallen in love with the thirteen-year-old coltish Clarissa, who was already fulfilling her father's prophecy as gauche fifteen-year-old Scots blushed in her presence.

The final result of the election did not become clear until four o'clock on the Friday afternoon as several recounts took place up and down the country.

"It will be a hung Parliament," David Dimbleby told the viewers tuned into the BBC "Election Special" program that afternoon. He repeated the detailed figures for those people still returning from work:

Conservative	313
Labour	285
Liberal/SDP Alliance	31
Irish/Ulster Unionist	17
Speaker and others	4

Dimbleby went on to point out that there was no necessity for Mrs. Thatcher to resign as she was still the leader of the largest party in the Commons. But one thing was apparent, the SDP might well hold the balance at the next election.

The Prime Minister made very few changes to her frontbench team as she clearly wished to leave an impression of unity despite her small majority. The press dubbed it 'The cosmetic Cabinet." Charles moved to the Home Office while Simon became Foreign Secretary.

Everyone at Westminster was thankful when a few weeks later Parliament broke up for the summer recess and politicians returned home for a rest.

That rest was to last a complete week before Tony Benn rolled a thundercloud across the clear blue summer sky by announcing he would contest the leadership of the Labour party at the October conference.

Benn claimed that Kinnock's naïveté and gauche approach as leader had been the single reason that the Labour party had not been returned to power. There were many Socialists who agreed with this judgment, but they also felt they would have fared considerably worse under Benn.

What his announcement did, however, was to make respectable the claim of any other candidates who wished their names to be put forward. Roy Hattersley and John Smith joined Benn and Kinnock for the first ballot. Many Members of Parliament, trade union leaders, and constituency activists pressed Raymond to stand for the leadership.

"If you don't stand now," Joyce told him, "you'll have no chance in the future."

"It's the future I'm thinking about," replied Raymond.

"What do you mean?" she asked.

"I want to stand for deputy leader against Michael Meacher and John Cunningham, and that will secure me a power base in the party which would afford me a better chance next time."

Raymond waited another week before he launched his candidacy. On the following Monday, at a packed press conference, he announced he would be standing for deputy leader.

With four candidates in the field for the leadership no clear favorite emerged although most prophets accepted Benn would lead after the first ballot. Hattersley came to an agreement with Smith that whichever one of them captured the most votes in the first round the other would drop out and support the leader of the right in the final ballot.

When the vote had been counted Benn, as predicted, topped the first ballot, with Kinnock in third place. To everyone's surprise when Kinnock dropped out he advised his supporters not to back Benn as he felt it could only spell a further prolonged period of Opposition for the Labour party.

A few hours later the party chairman announced that Tony Benn had been soundly beaten. The Labour party had a new moderate leader.

The vote then took place for the deputy leadership and although the new leader made clear his preference for Raymond everyone still expected it to be close. Joyce spent the last hour running from delegate to delegate while Raymond tried to appear calm. At eleven o'clock that Sunday night the chairman of the Labour party's National Executive announced that by a mere three percent Raymond Gould was the newly elected deputy leader of the Labour party.

The new leader immediately appointed Raymond Shadow Chancellor of the Exchequer.

Among the many letters and telegrams Raymond received was one from Kate, which read: Congratulations. But have you read standing order no. 5(4) of the party constitution? Raymond replied: Hadn't. Have now. Let's hope it's an omen.

In their first twelve months the new Labour team looked fresh and innovative as Mrs. Thatcher began to look tired and out of touch. She was not helped in her cause by the election of Gary Hart to the White House in November 1988. President Hart's avowed intention to lower unemployment and spend more of the nation's wealth to help "genuine Democrats" left Britain with a handful of new problems. The pound strengthened against the dollar overnight, and large export orders sat gathering dust in dockside warehouses.

But what threw her economic forecasts into total disarray was the decision of the recently elected Governments of Brazil and Argentina to refuse to repay any of the loans negotiated by their former military rulers leaving the Bank of England with what could only be described as an overdraft.

During the long cold winter of 1988 the Conservatives lost several votes on the floor of the House and many more upstairs in committee. The Prime Minister seemed somewhat relieved to find herself spending Christmas at Chequers.

The relief did not last long as two elderly Conservative members died before the House convened in January. The press dubbed the Government the "lame drake" administration.

Both of the pending by-elections were held in May: the Conservatives fared far better than might have been expected, holding on to one and just losing the other. For a third time Mrs. Thatcher plumped for a June election.

After a decade of the lady from Grantham Raymond sensed the mood was for change. The monthly unemployment, inflation, and import/export figures announced at regular intervals during the campaign all augured badly for the Conservatives.

The Prime Minister's reiterated plea that a Government shouldn't be judged on one month's figures now sounded unconvincing, and by the final week the only point of contention was whether the Labour party would end up with a decent working majority.

Raymond woke up on the Friday morning after the election to be told by Joyce that the computer predictions indicated an overall majority of four seats. Together they toured the constituency that morning before joining Raymond's parents for a late lunch. When they left the little butcher's shop that afternoon there was a crowd of well-wishers awaiting them on the pavement who cheered them all the way to their car. Raymond and Joyce traveled down to London and were back in Cowley Street in time to watch the first Labour Prime Minister since 1979 emerge from Buckingham Palace with the television cameras following him all the way back until he took up residence at 10 Downing Street.

This time Raymond did not have long to wait for a telephone call because the first appointment the new Prime Minister confirmed was his Chancellor. Raymond and Joyce traveled to No. 11 later that afternoon, instructing estate agents to lease their Cowley Street house on a six-month let that might or might not be renewable. Joyce spent hours checking over her new home and replacing some of the objects she had inherited from Diana Brittan while Raymond called his team over from Transport House to prepare the Labour party's first budget, and replace even more of what Leon Brittan had left behind.

After Raymond's advisers returned to Transport House that night he started to go over the hundreds of letters and telegrams of congratulations that had been flooding in throughout the day. One from America made him particularly happy, and he returned his own best wishes to Mrs. Kate Wilberhoff.

Andrew had defeated Frank Boyle for a third time and the left-winger announced that he would not be standing again.

Andrew had also spent a weekend thanking all his helpers. When he returned to the Commons on the Monday morning he found a note awaiting him on the Members' Letterboard.

Over lunch in the Members' Dining Room David Owen informed him privately that he would not be seeking reelection as leader of the SDP: seven years had been quite enough. Although the party had slightly improved their position in the House he accepted that they now faced a five-year Parliament, and he wanted Andrew to take over.

As soon as Owen had issued an official press statement Geoffrey Parkhouse of the *Glasgow Herald* was the first to phone and ask Andrew, "When will you be announcing your bid for the SDP leadership?"

Leaving the Home Office came as a great blow to Charles. His period of time there had been so short that he felt he had achieved very little. The civil servants had procrastinated over all major decisions as they waited for another general election and a clear mandate. He informed Amanda over breakfast on the Monday after the election that he would be returning to Seymour's Bank and that his salary would once again be sufficient for her allowance to remain constant—so long as she kept to her part of the bargain. Amanda nodded and left the breakfast table without comment just as Harry came in.

It was an important morning for Harry as he was to be taken to his first day of prep school at Hill House to begin the academic course mapped out for him by his father. Charles tried to convince him that it would be the start of a wonderful future, but Harry looked apprehensive. Once he had deposited a tearful eight-year-old with his first headmaster Charles continued on to the City, cheerful at the prospect of returning to the world of banking.

When he arrived at Seymour's, he was met by Clive Reynolds's secretary who immediately took him through to the boardroom and asked him if he would like a coffee.

"Thank you," said Charles, taking off his gloves, placing his umbrella in the stand, and settling himself in the chairman's seat at the head of the table. "And would you tell Mr. Reynolds I'm in?"

"Certainly," said the secretary.

Clive Reynolds joined him a few moments later.

"Good morning, Mr. Seymour. How nice to see you again after such a long time," he said, shaking Charles by the hand.

"Good morning, Clive. It's nice to see you, too. First I must congratulate you on the manner in which you have conducted the bank's affairs in my absence."

"It's kind of you to say so, Mr. Seymour."

"I was particularly impressed by the Distillers takeover; that certainly took the City by surprise."

"Yes, quite a coup, wasn't it?" said Reynolds, smiling. "And there's another one in the pipeline."

"I shall look forward to hearing the details."

"Well, I'm afraid it remains confidential at the moment," said Clive, taking the seat beside him.

"Of course, but now I have returned I had better be briefed fairly soon."

"I'm afraid shareholders cannot be briefed until we are certain the deals have been concluded. We can't afford any rumors harming our chances, can we?"

"But I'm not an ordinary shareholder," said Charles sharply. "I am returning as chairman of the bank."

"No, Mr. Seymour," said Reynolds quietly. "I am chairman of this bank."

"Do you realize whom you are addressing?" said Charles.

"Yes, I think so. A former Foreign Secretary, a former Home Secretary, a former chairman of the bank, and a two percent shareholder."

"But you are fully aware that the board agreed to have me back as chairman when the Conservatives went into Opposition," Charles reminded him.

"The composition of the board has changed considerably since those days," said Reynolds. "Perhaps you've been too busy running the rest of the world to notice minor comings and goings in Cheapside."

"I shall call a board meeting."

"You don't have the authority."

"Then I shall demand an Extraordinary General Meeting," said Charles.

"And tell the shareholders what? That you had a standing order to return as Chairman when you felt like it? That won't sound like a former Foreign Secretary."

"I'll have you out of this office in twenty-four hours," Charles continued, his voice suddenly rising.

"I don't think so, Mr. Seymour. Miss Trubshaw has completed her five years and left us on a full pension, and it won't take you long to discover that I don't possess a Swiss bank account or a well-compensated mistress."

Charles went red in the face. "I'll get you removed. You don't begin to understand how far my influence stretches."

"I hope I'm not removed, for your sake," said Reynolds calmly.

"Are you threatening me?"

"Certainly not, Mr. Seymour, but I would hate to have to explain how Seymour's lost over £500,000 on the Nethercote account because of your personal wish to ruin Simon Kerslake's career. It may interest you to know that the only thing the bank gained from that fiasco was goodwill, and we only managed that because I recommended that Morgan Grenfell pick up the pieces."

Charles couldn't resist a smile. "When I make that public it will finish you," he said triumphantly.

"Perhaps," said Reynolds calmly, "but it would also stop you from becoming Prime Minister."

Charles turned, picked up his umbrella, put on his gloves, and walked away. As he reached the door, a secretary walked in holding two cups of coffee. Charles passed her without a word and slammed the door.

"I'll only be needing one, Miss Bristow."

During the first week after the Queen's Speech Andrew was pleased to discover that a majority of his colleagues wrote to say that they would support him if he put his name forward for the leadership of the SDP.

At their weekly parliamentary meeting the party Whip asked that names for the post of party leader be submitted to his office within seven days. Each candidate had to be proposed and seconded by Members of Parliament.

For the next week the popular press tried to suggest, conjure up, or even invent a rival for Andrew. Louise, who believed almost everything she read in the papers, took to perusing the *Morning Star*, the only paper which showed no interest in the outcome. But by five o'clock on the seventh day it had become obvious that Andrew was to be the sole nomination.

At the next parliamentary meeting of the SDP he was not so much elected as anointed. On the following Saturday, having been made a Privy Councillor the day before, Andrew addressed the party faithful at a packed Albert Hall. After a well-received speech, the press unanimously predicted—yet again—an SDP-Liberal revival. One or two journalists were quick to point out that if the balance of power did ever rest in his hands the Right Honorable Andrew Fraser might not know which way to jump: with on the one hand a father who was a distinguished Tory, while on the other having been a member of the Labour party himself for twenty years, which party would he consider the lesser of the two evils? Andrew always told the press that he would worry about that when the problem arose, because the SDP might not even be able to come to an agreement with the Liberals.

Numerous articles on the new SDP leader appeared in newspapers and magazines across the country. They all reported the stories of his attempt to save his son's life, the gradual recovery of his wife after Robert's death, the successful adoption of Clarissa, and his reelection to Parliament on the toss of a golden sovereign.

All the publicity made Clarissa feel like a film star, she told her father. She was the most popular girl in school, she added, so he had better become Prime Minister. He laughed but proceeded to lead his party with a determination and energy that caused him to be talked of in the same breath as the leaders of the two main parties.

No sooner had the publicity over Andrew's election died down than the press started speculating as to whether Mrs. Thatcher would now make way for a younger man.

"Don't you know any other restaurant?"

"Yes, but they don't know me," replied Ronnie Nethercote, as the two men strolled into the Ritz for the first time in a couple of years. Heads turned as people leaned forward and whispered Simon's name to their guests.

"What are you up to nowadays? I can't believe Opposition fully occupies you," Ronnie said as they took their seats.

"Not really. I might also be described as one of the four million unemployed," replied Simon.

"That's what we're here to talk about," said Ronnie, "but first I recommend the country vegetable soup and the . . ."

"Beef off the trolley," interjected Simon.

"You remembered."

"It's the one thing you've always been right about."

Ronnie laughed more loudly than people normally did in the Ritz before saying, "Now you no longer have the entire armed forces at your disposal or ambassadors to call you Your Eminence or whatever they call you now, why don't you join the board of my new company?"

"It's kind of you to ask, Ronnie, but the answer has to be no."

They both broke off their conversation to allow the head waiter to take their orders.

"There's a salary of £20,000 a year that goes with it."

"I can't deny that Elizabeth and I could do with the money. With Peter staying up at Oxford to do a D.Phil. and Michael bent on being an actor I wonder if my bank account will ever be in credit."

"Then why not come in with us?" asked Ronnie.

"Because I'm a committed politician," said Simon, "and I no longer want to involve myself in any commercial activities."

"That might stop you becoming Prime Minister?"

Simon hesitated at the bluntness of Ronnie's question then said, "Frankly, yes. I've got a better than outside chance and I'd be foolish to lengthen the odds by becoming involved in anything else right now."

"But everyone knows that as soon as Margaret announces she's going to pack up you'll be the next leader. It's as simple as that."

"No, Ronnie, it's never as simple as that."

"Then tell me, who could beat you?"

"Charles Seymour, for one."

"Seymour? He's a toffee-nosed git," said Ronnie.

"He has a lot of friends in the party, and his patrician background still counts for something with the Tories. Sir Alec remains the best loved of our most recent Prime Ministers."

"Yes, but he was given the leadership by the magic circle," said Ronnie. "You'd kill Seymour with every elected member of the party having a vote."

"Time will tell," said Simon, bored with a conversation he had had with so many people lately. "But what have you been up to?" he asked, deliberately changing the subject.

"I've been working my backside off in preparation for going

public in about a year's time, which is why I wanted you on the board."

"You never give up."

"No, and I hope you haven't given up your one percent of the company."

"Elizabeth has it locked away somewhere."

"Then you had better find the key."

"Why?" asked Simon.

"Because when I put out ten million shares on the market at three quid a time, your one original share will be exchanged for 100,000 shares of common stock. I know you weren't ever Chancellor but that's £300,000 of anyone's money."

Simon was speechless.

"Well, say something," said Ronnie.

"Frankly I'd forgotten the share existed," Simon finally managed.

"Well, I think I can safely say," said Ronnie, parodying one of Mrs. Thatcher's favorite phrases, "that's not a bad investment for a pound, and one you will never regret."

As the budget debate drew nearer Raymond found twenty-four hours each day were not enough, even without sleep. He discussed the changes he required with the Treasury mandarins, but it became more obvious as each week passed that he would have to make sacrifices. He was sick of being told that there would always be next year, feeling he had waited far too long already. He often went over to Transport House to discuss with his party researchers those promises in the manifesto which they considered the top priorities. Raymond had been pleased by the party's decision to leave Walworth Road and return to Transport House as the party headquarters soon after their victory at the polls.

As the weeks passed, compromises were reached and cutbacks agreed but Raymond managed to cling to the changes about which he felt most passionate. By the Friday morning before the budget the mandarins had handed him his speech.

It ran to 143 pages and they estimated it would keep him at the dispatch box for two and a half hours.

On the Tuesday morning of Budget Day he spelled out his tax changes to the Cabinet, who traditionally did not hear the full details until a few hours before the budget was presented to the House.

Budget Day in the House of Commons is a traditional affair. Ambassadors, diplomats, bankers, and members of the House of Lords rub shoulders with the general public in the tiny Strangers' Gallery. The queue for seats often stretches for a quarter of a mile from St. Stephen's to Westminster Bridge, but only half a dozen people at the front of the line actually hear the Chancellor's speech, because every other place has been allocated even before the queue has begun to form. The Chamber itself is usually packed by two-thirty although the Chancellor does not rise until an hour later. The Press Gallery is equally overcrowded with correspondents ready to run to the nearest phone as soon as any change in taxation is announced. Back-benchers, who because of the size of the Chamber cannot be guaranteed their normal places, are mostly seated by two-twenty-five. Conservatives can reserve their seats by filling in a small prayer card during the morning and leaving it on the place they wish to occupy. Socialists, who consider the system undemocratic, refuse to use the prayer cards and make a mad rush for places at two-thirty. The atheists on both sides wait for the chaplain to finish prayers before they charge in, hoping to find their usual places free.

Budget Day is also traditionally one for eccentric dress. A few top hats can be observed on the Conservative benches and the odd miner's helmet rests on a Labour head. Tom Carson arrived in a boiler suit with a Liverpool scarf around his neck, while Alec Pimkin satisfied himself with a red silk waistcoat and a white carnation in the buttonhole of his morning coat.

The green leather of the two front benches begins to disappear long before three o'clock, and by then any straggling back-bencher will be relegated to the floor or to the upstairs galleries, known as the "Members' Side Galleries," which lack the atmosphere of the House and from which members traditionally do not rise to interrupt or make a speech.

At ten past three Raymond stepped out of No. 11 and held the famous battered budget box, first used by Gladstone, high above his head, so that the press photographers could take the traditional picture before he was driven off to the Commons.

By three-fifteen, when the Prime Minister rose to answer questions, the Chamber had taken on the look of an opening night in the West End, for what members were about to experience was pure theater.

At three-twenty-five Raymond entered the Chamber to be greeted by cheers from his own side. Every place in the Commons except his had been filled. He looked up to see Joyce in the Strangers' Gallery, and smiled. At three-thirty, when the Prime Minister had finished answering questions, the chairman of Ways and Means—who traditionally takes the Speaker's place for a budget debate as the Speaker, being "the King's man," does not preside over money matters—rose from his chair and called:

"Budget statement, Mr. Chancellor of the Exchequer."

Raymond rose and placed his speech in front of him. He began with a review of the world economic position and went on to inform the House of the philosophy behind his first budget, namely to bring down unemployment without driving up inflation. He spoke for the first hour and a half without divulging to the House any of the fiscal changes that he would be making, so abiding by the tradition that no irreversible decisions could be considered until the Stock Exchange had closed, but also giving him the opportunity to tease the House with the odd hint or suggestion.

Raymond took a sip from the glass of water by his side when he had turned page seventy-eight. He had finished with the theory and was now ready to start on the practice.

"Old-age pensions will be raised to a record level," he declared, "as will allowances for single-parent families and disablement grants." Raymond paused and taking a faded sheet from his inside pocket read from the first speech he had ever delivered in public. "No woman whose husband has sacrificed his life for his country shall be allowed to suffer because of an ungrateful nation. War widows' pensions will go up by fifty percent and war bonds will be honored at their full face value." The cheering after this statement lasted for some considerable time. Once the House had settled again he continued. "The tax on beer, cigarettes, petrol, and perfume will go up by five percent. Taxes on salaries of more than £30,000 a year will be raised to eighty-five percent and capital gains tax to fifty percent." Several Conservatives looked glum. The Chancellor went on to announce an expansion program in the regions to stimulate employment. He detailed his plan region by region, to cheers from different sections of the House.

He ended his speech by saying, "My purpose as the first Labour Chancellor for ten years is not to rob the rich and give to the poor, but rather to make those who live in comparative ease pay taxes that will alleviate the plight of those in genuine need. Let me tell those Honorable members who sit on the benches opposite that this is only a fifth of what I intend to achieve in the lifetime of this Parliament, and by then Britain can hope to be a more equal and just society. We intend to create a generation in which class is as outdated as the debtors' prison, in which talent, hard work, and honesty are their own reward, a Socialist society that is the envy of the East as well as the West. This budget, Mr. Speaker, is nothing more than the architect's plan for that dream. I look forward to being given enough time to build the reality."

When Raymond resumed his seat after two hours and twenty minutes, the length of time it takes to run a world-class marathon, he was greeted by cheers and the waving of order papers from the benches behind him.

The leader of the Opposition was faced with the almost impossible task of an immediate response, and couldn't hope to do more than pick up one or two weaknesses in the Chancellor's philosophy. The House did not hang on her every word.

BOOK FIVE

1989–1991
PARTY LEADERS

CHAPTER
THIRTY-TWO

AFTER THE SUCCESS of Raymond's first budget the leader of the Opposition made changes to her Shadow Cabinet as quickly as was diplomatic. She moved the former Chancellor to cover the Foreign Office, Simon to tackle Home Affairs, and Charles to counter the formidable problems now raised by Raymond Gould at the Treasury.

Raymond soon discovered his task of pushing legislation through became that much harder when Charles had added the enthusiasm of his new young team to his own considerable experience of financial matters.

Raymond's success continued, however, even if it was at a slower pace than that for which he would have hoped. Labour won the first two by-elections occasioned by members' deaths, which in itself was remarkable in Government. The by-election results only started a fresh round of rumors that Denis Thatcher was pressing his wife to retire.

Charles Seymour knew that when such moves were finally made they could happen so suddenly that everyone seemed unprepared and uncertain what to do next. By the time Mrs.

Thatcher announced her resignation he had been building up a loyal team around him for several months.

The former Prime Minister sent a letter to Sir Cranley Onslow, the new chairman of the 1922 Committee, letting him know that she would not be putting her name forward for reelection. She explained that she would be over sixty-five at the next election and had already led the party for fourteen years, the longest period for any Conservative since Churchill, and that she now felt she was ready to pass the leadership on to new blood.

The moment everyone in the party had said the usual phrases about the retiring leader being the greatest Prime Minister since Churchill, they proceeded to look for the new Churchill.

Within hours of Mrs. Thatcher's resignation both Charles Seymour and Simon Kerslake had received calls and messages from about fifty or sixty supporters, and been contacted by all the leading political journalists. Charles went about his campaign in the thorough manner in which he approached everything, appointing lieutenants to cover each intake of new members since 1964. Simon had invited Bill Travers to organize his backup team. Travers, like any farmer, rose early each morning to gather in his harvest.

Both Simon and Charles were nominated within twenty-four hours of the necessary seven days, and by the weekend none of the rumored third candidates had appeared in the lists which convinced the press it would be a two-horse race.

The *Financial Times* went one better than its rivals. Its political editor, Peter Riddell, spent the whole week trying to contact the 289 Tory members. He succeeded in reaching 228 of them and was able to report to his readers that 101 had said they would vote for Simon Kerslake, ninety-eight for Charles Seymour, while twenty-nine had refused to give any opinion. The article's headline read "Narrow lead for Kerslake," and went on to point out that although the two men were polite about each other in public no one pretended they were friends.

"King Kerslake" ran the banner headline in the Monday editions of the *Sun*, and its political editor predicted Simon would win by 116 to 112: Simon suspected that they had done little more than divide the *Financial Times*'s don't-knows down the middle. With eight days to go he was being quoted at two-one on with Charles eleven-eight against by the veteran ex-Labour MP Lord Mikardo, who had run a book on the last fourteen leadership contests irrespective of party. When Elizabeth told him the odds Simon remained sceptical, as he knew from bitter experience that it never paid to underestimate the Right Honorable member for Sussex Downs. Elizabeth agreed and then pointed to a small paragraph in the paper which he had overlooked. Ronnie's new company was going public, and the shares looked certain to be well over-subscribed.

"That's one prediction that's turned out to be accurate," said Simon, smiling.

With twelve hours to go to the close of nominations a new candidate appeared in the lists, which came as a shock to everyone because until that moment the general public were entirely unaware of Alec Pimkin. Some of his colleagues even expressed surprise that he had been able to find a proposer and a seconder. As it had been assumed that Pimkin's supporters were all men who would have backed Charles it was considered a blow to his cause, although most political pundits doubted if Pimkin could scrape together more than seven or eight out of the 289 votes to be cast.

Charles pleaded with Pimkin to withdraw but he stubbornly refused, admitting to Fiona that he was thoroughly enjoying his brief moment of glory. He held a press conference in the Commons, gave endless interviews to television, radio, and the national press, and found he was receiving considerable political attention for the first time in his life since the Common Market debate. He even enjoyed the cartoon that appeared in the *Daily Telegraph* of the three candidates in the 100 meters which had Charles portrayed as a string bean, Simon as a jumping bean, and Alec as a has-bean waddling in a long way behind the other two. But Alexander Dalglish remained puzzled as to what had made Pimkin place his name in the lists in the first place.

"My majority in Littlehampton had plummeted from over 12,000 to 3,200 since I was first elected, and frankly the Social Democrats have been getting a little too close for comfort. That tiresome fellow Andrew Fraser is in Sussex once a month making speeches on behalf of his candidate and there are still over four years to go until the election."

"But how many votes can you hope to pick up?" asked Fiona.

"Many more than those drunken scribblers realize. I have nine votes already pledged, not including my own, and I could well end up with as many as fifteen."

"Why so many?" asked Fiona, immediately realizing how tactless the question must have sounded.

"Dear, simple creature," Pimkin replied. "There are some members of our party who do not care to be led either by a middle-class pushy minor public schoolboy or an aristocratic, arrogant snob. By voting for me they can lodge their protest very clearly."

"But isn't that irresponsible of you?" asked Fiona, annoyed by the "simple" quip.

"Irresponsible it may be, but you can't begin to imagine the invitations I have been receiving during the last few days. They should continue for at least a year after the election is over."

Bombshells occur in the House of Commons only on rare occasions, mainly because the elements of bad luck and timing have to come together. Something that will create a headline one week may be hardly worthy of a mention the next. On the Thursday before the leadership election the House was packed for questions to the Chancellor. Raymond and Charles were having their usual verbal battles across the dispatch box, Charles coming out slightly on top. As the Treasury wasn't his portfolio, all Simon could do was sit with his legs up on the table and listen while his rival scored points.

Tom Carson seemed extremely anxious to get in a supple-

mentary on almost any question that was down on the order paper. Between two-thirty and five past three he had leaped up from his place no less than a dozen times. The digital clock above the Speaker's chair had reached three-twelve when, out of exasperation, the Speaker called him on a seemingly innocuous question on windfall profits.

With Prime Minister's questions just about to begin Carson faced a packed House and a full press gallery. He paused for a moment before putting his question.

"What would be my Right Honorable friend's attitude to a man who invests one pound in a company and, five years later, receives a check for £300,000 despite not being on the board or appearing to be involved in any way with that company?"

Raymond was puzzled as he had no idea what Carson was talking about. He did not notice that Simon Kerslake had turned white.

Raymond rose to the dispatch box. "I would remind my Honorable friend that I put capital gains tax up to fifty percent which might dampen his ardor a little," he said. It was about the only attempt at humor Raymond had made at the dispatch box that year, which may have been the reason so few members laughed. As Carson rose a second time Simon slipped a note across to Raymond which he hurriedly skimmed.

"But does the Chancellor consider that such a person would be fit to be Prime Minister or even leader of the Opposition?"

Members started talking amongst themselves, trying to work out at whom the question was directed while the Speaker stirred restlessly in his seat, anxious to bring a halt to such disorderly supplementaries. Raymond returned to the dispatch box and told Carson that the question was not worthy of an answer. There the matter might have rested had Charles not risen to the dispatch box.

"Mr. Speaker, is the Chancellor aware that this personal attack is aimed at my Right Honorable friend, the member for Pucklebridge, and is a disgraceful slur on his character and reputation? The Honorable member for Liverpool Dockside should withdraw his allegation immediately."

The Conservatives cheered their colleague's magnanimity

while Simon remained silent, knowing that Charles had successfully put the story on the front page of every national paper.

Simon read the papers over breakfast on the Friday morning, and was not surprised by the coverage of Charles's bogus supplementary. The details of his transaction with Ronnie Nethercote were chronicled in the fullest extent, and it did not read well that he had received £300,000 from a "property speculator" for a one pound investment. Some of the papers felt "bound to ask" what Nethercote hoped to gain out of the transaction. No one seemed to realize that Simon had been on the previous company's board for five years, had invested £60,000 of his own money in that company, and had only recently finished paying off the overdraft.

By the Sunday Simon had made a full press statement to put the record straight, and most of the papers had given him a fair hearing. However, Sir Peter McKay, the editor of the *Sunday Express*, didn't help matters with a comment in his widely-read PM column on the center page.

I would not suggest for one moment that Simon Kerslake has done anything that might be described as dishonest, but with the spotlight turned so fiercely on him there may be some Members of Parliament who feel they cannot risk going into a general election with an accident-prone leader. Mr. Seymour, on the other hand, has made his position abundantly clear. He did not seek to return to his family bank in Opposition while he was still hoping to hold public office.

The Monday papers were reassessing the outcome of the ballot to take place the next day and were predicting that Seymour now had the edge. Some journalists went so far as to suggest that Alec Pimkin might profit from the incident as members waited to see if there would be a second chance to give their final verdict.

Simon had received several letters of sympathy during the week, including one from Raymond Gould. Raymond assured Simon that he had not been prepared for the Carson supplementary and apologized for any embarrassment his first answer might have caused.

"It never crossed my mind that he had," said Simon, as he passed Raymond's letter over to Elizabeth.

"The Times was right," she said a few moments later. "He is a very fair man."

A moment later Simon passed his wife another letter.

15 May 1989

Seymour's Bank,
202 Cheapside,
London, EC1

Dear Mr. Kerslake,

I write to correct one fact to which the press have continually referred. Mr. Charles Seymour, the former chairman of this bank, did seek to return to Seymour's after the Conservatives went into Opposition. He hoped to continue as chairman on a salary of £40,000 a year.

The board of Seymour's did not fall in with his wishes.

Yours sincerely,
Clive Reynolds.

"Will you use it?" asked Elizabeth, when she had finished reading the letter through.

"No. It will only draw more attention to the issue."

Elizabeth looked at her husband as he continued to read the letters, and remembered the file that she still possessed on Amanda Wallace. She would never reveal its contents to Simon; but perhaps the time had come to make Charles Seymour sweat a little.

On the Monday evening Simon sat on the front bench listening to the Financial Secretary moving those clauses of the short Finance Bill which were being taken in committee on the floor of the House. Charles never let any of Raymond Gould's team get away with a phrase or even a comma if he could see a weakness in their case, and the Opposition were enjoying every moment. Simon sat and watched the votes slipping away, knowing he could do nothing to stop the process.

Of the three candidates only Pimkin slept well the night before the election.

Voting began promptly at nine o'clock the next day in the Grand Committee room of the House of Commons, the party Whips acting as tellers. By three-ten all but one of those entitled to vote had done so. John Cope, the Chief Whip, stood guard over the large black tin box until Big Ben struck four, when it became apparent that Mrs. Thatcher had decided to remain neutral.

At four o'clock the box was removed to the Chief Whip's office and the little slips were tipped out and checked twice in less than fifteen minutes. As John Cope left his room he was followed, Pied Piper-like, by lobby correspondents hoping to learn the result, but he had no intention of divulging anything before he reached the 1922 Committee who were keenly awaiting him.

Committee room fourteen was filled to overflowing, with some 280 of the 289 Conservative Members of Parliament present. Their chairman, Sir Cranley Onslow, welcomed the Chief Whip and asked him to join him on the small raised platform. He did so and passed over a folded piece of paper. The chairman of the 1922 Committee rose, faced the committee, unfolded the piece of paper, and pushed up his glasses. He hesitated as he took in the figures.

"The result of the ballot carried out to select the leader of the parliamentary party is as follows:

Charles Seymour	138
Simon Kerslake	135
Alec Pimkin	15"

There was a gasp followed by prolonged chatter, which lasted until members noticed that the chairman remained standing as he waited for some semblance of order to return among his colleagues.

"There being no outright winner," Sir Cranley continued, "a second ballot will take place next Tuesday without Mr. Pimkin."

The national press surrounded Pimkin as he left the Commons that afternoon, wanting to know whom he would advise his supporters to vote for in the second ballot. Pimkin, obviously relishing every moment, declared a little pompously that he intended to interview both candidates in the near future and ask them one or two apposite questions. He was at once dubbed "Kingmaker" by the press, and the phones at his home and office never stopped ringing. Whatever their private thoughts, both Simon and Charles agreed to see Pimkin before he told his supporters how he intended to cast his vote.

Elizabeth sat alone at her desk willing herself to go through with it. She glanced down at the faded file that she had not looked at for so many years. She sipped the brandy from the tumbler by her side, both of which she had discovered in the medicine cabinet a few minutes before. All her years of training and commitment to the Hippocratic oath went against what she felt she must now do. While Simon had slept soundly she had lain awake considering the consequences, then made the final decision. Simon's career came first. She picked up the receiver, dialed the number, and waited. She nearly replaced it at once when she heard his voice.

"730-9712. Charles Seymour speaking."

"It's Elizabeth Kerslake," she said, trying to sound confident. There was a long silence in which neither of them spoke.

Once Elizabeth had taken another sip of brandy she added, "Don't hang up, Mr. Seymour, because I feel confident you'll be interested in what I have to say."

Charles still didn't speak.

"Having watched you from a distance over the years I am sure that your reaction to Carson's question in the Commons last week was not spontaneous."

Charles cleared his throat but still didn't speak.

"And if anything else happens this week that could cause my husband to lose the election, be assured I shall not sit by and watch."

There was still no reply.

"I have a file in front of me marked 'Miss Amanda Wallace' and if you wish all its contents to remain confidential I would advise you to avoid any repercussion of your antics. It's packed with names *Private Eye* would wallow in for months."

Charles said nothing.

Elizabeth's confidence was growing. "You needn't bother to inform me that such an action would get me struck off the medical register. That would be a small penalty for watching you have to suffer the way my husband has this week." She paused. "Good day, Mr. Seymour."

Charles still didn't speak.

Elizabeth put the phone down and swallowed the remainder of the brandy. She prayed that she had sounded convincing because she knew she could never carry out such a threat.

Charles took Pimkin to dinner at White's—where Alec had always wanted to be a member—and was escorted to a private room on the first floor.

Charles didn't wait long to ask, "Why are you going through with this charade? Don't you realize I would have won it in the first round, if you hadn't stood?"

Pimkin bridled. "No doubt, but I haven't had so much fun in years."

"Who the hell got you your seat in the first place?"

"I well remember," said Pimkin. "And I also remember the price you exacted for it. But now it's my turn to call the tune, and this time I require something quite different."

"What are you hoping for? Chancellor of the Exchequer in my first administration?" said Charles, barely able to keep the sarcasm from his voice.

"No, no," said Pimkin, "I know my worth; I am not a complete fool."

"So what do you want? Membership of White's? Perhaps I could fix that."

"Nothing as mundane. In return for putting you into Downing Street I expect to be translated to the House of Lords."

Charles hesitated. He could always give Pimkin his word; and who other than Pimkin would notice if in three years' time he didn't carry it through?

"If you and your fifteen men vote for me next Tuesday I'll put you in the Lords," said Charles. "You have my word on it."

"Good," said Pimkin. "But one small thing, old chum," he added as he closely folded his napkin.

"Christ—what do you want now?" asked Charles, exasperated.

"Like you, I want the agreement in writing."

Charles hesitated again, but this time he knew he was beaten. "I agree," he said.

"Good, then it's a deal," said Pimkin. Looking round for a waiter he added, "I rather think champagne is called for."

When Pimkin put the same proposition two days later Simon Kerslake took some time before he answered. Then he said, "That's a question I would have to consider on its merits at the time, if and when I became Prime Minister."

"So bourgeois," said Pimkin as he left Simon's room. "I offer him the keys to No. 10 and he treats me like a locksmith."

Charles left the Commons that night having spent his time going round a large cross-section of his supporters, and he was reassured to discover they were standing firm. Wherever he went in the long Gothic corridors members singly or in groups came up to pledge their support. It was true that Kerslake's windfall of £300,000 was fast becoming yesterday's news, but Charles still felt enough blood had been let from that wound to ensure his final victory, even though he still cursed Pimkin for holding up the result. One anonymous note, with all the necessary details, sent to the right Labour member, had certainly proved most effective. Charles cursed as he realized Elizabeth Kerslake had successfully stopped any further covert attacks on his rival.

When he arrived home he was appalled to find Amanda waiting for him in the drawing room.

"I thought I told you to stay away until the middle of next week?"

"I changed my mind, Charlie," said Amanda.

"Why?" he asked suspiciously.

"I think I've earned a little reward for being such a good girl."

"What do you have in mind?" he asked as he stood by the mantelpiece.

"Fair exchange."

"For what?"

"For the world rights to my life story."

"Your *what?*" said Charles in disbelief. "Who is going to be the slightest bit interested in you?"

"It's not me they're interested in, Charlie, it's you. The *News of the World* have offered me £100,000 for the unexpurgated story of life with Charles Seymour." She added dramatically, "Or what it's like to live with the second son of an earl who will go to any lengths to become Prime Minister."

"You can't be serious," said Charles.

"Deadly serious. I've made quite a few notes over the years. How you got rid of Derek Spencer but failed to pull the same trick on Clive Reynolds. The extremes you went to trying to keep Simon Kerslake out of the House. How your first wife swapped the famous Holbein picture of the first Earl of Bridgwater. But the story which will cause the most interest is the one in which the real father of young Harry Seymour is revealed because his dad's life story was serialized in the *People* a couple of years ago, and that seems to be one episode they missed out."

"You bitch. You know Harry is my son," said Charles, advancing toward her. But Amanda stood her ground.

"And perhaps I should include a chapter on how you assault your wife behind the closed doors of your peaceful Eaton Square mansion."

Charles came to a halt. "What's the deal?"

"I keep quiet for the rest of my life and you present me with £50,000 now and a further £50,000 when you become leader."

"You've gone mad."

"Not me, Charlie, I've always been sane. You see, I don't have a paranoia to work out on dear harmless brother Rupert. The *News of the World* will love that part now that he's the fifteenth Earl. I can just see the picture of him wearing his coronet and decked out in his ermine robes."

"They wouldn't print it."

"They would when they learn that he's as queer as a two-pound note, and therefore our only son will collect the earldom when he's not entitled to it."

"No one would believe it, and by the time they print the story it will be too late," said Charles.

"Not a bit," said Amanda. "I am assured by my agent that the true reason behind the resignation of the leader of the Conservative party would be an even bigger scoop than that of a one-time contestant."

Charles sank down in the nearest armchair.

"Twenty-five thousand," he said.

"Fifty thousand," replied his wife. "It's only fair. After all, it's a double deal: no story to the press and you become leader of the Conservative party."

"All right," whispered Charles, rising to leave the room.

"Wait a minute, Charlie. Don't forget I've dealt with you in the past."

"What else are you hoping for?" said Charles, swinging round.

"Just the autograph of the next Tory leader," she replied producing a check.

"Where the hell did you get hold of that?" asked Charles, pointing to the slip of paper.

"From your checkbook," said Amanda innocently.

"Don't play games with me."

"From the top drawer of your desk."

Charles snatched it from her and nearly changed his mind. Then he thought of his brother in the House of Lords, his only son not inheriting the title, and having to give up the leadership. He took out his pen and scribbled his name on the check before leaving his wife in the drawing room holding £50,000. She was checking the date and the signature carefully.

Simon and Elizabeth spent a quiet weekend in their country cottage while the photographers pitched camp in Eaton Square. They had received a leak from an "authoritative" source that Pimkin would come out in support of his old school chum.

"A brilliant move," said Elizabeth over breakfast on the Sunday morning admiring the picture on the front page of the *Observer*.

"Another photo of Seymour telling us what he will do when he's Prime Minister?" said Simon, not looking up from the *Sunday Times*.

"No," said Elizabeth, and passed her paper across the table. Simon stared at the Holbein portrait of the first Earl of Bridgwater under the headline "A gift to the nation."

"Good God," said Simon. Are there no depths he will not sink to, to win this election?"

"My dear, by any standards you have delivered the coup de grace," said Pimkin to Fiona over lunch that Sunday.

"I thought you would appreciate it," said Fiona, pouring him another glass of his own wine.

"I certainly did and I particularly enjoyed the director of the National Gallery's comments—'that Charles's gesture of presenting the priceless painting to the nation was the act of a selfless man.' "

"Of course, once the story had been leaked to the press Charles was left with no choice," said Alexander Dalglish.

"I realize that," said Pimkin, leaning back, "and I would have given a dozen bottles of my finest claret to have seen Charles's face the moment he realized the first Earl of Bridgwater had escaped his clutches forever. If he had denied giving the earl to the nation the publicity that would have followed would have certainly ensured defeat in the election on Tuesday."

"Win or lose next week, he daren't then suggest it was all done without his approval," said Alexander.

"I love it, I love it," said Pimkin. "I am told that Princess Diana will be unveiling the portrait on behalf of the nation—and rest assured that when she performs the official ceremony, I shall be there to bear witness."

"Ah, but will Charles?" asked Fiona.

On Monday morning Charles's brother phoned from Somerset to ask why he had not been consulted about donating the Holbein to the nation.

"It was my picture to dispose of as I pleased," Charles reminded him and slammed down the phone.

By nine o'clock on Tuesday morning, when the voting took place for the last time, the two contestants had spoken to nearly every member twice. Charles joined his colleagues in the Members' Dining Room for lunch while Simon took Elizabeth to Locketts in Marsham Street. She showed him some colored brochures of a holiday on the Orient Express which would be the most perfect way to see Venice. She hoped that they wouldn't have time to go on the trip. Simon hardly mentioned the vote that was simultaneously taking place in the Commons but it never was far from either of their minds.

The voting ended at three-fifty but once again the Chief Whip did not remove the black box until four o'clock. By four-fifteen he knew the winner but did not reveal his name until the 1922 Committee had assembled at five o'clock. He informed their chairman at one minute to five.

Once again, Sir Cranley Onslow stood on the small raised platform in the committee room fourteen to declare the result. There was no need to ask if the people at the back could hear.

"Ladies and gentlemen," he said, his words echoing round

the room, "the result of the second ballot for the leadership of the Tory Party is as follows:

> Charles Seymour   130
> Simon Kerslake   158."

Just over half the members present rose and cheered while Bill Travers ran all the way to Simon's room to be the first to report the news. When he arrived Simon swung round and faced the open door.

"You look and sound as though you'd run a marathon."

"Like Pheidippides, I bring great news of victory."

"I hope that doesn't mean you're going to drop down dead," said Simon, grinning.

The new leader of the Conservative party said nothing more for a few moments. It was obvious that Pimkin had come out in favor of him. Later that night, one or two other members also admitted that they had changed their minds during the second week because they hadn't liked the blatant opportunism of Charles presenting a priceless portrait to the nation only a few days before the final vote.

The following morning Fiona phoned Pimkin to ask him why he had acted as he did. "My dear Fiona," he replied, "like Sidney Carton I considered it would be good to go to my grave knowing I had done one honorable thing in my life."

It took only a week for Simon's little house in Beaufort Street to be transformed. He could not as much as turn his head without facing a camera. Everywhere he went he was followed by a platoon of press men. He was surprised how quickly the experience became part of his daily routine, although Elizabeth never found it an edifying experience. She was, however, as booked up as Simon and once again they seemed only to meet in the evenings. He spent his first two weeks selecting the Shadow Cabinet he wanted to take into the next general election. He was able to announce the composition of his new team to the press fourteen days after his election as leader of the Conservative party. He made one sentimental appointment: that of Bill Travers as Shadow Minister of Agriculture.

When asked at a press conference why his defeated rival would not be serving in the team Simon explained that he had offered Charles Seymour the deputy leadership and any portfolio of his choice, but Charles had turned the offer down, saying he preferred to return to the back benches for the present time.

Charles had left for Scotland the same morning for a few days' rest by the river Spey, taking his son with him. Although he spent much of their short holiday feeling depressed about the final outcome of the leadership struggle, Harry's original efforts at fishing helped deaden some of the pain. Harry even ended up with the biggest fish.

Amanda, on the other hand, realizing how slim her chances were of coaxing any more cash out of her husband, reopened negotiations over her life story with the *News of the World*.

When Nick Lloyd, the editor, read through Amanda's notes he decided on two things. She would require a ghostwriter and the paper would have to halve their original offer.

"Why?" demanded Amanda.

"Because we daren't print the better half of your story."

"Why not?"

"No one would believe it."

"But every word is true," she insisted.

"I'm not doubting the veracity of the facts," said Lloyd, "only readers' ability to swallow them."

"They accepted that a man climbed the walls of Buckingham Palace and found his way into the Queen's bedroom."

"Agreed," replied Lloyd, "but only after the Queen had confirmed the story. I'm not so sure that Charles Seymour will be quite as cooperative."

Amanda remained silent long enough for her agent to close the deal.

The watered-down version of "My Life with Charles Seymour" appeared a few months later to coincide with Charles's much-publicized divorce, but it made no more than a faint ripple in political circles. Now that Charles had no prospect of leading his party it was very much yesterday's news.

Amanda came out of the divorce settlement with another £50,000 but lost custody of Harry, which was all Charles really cared about. He prayed her irresponsible remarks reported in the papers concerning the boy's claim to the title had been quickly forgotten.

Then Rupert phoned from Somerset and asked to see him privately.

A week later they sat facing each other in Charles's drawing room at Eaton Square.

"I am sorry to broach such an embarrassing subject," said Rupert, "but I feel it is my duty to do so."

"Duty, poppycock," said Charles, stubbing out his cigarette. "I tell you Harry is my son, and as such will inherit the title. He's the spitting image of great-grandfather and that ought to be enough proof for anyone."

"In normal circumstances I would agree with you, but the recent publicity in the *News of the World* has been brought to my notice and I feel . . ."

"That sensationalist tabloid," said Charles sarcastically, his voice rising. "Surely you don't take their word before mine?"

"Certainly not," said Rupert, "but if Amanda is to be believed Harry is not your son."

"How am I meant to prove he is?" asked Charles, trying to control his temper. "I didn't keep a diary of the dates when I slept with my wife."

"But it seems Amanda did so I have had to take legal advice on the matter," continued Rupert, "and am informed that a blood test is all that will prove necessary to verify Harry's claim to the title. We both share a rare blood group as did our father and grandfather, and if Harry is of that group I shall never mention the subject again. If not, then the title will eventually be inherited by our second cousin in Australia."

"And if I don't agree to put my son through this ridiculous test?"

"Then the matter must be placed in the hands of our family solicitors," said Rupert, sounding unusually in control. "And they must take whatever course they consider fit."

Chapter
Thirty-Three

Simon's first year as leader was one of unbounded energy and ideas which bore fruit as the Conservatives picked up three seats at by-elections and whittled away the Government's majority. The press were already predicting that the Socialists wouldn't be able to complete their full five-year term, which moved Simon to goad Central Office into a perpetual state of readiness for an election.

Raymond continued to gain respect at the Treasury as his policies began to show results. He had to cut back on some of the more ambitious projects as his gloomy predictions about American interest rates and the drop in the production of North Sea oil proved daily more accurate. After his second budget the financial press felt he had done all that was possible, given the world situation. When unemployment fell below two million and strikes to their lowest level since the Second World War some members hailed Raymond as the unions' Messiah, while others noted that he had been shrewd enough to steal some of the Opposition's co-inflation clothes in the absence of Charles Seymour.

As Raymond entered his third year as Chancellor the opinion polls showed the two main parties neck and neck again, with a surprising proportion of people saying that they would vote for the Alliance for the first time.

The Liberals still held sixteen seats in the Commons but, as in the past three elections, they had decided to fight under the collective banner as the Social Democrats during the general election campaign.

As the time for election drew near both small parties knew they would have to declare their choice for overall leader if a combination of Liberals and Social Democrats ever held the balance of power in Parliament. When the pollsters dug a little deeper it transpired that Andrew Fraser had become the most popular political leader in the country despite the fact he only led forty-two members in the Commons.

Andrew spent a lot of his time addressing meetings all over the country trying to convince the voters that at the next election the political balance would change. He said it so often he began to believe it himself, and two good by-election victories early in 1990 helped his supporters feel it was possible, too. The press began to take such claims seriously when at the local election in May the Alliance captured 102 council seats at the expense of both the major parties.

"Daddy, Daddy, open my school report."

Charles left the morning mail unopened as he held Harry in his arms. He knew nothing could ever part them now but he dreaded Harry finding out that he might not be his real father.

"Please open it," pleaded Harry, wriggling free.

The school doctor had been asked to take a sample of Harry's blood along with six other boys from his form so that he would not consider the request unusual. Even the doctor hadn't been told the full significance of the action.

Harry extracted the envelope from the pile by Charles's side—the one with the school crest in the top left-hand corner—and held it out for his father to open. He looked excited and seemed hardly able to contain himself. Charles had promised he would phone his brother as soon as the result of the blood test was confirmed. He had wanted to phone the doctor a hundred times during the past week but had always stopped himself, knowing it would only add to the man's curiosity.

"Come on, Dad, read the report and you'll see it's true."

Charles tore open the letter and removed the little book which would reveal the result of all Harry's efforts during the term. He flicked through the pages—Latin, English, History, Geography, Art, Divinity, Games, Form master, Headmaster. He reached the last page, a small yellow sheet headed: "Term medical report." It started: Harry Seymour, age eleven, height four feet nine inches—he's suddenly sprung up, thought Charles—weight five stone four pounds. He glanced up at Harry who looked as if he was about to burst.

"It is true, Dad, isn't it?"

Charles read on without answering the boy's question. At the foot of the page was a typewritten note signed by the school doctor. Charles read it twice before he understood its full significance and then a third time. "As requested I took a sample of Harry's blood and analyzed it. The result shows that Harry shares a rare blood group . . ."

"Is it true, Dad?" asked Harry yet again.

"Yes, my son, it's true."

"I told you, Dad—I knew I'd be top in the class. That means I'll be captain of the school next term. Just like you."

"Just like me," said his father, as he picked up the phone by his side and began to dial his brother's number in Somerset.

When the Prime Minister went into hospital for a minor operation the press immediately started to speculate on his resignation. Ten days later when he walked out looking better than ever the rumors ceased immediately. In the Prime Minister's absence as deputy leader Raymond chaired Cabinet meetings and stood in for him during questions in the Commons. This gave the lobby correspondents a chance to proclaim, like Caesarian soothsayers plucking at entrails, that Raymond was *primus inter pares.*

Raymond enjoyed presiding over the Cabinet, but was surprised that the civil servants expected him to spend his entire Tuesday and Thursday mornings preparing for Prime Minister's questions.

Both Simon Kerslake and Andrew Fraser had gained formidable reputations during Prime Minister's questions, and Raymond found the fifteen-minute encounter more demanding than a full winding-up speech in a major debate; in retrospect, he was relieved that he had prepared so thoroughly. The lobby correspondents seemed to be in agreement that Raymond had held his own on both occasions and that, if anything, Simon Kerslake had underestimated him.

The Prime Minister returned to Downing Street the following week and assured Raymond that the operation had been a success and the likelihood of any recurrence of the trouble was, in the surgeon's opinion, minimal. He admitted to Raymond that he hoped to lead the party to a second victory at the polls, by which time he would be within a few years of his seventieth birthday and ready to bow out quietly. He told Raymond bluntly that he hoped he would be his successor. But Raymond couldn't help remembering that Neil Kinnock was eight years younger than he was.

Raymond returned to the Treasury to prepare for what looked like his final budget before the general election. His stewardship had made it possible to loosen the reins slightly with an election in mind. He described the loosening to the Cabinet as no more than a percentage point or two; he had no intention, he assured them, of letting three years' hard work be sacrificed at the altar of vote-catching. Some of his colleagues round the Cabinet table wished he were not quite so unbending at times.

Whenever Raymond spoke around the country more and more people approached him about standing for the leadership. He always thanked them courteously but maintained his loyalty to the Prime Minister, which loyalty, he added, would remain constant until he chose to resign.

Simon and Andrew also spent every weekend in planes, cars, or trains fulfilling speaking engagements right up until the party conferences in October.

Andrew, in his summing-up speech to the SDP conference at Weston-super-Mare, told the delegates that they should expect to hold the balance of power between the two major parties after the next election. For the first time, he told them, they would have the chance to participate in a national Government. He sent the delegates home warning them to prepare for an election within the coming twelve months, by which time they would be able to welcome SDP Members of Parliament who would already be playing a major role in the running of the nation. Andrew's supporters left the West Country keyed up for battle.

The Labour party conference followed a week later at Brighton and Raymond delivered a keynote speech on the state of the nation's finances. He pressed the unions to continue supporting their Government by keeping the twin evils of inflation and unemployment at acceptable levels. "Let us not pass on three years of achievement to be squandered by a Conservative Government," he told the cheering delegates. "Brothers, I look forward to presenting five more Labour budgets that will make it impossible for the Tories to imagine a future victory at the polls."

Raymond received one of the rare standing ovations to be given to any Cabinet minister at a Labour party conference. The delegates had never doubted his ability, but over the years they had grown to respect his sincerity as well as his judgment.

Seven more days passed before Simon addressed the Tory faithful at the Conservative party conference in Blackpool. By tradition, the leader always receives a four-to-six-minute standing ovation after he completes his speech on the final day. "He'd still get four minutes," said Pimkin to a colleague, "if he read them *Das Kapital.*"

Simon had spent six weeks preparing for the occasion since, like Andrew, he was convinced this would be the last conference before the election. He was pleasantly surprised to find

Charles Seymour coming forward with new ideas on tax reform which he hoped might be considered for inclusion in the leader's speech to the conference.

Charles had recently been making useful contributions in the House during finance debates, and Simon hoped that it would not be long before he would be willing to return to the front bench. His main preoccupation in the House had been as a member of the Chairmen's Panel from which committee chairmen were recruited for each bill. Charles had mellowed considerably during his time on the back benches and many of his friends feared he had lost his ambition for high office and might not even stand at the next election. Simon hoped this wasn't the case as he desperately needed someone of Charles's ability to counter Raymond Gould at the Treasury. Simon included Charles's suggestions in the final draft of his speech and dropped him a handwritten note of thanks.

On that Friday morning in Blackpool, in front of 2,000 delegates and millions more watching on television, Simon presented a complete and detailed plan of what he hoped to achieve when the Conservatives were returned to Government.

"*Power* is what we want and *power* is what we seek," he told a mesmerized audience. "For without *power* we cannot serve."

After the peroration the delegates duly rose for a genuine six-minute ovation. When the noise had died down Pimkin was heard to remark, "I think I made the right decision."

The conference season over, members made their way back from the three seasides to Westminster. Sadness overcame the House in their first week back when the aging Mr. Speaker Weatherill suffered a minor heart attack and retired to the Lords. The Government's overall majority was only two at the time and the Labour party Chief Whip feared that if they supplied the new Speaker from their own ranks and the Conservatives were to retain the old Speaker's safe seat the Government majority would cease to exist.

Simon reluctantly agreed that the Speaker should come

from his own benches and asked his Chief Whip to suggest a suitable candidate.

When Charles Seymour asked to be granted a private interview with the leader Simon agreed immediately.

Charles arrived at the Opposition leader's office the following morning. It was the first time they had talked alone since the leadership battle. A head of white hair had grown from the roots of Charles's once Odyssean locks, and the deeper lines in Charles's face gave him a more gentle look. Simon couldn't help noticing a slight stoop had replaced his ramrod bearing. Looking at them now no one would have suggested they were contemporaries. Charles's request came as a shock to Simon for he had never once considered his great rival as a candidate for that particular job.

"But I want you to return to the front bench and be my Chancellor," said Simon. "You must know I would be delighted to have you back in the team."

"That's considerate of you," said Charles. "But I would prefer the more restful life of being an arbitrator rather than an antagonist. I've lost that desire always to be on the attack. For over twenty years you've had the advantage of Elizabeth and two sons to keep your feet on the ground. It's only quite recently that Harry has done the same for me."

All men are thought to have one great moment in their careers in the House, and for Alec Pimkin it was to be that day. The election of a Speaker in the Commons is a quaint affair. By ancient tradition no one must appear to want the honor, and it is rare for more than one person to be proposed for the post. During Henry VI's reign three Speakers were beheaded within a year, although in modern times it has been more the heavy burden of duties that has often led to an early grave. This tradition of reluctance has carried on through the ages, and for that reason a future Speaker frequently does not know who has sponsored him. Dressed in a smart blue suit, sporting a red carnation and his favorite pink-spotted bow tie, Alec Pimkin rose from his seat on the back benches to move that "the Right

Honorable Charles Seymour does take the chair of this House as Speaker." His speech was serious yet witty, informed but personal. Pimkin held the House in his grasp for nine minutes and never once let it go. "He's done his old friend proud," one member muttered to another across the gangway when Pimkin sat down, and indeed the look on Charles's face left no doubt that he felt the same way, whatever had taken place in the past.

After Charles had been seconded the tradition of dragging the Speaker-elect to the chair was observed. This normally humorous affair, usually greeted with hoots of laughter and cheering, became even more of a farce with the sight of the small, portly Pimkin and his Labour seconder dragging the six-foot-four former Guards' officer from the third row of the back benches all the way to the chair.

Charles surveyed the Commons from his new vantage point. He began by expressing his grateful thanks for the high honor the House had bestowed on him. From the moment he rose and stood his full height, every member knew they had selected the right man to guide them through the parliamentary calendar. The sharpness of his tongue may have gone but there remained a firm delivery and natural authority that left none of his colleagues in any doubt that Mr. Speaker Seymour intended to keep "order" for many years to come.

The Conservatives held the Croydon North-East seat comfortably at the by-election, and captured a marginal six weeks later. The press pointed out that it only needed the Tories and the SDP/Liberal Alliance to join together for the Government and Opposition to be in equal numbers, leaving the seventeen Irish members to decide the fate of the Parliament. Raymond was determined that the Government should hold on for another few weeks so that he could deliver his third budget, which he was convinced would act as a launching pad on which to fight the election.

Andrew had realized that Raymond's next budget might help Labour's chances at the polls, and he sought an official meeting with the leader of the Opposition to discuss the possibility of a "no confidence" motion.

Simon agreed with Andrew's suggestion and thought that they should time the debate for the end of March. If they won that would ensure an election before the budget.

Raymond had accepted an invitation to address a large Labour rally in Cardiff the weekend before the vote of "no confidence." He boarded the train at Paddington, settled into his compartment, and began to check over his speech. As the train pulled into Swindon a railway official stepped on board and, having discovered where the Chancellor of the Exchequer was seated, asked if he could speak to him privately for a few minutes. Raymond listened carefully to what the man had to say, replaced the speech in his brief case, got off the train, crossed the platform, and returned by the first available train to London.

On the journey back he tried to work out all the consequences of the news he had just been told. As soon as he arrived at Paddington he made his way through the waiting photographers and journalists, answering no questions. A car took him straight to Westminster Hospital. Raymond was shown into a private room, to find the Prime Minister sitting upright in bed.

"Now don't panic," he said before Raymond could speak. "I'm in fine shape considering I'm over sixty and with all the pressure we've been under this last year."

"What's wrong with you?" asked Raymond, taking a chair next to the bed.

"Recurrence of the old trouble, only this time they say it will take major surgery. I'll be out of this place in a month, six weeks at the most, and then I'll live as long as Harold Macmillan, they tell me. Now, to more important matters. I want you to take over for me again, which will mean you will have to speak in my place during the 'no confidence' debate on Wednesday. If we lose the vote, I shall resign as leader."

Raymond tried to protest as he had already worked out the implications the moment he had heard his leader was ill again. The Prime Minister held up his hand and continued talking. "No party can fight an election with its leader laid up in bed for six weeks, however well he might be when they release him. If there is to be an election, the voters have the right to know who is going to lead the party in Parliament, and of course in such an emergency under standing order number five (four) of the Labour party's constitution," continued the Prime Minister, "the National Executive would meet and automatically select you to take over as party leader."

Raymond raised his head. "Yes. The importance of that particular standing order has already been pointed out to me."

The Prime Minister smiled. "Joyce, no doubt."

"Her name was Kate, actually."

The Prime Minister looked puzzled and then continued. "I think you must get used to the idea, Raymond, that you may well be running for Prime Minister in three weeks' time. Because if we lose the 'no confidence' vote on Wednesday I am given no choice but to advise the Queen to call an immediate general election."

Raymond remained silent.

"I can assure you," continued the Prime Minister, "the National Executive will not want an internal bloodbath three weeks before a general election. Nothing could be more certain to guarantee a Tory victory. If, however, we do win the 'no confidence' vote then it's a different matter altogether because I'll be back and running the ship long before the Easter recess is over. That will give us enough time to call the election after you've delivered your third budget. So make sure you win on Wednesday."

"I am unable to express how much we will all miss your leadership," said Raymond, without guile.

"As every member of the House except the Irish will know which lobby they'll be voting in long before the debate begins, my leadership may turn out to be less important than any single vote. And don't forget it will be the first occasion at which they've allowed television on the floor of the Commons, so make sure Joyce picks out one of those smart shirts you sometimes wear."

Raymond spent the final few days before the "no confidence" vote preparing his speech. He canceled all the engagements in his diary except for the Speaker's dinner to celebrate the Queen's sixty-fifth birthday, at which he would be standing in for the Prime Minister.

The Government and Opposition Whips spent Monday and Tuesday checking that every member would be present in the House by ten o'clock on Wednesday night. The political journalists pointed out that, if the vote were a tie, Mr. Speaker Seymour had already made it clear that he would abide by the ancient tradition of giving his casting vote to the Government of the day. Charles was armed with precedents from Speaker Addington in the eighteenth century to Speaker Denison in the nineteenth. Charles pointed out that, in line with the principle, he must vote in such a manner as not to make the decision of the chair final.

Simon was to open the debate for the Opposition while Andrew was being allowed to wind up, the only concession Simon had granted the SDP/Liberal Alliance for ensuring their support in the lobbies. Neil Kinnock was to open for the Government with Raymond winding up.

When Raymond read his speech out to Joyce on the Tuesday night the entire rehearsal took only twenty-four minutes, but he explained to her that with the noise and interruptions that would occur in the Chamber he would be on his feet the full thirty minutes. In fact he might have to cut short some lines on the night.

The following day members began arriving hours before the debate was due to begin. The Strangers' Gallery had been booked days in advance, with many senior ambassadors and even some Privy Councillors unable to be guaranteed a seat. The Press Gallery was filled and editors were sitting at the feet of their political journalists' desks. The Commons itself was like a stand at a cup final where twice as many tickets had been sold as there were seats. The only difference from a Budget Day was that the House was taken up with lighting equipment that had been tested a dozen times that morning.

Between two-thirty and three-thirty Mr. Speaker Seymour had been unable to stop members chattering during questions to Mr. Meacher, the Secretary of State for Education, but at three-thirty he duly shouted for "Order" and did not have to wait long for silence before calling: "The leader of the Opposition."

Simon rose from his place on the front bench to be greeted with cheers from his own side. He was momentarily surprised by the brightness of the arc lights which he had been assured he would hardly notice, but soon he was into his stride. Without a note in front of him he addressed the House for fifty minutes, tearing into the Government one moment, then switching to the policies he would implement the next. He ended his peroration by describing the Labour party as "the party of wasted opportunity" then added—jabbing his finger at Raymond—"but you will be replaced by a party of ideas and ideals."

He sat down to the cheers of his back-benchers who thought they had already won the vote—if not the next election as well. The noise continued for some time before Charles could bring the House back to order and call the next speaker.

Neil Kinnock had always reveled in his Welsh ancestry and had often been compared by older members to Aneurin Bevan. The bête noire of the Tories set in to the Opposition leader with a vengeance, expounding his beliefs and rousing his own side to cheers when he said that the Tories would be routed and would regret this no confidence "trick" for a decade. "The Right Honorable Gentleman," he said, pointing at Simon, "has the nerve to call us the party of wasted opportunities. For the past two years it is he who has led the party of opportunists, and who will be the leader of the Opposition until it is time for him to be replaced." When Kinnock sat down the television producers couldn't be blamed for thinking that they were covering a lions *v.* Christians slaughter. Again it took the Speaker several minutes to bring the House back to order.

The back-benchers also rose to the occasion with speeches from past ministers quoting precedent and from young turks demanding change, which helped confirm old and established new reputations. The House remained packed that night right up until nine o'clock when the Speaker called Andrew Fraser to wind up for the Opposition.

Andrew delivered a "plague on both your houses" speech and shouted above the protests from the two main parties, "When the time comes you will both need to call on an honest broker." At nine-thirty when he resumed his seat Andrew was cheered as loudly as forty-two members in unison could manage.

When it came to Raymond's turn to wind up, members wondered how he would make himself heard above the noise that greeted him. He rose to the dispatch box and, looking grave, with head bowed, almost whispered his first words, "Mr. Speaker, I know the whole House would wish me to open my speech by saying how sad we all are that the Prime Minister is unable to be present tonight. I am sure all Honorable members will want to join me in sending him, his wife, and family our best wishes as he prepares for his operation."

Suddenly the House was silent and, having caught its mood Raymond raised his head and delivered for the eleventh time the speech he had prepared so assiduously. When he had seen Simon give his apparently impromptu speech Raymond had torn up his notes. He spelled out the achievements of the Government during the past two and a half years and assured the House that he was only halfway through his time as Chancellor. "I have not been able to achieve equality in three years, but of one thing I am certain: I look forward to delivering my next budget whatever the outcome of the vote tonight. We shall not see the opportunist Government of the Conservatives or the Alliance's so-called 'honest broker.' Indeed, looking at the Alliance I can say there is no one less honest and no one more broke. We, Mr. Speaker, will see the return of a Labour Government for another full Parliament." Raymond sat down as the clock reached ten. He found, like the speakers before him, that he was drenched in sweat from the heat sent out by the powerful arc lights.

The Speaker rose and his first words were lost as he put the question:

"This House has no confidence in Her Majesty's Government. As many as are of that opinion say Aye, to the contrary, No. I think the Ayes have it."

"No," hollered back the voices from the Government benches.

"Clear the lobbies," called the Speaker above the cheers for Raymond Gould. Members departed to the lobbies to cast their votes. The Irish members surprised no one by dividing among themselves. Fourteen minutes later the tellers returned to a noisy Chamber to give the result of the division to the clerk at the table who then entered the figures on a division paper. The four tellers lined up and advanced toward the table from the bar of the House. They came to a halt and bowed for a third time. One of the Opposition Whips read out: "Ayes to the right 323, Noes to the left 322" and passed the piece of paper to the Speaker who tried to repeat it above the bedlam. Few members heard him say:

"The Ayes have it, the Ayes have it."

Raymond sat on the front bench and watched the delighted Tories bobbing up and down like children on a carousel. He reflected that if the Prime Minister had been present to register his vote the Government would have saved the day.

Her Majesty the Queen visited her Prime Minister in hospital twenty-four hours after his successful operation. He advised the monarch to dissolve Parliament immediately and asked that the general election be set for 9 May. He explained to the Queen that he intended to resign as leader of his party that morning and would relinquish the office of Prime Minister as soon as the outcome of the election was clear.

Before she left the Westminster Hospital the Queen spent some time discussing a private constitutional issue with the Prime Minister. He suggested that when the Labour party had confirmed their new leader he must be the man to offer her advice on such a personal matter.

*   *   *

The National Executive of the Labour party met behind the closed doors of Transport House in Smith Square at ten o'clock the following morning to select their new leader.

Three hours and twenty minutes later the committee issued a one-line press statement: "Mr. Raymond Gould has been invited to lead the party at the forthcoming general election."

Although no one was in any doubt about the fierce arguments that must have taken place during the meeting the press were met by a unified voice once the committee finally broke up.

As Lord Broadstairs, the former Prime Minister, wrote in the center page of the *Sunday Express* that weekend, "The Labour party in selecting their leader resembled nothing less than the old-fashioned magic circle of Lord Rosebery in their determination to prove unity." The only leak he had managed to gather from the meeting was that Raymond Gould's acceptance speech had impressed every one present.

But Lord Broadstairs went on to point out that if the Labour party should lose the general election Raymond Gould could be the shortest serving leader in the Labour party's history, as under standing order five (four) of the constitution his appointment had to be confirmed by the delegates at the next party conference in October.

It had been two hours before Raymond was able to leave Transport House and escape the press. When he eventually got away he went straight to Westminster Hospital to visit the Prime Minister. The operation had visibly aged him. He was in good spirits, but admitted that he was glad not to be facing a grueling election campaign. After he had congratulated Raymond on his new post he went on to say: "You're dining with the Queen tonight?"

"Yes, to celebrate her sixty-fifth birthday," said Raymond.

"There's more to it than that," said the Prime Minister gravely and he then revealed the private conversation that he had had with the monarch the previous day.

"And will her decision depend on the four people in that room?"

"I suspect it will."

"And what's your attitude?"

"That's no longer relevant because I shall resign as Prime Minister the day after the election, so it's more important the new Prime Minister considers what is best for the country."

For the first time Raymond felt like the leader of the party.

CHAPTER
THIRTY-FOUR

ELIZABETH STRAIGHTENED SIMON'S white tie and took a pace back to look at him.

"Well, at least you *look* like a Prime Minister," she said, smiling.

Her husband checked his watch. Still a few minutes to spare before he needed to be at the Speaker's private apartments—not that he was willing to risk being late for this particular birthday celebration. Elizabeth helped him on with his overcoat and after a search realized he had lost another pair of gloves.

"I do hope you can take care of the nation's belongings a little better than you do your own." She sighed.

"I'm sure I'll find it hard to lose a whole country," said Simon.

"Do remember that Raymond Gould will be trying to help you," said Elizabeth.

"Yes, that's true. I only wish I was fighting Kinnock."

"Why?" she asked.

"Because Gould was born into the wrong party," said Simon as he kissed his wife and walked toward the front door, "and a lot of the electorate have already reached the same conclusion."

The policeman on the gates of New Palace Yard saluted as Simon was driven into the courtyard and dropped at the Members' Entrance. He glanced at his watch again: ten minutes to spare. He never could resist checking how many people were in the Chamber or what the latest news was on the ticker-tape machine.

He put his head round the door of the smoking room. A few members were scattered around, mainly from safe seats they felt did not need nursing. Pimkin, surrounded by his usual cronies, hailed him. His face lit up when he saw Simon formally dressed. "I say, waiter, mine's a double gin and tonic." His companions duly laughed. Simon responded by asking the barman to give Mr. Pimkin a large gin and tonic and to charge it to his account.

He spent a few minutes moving from group to group chatting to members about how the election might go in their constituencies. Pimkin assured Simon that the Tories would return in triumph. "I wish everyone was as confident as you are," Simon told him before leaving for the Speaker's private apartments as Pimkin ordered another gin.

He strolled along the library corridor, lined from floor to ceiling with venerable old journals of the House, until he reached the Speaker's office, which is the route members take to the Speaker's private rooms. When Simon reached the Grand Stairway dominated by Speaker Addington's portrait he was met by the Speaker's train-bearer clad in white tie and black tails.

"Good evening, Mr. Kerslake," he said and led Simon down the corridor into the antechamber where a relaxed Charles Seymour stood ready to receive his guests. Charles shook Simon's hand warmly. Simon thought how well his colleague looked compared with their meeting of a few months before.

Andrew Fraser had already arrived and soon the three men were deep into a discussion about the course the election would take when another guest walked in.

"The Right Honorable Raymond Gould," announced the train-bearer. Charles went over to greet his guest.

"Many congratulations on your election as leader," were his first words. "You've had one hell of a week; you must be exhausted."

"Exhilarated, to be honest," replied Raymond.

He moved toward Simon, who in turn offered his congratulations. The two men shook hands and for a moment resembled medieval knights who had lowered their visors before the final joust. The unnatural silence that followed was broken by Andrew.

"Well, I hope it's going to be a clean fight," he said. Both men laughed.

The train-bearer came to the Speaker's side to inform him that Her Majesty had left Buckingham Palace a few moments earlier.

Charles excused himself while the three leaders continued their conversation.

"Has either of you been told the real reason why we are bidden here this evening?" asked Raymond.

"Isn't the Queen's sixty-fifth birthday enough?" said Simon.

"No, that's just an excuse for us to meet without suspicion. I think it might be helpful for you both to know that Her Majesty has a highly sensitive question to put to us."

Simon and Andrew listened as Raymond revealed the substance of his discussion with the Prime Minister.

Charles waited in the entrance of the courtyard of the Speaker's House to welcome the Queen.

It was only a few minutes before he spotted two police outriders entering the gates of New Palace Yard followed by the familiar maroon Rolls-Royce, which displayed no numberplate. A tiny white light on the center of the roof blinked in the evening dusk. As soon as the car had come to a halt a footman leaped down and opened the back door.

The Queen stepped out, to be greeted by the commoner history had judged to be the monarch's man. She was dressed in a simple cocktail dress. The only jewelry she wore was a string of pearls and a small diamond brooch. Charles bowed before shaking hands and taking his guest up the carpeted staircase to his private apartments. Her three party leaders stood in line waiting to greet her. She shook hands first with the new leader of the Labour party and congratulated him on his election that afternoon before inquiring how the Prime Minister was faring. Then she shook hands with her leader of the Opposition and asked how his wife was coping at Pucklebridge General Hospital after the new National Health cutbacks. Simon was always amazed by how much the Queen could recall from her past conversations, few of which could ever last more than a few moments. She then moved on to Andrew whom she teased about his father's recent speech in Edinburgh on the Social Democrats' greatest weakness being their lack of leadership.

"He's very old, ma'am," insisted Andrew.

"Not as old as Gladstone when he formed his last administration," she replied.

She removed the gin and tonic offered to her on a silver tray and looked around the magnificent room. "My husband and I are great admirers of the Gothic revival in architecture, though being infrequent visitors to Westminster we are, however, usually forced to view the better examples from the outside of railway stations or from the inside of cathedrals."

The four men smiled and a few minutes later Charles suggested they adjourn to the State dining room where five places were set out round an oval table covered with silver which glittered in the candlelight. The four men waited until the Queen was seated at the head of the table.

Charles had placed Raymond on the Queen's right and Simon on her left while he and Andrew filled the other two places.

When the champagne was served Charles and his colleagues rose and toasted the Queen's health. She reminded them that her birthday was not for another two weeks and remarked that she had twenty-four official birthday engagements during the month, which didn't include the family's private celebrations. "I would happily weaken but the Queen Mother attended more functions for her ninetieth birthday last year than I have planned for my sixty-fifth. I can't imagine where she gets the energy."

"Perhaps she would like to take my place in the election campaign," said Raymond.

"Don't suggest it," the Queen replied. "She would leap at the opportunity without a second thought."

The chef had prepared a simple dinner of smoked salmon followed by lamb in red wine and aspic. His only flamboyant gesture was a birthday cake in the shape of a crown resting on a portcullis of sponge. No candles were evident.

After the meal had been cleared away and the cognac served the servants left them alone. The four men remained in a light mood until the Queen without warning put to them a delicate question that surprised only Charles. She waited for an answer.

No one spoke.

"Perhaps I should ask you first," said the Queen, turning to Raymond, "as you are standing in for the Prime Minister."

Raymond didn't hesitate. "I am in favor, ma'am," he said quietly.

She next turned to Simon.

"I would also support such a decision, Your Majesty," he replied.

"Thank you," said the Queen, and turned to Andrew.

"At heart I am a traditionalist, Your Majesty, but I confess to having given the subject a great deal of thought over the last few years and I have come round to supporting what I think is described as the 'modern approach.'"

"Thank you," she repeated, her eyes finally resting on Charles Seymour.

"Against, ma'am," he said without hesitation, "but then I have never been a modern man."

"That is no bad thing in Mr. Speaker," she said, and paused before adding: "Some years ago I asked a former Lord Chancellor to draw up the necessary papers. He assured me then that if none of my parliamentary leaders was against the principle the legislation could be carried through while both Houses were still in session."

"That is correct, ma'am," said Charles. "It would require two or three days at most if all the preparations have already been completed. It's only a matter of proclamation to both Houses of Parliament: your decision requires no vote."

"Excellent, Mr. Speaker. Then the matter is settled."

BOOK SIX

1991

PRIME MINISTER

CHAPTER
THIRTY-FIVE

HER MAJESTY'S PROCLAMATION passed through the Lords and Commons without a division.

Once the initial shock had been absorbed by the nation the election campaign took over. The first polls gave the Tories a two-point lead. The press attributed this to the public's unfamiliarity with the new Labour leader, but by the end of the first week the Tories had slipped a point while the press had decided that Raymond Gould had begun his stewardship well.

"A week is a long time in politics," he quoted.

"And there are still two to go," Joyce reminded him.

The pundits put forward the theory that Raymond had increased his popularity during the first week because of the extra coverage he had received as the new leader of the Labour party. He warned the press department at Transport House that it might well be the shortest honeymoon on record, and they certainly couldn't expect him to be treated like a bridegroom for the entire three weeks. The first signs of a broken marriage came when the Department of Employment announced that inflation had taken an upturn for the first time in nine months.

"And who has been Chancellor for the last three years?" demanded Simon in that night's speech in Manchester.

Raymond tried to dismiss the figures as a one-off monthly hiccup but the next day Simon was insistent that there was more bad news just around the corner.

When the Department of Trade announced the worst deficit in the balance of payments for fourteen months Simon took on the mantle of a prophet and the Tories edged back into a healthy lead, but with the Social Democrats stealing a point from both of them.

"Honeymoon, broken marriage, and divorce, all in a period of fourteen days," said Raymond wryly. "What can happen in the last seven?"

"Reconciliation, perhaps?" suggested Joyce.

During the campaign all three leaders managed to visit most of the one hundred marginal seats in which the outcome of any general election is decided. None of them could afford to spend too much time worrying about those 550 of the 650 seats that could not change hands without a swing of at least eight percent.

Andrew was willing to make one exception to the eight percent rule in the case of Alec Pimkin's seat in Littlehampton, which he had considered vulnerable for some time. The Social Democrats had selected an able young candidate who had nursed the constituency assiduously over the past three years and couldn't wait to take on Pimkin.

Alec Pimkin eventually made an appearance in Littlehampton—only after the local chairman had tracked him down to his London flat to say they were becoming desperate. The Alliance yellow lines were almost as abundant on the canvass returns as the Conservative blue ones, he warned.

"Don't you realize that I have had grave responsibilities in the Commons?" Pimkin declared. "No one could have anticipated that members would have been called back for a special declaration by the monarch."

"Everyone knows about that," said the chairman. "But the bill commanded by the Queen went through all its three readings last week without a division."

Pimkin inwardly cursed the day they allowed television into the House. "Don't fuss," he soothed. "Come the hour, cometh the man and the voters will remember that I have had a long and distinguished parliamentary career. Damn it, old thing, have you forgotten that I was a candidate for the leadership of the Tory party?"

No, and how many votes did you receive on that occasion, the chairman wanted to say, but he took a deep breath and repeated his urgent request that the member visit the constituency as soon as possible.

Pimkin arrived seven days before the election and, as in past campaigns, settled himself in the private bar of the Swan Arms—the only decent pub in the constituency, he assured those people who took the trouble to come over and seek his opinion.

"But the Alliance candidate has visited every pub in the division," wailed the chairman.

"More fool he. We can say that he's looking for any excuse for a pub crawl," said Pimkin, roaring with laughter.

From time to time Pimkin did stroll over to his local committee headquarters to find a few loyal workers, licking envelopes and folding election messages. On the one occasion on which he ventured into the high street he was appalled to discover Andrew Fraser standing on an upturned box extolling the virtues of the Alliance candidate to a large crowd. Pimkin wandered over to listen to what Andrew had to say and was not pleased to find that hardly anyone in the crowd recognized him.

"Humbug," said Pimkin at the top of his voice. Andrew waved back. "Littlehampton needs a member who lives in the constituency," declared Andrew genially, and went on with his speech. Pimkin turned to retreat to the warmth of the fireside at the Swan Arms. After all, as the landlord had assured him, put up a donkey with a blue ribbon as the Conservative candidate in Littlehampton and they would elect it. Pimkin had not been overwhelmed by the analogy.

With six days to go Andrew held a meeting with the Liberals to discuss tactics. The Alliance began to record over twenty-two percent in some polls while the Labour and Conservative vote remained neck and neck with thirty-eight percent each. Andrew's continual claim that he would hold the balance of power in the next Parliament was analyzed seriously by the *Observer* and *Sunday Times* over the last weekend of the campaign, and few political pundits were now disagreeing with him. Both the BBC and ITV were already trying to book him for the first interview after the election. Andrew made no commitment.

He traveled up from Liverpool to Glasgow on the Monday before the election and then trekked across Scotland, pursued by a pack of journalists, until he reached Edinburgh on the Wednesday night.

The same evening Simon returned to Pucklebridge to deliver his last speech of the campaign in the local village hall. Four hundred and eighteen sat inside to hear his speech. Four thousand more stood outside in the cold listening to his words being relayed by loudspeaker. Simon's final message to his supporters all over the country was, "Be sure you go to the polls tomorrow. Every vote will be vital."

The statement turned out to be the most accurate any of the three leaders had made during the entire three-week campaign.

Raymond had returned to Leeds on the evening and was met on the platform of Leeds City station by the Lord Mayor and over half the Corporation. He was driven to the town hall to deliver his last appeal to the electorate before an audience of 2,000 people. Somehow he raised himself to give one more speech, and the cheers that greeted his arrival at the town hall made him forget he hadn't had more than four hours' sleep a night during the last month. Introducing the Labour leader the Mayor said, "Ray has come home."

Raymond stood up and delivered his speech as vigorously as if it were the opening day of the campaign. When he sat down forty minutes later he felt his legs give way. As soon as the hall was cleared Joyce and Fred Padgett took the exhausted candidate home. He fell asleep in the car on the way back so the two of them helped him upstairs, undressed him, and let him sleep on until six the next morning.

All three leaders were up by six preparing for interviews on both breakfast television channels followed by the obligatory photo of each arriving at a polling station accompanied by his wife to cast their votes.

Andrew enjoyed being back in Edinburgh where for a few hours he was allowed to recall the days of recounts and catch up with the many old friends who had made it possible for him to remain in Parliament. Once again he ended up on the steps of the final polling station as the city hall clock struck ten. No Mrs. Bloxham was there to remind him that she only voted for winners; she had died the previous year. Andrew, Louise, and Clarissa walked back to the local SDP headquarters arm in arm to join their supporters and watch the results as they came in on television.

Raymond and Joyce remained in Leeds overnight while Simon and Elizabeth returned to London to follow the outcome at Central Office in Smith Square. Raymond couldn't remember when he last watched television for three hours without a break. The first result came from Guildford at eleven-twenty-one, and showed a two percent swing to the Conservatives.

"Not enough," said Simon from the party chairman's room at Central Office.

"It may not be enough," said Raymond when the next two seats delivered their verdict, and the swing remained the same. The first shock came a few minutes after midnight when the Social Democrats captured the Labour seat of Rugby, and less than thirty minutes later followed it by taking Billericay from the Conservatives. When the first hundred seats had been declared the pundits were certain of only one thing: they were uncertain what the final outcome would be. Opinions, expert and amateur, were still fluid at one o'clock that morning, by which time 200 results were in, and remained so at two o'clock when over 300 constituencies had selected their member.

Raymond went to bed with a lead of 236-191 over Simon, knowing it would be offset by the county shires the next day. Andrew had gained four seats and lost one, to give the Alliance thirty-two seats overnight.

The next morning pundits were back on radio and television by six o'clock, all agreeing with the *Daily Mail*'s headline "Stalemate." Raymond and Joyce returned to London on the early morning train while the rural seats were proving their traditional loyalty to the Conservatives. Simon traveled down to Pucklebridge to acknowledge a record majority. He wished he could have sacrificed a couple of thousand for the marginals that weren't going his way. By twelve-thirty-three when Raymond had reached No. 11 Downing Street, the Labour lead had fallen to 287-276 while the Alliance had captured forty-four seats.

At twelve o'clock that Friday morning, the cameras from all four channels swung over to Edinburgh where the Sheriff was declaring that Andrew Fraser had been returned to the House with a majority of over 7,000. The cameras moved on to show the victor, hands high above his head. The number on the SDP chart flicked up to forty-five. By one o'clock the Social Democrats had notched up their forty-sixth victory by a mere seventy-two votes, a result which saddened Simon.

"The House won't be quite the same without Alec Pimkin," he told Elizabeth.

At two-twenty-three that Friday afternoon both the major parties had 292 seats with only two safe Tory-held seats still to be declared. Simon retained the first but Andrew picked up the last after three recounts.

At four o'clock Lord Day of Langham announced from the BBC studios the final result of the 1991 election:

Conservative	293
Labour	292
SDP/Liberal	47
Irish	17
Speaker	1

Lord Day went on to point out that the popular vote made the outcome even more finely balanced with Labour taking 12,246,341 (35.2 percent), Conservatives 12,211,907 (35.1 percent) and the Alliance 8,649,881 (25.4 percent). He told viewers that he had never experienced a result like it in his thirty-six years as a political journalist. He apologized for his failure to get an interview with Andrew Fraser who now held the key as to who would form the next Government.

Andrew phoned Simon first, then Raymond. He listened intently to both men and what they were willing to offer before telling them that he intended to hold a meeting of his members in London on Sunday and relay their comments. He would report back with their decision in the hope that a Government could be formed by Monday.

Andrew and Louise flew down from Edinburgh on the Saturday morning together with a planeload of journalists but by the time Andrew disappeared outside Terminal One into a waiting car the press had nothing new to report.

Sir Duncan had already told the *Scotsman* that his son would naturally back the Conservatives, while the former Prime Minister announced from his bedside that Andrew had always been a good Socialist at heart and would have nothing to do with the capitalist cause.

On the Saturday Andrew held several informal meetings in Pelham Crescent with senior members of the Alliance to ascertain the views of his colleagues, old and new. By the time he went to bed he still had no clear mandate and when a newscaster said no one was sure how the SDP/Liberal Alliance would vote the following day in their private meeting Andrew added out loud, "Me included." Even so he had decided after much deliberation on the qualities of the two men and what they stood for and that helped him make up his mind which party he thought should form the next Government.

At the Commons the next morning he and every other SDP and Liberal member had to run the gauntlet of journalists and photographers on the way to a closely guarded committee room on the third floor. The Whip had deliberately selected one of the less accessible rooms and had asked the Serjeant-at-Arms to be certain the recording machines were disconnected.

Andrew opened the meeting by congratulating his colleagues on their election to the House of Commons. "But it is important to remember," he continued, "that the nation will never forgive us if we are irresponsible with our new power.

We cannot afford to say we will support one party, then change our minds after only a few weeks, causing another general election. We must be seen to be responsible. Or you can be sure that when the next election comes every one of us will forfeit our seats."

He went on to describe in detail how both the major party leaders had accepted the general direction in which he felt the new Government should be moving. He reported that they had both accepted that two members of the Alliance should have seats in the Cabinet. Both had also agreed to back a motion in the Commons for a referendum on proportional representation. For three hours the SDP/Liberal members gave their views, but by the end of that time Andrew was still unable to steer them to a consensus and had to call for a ballot. Andrew did not vote himself and left the SDP Liberal and Chief Whips to count the votes and announce the result.

Twenty-three votes each was the decision of his members.

The Chief Whip informed the parliamentary party that they would have to allow their elected leader to make the final decision. He, after all, was the biggest single reason they had been returned to the House in such relatively large numbers. After twenty-seven years in the Commons he must have the clearest view of which man and which party was most capable of governing the country.

When the Chief Whip sat down, the word "Agreed" came over clearly from the lips of the members sitting round the long table, and the meeting broke up.

Andrew returned to Pelham Crescent and told Louise which man he had decided to support. She seemed surprised. Later that night he left for a quiet dinner at the Atheneum with the sovereign's private secretary. The equerry returned to Buckingham Palace a little after eleven o'clock and briefed the monarch on the salient points of their discussion.

"Mr. Fraser," the private secretary said, "is not in favor of another quick election and has made it quite clear which party the Social Democrats are willing to support in the Commons."

The monarch nodded thoughtfully, thanked his private secretary, and retired to bed.

CHAPTER
THIRTY-SIX

KING CHARLES III made the final decision.

As Big Ben struck ten o'clock on that Saturday morning, a private secretary to the Royal household phoned the Right Honorable Simon Kerslake and asked if he would be kind enough to attend His Majesty at the palace.

Simon stepped out of the Conservative party headquarters on the corner of Smith Square and into the clear morning sunlight to be greeted by crowds of well-wishers, television cameras, and journalists. He only smiled and waved as this was not the occasion to make a statement. He slipped quickly through the police cordon and into the back of his black Rover. Motorcycle outriders guided the chauffeur-driven car through the dense crowds slowly past Transport House. Simon wondered what would be going through Raymond Gould's mind at that moment as he considered the decision Andrew Fraser must have made.

The chauffeur drove on to Millbank past the House of Commons, round Parliament Square, and left into Birdcage Walk before reaching the Mall.

Scotland Yard had been briefed as to which party leader

had been called to see the King and the car never stopped once on its journey to the palace.

The chauffeur then swung into the Mall and Buckingham Palace loomed in front of Simon's eyes. At every junction a policeman held up the traffic and then saluted. Suddenly it was all worthwhile: Simon went back over the years and then considered the future. His first thoughts were of Elizabeth and the children. How he wished they could be with him now. He recalled his selection at Coventry, the loss of his seat, and the continual rejections before Pucklebridge. The financial crisis, the resignation letter that Archie Millburn had promised to return the day he became Prime Minister. The Irish Charter, *Broadsword,* and his final battle with Charles Seymour.

The Rover reached the end of the Mall and circled the statue of Queen Victoria before arriving at the vast wrought-iron gates outside Buckingham Palace. A sentry in the scarlet uniform of the Grenadier Guards presented arms. The huge crowds that had been waiting round the gates from the early hours craned their necks in an effort to see who had been chosen to lead them. Simon smiled and waved. In response some of them waved back and cheered more loudly while others looked sulky and downcast.

The Rover continued on its way past the sentry and across the courtyard through the archway and into the quadrangle before coming to a halt on the gravel by a side entrance. Simon stepped out of the car to be met by the King's private secretary. The silent equerry led Simon up a semicircular staircase, past the Alan Ramsey portrait of George III, and down a long corridor before entering the audience chamber. He bowed and left Simon alone with his new sovereign.

Simon could feel his pulse quicken as he took three paces forward, bowed, and waited for the King to speak.

The forty-three-year-old monarch showed no sign of nervousness in carrying out his first official duty, despite its unusual delicacy.

"Mr. Kerslake," he began, "I wanted to see you first as I thought it would be courteous to explain to you in detail why I shall be inviting Mr. Raymond Gould to be my first Prime Minister."

A New York Times bestselling novelist
faces the harsh reality of prison life.

A PRISON DIARY

JEFFREY Volume 1
ARCHER

NEW YORK TIMES BESTSELLING
AUTHOR OF *SONS OF FORTUNE*

On July 19, 2001, Jeffrey Archer—international bestselling author, now known as Prisoner FF8282—was sentenced to four years in prison and spent the first 22 days in HMP Belmarsh, a high-security prison that houses some of Britain's most violent criminals.

During those three weeks, Archer contemplates suicide; he's moved to the lifer's wing because it's the only place with enough security to protect him; his cellmate sells a story to the tabloids, prompting Archer's move to solitary; and prisoners and guards routinely line up outside his cell to ask him to sign books.

A Prison Diary, Volume 1, is his fascinating account of these events.

"A tale that is not only important but true."
—*The Washington Post*

"Compelling reading. . . . Archer knows how to tell a story."
—*Houston Chronicle*

ISBN: 0-312-32186-4

**AVAILABLE WHEREVER BOOKS ARE SOLD
FROM ST. MARTIN'S GRIFFIN**   PD1 12/03

Bestselling novelist Jeffrey Archer shares his
experiences of prison life, critiquing the British penal system.

PURGATORY
A Prison Diary: Volume 2

JEFFREY ARCHER

NEW YORK TIMES BESTSELLING AUTHOR OF
SONS OF FORTUNE

On August 9. 2001, 22 days after Archer—now known as
Prisoner FF8282,was sentenced to four years in prison for
perjury, he was transferred from a maximum security prison
In London to HMP Wayland, a medium security prison in
Norfolk. For the next 67 days, as he waited to be reclassified
for an "open," minimum security prison, he encountered not
only the daily degradations of a dangerously overstretched
prison system but also the spirit and courage of his fellow
inmates.

Purgatory: A Prison Diary, Volume 2 is Archer's frank,
shocking, sometimes humorous, sometimes horrifying,
account of those 67 days.

"His dialogue sparkles, his narrative is taut and compelling
while his cast of criminal characters stays credible."
—*Mail On Sunday*

**AVAILABLE WHEREEVER BOOKS ARE SOLD
FROM ST. MARTIN'S GRIFFIN**

PD2 10/06

CPSIA information can be obtained
at www.ICGtesting.com
Printed in the USA
LVHW100733021022
729760LV00018B/78

9 781250 101990